# Rick Green, Esquire

# Rick Green, Esquire

## Harvey Sawikin

RIVERINE BOOKS     NEW YORK     2016

Riverine Books, September 2016

Library of Congress Control Number: 2016952841

ISBN 978-0692752760

Designed by Eliad Design

Riverine Books

New York, New York

*To Chaim and Miriam*

# Acknowledgments

I would like to thank, for their support and encouragement during the writing of this book, Georges and Anne Borchardt, Dominick Anfuso, Phyllis Levy, Cassie Jones, and in particular, my wife and first editor, Andrea Krantz. I would also like to thank, for their helpful comments on various drafts, Lauren Albert, Brom Keifetz, Barbara Schwartz, Ed Rudofsky, Wayne Carlin, and Judy and Benjamin Fein.

# From the diary of Rick Green

*American Lawyer* called. They saw the *Times* article and want to run a long profile. "Fall of a Young Superstar" was their tentative (corny) title. When I hesitated, the reporter, Andy Abrams, swore he had no intention of doing a hatchet job; on the contrary, he thought a sympathetic story might be "refreshing." I could state "my version," meaning, of course, exonerate myself to the profession.

The point, though—which Abrams obviously was too cynical even to imagine—is I accept full responsibility for my crimes and don't feel I *deserve* absolution. It's taken me months to stop blaming everyone else; I'm afraid if I hang around long enough with a reporter working his "Green as victim" angle, I'll lose ground.

The other problem is that "my" version remains a jumble. Just today I spent two hours staring at the ceiling, trying to pinpoint the exact moment when I set in motion the events that ruined my life. I couldn't. (Maybe I still lack the necessary distance; or maybe self-destruction, like many forces of nature, occurs at a gradual, imperceptible rate. So your disastrous decision may finally come on X date but, like a river bursting through rock, it's the inevitable climax of years of silent drippage.) If *I* haven't been able to form a clear picture of what happened, how can I expect Abrams to convey it to thousands of magazine readers?

One more, kind of embarrassing, reason to decline: I've been fantasizing about writing my own autobiography someday. That whole poor-boy-makes-it-big story. It could begin:

> *I was born, to immigrant parents, in a log apartment building on West 72nd, on the banks of the mighty Hudson River.*

Sounds good.

# Part One

I pray you, in your letters,
When you shall these unlucky deeds relate,
Speak of me as I am. Nothing extenuate,
Nor set down aught in malice. . . .

—*OTHELLO*, ACT 5, SCENE 2

# Chapter 1

*June 1987*

G reen reclined in his $10,000 Swedish chair, and it molded pleas-
ingly—ergonomically—to his back. Swivelling, he looked down
at the yellow taxis swarming up Park, then stood and hung a poster,
from a play he'd once seen, that showed the young Elvis tongue-kiss-
ing a pretty fan. Slipping a Clash CD into his boom-box, he strutted
around forming pretend chords, but dropped his air guitar when a man
appeared in the doorway. "I'm Lou Mandel."

"Rick Green."

"I know," Mandel said, nodding to Green's nameplate while offering a moist shake. "You're gonna work for me."

Green followed Mandel's eyes to the radio, now blasting "London Calling," then weighed his options. Turn it off immediately? Or
ignore it?—as if to say that rock music should be tolerated at Crank,
Wilson & Shapiro when it assists a lively young lawyer in the production of work. That sounded right, and Green relaxed.

Mandel did a double take at the Elvis poster, then angled his
chubby, stubbly, blunt-featured face—which suggested a tougher Fred
Flintstone—toward Green, for a better view of the lawyer who would
decorate his office so oddly. Green blinked once and grinned. Mandel

shrugged, said, "Whatever," then jammed his hands in the pockets of his baggy suit pants and shook them, producing a jingle of coins. "Anyway, tomorrow we're flying to Pikeville, it's in Georgia, to meet with the CEO of Lee Textiles—y'know, Premier sheets and those big nice towels?—to discuss an LBO. It's top secret," he explained, searching Green for signs of treachery.

"Do me a favor and bring Lee's last 10-K." Green had no clue what Mandel meant, though his tone implied that "10-K" was, to a corporate attorney, elementary as pen and paper. Mandel stared for a second, already out of things to say to this new boy. He turned to leave, added, "Good to have you aboard," then as an afterthought jerked his head at the radio. "Do me another favor and shut that off. Nobody can work." He jingled out and down the hall.

The singing voices echoing in the empty office suddenly sounded thin and whiny, the backup instruments amateurish. Green pressed STOP, then hid the Elvis poster behind a metal cabinet.

He spent several hours filling out forms, which covered his history and physiology in enormous detail. He didn't mind the effort, though. Crank was paying a large sum for him, after all, and was entitled to know what it had bought. Also it felt . . . comforting, to see his particulars assembled in a neat pile. After finishing, he rewarded himself with a trip to the fortieth-floor kitchen, which he'd been elated to find stocked with fresh coffee, cold sodas, and, opulently, shelves of Pepperidge Farm cookies. He couldn't quite wrap his mind around the concept that whenever he wanted a cookie—*whenever*—he could take one, or more, all free. Now, as he filled his fists with Mint Milanos, he had a notion: They weren't just cookies, but symbols of the new, abundant life he had earned through hard study.

His secretary, a slim young Puerto Rican with earrings like gladiators' shields, was annoyed. "Rick, you ran off, but the rule here is when you leave your desk, you say where you're going. I must know your whereabouts at all times."

"Why don't they implant a transmitter in my skull?"

"You're gonna be trouble." She chuckled.

Green peeped into the next office, which said "Mr. Murphy" and was a volcano of old food containers, cans, and paper. Murphy was yelling, "I'll fax it first thing!" at a speakerphone and simultaneously shoving a Ring Ding Jr. into his mouth. Stress relief, Green figured. Murphy was a fat young man.

He disconnected and raised his red-rimmed eyes. "Rick? Jeff. I meant to say hi but things're going nuts." Green sat on the one un-littered chair. "We've got twenty new associates, but most of 'em won't show till September. Didn't you want the summer off?"

Green shrugged. "I'm deeply in debt from school. Anyway I get nervous, waiting around. I need—structure."

"You may regret it. It's hard to swing a vacation."

"They said we get four weeks!"

Murphy nodded. "Someone told me you're a Fineman survivor," referring to the federal judge Green had worked for out of law school. Leo Fineman was known to the public for sending a Communist couple, the Funiculars, to the electric chair for treason in the 1950's; but inside the courthouse for torturing his clerks to the point where almost half quit or were fired midway through the year. Green had toughed it out by reacting to Fineman's often bizarre directives by telling himself, "Don't argue, just let him."

Murphy said, "Unusual for an ex-clerk to pick the corporate department."

"Litigation seemed pointless. Battling for years, running up fees . . . and I thought, doing deals you help companies." Green cast his eyes down, shy to state noble principles. But Murphy stared as if he'd just described his recent trip to Jupiter, then asked, "So which pillar of American business are you assigned to?"

"Mandel."

Murphy banged the desk. "The Adjuster! Did you notice him play pocket pool?"

Green smiled weakly. "So we're traveling tomorrow, and I'm sup-posed to get a . . . 10-K?"

"Call the library and they'll bring it to you."

"Huh? They just bring . . . ?"

"That's how Crank operates. Malfunctioning kidney? They bring dialysis. Anything to keep you at your desk."

Green snickered.

"I'm not kidding! The famous story: Roth, a former associate, one night he had horrible stomach pains. This crazy partner insisted he finish a brief, so the firm paid a private ambulance to park outside. By the time he got to the hospital he had a burst appendix and almost died."

"Jesus." Green pictured Roth, a Bob Cratchit in dusty jacket and battered hat, crawling to his special ambulance, leaving a trail of red ink. "Why did he leave? Too crazy?"

"No. He didn't make partner. They were afraid he couldn't physically handle the hours anymore. So," Murphy concluded, "welcome to the NFL."

"Yeah," Green said. "Um, one more thing. I was gonna register with the pro bono coordinator. Would you know which volunteer projects people like best?"

Again Murphy gave him the oddity stare. "I really don't. You're not gonna have a *lot* of extra time, is the thing—" Murphy's secretary appeared, saying he was wanted in the office of George Wilson: the senior partner. He leaped from his chair, belly shaking, and without another word lunged into the hall.


At six-thirty Green thought it respectable to go, but first, dividing $80,000 by 365, calculated that he'd made $219 today. Almost one payment on loan number two; more, in fact, than Fievel used to take home in a week, as bookkeeper for a *schmatte* company. That felt weird.

On his way out, he observed almost every associate still in his or her office, hunched over a document or banging on a keyboard. Passing the kitchen, he saw that a long dinner table had been set up with about thirty plastic place settings. Murphy, digging in a bag of Lidos, found Green's departure amusing. "Half day?"

"I have a pain in my appendix." Green smiled, though Murphy's story had in fact disturbed him all afternoon.

"Well, enjoy it. They'll hammer you soon enough. Good luck on your trip. By the way, Mandel's funny around new people. He may decide he wants to talk to you, but otherwise don't even try."

"Who is he—I mean, the great and powerful Oz?"

"Just take my advice." Green nodded dubiously, priding himself on his ability to get along with anyone. It was merely a matter of discovering Mandel's interests, outside the law.

·  ·  ·

Shelly sipped white wine, licking a drop off her lip. "So what's your first impression?"

"Incredible," Green said, settling in beside her on his couch. "I have my own office, and the support staff is huge and, like, hovers around waiting to do anything you want. There's all this food—cookies and sodas. On top of the salary."

"Sounds great."

"Yeah! Except, I knew it was a kind of . . . sweatshop. I've heard some stuff, though . . ." He trailed off but, seeing her intrigued, went on, "Oh, like one lawyer worked so hard he almost died." Shelly tilted her head, uncomprehending, and he quickly added, "I'm sure it's an apocryphal story."

"I hope you haven't committed yourself to some asylum." He tittered. "Anyway, what company are you visiting tomorrow?"

"I'm not supposed to say."

"Wow. You are important." Green blushed; he had felt important, telling her that. "Okay," she explained, "when you get outside Manhattan you'll see these wood things with green stuff hanging all over them. Don't get scared, they're called 'trees.'"

He laughed. "What are you, a farm girl? Don't make it like Chicago's some bucolic—"

"Not Chicago. Winnetka."

"It's all the same to me. It's—"

"We had one tree in our yard that was taller than this whole building."

"I'm not surprised. You're so way out in the Diaspora, there must be all sorts of wonders. Y'know, eggplants the size of children . . ."

She snuggled up to his chest, stroking his arm with her delicate hand. "Speaking of Chicago, I heard from David. He's happy at his firm, so if you don't like Crank, you can go west to seek your fortune."

Feldman, Green's law school roommate, was Shelly's older brother. At commencement, on the wide, freshly watered lawn, David had introduced his parents, almost faint with *naches*, and Shelly. Seeing her, Green had gasped—her heart-shaped face, green eyes, and black hair conjured some Bible-comic version of a Hebrew princess. It turned out she'd graduated from Northwestern and had just moved to New York for a job at an ad agency, as a graphic artist. "Maybe," said

Green with a cough, "we could meet in the city, maybe, if you . . ." She'd smiled and nodded.

But Green, whose fear of female rejection was great and unreasoning, agonized for almost the entire Fineman clerkship year, keeping her number taped up above his phone, where it would be instantly handy should he flood with courage. When he finally called and they met for dinner at a brick-walled trattoria, he found her charming, even lovelier than he'd remembered and, unlike the girls he'd known growing up, a regular American (with a Midwestern accent!), free of evident neuroses. Her disposition was so sweet, it was as if invisible Disney birdies chirped around her head. After three glasses of Chianti, he wanted to caress her smooth hair and kiss her over the candle.

He had so rarely heard, in the two months of courtship that followed, an unkind or cynical word from Shelly that it came as a mild shock when, in the last week, she'd begun to display a darker side. A troubled look would cross her face, he'd ask if he'd done something wrong, and she'd swear he hadn't, then kiss him, unable or unwilling to express her emotions. In a minute she'd brighten, but he'd remain nervous, and very curious.

Tonight she seemed her usual self. "I took your advice and rented *Chinatown,*" she was saying.

"Great, huh?"

"Not bad." He wheezed surprise, and she explained, "It's just— Jack Nicholson solves this mystery, and then what happens? She gets shot? What's the point?"

"What do you mean?"

Shelly sat up, brushing her hair back off her temples. "What lesson is taught?"

"I guess . . . that the world's corruption is so vast, one honorable man is no match for it."

"That's a point, not a *lesson*. Nobody's forced to make a moral choice. That's, to me, what great drama is. This, you're interested while you're watching, but you walk out and feel, blah."

Green sipped his wine, trying to picture the kind of drama she meant, but all that came to mind was Yiddish theater: sappy, weepy, unbearable. "I think art should reflect life," he said. "And most experience is random, bouncing around. Who makes moral choices?"

"We all do, all the time! But they're subtle. It's not, you know, cymbals crash and cellos play." He nodded, but actually felt she was schmaltzing up reality. "Want a good movie?" she asked. *"Kramer vs. Kramer."* He groaned. "No, and the reason is you have people struggling to make difficult decisions. Dustin Hoffman has to choose whether—"

"All Hoffman had to choose was salary or gross points." He shrugged, wishing he could change the subject. Clearly she meant to pursue this argument to the end, and he wasn't up to it.

Another trait of Shelly's that he'd only recently noticed was her tendency, when an issue caught her fancy, to turn it into a fixation. As she got started on such a topic, her eyes would flash, her cheeks color, and every trace of skepticism vanish. These passions bewildered Green and vaguely frightened him, just as the glazed chanting of Hare Krishnas did. He preferred moderation.

One such subject was Israel. A month earlier they had watched a documentary on Jerusalem, which had so moved Shelly that she'd discussed it for days afterward. He'd thought it would die down, but instead she'd slogged through an armload of library books and now knew as much about the Zionist state, probably, as Abba Eban. She assumed that Green, as a Jew, would naturally share her interest. But he didn't.

"We should go," he said, before she could persist. "There's no concept of 'fashionable lateness' in my parents' universe."

They lived within hocking distance—as Green liked to say—in a rent-controlled two-bedroom off West End. Fievel kissed Shelly fervently at the door, saying, "Come in, beauty." He and Green leaned toward each other, then shook. "Big lawyer, *vus machste?*"

The long hallway overflowed with books, in English, Yiddish, Russian, Hebrew. Because the Greens couldn't imagine throwing a book out, there were scores of hardcovers from the sixties, hundreds of ninety-five-cent paperbacks, and the odd ones nobody could remember acquiring, like a ten-volume cyclopedia, copyright 1900, that lacked entries for airplanes, Hitler, and television.

Rachel made her usual entrance: from the kitchen, soup spoon in hand. The source of her son's coloring, she was dark-eyed and -complexioned, with a plump, unlined face and the well-balanced body of a durable fullback. Her hair, brown and long in faded album photos, was now spun up into a red bale. Green bent way down to kiss her, stunned at how short she seemed; Fievel, too, was shrinking to fit the body of somebody else's old, frail dad. Though a shade under six feet, Green had begun to feel like the Jewish giant he'd once seen in a picture, towering over his confused parents.

In the living room, bowls of fruit and nuts sat on a coffee table with a curved shape that had been stylish in the Kennedy era and was now coming back. Tchotchkes of all types—ceramic owls, fabric roses, Van Gogh coasters—gathered dust atop the hi-fi cabinet and the mantel over the fake fireplace. (The fireplace, of white tile, contained a glued arrangement of fake logs, inside which a red bulb could simulate the hearth's glow.) Green and Shelly went to the window and looked left, across Riverside Park, at the Hudson. Fievel directed their attention to the on-ramp for the West Side Highway, beneath which Green discerned, clumped in huge piles, the dark shapes of . . . boxes? Shopping carts? "A homeless camp," explained Fievel. "Yes my friend, in America. Your Reagan. I hope you're enjoying your *goylem* in the White House."

"He's not 'my Reagan.'" Green didn't know why his father always used that expression, because he'd voted the straight Democratic line since coming of age. But it seemed to give him pleasure.

"The shelters aren't much better," Shelly said, and Green experienced a burst of pride. She spent three nights a month at the armory downtown, distributing blankets and hot food. He'd gone along once, but had found it dull and the men ungrateful. Also it smelled.

Fievel poured Vodka Wyborowa for Green and himself, and Kedem concord grape for the ladies. Then he toasted to good fortune at Crank and they all sipped, the alcohol knifing its way down Green's gullet. "So, *artist*, how's the advertising game?" Fievel's gray eyes twinkled beneath bushy gray brows.

Shelly shrugged. "Nothing I'm doing's going to end up hanging in the Met."

"Don't belittle yourself," Green said. "You're very talented. Not only your layout stuff; the fine art, too." Once she'd drawn him in charcoal, superbly, though he'd been upset because she'd shaded his nose so it looked the size of a banana.

"I'm really not," she protested, then told Fievel, "I still want to sketch you someday, even so."

"A pleasure." He half-bowed in his chair, suggesting a Prussian diplomat, and Green said, "Get a deal in advance on the nose." Shelly whacked his arm, laughing.

"Neither of you has a big nose," Rachel proclaimed, then headed to the kitchen, tying her apron. Shelly offered to help, provoking from Rachel a honk that expressed the simplicity of her task.

Fievel tugged at his wood-buttoned blue knit vest, then smoothed his unruly shirt collar. "So Shelly, what'll you think of the latest crack-down?" Green moaned: his father, who believed Israeli West Bank policy disgraceful, loved to press Shelly, a new supporter of Likud.

"It's hard to tell," she said, "because the media's incredibly biased. Have you watched the *ABC News* lately?"

"There I must agree. That Jennings is some anti-Semit. A Cana-dian, you know." Green had to smile, recalling how Fievel had once ranked the world's nations based on anti-Semitism. He'd put Germany first, Poland second, Russia third, then had thrown up his hands and declared a twenty-way tie for fourth.

The Israel debate continued and after ten minutes Shelly, stymied by Fievel's elliptical, prodding technique, exhaled and said, "Maybe you're right. I'm all confused now."

"No, you made good points," he said graciously.

Green could've told her, you didn't want to tangle with Fievel . . . he kept his knowledge tuned up, hard-earned as it was. Though he'd attended school only through ninth grade, at which point he'd escaped the Nazi invasion of Poland, he was an autodidact—an authority, in fact, on subjects ranging from botany to medieval history. People were surprised sometimes at his varied areas of expertise, but Green knew the code: it depended what books he'd happened to find, discarded down in the garbage room.

On the other hand, he often came out with opinions so unexpected, so angled, they implied lunacy—or utter genius. He'd hone, polish, then publish them in the remaining Yiddish periodicals; those that, as the joke went, printed one fewer copy every time an old Jew died. This month he had a piece in *Unser Tsait* on the Trilateral Commission. "That's some conspiracy," he explained, "funded by the Rockefellers, that decides everything: how much will be spent on defense, who'll be the president—"

"Who'll win the Super Bowl . . ."

"Make fun, but do you know who's involved?" He ticked them off: "Kissinger, Nixon, your Reagan, Charlton Heston—"

"Wait a minute, why would he—?"

"Heston has the tippy-top security clearance, because he narrates Pentagon movies!" Green exchanged a sidelong grin with Shelly, but before they could probe further, Rachel announced dinner. She loved to cook, and had begun experimenting with Indian spices; Fievel, however, insisted each meal contain meaningful Jewish content. So tonight we have the happy marriage of curry, cardamom, and brisket, Green thought as he sawed at the meat.

Fievel lay down his fork. "Let's talk *takhles*. About your apartment, with the exposed wiring."

"I wanna settle into Crank before I jack up my living expenses. And you're unaware, since you have the deal of the century—what're you paying now, twenty-eight dollars a month?—but prices are wild. Right Shelly?" Her one-bedroom, in a monstrous slab of a building on Second Avenue, was less miserable than his studio; but she shared it with a roommate, forcing the women to alternate sleeping behind a pathetic curtain in the living room.

"All right," Fievel said, completing his syllogism, "then you'll move back in here."

Green's head drooped. "Not this again."

"Yes this again! Why should you pay so much to live with roaches?"

"You have roaches, too." He poked his knife toward the baseboard cracks that served as their portals.

"But ours you know. They were like your pets." Green laughed, resting his forehead on his palm. Getting him back home had long been Fievel's quixotic goal, and perhaps to that end, Green's room seemed frozen on the black day when he'd left for the Columbia College dorm: his Monopoly and Risk still on the shelf, his shoeboxes of baseball cards filling the closet. He glanced at Shelly, who was amused by the crazy tug-of-war, and vowed someday to explain Fievel's reasons. He'd tell her, "Watch *your* family perish and you, too, will create your own, permanent, life-logic." How surprising if Fievel's logic demanded that he keep, right by him, his only child, born late and accidentally, Green had to assume in light of his parents' oft-expressed view that children should not be brought into this horrible world.

Fievel waggled his eyebrows; Green shrugged; Rachel intervened tentatively. "I can understand why he wants his own place. He wants 'independence.'"

"He can have it here! Nobody bothers him!" Rachel gave her son an eye pop that meant: Don't worry, we'll talk later. Spotting her expression, Fievel shouted, "Don't drag me down!"—his customary accusation when she opposed his ideas.

She created a diversion. "Daddy, tell about Mrs. Jones."

"Huh? Oh!" He rubbed his palms together, then began: "A rich widow, Sadie Katz, wants to stay by a fancy hotel that's restricted. From Jews, restricted. So she registers as 'Mrs. Jones,' gets a room lookin' over the whatever, the polo, the field where they play polo. Anyway, at dinner she's seated with some Gentile ladies, very nice, and with the most fancy accent she asks, 'Could you be so kind and pass the butter?' But as they pass, it falls in Sadie's lap. '*Oy vey!*' she yells, then adds, very sweet, 'Whatever *that* means.'" Fievel burst out laughing, then Shelly, but Green just nodded. He'd heard Sadie Katz's story, and those of the many other Jews peopling Fievel's gallery of failed assimilationists, at least ten times apiece.

As they ate, the men continued the jokes, most of which were aborted after the first line, when the listener raised his palm: I know it. Though Fievel had the broader repertoire, his son had the topper tonight, a Jew and an Arab on a plane. "You win!" Fievel cried. "'Pissing in Cokes,' ha-ha."

After fruit cocktail, the women cleared. Fievel sipped seltzer from his favorite glass, one of a set bought cheap at a Sunnyside flea market and cut with the irrelevant initials JLV. "So the job is good. The job is good."

Green chewed a macaroon. "It seems. One thing—I get the impression it's going to be really hard. The hours."

"Hard," Fievel repeated, stroking his bald scalp as if arranging hair. "Try bein' a Appalachian coal miner, or pick grapes, then you'll see hard."

"I'm not comparing myself with the migrant workers! Jesus! It's just—you know what? Forget it. You asked, I answered, and forget it." He fingered the wine-stained lace tablecloth that was their only heirloom.

"Let me put it different. Never mind hard, never mind hours. You should be glad to have a profession. If, God forbid, something should happen, you'll always be okay!"

"What'll happen? A pogrom? I'm not aware of one brewing, are you?"

"Not what I meant. Although—" Fievel looked away, as if picturing the unfortunate chain of events that could lead to a pogrom, then came back around. "Let's not argue. I know you, and you'll like it, and you'll succeed. Because you're a winner! Not like me, the schlimazel from all schlimazels." His grimace conveyed a somewhat theatrical self-loathing.

"Speakin' of me, I forgot to tell you: I'm takin' semi-retirement. Live a little. Also I'll get Social Security, since they think I'm sixty-five."

"How'd you accomplish that?"

Glancing toward the kitchen, he whispered, "I said the birth records were destroyed in the war. What'll they do, go to Lodz and check?"

"I'm . . . surprised at you, Dad. It's not—"

"Anyway I *can't* say what year I was born. I think it was fall of '23, but we didn't celebrate, so I'm not sure. My cousin Julian in Ow-stralia says it was in spring. Means 1924."

Green felt shaken. He'd known his father's birthday was a mystery, but had always thought the year, at least, was definite. "Who cares?" Fievel asked, and said, tapping his temple, "In here I see myself a teenager.

"Back to the subject. A group from the Bund—Moishe and Sonya, Zweig, a few others you don't know—we pooled pension money in an investment club." Green had always liked his parents' comrades from the labor organization. As a kid he'd sit among them, some Sundays down in the Garment District, and listen to wild-haired old speakers heaping abuse on the unjust American system. Afterward, coffee and cake.

"So they voted me manager. I'm makin' investments, and lookin' for more. So if you hear of a company that's gonna be taken over, you'll tell me?" Green checked to see if he was joking, but Fievel's face was untroubled, as if he'd asked the weather.

"You—are you aware it'd be illegal for me to give you that kind of information?"

"Who could connect you to the club?"

"Whether you get away with it's not the issue, you know that! It's wrong."

"Wrong. What do you think they do on the golf course, the executives from IBM and Exxon, just play golf? That's fun? Why shouldn't the little pisher get a chance?!"

"Please drop it!" Green studied his father. "I can see you're fooling around, so cut it out."

Fievel dipped his head, then smiled "Okay, but—serious now—I got clipped all my life. One time I'd like to clip back a little." For as long as Green could remember, his father had bemoaned the trusting nature that had made him a "big sucker" in even the most minor business dealings, as well as the Good Samaritan instincts that had gotten him nothing but trouble—that had, in fact, gotten him mugged on several occasions.

What was the source of Fievel's volunteerism? Why did he supervise the seniors' center lunch program, the West Side Folk Dancers, and the Workmen's Circle Yiddish lending library? It made him feel good, certainly, though Green knew that he did it just as much to satisfy his need for—addiction to—the praise of his peers. At home, of course, he cursed, loudly and often, this putzy propensity to take on unpaid responsibilities, as if a *smart* man would use his free time for entrepreneurial startup projects.

"Clipped my whole life," he repeated.

"I don't call it being clipped. I call it keeping a sense of morality in your dealings."

"Yeah. From such a sense you get only poorer. I just pray you won't take after me, in your career. Get that killer instinct!" He tried to look hard, but soon reached over to caress his son's face, saying, *"Scheyn yingl."*

Green averted his eyes, ashamed that parental affection still gave him such pleasure. "I'm glad to help the investment club any other way I can. Maybe general, y'know, market advice."

"Thanks. I may call. Good."

The women returned, and Rachel, fixing them with a detective's eye, asked, "Why the yelling?" Fievel blinked once at Green: This is a you-and-me thing. You-and-me things had been Fievel's favorite ever since the days when he'd come into Ricky's room and detail some scheme, usually involving a money-saving angle, which must at all costs be kept from Rachel. He'd feared her silent disapproval, the judging eyes that dragged him down.

What he'd never known was that Rachel had her own plans, divulged to Ricky in kitchen whispers. Sometimes it had felt like having enemy spies for parents. Like the suit debacle; Green could never forget that.

Ten now, Ricky was being invited to weddings, bar mitzvahs. In a blazer you can't go. His dad had a suit place, but his mom whispered, "I'll take you when he's at work, to a real store. Don't worry about his junk shop." The real store was near the Bund, so why not stop up first? Something a boy should see. The men had hair in their noses and ears. They asked did he get A's, and what he'd be. He said he wanted to be a movie-reviewer, like Gene Shalit.

His mom showed him old pictures of men and explained, "Each working person, nobody hears him. Like in school if you sing alone, you don't sound too loud. But if you put all the voices together, it's loud, right? So these men, they put the voices together, in what's called a union."

Ricky pointed. "Is that Zeyde?"

"No, remember the candy store?" He nodded. When Zeyde and Bubbe came to America, they opened a place in the Bronx with pretzel logs and milk shakes. His mom worked there after school, as a "soda jerk." Ricky wished they still had the store; then he could get as much ice cream and stuff as he wanted, all free.

"But Zeyde believed in unions." Whenever she talked about him, she got sad, because he was the nicest man you could ever meet—not that fake kissing-and-touching kind, but *real*. And smart, so smart he saved the family from Hitler, all right? And funny! with his faces and voices. Then one morning he died in the street. He was walking, then

just collapsed with a heart attack. "I wish he could see you up here."
Ricky's mom wiped her eye with a tissue.

Another lady spoke to her in Yiddish. Ricky didn't understand,
so he sat at a desk and finished his review of *The Last Picture Show*, a
movie he'd seen at the Symphony. He gave it four stars. Soon the lady
handed him a book and said, "This'll be hard, but I hear you're intelligent." He smiled; he liked to be called intelligent. The book was about
a man with a funny name: Debs.

Just as they were leaving, Ricky's dad came in. He was on lunch
break from Fabulous Fashions, and where were they going? To get a
suit, Ricky's mom answered, like a double dare. He said they'd all go
to his place, where it was the same suits, didn't she understand? At half
the price.

His dad's place was one room, behind a gate, with a million suits. A
little man ran to buzz them in. On the side, men sat at sewing machines
with pins sticking out of their mouths. The little man slipped between
racks into a tunnel of suits. "His size, all. All come with the vests."

His dad liked one jacket and vest on Ricky. "Now try the pants."
You changed behind a big box, and Ricky put the Debs book on top.
The legs were too long, so he folded them up, then walked out to the
mirror. He looked good. While his dad felt the shoulders, his mom
ran her hand down the back and yanked the bottom. Ricky flapped his
arms, and his dad asked if it felt tight. It didn't.

His dad asked the little man, "Seventy-nine?" Of course, he said,
and wrote a ticket. When his dad read it, his eyes popped out. "You
say seventy-nine—so where do we come to eighty-five?" The man said
sales tax. "I don't pay tax!" he yelled, like everybody knew it. "I pay
*cash!*" Ricky's mom asked, please don't start over six dollars, and he
gave her an angry look. The man said tax was the law. Ricky's mom
whispered, but his dad kept shaking his head, asking what was he, a
sucker? "Take off the pants," he said, and Ricky went back behind the
box, ashamed, and also afraid—afraid for his parents, who seemed so
unlucky.

At first the man wouldn't buzz them out, wailing, "Here's some for
sixty-nine! Please just look, that's all I ask!" But Ricky's dad rattled the
gate, and kept rattling until the man opened up, nodding at them to
say: You'll be sorry. Downstairs Ricky's mom said, "I don't understand

you, over six dollars." His dad's face was red. "It's the principle! And I could've got, but you fucked me up!"

Ricky worried his dad might have a heart attack, and wanted to calm him down. "It was tight when I flapped, anyway."

Outside the subway, his dad asked his mom, "Maybe we'll go and pay the shitty tax? Otherwise he just has to come back downtown." He bit his lip like he hated himself.

"You have to go to work. I'll try with him again next week." She turned to Ricky. "Show Daddy your movie review." He handed it over and his dad read it, nodding and grinning. Ricky wanted to know which parts were making him grin . . . which were best? When his dad finished he said, "That's so professional! But you really think the movie's a four-star?"

"Yes," Ricky said, happy and proud. "The performances were superb."

"*Ja*," said Ricky's dad, and quoted the review: "'Ellen Burstyn's performance clicks like a pair of castanets. If she doesn't win an Oscar, there is no God.'" He giggled and squeezed the back of Ricky's head. He said he had to go.

Ricky's mom took him down into the subway station. Just through the turnstile, he remembered his new Debs book, still on top of the big box. He wanted to tell, but his mom was leaning over the track, searching for the RR train, and he decided to keep quiet. It was time to go home.


Rachel brought out a sponge cake. "You forgot my cookies," Fievel said.

"Not those lousy ones for company."

He fetched them, insisting there was nothing wrong. The cookies were all in blue-and-yellow-frosted pieces. At a bakery Fievel knew downtown you got a big plastic bag of broken cookies for a dollar fifty. Green looked from the bag to Shelly, suddenly delighted at her exposure to the cookies, and her amused response.

Fievel bit into one, nodding to convey its deliciousness, then nudged the bag toward Shelly. "Please, beauty. At *least* try."

. . .

Later, lying on Shelly's pink bedcover, Green ran his hand along the soft curve of her back. She pressed her chest against his, making him tingle. If only they could undress completely. He wouldn't have to go inside her; they'd hold each other, and he could— No, gross. Anyway, there was no point getting worked up, because she'd clearly expressed her feelings about sex at this stage of a relationship, and he was resigned. They'd had just one fight, early on, when in a frenzy of frustration he'd called her a puritan nun, or something equally inane. He'd made her cry, then had felt awful and sworn never to do it again.

Now she kissed his neck. Okay, he was too excited; he rolled over, thinking how cruel it was that the female he'd found most attractive in his life lay inches away, yet off-limits. There was, however, a glorious tradition behind this sweet torment. He'd read the metaphysical poets; they'd been there. Also, he had to admit that he'd responded partly *to* Shelly's modesty, which, for all he knew, was inseparable from her best qualities: her kindness, honesty, optimism.

He'd never been a sex nut anyhow, even at the start, with Diane Perchik, sophomore year. Sleeping with her had been fine; he'd just never bought the hype surrounding the act itself. And without love? The two one-night stands he'd lurched into were thrilling at the time, sure, but had left him disgusted and guilty the next day. And maybe he and Shelly would stick it out, which raised another point the poets had made: when one finally possessed one's desire, the ecstasy was proportionate to the wait. Now, catching a lock of her hair between his lips, he pictured them married—a suburban house, a car, a brown-haired boy and girl costumed for a school play—and his cheeks warmed.

But did he love her? He felt something, a sort of falling in his heart. Maybe he'd resisted labeling it because he had, as they said in *Cosmo* (which read like an enemy's book of codes and stratagems), the male fear of commitment. Anyway, why should he assume *she* loved *him?*

He turned to her—staring at the ceiling, distracted—and asked what she was thinking. "Oh, lots of things were running around my mind."

"Tell me one."

"How sweet you and your father are together, and how he loves you. Do you realize how much?" Green didn't answer. "Well, one day you might."

"What else?"

"That I hope your job doesn't affect our relationship." She continued softly: "Because I've never been so—comfortable with anyone before."

He kissed her. "I won't let it."

After a pause she said, "Remember Dvorah Weissbart, the Orthodox woman I told you about from my agency? Her brother's a lawyer, and he just made aliyah—you know, moved to Israel."

Green nodded, unsure of her point. "Are you advising me to relocate?"

"Not really. It's just, sometimes I feel . . ."

"What?"

"I don't know." Her eyes closed. "I've lived in Winnetka and Evanston and Chicago. And now New York, in my sad little apartment. But I've never felt a part of anything."

"You were, though. Your father was a big shot in town, right?" Shelly had shown pictures of Marv's restaurant-supply business and of the two-story colonial with the Mercedes fleet out front. Green estimated that his parents' apartment could fit twice inside Marv's first floor alone.

"So for twenty years he's made sure the North Side is fully stocked with paper napkins. And now me. I go in every day and design, and what am I contributing to? To selling tampons?"

"You make a contribution," Green protested.

She sighed. "I have nothing meaningful in my life."

"And what am I, a pile of shit over here?"

She laughed, kissing him. "Of course, you." Then they lay quietly until she said, "You visited Israel, right? Weren't you happy there? Like you belonged for the first time?"

"*Kind* of." But that wasn't strictly true. In fact when he'd toured the Holy Land with his parents in '71, he hadn't liked it much. There was a punishing, wavy heat, and sand in everything, and he'd grown crankier and crankier until, at the Dead Sea, he'd blown up at Fievel, throwing a sandal at him. (Though, to be fair, his childhood memories of places depended on what he'd gotten to eat. So Tel Aviv was an uninspiring town of salads and hummus, whereas Palisades Amusement Park was a hot-dog-and-peanut paradise.)

The bigger problem was he detested Israeli men, at least those he'd encountered in New York. They always tried to cheat him at the electronics stores, one time selling him a Nikon camera that he only later noticed was a Nikono, some Hong Kong knockoff. When he tried to return it, they claimed not to recognize him or the merchandise. In summer he watched them at Jones Beach, with their kinky hair, hitting on the Queens high school girls—just walking from one to the next as if failure were wholly unimportant. After striking out they'd shrug: You must be lesbian, anyway. It'd be terrible to live with a countryful of guys like that.

"I belong right here," Green said. "In America."

# Chapter 2

The cute stewardess checked Green's boarding card, then flashed a smile like a secret and directed him to the aisle seat in the first row of first-class. Settling into its comfort, he was astounded by the sheer space. He wanted to stay a long time, just floating over the clouds with his legs stretched out. In the past he'd always been stuck in a seat like 37E, next to the malodorous lavatories and pressed between two obese Americans. His arm would be nudged off the rest by a Stetson-hatted man, while the woman on his other side would sleep, her pudgy, unpleasant head sagging onto his shoulder. By the time the meal cart got to the back, the cereal would be gone, and all he could get was a soggy omelet, oozing grease and Velveeta.

Up here, the stewardess asked if he wanted a drink *before* takeoff, then perkily brought an orange juice. Once they were airborne and the curtain of envy separating the two cabins closed, the luxury began in earnest. Green chose a warm muffin from a basket, but the stewardess, observing his desirous eyes, insisted he take a sourdough roll as well. French toast was served, with strawberries and real maple syrup. Picturing the coach passengers unpeeling their foil eggs, Green sincerely pitied them.

Mandel had run on ten seconds before they sealed the hatch, muttering about the "fershtunkener Grand Central," then opened his *Wall Street Journal* and didn't speak again until he gave his food order. "Special meal," he said, staring at the stewardess's breasts frankly, as if they had asked the question. The special meal turned out to be a kosher bagel-and-lox plate, which he devoured while holding the newspaper.

Feeling it might impress Mandel if he prepared for the meeting, Green produced Lee Textiles' annual report—glossy, with a color photo of a loom in action—and laid it on the tray-table. When Mandel abruptly reached over and flipped it facedown, Green scratched his head, mortified; the LBO was top secret, and here he was with a billboard. On the other hand, communication of a sort had been established. "So, Lou, traffic coming out? I always say the LIE's the eighth ring of hell." Green chuckled, but Mandel just gave a half nod. Okay, Green thought, a man who doesn't speak.

No more words were exchanged until after they'd landed and caught a cab out to the company. Mandel blurted, "I met Ben Lee once before, but today I take his measure. See, Rick, working for me you'll learn that to be a good deal-lawyer you not only have to know the law inside out, you also have to be a psychologist. To know what kind of man your client is: strong, weak, honest, a fuckin' liar? And your adversary, too. You plan your strategy based on what you expect all the players to do when the shit flies. Get it?"

"Uh-huh. You—"

"Fuckin' humid town," Mandel said, squirming in the seat.

Pikeville's immaculate streets and trimmed lawns fascinated Green. The trees were portly, and drunk with leaves; rich Gentile cousins to the dogshit-choked sticks that stooped over Seventy-seventh. Before this, the farthest south he'd been was when his parents took him, at age eight, on a Workers' Bund bus trip to Colonial Williamsburg, and his only memory of that was having his picture snapped proudly sporting a three-cornered hat.

Lee headquarters, a one-story black-glass building set in a "corporate park" abutting a well-to-do residential neighborhood, featured in its lobby display cases containing samples of the company's fabric, and a painting of a jolly, jowly old man named Lucius Lee, Jr. (1899-1979).

Behind a low marble barrier sat an adorable, feline-faced reception-ist who wore, over straight blond hair, a headset into which she kept saying, "Lee Textiles, may I he'p you?" Mandel jingled up, told her breasts he was here for Mr. Lee, and she dialed an extension. "A Mr. Man-dle. And your name sir?" When Green told her, she smiled with a flutter of lashes. "Would y'all please have a seat?" *Y'all*, he thought . . . adorable.

On the couch, leafing through a big hook entitled *Lee Textiles: 150 Years of Quality*, Green saw that "The 1800's" had nothing about slave labor or any of that fun stuff, though there was a grainy photo of some cotton pickers enjoying a smoke. He imagined a rifleman outside the frame, yelling, "Smile, niggers!" and wished he could bring the book home; Fievel would clip the picture for his "Oppression of Negroes, Southern" research file. Glancing up, he caught the receptionist star-ing. She looked away, saying, "Lee Textiles, may I he'p you?"


In the small, drab conference room, a sandy-haired suspendered man jumped to greet them. "Lou! How're you?!"

"Some fuckin' humid town."

"Better get used to it. We'll be here a lot the next few months." He thrust his hand at Green. "Will Baxter. With Tate McMahon."

Baxter and Mandel poured coffee from a service set on the round wood table, then reminisced about the last deal in which they'd been the legal/investment banking team. Though Baxter flung jargon around ("The raider triggered the chutes in the squeeze-out" was one especially ripe phrase), something in his tone gave Green the impres-sion he wasn't too smart. And his worshipful treatment of Mandel made Green proud, as if his very presence at Lou's side gave him intel-lectual status. He felt, all at once, an overwhelming desire to attain Mandel's favor.

Another man entered, so heavy the walls shook. "Lou, Will," he said, then faced Green. "We haven't met." Clasping Green's hand like a long-lost brother, he added, "Ben Lee. I'm in charge of this mess." Appraising Lee, Green saw that he wasn't really heavy, after all; his importance alone must shake the walls around here. Fiftyish, with blond, gray-streaked hair, Lee had an upturned nose and jowls similar to those of the man in the lobby portrait, obviously his father. He introduced two silver-haired executives: Gilbert Houser, who was lanky, with elegant features and tinted aviator-style glasses, and Joe McCoy, a ruddy fireplug wearing a brown suit and a chunky college ring.

After they sat, Lee apologized for the weather. "I hope you all don't find it oppressive."

"It is fu—quite humid," said Mandel. Lee apologized again, and when he let the small talk trail off and turned to business, there was a shift in the room, like a veil dropping. "Will, I think it's time we seriously consider your idea of a management buyout."

Baxter sounded excited. "Good, since it's the answer."

Lee smiled. "Well, that's what we're here to figure out." Baxter's nod was an admission, and his eyes met Mandel's. Green sensed some deep dynamic in the room, one he lacked the experience to identify. Lacing his fingers on the table, Lee continued in a courtly voice. "Ever since my father first took the company public in the forties, we've enjoyed a fine relationship with our stockholders. They've supported our approach to growth. But today's market—"

"It's a short-termism," Mandel said.

Lee cocked his head, liking the expression. "Right on. See, the market screams for profits now, with no eye to the long run. Example: our two largest holders, mutual-fund managers, called me to say *they* decided we oughta shut the Pikeville plant and combine its capacity into Louisiana. Like they ever run anything!" Riled, he'd abandoned his genteel tone. "Sit in New York with their calculators, what do they know 'bout the effect of layoffs in a small town?!"

Mandel nodded. "They're all over you nowadays."

"Even had the nerve to criticize our charity work! We got a Lee Children's Hospital over to Boland they want us to cut off. Heartless bastards." He drained his coffee and banged the cup down. "Sick kids," he added, repulsed. "Guess it's plain, I think the company needs to get out from under these kinds of stockholders. Question is, if we did a buyout, how much we'd have to pay. And where we're at, is thirty-one bucks a share."

Baxter coughed. "I was thinking in terms of forty."

Houser noticed Green scribbling. "Son, might be best if you stopped taking notes at this particular time." Mandel grabbed Green's pad away like a child's toy, and embarrassment flowed, hot as lava. They didn't want a record of all this sensitive talk! Could he possibly be any dumber?

"Now how we got to thirty-one," Lee said, courtly again. "We think a thirty-six dollar payout's quite fair. We assume whatever we bid, the board will feel bound to negotiate us up a few bucks. So by opening at thirty-one we have some leeway."

Mandel sucked his tooth. "Can I cut through the shit here for a second? If your board'll agree to thirty-six, mazel tov. I don't do valuations. But I do know strategy, and the way to win is to go at a slam-dunk price. If you low-ball, every bank on the Street's gonna cry, 'He's stealing the company!' Then they drag out Joe Schmo Textiles to compete, and you're in a bidding war."

Lee grinned patiently. "Maybe you're unfamiliar with how business is done in this part of the country. If my board agrees to sell to me at thirty-six, then we're gonna complete that deal come hell or high water." He folded his arms. "I must say I resent the claim that I'm, quote, stealing the company."

Mandel shrugged, as if apologetically, and Lee added, "I swear, all I'm trying is to do this at a sane price, so I don't smother the business with debt. If I thought that was necessary. I'd stop right now." Suddenly, for no reason, Green felt fearful over the buyout, but then reminded himself: Lee was a smart, powerful man. Had Mandel taken his measure yet?

"Well," said Baxter, plucking his suspenders like bowstrings, "Tate McMahon can definitely support a deal at thirty-six!" Green wondered why he was so gung-ho. "Lou?" Baxter asked.

"Sure. If that's what everybody wants," he added, and they then went on to discuss the deal's financing. Tate would end up owning half the $2 billion company—which perhaps explained Baxter's lust—and management the other half. In the process of liberating his company from the market's "short-termist" demands, Ben Lee stood to become superrich.

Hearing Mandel draw on an apparent knowledge of every LBO in history and detail complex alternate strategies, Green got the troubling impression that nothing he had learned in law school would be of any use at Crank. He had zero feel for business—he'd been an English major, for God's sake! But he relaxed, thinking he'd just watch Mandel and absorb.

He slipped out to the lobby, where the receptionist put aside a paperback. "More coffee?"

"The opposite, actually. The men's—facility?"

She pointed. "Sure you don't need anything else?"

"Well, um, maybe you should tell me your name . . . in case someone needs something."

"Bonnie. Like 'Lies Over the Ocean.'"

"Are ye a Scottish lass?" he asked, dusting off an imitation of Jackie Stewart, the driving ace. But he hadn't committed to it, so he just sounded strange.

She laughed anyway, her curtain of hair trembling. "I canna tell ye ha' glad I am to meet a kinsman—" The phone board bleated, and with a comely blink, she said, "May I he'p you?" southern again. Green smiled, confused; her Scottish accent had been far superior to his. Heading off to the bathroom, he peeked over the partition, figuring her book would provide instant access to her mentality. If it was Jackie Collins or some love-astrology guide, then she was a ninny. He hoped it might be a quality epic but tripped slightly when he saw that it was *Death in Venice*.

At noon an old red-jacketed black man brought in a tray of ham sandwiches on white. Mandel examined each as if a nice kosher salami might miraculously appear, then gave up and made a plate of lettuce and potato chips. As Lee, Houser, and McCoy happily consumed their ham, squeezing on extra mayo, Green pictured them all on gurneys, rolling in for the bypass. The men kept strategizing as they ate. Green tried to follow, but they used too many technical terms, and finally he let his mind drift to Bonnie, her burr, and her *Death in Venice*.

Late in the afternoon Houser said, "Lou, I assumed you'd want to start analyzing our data, so I set up a room."

Mandel turned to Green. "You'll stay on a couple days." Then he frowned. "Ah, shit. Tomorrow's yontev."

Green vaguely recalled that a Jewish holiday fell in early June, some celebration involving figs, or dried fruit generally. "It's okay,

I don't celebrate—y'know, this one." He looked, as if for some kind of praise, to Houser, who said that'd be just fine.

Before leaving, Mandel took Green aside. "Know what to do in the data room?" When he shrugged confessionally, Mandel winced, then said, "You'll find shit like contracts. Read 'em to see if . . . know what? Just go through the shit, then get 'em to Xerox it all and ship it up to the office. I'll draft someone more senior into the deal." Green felt bad that he needed rescuing, but also relieved at the insertion of a buffer between his ignorance and Lou's genius.

"And listen, around Houser pretend you know what you're doing, and don't say this is your first week." He patted Green's back, amused. "You'll learn."

Out in the soupy heat, watching Baxter and Mandel ride off, Green got a lump in his throat, as he used to on one of the rare occasions when his parents had left him with a sitter. He was alone, and in a moment he'd return to a roomful of documents he didn't understand. "Alone at last," Houser said. He seemed about to make a joke, but thought better of it and added, "Let's get you a hotel."

Inside, Bonnie called the local Ramada. "The honeymoon suite's all they've got. That okay?" She booked it, then said, "So, stuck in scintillatin' Pikeville. Well, at least you'll have the heart-shaped Jacuzzi."

"The Magic Fingers. Is there—?"

"Oh, sure, everything's up-to-date. If you want some real excitement you might play bingo at the First Baptist hall or get a Slush Puppie at the Route 29 Seven-Eleven." She twirled a lock of hair between two fingers and let out a tiny giggle. Green blushed, forming an idea. No, it was impossible and stupid.

"Or," she said, blinking pale blue eyes, "maybe I could, y'know, give you the grand tour." She stared at his tie.

"Thank you, that's—but I have work here, to do." He gestured toward the offices. She nodded, smiling at herself. "But thanks." He tried to walk away normally, though his heart pounded and his leg muscles were so tense they ached.

The data room contained ten paper-stuffed boxes laid out on a long table. Green stepped up and down, searching for any document that looked easy, but all were equally unfamiliar. Finally he chose a hundred-pager called an "Indenture," which detailed the rights of an issue of Lee's bonds. Bonds, he knew, were like stock, except they paid interest and they . . . well, fuck, he'd pick it up.

Though he'd thought himself comfortable with legalese, he found this Indenture—which led off with the sentence "Issuer has duly authorized the creation of an issue of Debentures of substantially the tenor hereinafter set forth"—impenetrable, and after an hour he'd read only ten pages, fathoming little. Part of the problem was that he kept imagining Bonnie, now in a swimsuit, now in some petticoat-and-hoop concoction, now naked. Had she really asked him out? *Her?* Probably she was being neighborly, as they were down South. Anyway he had a girlfriend, plus he'd be digging through these boxes all night.

But at six, just as he'd begun to make progress, Houser announced that the office was closing and he'd have to leave. Pikeville folk did keep genteel hours, he thought, picturing Mandel at that moment rolling up his sleeves for an evening's work "How's our data look so far?" Houser asked.

"Standard," said Green, nodding confidently. "You run a tight ship." Houser grinned and said, "Try to. Try to."

Green gathered a few contracts to study at the hotel. As he passed Bonnie, straightening up her phone bank, she gave him a smile that caused a jolt in his groin.

Though the suite didn't really have a heart-shaped bath, two teddy bears, preciously clad in wedding clothes, did repose on the king-size bed. More important to Green was the goodie-jammed minibar, from which he withdrew a Heineken and a jar of cashews, amazed by the endless bounty of free food in this job.

He struggled to focus on his documents, but there were too many distractions. A sort of ark contained a cable TV, atop which a garish display promised "adult programming" after midnight. In the living room were a couch, desk, and second TV. Green kept moving from room to room, from couch to bed to desk, unable to decide which was best.

From the three-line speakerphone, he called Murphy in New York. "So I'm stranded, and I didn't bring a bag. I have no casual clothes, no clean shirt or underwear, not even a toothbrush."

"Happens all the time. What you do is go to a store and charge everything to Lee Textiles."

"To *Lee*?"

"You're there for their convenience, right?"

"I guess, but it seems—"

"Listen, a shirt? A toothbrush? That's bullshit. Once I was in L.A. on a deal and the client invited me to a party, so I got a tux at Armani, on them. It's still in my closet. But I outgrew it."

Green headed out into the purple Pikeville twilight, then walked down Route 29 to a nearby mall with a McDonald's, KFC, Fotomat—everything, in fact, seemed a franchise, as if they'd run fresh out of new ideas. An immense one-level department store offered food, furniture, and, shockingly, firearms (a Pikeville housewife with her list: "Froot Loops, Skippy . . . oh, the ammo!"). Loading a basket with clothes and toiletries, he put it all on his shiny, stiff, sea-green corporate credit card, sensing that a long, satisfying relationship had just begun between him and it.

Back at the Ramada he managed a few more hours of work, interrupted by a room-service dinner—bacon cheeseburger, fries, onion rings, Caesar salad, and cherry pie—then went to bed, gassy and too tired even to watch the porno movie.

The next day in the data room he bore down, filling a pad with summaries of the Lee documents and noting in the margins dozens of questions to ask Houser. Even the Indenture started making sense. He imagined delivering his precociously astute analysis to Mandel and receiving startled praise.

Several times he stepped out to chat with Bonnie. They did their Scottish voices, she ridiculed Pikeville's backwardness, and in the evening, when he asked her to call a cab to the hotel, she offered a lift instead. Her car, a filthy, rust-eaten Chrysler LeBaron, had dents in each fender and a front seat littered with lipsticks, empty Marlboro packs, and Dr. Pepper cans.

As Green cleared off the passenger side, she said, "Sorry about the Lebanon."

"What?"

"That's what I call my car. Lebanon."

"Oh, ha," he said, deciding to be cool and eschew the seat belt. Bonnie surprised him, clicking hers in place; but now he felt it would be too embarrassing to change his mind. Of course, he realized as she wheeled out, this would be the one time he'd get in a wreck, his face ending up steak tartare on the windshield.

"So you live in town?" he asked.

"I go to Vanderbilt University, in Tennessee?"

"Good school," he said, nodding.

"I took last semester off, and I've been staying with my parents." Her southern accent, so strong at the reception desk, had now mostly disappeared. Could she just switch it on? When was it most useful, answering Lee phones? Or sweet-talking a state trooper?

"You decided you needed a break?"

"Sort of. I had an—illness. Came home to recover."

Questions crowded his mind. "What year are you?"

She glanced over. "I'm twenty. You'd be about twenty-five?" She grinned, proud of her talent.

"Are you reading *Death in Venice* for Vanderbilt?"

"No, I have insomnia, and I saw the movie one night late. So now read the book, right? I do like it. Might read more Thomas Mann, but the library only had this one. As you might imagine, there ain't much call for him heah in Pikeville. None of that Kraut fairy stuff." Green laughed, then allowed himself a longer look at Bonnie. Very pretty. God, she was. And where in town did she find this wit, anyway?

"Sorry you didn't get the scenic tour," she said as she pulled up to the Ramada. "That's a dollar extra."

He fiddled with the door handle, staring at the glove compartment and picturing another night in the climate-controlled room, maybe watching the local news with its dolt of an anchorman and its bumpkin omission of the Mets score. "Offer still good?" he asked finally, the words sounding to him as disconnected as if they'd drifted through the window.

Two hours later he was waiting in the hotel lobby, watching as name-tagged, corpulent businessmen waddled around with cocktails, pressing flesh. He felt excited, but also guilty: Was he cheating on Shelly? They'd never explicitly agreed not to see other people, though it was kind of understood. On the other hand, it wasn't as if anything would *happen* with Bonnie. It was that whole, that whole—neighborly attitude.

She entered, wearing a clingy white minidress, her legs tanned and bare and her hair in a ponytail. Feeling chest constriction, Green hurried toward her, as if he needed to outrace the other men in the room, and tried to sound jaunty. "I thought we'd have a drink in the bar first, if—"

"I'm not that kind of girl." She grinned at his stricken expression. "I mean, I hate this scene. Let's take that ride." She offered the car keys, he admitted he couldn't drive a stick, and she mumbled something about him being quite the New Yorker.

She merged onto the highway, then right off, to a convenience store called the Hungry Dawg. Past the aisles of groceries, whose alien brand names and wrappers gave Green a sharp sense of dislocation, was a refrigerator case from which Bonnie took a six-pack of Grolsch. Ahead, in the register line, hulked a bearded Goliath in a cap with the motto, Kill 'Em All, Let God Sort 'Em Out, under a skull. Green pictured himself defending Bonnie—being beaten to death, actually—but when the man turned, he said, "Evenin', sir, 'scuse me please."

They rolled along Pikeville's deserted streets. She asked where he'd gone to law school, and he answered, "Harvard," like no big deal. He usually said it that way, instead of posing it as a question, or confessing it as a kind of sin.

Bonnie was unfazed. "So you could've done whatever you wanted, I guess. And you picked a big firm." She exited onto an unlit, winding two-lane. "See, to me you seem the type who'd do ACLU or civil rights or something."

"I did volunteer poverty law in school," he said, aware that he hadn't addressed her point. "And Crank has a strong—a pro bono program." That one had rung false. "No, the truth? They're paying a ton of money. What can I say? I'm ashamed now."

"Don't be. A hypocrite's the only thing I can't stand. Anyway, maybe you can do this awhile and change."

"That's my plan," he said, though he'd never exactly formulated such a plan. Heard aloud, though, it was a fine plan. "I don't see myself getting caught up in the law firm, ambition thing. I don't worship money. I'm not—"

"Work awhile, you can pay off your loans. You got loans?"

"Billions," he said, exhaling.

They climbed a dirt road. Branches cracked and popped beneath the tires, and sweet nature odors blew in the windows. "Good smells," he said. Bonnie explained all the blossoming flowers, whose names, like magnolia and wisteria, were familiar. (Green used to watch *The Waltons*, and John-Boy's fiction mentioned them.)

"In New York we have a plant that blooms in the subway: 'Urinalia,' or the urine flower. Quite fragrant."

She snickered and repeated, "The urine flower. Like it."

They stopped at a clearing, where some longhaired teenagers lazed in the gate of a pickup, passing a bottle of Rebel Yell. Bonnie slipped through foliage onto a footpath, pitch-dark except for shafts of moonlight. Green tripped over a root and almost dropped the beer. "Careful, darlin'," she said, grabbing his hand. He held on firmly, as if steadying himself, and without any squeezing that might come off flirtatious or sexy.

Soon they emerged onto a huge boulder, below which the town stretched out for miles, lights twinkling on all the empty streets. Bonnie made a sweeping gesture. "There it is—Dullville, U.S.A. And those echoing sounds of laughter? People watching *Hee Haw*, which is shown here on the educational station. Regular TV, of course, is twenty-four-hour fishin' shows and rasslin'."

She sat and sipped a Grolsch. "Another feather in our town's cap is we were the last in Georgia to integrate the lunch counters. Why I mentioned civil rights law." She leaned back on her elbows, her white dress glowing against the rock, and appraised him. "You seem too young to have a serious corporate job. Didn't you want to have some fun first?"

"Well, my life's not *over*."

"No, I know. The attraction of—what's the word? Stability." Then they were quiet.

"This is nice," he said, but had nothing to add. The whites of her eyes shimmered, her front teeth indented her lower lip, and a kind of invisible blood flowed between them. Suddenly they were kissing, and he was smelling her hair: flowers, all those John-Boy flowers. She pushed him onto his back.

He got dizzy, like floating in circles under water . . . then remembered Shelly and, pierced, came awake. This wasn't right. He applied upward pressure to Bonnie's head, but stopped, again asking himself: *Did* he and Shelly have an agreement? The tip of Bonnie's tongue ran over his lips—it was very, very tough to believe this was happening. The fact was they'd never struck a deal.

He groped under Bonnie's dress. She tugged at his jeans, he clawed them around his ankles, and soon she straddled him, got up on her knees and began rocking. He saw her ponytail swinging and the sky sprayed with stars. It was too much to stand; it was over in a minute.

She lay beside him. The quiet made him uncomfortable. "To be gouged by a rock is always romantic," he said with a little laugh. She seemed surprised at his tone. "It'd be better in a bed," he added. "We could go to the honeymoon suite."

"Well . . . I don't have birth control."

"Huh?"

"Yeah, what're the odds, right?" He felt like screaming. What was she, crazy?! Well, but she was right: Would he shoot a bull's-eye the first time? Then he pictured the rubber in his wallet, so old it had probably dried out and cracked, so old it was really comical. "I have something."

"Hmm. Wouldn't've thought you were the type to bring that." She sighed. "Okay, but my parents'll go wild if I don't come home, so I'll stop there and sneak out again."

Green felt unstable on his feet, as if experiencing a series of aftershocks. In the clearing the teenagers were still guzzling their way toward lifelong penury, and one winked at him. They didn't seem to mind him poachin' their womenfolk, though after he passed he worried they might jump him from behind.

Unsure what one said in this situation—and Bonnie appearing out of it, anyhow—he stayed silent the whole ride back to the hotel. She hugged him hard, as if they were parting forever. He said he'd see her in a little while, then looked back from the revolving door. She blew a kiss and jerked the Lebanon away.

· · ·

She didn't come. He waited in bed, naked, watching a movie called *Stockholm Girls' School* that had crappy production values, the set resembling less Stockholm than a vacant lot in Long Island City. It seemed silly, especially in the circumstances, and at two he turned it off, a bit angry but mainly let down. The next morning he hurried through checkout, eager to get to Lee reception. But she hadn't shown there, either, and the headset was now worn by a high-collared brunette whose smile suggested skin stretched over a fist. He thought of calling Bonnie at home, but had never asked her last name.

Paging through contracts in the data room, he visualized Bonnie, her hair swinging, and all the stars. Whenever he remembered Shelly, his stomach dropped. How could he have done it?! Deal or no deal, it felt awful. But it had happened so fast—Bonnie had given him such a shock—that he hadn't thought it through. Anyway, too late; his penis had won this round. As long as she wasn't pregnant. Oh God! Then he calmed himself: very unlikely.

Finally it was time to go. Riding to the airport, he searched the roadsides as if Bonnie might appear, hitchhiking or selling peaches and boiled peanuts. After takeoff he drank two scotches and fell asleep, sinking down in the big leather seat.

Soon after Green got home, Peter Rosen called from the booth at Big Nick's Pizza Joint, asking him to come downstairs. Green protested, "I ate on the plane and I'm tired—"

"Aw, man! Don't make me have dinner alone!"

Green moaned, but Rosen pestered him until he agreed.

At their usual table, beneath a mosaic of yellowed glossies promoting actors whose failed careers now rendered pathetic their chipper poses, Green watched Rosen grapple with two slices so huge they lolled off the sides of the plate.

"So Crank's good?" he asked.

"Petey, I mean I've been there four days, and three of them I spent in Pikeville, Georgia." He shrugged. "No, it's great. It'll be great. But it's tough."

Rosen flicked a searing pizza chunk around his mouth and then doused it with a cooling wash of Sprite. "Well, believe me, nobody's giving money away. So if they tell you to work buried in dogshit, you say, 'Yes, sir!'" He smiled, eyes crinkling, freckles merging at the corners. His freckles, which, together with his carrot hair, had gotten him commercials as a kid, now gave him the look of someone who'd never finished growing up. This wasn't helped by his five-foot-five height, colorful snap-and-buckle clothes, and white high-tops with Velcro fasteners. In the old days Ricky had envied Petey's TV work, paid at $1,000 a shot—to a boy, measuring wealth in Topps and Bazooka, a mind-boggling sum—but now it didn't seem worth it. It must be tough to be taken seriously, as an adult freckle-face.

On the way out, as Rosen passed Big Nick—behind his red-speckled counter, surveying his domain of fats—he shouted, "High-five, my man!" Green was embarrassed, but when their palms smacked, felt a jealous twinge. He could imagine no scenario in which he'd get five from Big Nick.

Early-evening shoppers milled around the fruit stalls just outside on Broadway. Rosen sidled up to a blonde in tight jeans sniffing a cantaloupe and said, "Smell good?"

Green whispered, "Come on!" but Rosen waved him away, and he edged to a nearby newsstand.

The woman ignored Rosen, who then shook a melon beside his ear, saying, "I only like ripe, juicy things." As if betraying her, the corner of her mouth turned up. "There it is!" he cried. "Your boyfriend tell you you got a beautiful smile? You must have a boyfriend—!" Tuning out the patter, Green found he'd been unconsciously staring at the magazines devoted to oversized breasts. The Pakistani proprietor leered impertinently, and he shifted to the newsweeklies, annoyed at Petey, who couldn't even go out for a goddamn pizza without finding adventure. He skimmed an article on health-care policy.

Rosen appeared. "It's all set."

"What is?"

He nodded toward the market. "She said she'll come to your house. I told her you had a great stereo—she should check it out 'cause she's buyin' a new one."

"I have a shitty stereo! Some Malaysian—"

"She *knows?* Who's she, Edison? Anyway, she doesn't care about a stereo; she's comin' up to get laid. By us both." Green instantly pictured porno tableaux set to a soundtrack of vulgar guitar chords. Feeling a wave of nausea, he touched a trickle of sweat off his brow and said, "What makes you think that? Plus I have a girlfriend!"

Rosen got on tiptoes to speak in Green's ear. "How a two on one works is this: I do her first, then you come in from the other room, like you're surprised to see—"

"I live in a studio! Where would I be coming in from?"

"From the bathroom, okay? So you watch awhile. You're watching, you're watching, and when she doesn't complain? that means it's cool. Then you put your cock in her mouth, casually."

"*Casually* put my cock in someone's mouth. That's—that's . . . sure." *The Nation* clapped back in its slot.

Rosen eyed him. "Chill out, Grandpa, I was just playin' wit-choo."

Green shook his head—fucking Petey had always known how to get him. "You're hilarious. I have to go to bed." Rosen said he wanted to stop up and borrow some CDs. Green resisted, but finally agreed on the condition that he leave in five minutes.

Two hours later, Green was still on his couch, watching Rosen pick through his collection, spread out across the floor. He'd already segregated ten and was carefully examining the back of another. "Don't you have enough?"

"You got a two-CD limit? I need all kinds of tunes, all around me. A world of music." Rosen chuckled at himself, aware he'd gone overboard. He'd switched the radio to a power-disco station and now cranked the volume on a song with lyrics consisting of nothing but the words "I like you, I like you a lot," repeated ad infinitum. His hand moved in rhythmic waves. "Good one, Ricky?"

"No. It's annoying as hell, actually."

"I know, you prefer ancient music. How old is Mick Jagger now, anyway, ninety? But I live in the moment, and this tune is hot." Then he smiled.

They had met as kids, when their families "summered" at the same Catskills bungalow colony. During the school year they'd hardly seen each other; Green had refused to venture out to Canarsie, where Rosen lived, though Petey would come into Manhattan for concerts, like Pink Floyd at the Garden in '77. They'd lost touch when Rosen went off to the U of Miami, where, Green later learned, he'd slept through two semesters before dropping out. He'd stayed in Florida as a bartender, then a furniture salesman, and had returned to New York a couple of months ago. Green had been startled to hear his voice again.

Now Rosen drove in from Jersey every week to meet for pizza or sushi. (He owned the lowest-end Mercedes, which he'd chosen over a better American car in the same price range. "It makes an impact," he explained. "Gets you in the door with people.") Green found him hard to relate to, the ten years having laid a vast distance between them, but on the other hand his company was enjoyable—a sort of guilty pleasure, like a Schwarzenegger movie. And, for some reason, Rosen pursued their revived friendship energetically . . . and it was nice, Green thought, to be courted. Anyway, even if he did want out, it was hard to tell Petey no. Oblivious to subtlety, he only understood when you shouted the word in his face. Like tonight, relaxing on the floor and showing no sign of leaving.

"Nothing against the old songs. Other day I heard 'Light My Fire.' Still sounded great. J5, remember?"

Green nodded: the Silver Glen jukebox. "You are incredible."

"I remember because I was happy then."

"You were nine, of course you were."

Rosen rubbed his chin with a freckly wrist. "That's true. Your best time is when you're a kid, I think. Sometimes grown-up life seems like—war. Whatever you try, a fuckin' army fights you. You do X, expecting people to do Y? Instead they hit you with Z, always the meanest and most fucked-up reaction."

"I don't know. I don't think people are so bad."

Rosen popped a honey-lemon cough drop in his mouth. He wasn't sick; he just liked them. "Yeah, well, you had it easy the whole ride through school, because you had the brain. But now you's in the real worl', we gonna see how you git on!"

"Uh-huh." Rosen studied his face, then said, "I'm gonna tell you something, and it's crucial you learn it and live by it. This is it: The world is not your mother."

"Obviously."

"Obviously, but I see you don't understand, 'cause you always had—"

"Look, whatever you say. It's not my mother. Nevertheless, I have to work tomorrow, so—"

"How's Shelly?" Rosen crunched the cough drop. Twenty-five and he still wouldn't let candy melt; that, for some reason, irritated Green. "Get your dick wet yet?"

"Shut up! I told you, it doesn't matter."

"But you have manly needs. And it's everywhere! Right in my building I met this sixteen-year-old—"

"Listen. I need sleep!" Green had a fleeting urge to tell about Bonnie, but knew Petey would pump him for every detail, all the while smirking and making lewd remarks.

Rosen pulled on his Jordache windbreaker (his pants were Parachutes, his sneakers Nikes), baby blue with a Roman lace-up front. "Forgot to mention, I have a job interview."

"For what?" Sales, Green thought. Definitely sales.

"It's with Vincent Alfieri, the arbitrageur." Green gaped. "Y'know, an arb? Buys stocks low, sells 'em high?"

"I know what an arb is," Green said in a haughty tone, though he really didn't know, exactly.

"He's a friend of my stepfather." Rosen leaned on the door, CDs filling one arm. "Excellent field for me, 'cause it's people-oriented. In life you gotta emphasize your strengths—and I'm not a genius with books, but I'm decent at relationships. Why I always did well in sales." Rosen saluted and hopped down the stairs.

Green flossed, trying to picture Petey the disco lover dressed in business clothes, moving billions across the stock exchange. This was a man with one year of higher education, whose idea of polite conversation was to blurt out comments on his friend's sex life. Yes, he was trying to be funny, but certain things should be kept private. And the fact was, what he had with Shelly, Rosen couldn't begin to comprehend, in his world of wet dicks and casual putting-of-cocks in mouths.

Green watched Neil Mermelstein scrutinize a pad on which a "To Do" column listed thirty items in precise block letters. The fourth-year associate let out a "How will we ever finish?" groan, and Green's heart sank. That was one of his worst.

They were in a Crank conference room, surrounded by a mountain range of boxes sent from Pikeville. Green, studying the agreement between Lee and its truckers' union, reached a clause that provided: "There shall be no swearing on the loading dock." Reading it aloud, he joked, "Yeah, like: I dropped a winch on my foot! Sugar!'"

"That *is* funny," Mermelstein said, a smile cracking his sallow face, then returned to his pad. Green sighed. How could he not laugh?! He'd tried again and again, making quips about the material, but Neil always pressed on with little reaction, as if his brain automatically filtered frivolous data. Though it had only been a week. Green felt he'd already spent more time with him than anyone else, ever. He knew each black hair on the conical forceps-head and each line around the sunken eyes; he could distinguish, by slight variations in pitch, the array of groans and whimpers.

Now Mermelstein said, "Don't spend too much time on the truckers. That contract will be gone after the LBO."

"Why gone? It extends another two years."

"But when we acquire Lee, we get an opportunity to terminate unfavorable agreements. It was Mandel's idea," he added, as if that would end all dispute.

Green reflected. "Well, I doubt it'll work."

Mermelstein marked his place with a finger. "Why, is it prohibited?"

"Not exactly, but I mean the employees bargained for this contract, and it's not fair to just . . . blow it away."

"What do you mean, 'fair'?" He was genuinely stumped, forcing Green to consider: How did you explain the concept of 'fair' to a man who'd just landed from Mars?

"It means something that's understood, whether or not you put it explicitly in writing. It's a—like a spirit."

"That sounds nice, but the reality is, if the employees valued the kind of protection you want to give them, they could've negotiated for it, 'explicitly.' But then they'd have traded off something else. Right?" Green couldn't think of an answer, and Mermelstein continued, "As Lee's lawyers, our only question is: Can the union win a suit? By the way, don't use a term like 'spirit' in front of Lou, or he'll decide you're a yutz. Believe me, you don't want *that.*"

The phone rang: Mandel desiring them and expecting, of course, they'd be present and ready for action. They found him at his desk, examining the *Times* astronomical charts. "*Shabbes* starts at 7:42, so

I gotta leave. But I wanna bounce some ideas off you guys, so you'll come in my cab."

They searched among the blue Lincolns triple-parked outside the building until they found the one whose number matched the voucher flapping in Mandel's hand. In the backseat—which was plush, with darkened windows and a cellular phone—Mandel switched on the reading light, bent it up at the two associates, and commenced an interrogation. Neil displayed his knowledge of the Lee LBO like a young peacock fanning his tail, while Green, the pale chick, just listened, grasping maybe a third. It hadn't taken him long after returning from Pikeville to realize that despite his momentary optimism at Lee, he'd need years to achieve anything like the mastery of a Mandel, or even a Mermelstein.

The car crept along, stuck behind a hansom jockey and his frothing, diarrhetic nag. Mandel abruptly faced front. "Hey, you. What're we doing on Park?"

The driver spoke with a Russian accent. "Sir, all streets are bad traffic now. Park it's best."

"Second's better! I take this ride every day!"

The Russian shook his thick-sideburned head, chuckled, said, "You got it," and maneuvered the car over. Second was at a complete standstill. He looked back as if he expected an apology out of Mandel, who was oblivious, and finally said in a jocular tone, "See, sir. Second it's even worse than Park!"

Mandel cocked his ear: Excuse me? Then he screamed, "If you went the right way, this wouldn't've happened!" The Russian mumbled some pitiful apologies, but Mandel had already gone off on an anti-Ben Lee diatribe. "Every time I think about a thirty-six-buck bid I get sick! He has no strategy, to low-ball instead of slam-dunk!"

Green already knew this complaint by heart. The strange part was that despite his invective, Mandel claimed he still lacked sufficient information to take Lee's measure. "He's acting dumb now because he thinks he can eat his cake, too. But who knows what he'll be capable of when the shit flies?"

The Russian, meanwhile, was accelerating madly and weaving between cars, all the while cursing the other drivers in dialect. They raced across Long Island and then, after a James Bond climax, screeched into the circular driveway with a minute to spare. Getting out, Mandel noticed the Russian's fearful eyes and said, "Don't worry, Ivan, you did good," and shlumped to his stained-glass entry.

The Russian backed up, mopping his face. Mermelstein advised, "Next time you drive Mandel, follow his instructions, even if you think they're wrong. Then he's easy."

"Okay, sir. Thank you." Airing his collar, he went on: "Mr. Mandel, he is Jewish? I ask because he seems like anti-Semite." Mermelstein was tickled. "This 'anti-Semite' gave about $100,000 to Jewish charities last year. 'Kay?"

The Russian let out a low whistle. "He must be very unhappy man."

Though sick of discussing the deal, Green hadn't yet identified any other subject of interest to Mermelstein. When he mentioned a book, movie, or even the male New Yorker's least common denominator—the Mets—Neil would nod and then drift. "I see you're married," he now said, gesturing at Mermelstein's ring.

"Yeah. In fact Tuesday was my fifth anniversary."

"Ah, that's—congratulations." Tuesday they'd sat in the conference room until 4:00 A.M. "Kids?"

"A one-year-old." He showed a photo of a fat-cheeked boy in a bow tie and then, as if unwillingly, asked, "You?"

"I have a girlfriend."

"That's nice." He pulled a document from his case. "I'd love to chat more, but we're under the gun here."

"No problem. I forgot to bring my bag—" Mermelstein waved dismissively, adjusted the light, then got to work.

Looking out at the grim Queens streets, Green thought of Shelly, whom he hadn't yet seen since Pikeville. Last weekend he'd made an excuse; the Bonnie incident had been too fresh, and he hadn't felt prepared for the necessary lying. He was a lousy liar to begin with. When they did meet, tomorrow night, he'd have to keep cool. Not that she'd be suspicious. What he'd done was way beyond anything that might occur to her.

What he'd done. It was wrong, *wrong!* Yet he now replayed it for the thousandth time, freezing the best frames. Once this week he'd tried to call Bonnie, but Lee reception had said she'd quit. Would she ever pop up again? Well, probably it'd be better if she didn't. But what if she was—?

Mermelstein interrupted his seizure. "Me and Mandel are flying to Pikeville on Wednesday. We want you to go a day early, with Baxter. Nose around with Houser and them. Sorry." Green shrugged, has to be done, but actually felt elated to escape Neil's pasty face, even for twenty-four hours.

Back at the office, they found a gang of associates eating dinner in the fortieth-floor kitchen. Murphy called, "Hey, the *Shabbes* express! Join us—it's a pleasant way to spend a Friday evening." Green accepted a hunk of his one-pound lasagna, ordered from one of the gourmet takeouts that serviced Crank and the dozens of other firms where lawyers worked past dinner, night after night.

Another eighth-year, Aaron Josephson—thin-faced and balding, with tortoiseshell glasses, silver cuff links, and a vaguely aristocratic air—was saying that a new deal had come into the office that afternoon. "It's a bid for"—he glanced around, then lowered his voice—"International Shoe. By a Japanese company."

"What do they want with American shoes?" Murphy asked.

"Oh, Shoe sold its footwear operations years ago. They're just in financial services now. Anyway, the Japanese bid forty-five dollars. That's double the market price."

"Keep the deals rolling in," Murphy said, balancing a huge forkful of cheesy pasta. "I need a big bonus to pay for my liposuction." Green watched him stuff his mouth, wondering what his income really was. Last year Crank had paid its top associates over $200,000, and even this was peanuts compared to the partners, like Mandel, who'd supposedly made $1.5 million. It all seemed a bit insane to Green, but, as he'd admitted to Bonnie, that's why he'd come: to get on the gravy train.

Crank, Wilson & Shapiro hadn't always been a money machine. It had drudged along for a century, its lawyers mild WASPs in three-piece suits, but the formation in the late seventies of Bernard Shapiro's ethnic, fee-crazy mergers and acquisitions group had jolted the firm to life. Green's assignment to Mandel made him M & A property for the next two years, and he'd quickly discovered the group's Green Beret ethic, exemplified by Murphy, who loved nothing more than to hang out telling tales of the inhuman hours someone had put in on a deal or the obscene fee Shapiro had charged some client.

Now he said, "You caught a major break pulling Lou Mandel for your first rotation. He's great with clients."

"Him?" Green snorted. "He's rude, insulting—"

"Not what I mean. He knows how they think. And partly because of that he gets deals done, which gives him clout. So if he likes you, you're on track. He's been my big supporter all along."

"You're both up for partner in September, right?"

Their falling faces signaled an awkward topic, and finally Josephson nodded toward Murphy. "If you want to succeed, model yourself on Jeff. He's the ideal corporate lawyer—much like Leonardo's ideal man, physically and mentally harmonious."

"Yes, to the WASPs I am perfect—a perfect Catholic from Archie Bunker Queens and Hofstra Law."

Green said, "Obviously that doesn't matter anymore."

"They never forget your pedigree," Murphy said. "Like Aaron, Mr. Yale Law. Compared to me he's a prize Akita." Now that he'd started, Murphy rated the partnership chances of each eighth-year associate. Green found the discussion depressing, but consoled himself that he, at least, would never slip into this obsessive trap. He was at Crank for some experience, and some money—but eight years down the line? He hoped it'd be as he'd told Bonnie: repay his loans, then switch to public interest law.

For dessert he ate a brownie, a kiwi tart, and two chocolate chip cookies, and then, as he did every night, left the kitchen with a bellyache. He checked in with Mermelstein, who was bathed in brutal halogen lamplight and saying, "Should get out early. Eleven, maybe midnight, certainly not later than one. Can you stay?"

Green averted his eyes. "Neil, I mean, I've slept about fifteen hours in the last week."

"Welcome to the NFL." The firm's stock response to anyone who complained.

"I thought I'd go home and rest."

Neil grinned at "rest" as one might at an eccentric hobby, like ichthyology. "Okay, if you guarantee at least twelve hours tomorrow and ten on Sunday. Deal?" Green nodded, grateful, though unnerved at begging for sleep. It had a *Papillon* quality.

His phone rang while he was putting on his jacket. Rosen said, "You know, you're a jerk since you went to that firm. I leave messages, and you don't call back. I wanted to have sushi."

"I've been swamped."

"Sure, well, you're a big shot, I guess. Maybe I have a busy job, too. You don't even think to ask."

"Oh, did you get that arb job?"

"Yes, I got that arb job." Rosen sounded thrilled. "I'm working directly for Vince Alfieri, as a market analyst. Which means I call around to his contacts and say, 'What's the word on the Street? Any takeovers or LBOs comin' up?' Then if there's any action we get our bets down. You can hedge with some shorting, but still you gotta have brass balls to play with this kind of money. Fuckin' unreal amounts, man.

"But fuck the money. Know what I really like best about this job? Picture our office, right? With this amazing view of the harbor, and all jammed up with antiques and polished wood and all that shit. And you drink coffee from a china cup . . . and then put down in the middle of it a bunch of wild animals. 'Cause you'd fuck anybody to add a quarter percent to your return."

"That does sound delightful."

"But the point is, it's *honest*. Nobody pretends it's fair or nice."

"Let me ask a different question: Is all this legal?"

"Sure. Like they say, 'It's not what you know, it's who you know.' Like, for example, I know you."

"You know me. What does that mean?"

"It means access to information positions a person to make money."

Green paused: That wasn't a Rosen-constructed sentence. "I'm not sure what you're saying, but I *think* you're nuts. I don't feel like going to jail."

"I'm not talking about tips on secret deals! God! I just meant I might call once in a while for a general sense of the market—is it hot or cold?"

"No. Leave me alone." Rosen pretended not to hear, going on to tell how cool Alfieri was, with his Maserati, his Fifth Avenue duplex, and Hamptons house. Green could join the two of them sometime out at the beach.

"No, I can't." He hung up before Petey could object, then spent a minute considering his remark about access. The fact was, Green had it, at the top, to men like Ben Lee. But he was also in constant contact with nonlawyers—people not subject to the canons of ethics. He'd have to be very careful.

Just out of curiosity, he looked up International Shoe on the stock page: 22-3/8. If Josephson was right, in a few days it would double. That was incredible.

Saturday evening, after fulfilling his labor commitment to Mermelstein, Green rushed home, arriving not long before Shelly. She kissed him as she entered, saying, "I missed you last weekend."

"Oh, Crank is killing me." He grabbed his head for emphasis. "I thought I knew, but it's beyond—"

"Well, you'll adjust."

They brought wineglasses to the couch. "So what was Pikeville like?"

"Dull," he said, shamed by the trust in her face. "Have you decided what food?"

"Whatever. Italian. So did you see the sights, or were 'y'all' stuck in a conference room?" She smiled, but he winced. Who was she, Miss Marple with her questions?

"Oh, the townspeople were quite hospitable." He forced a laugh. "When I left the plane, I set off this buzzer—I guess that signals an important guest has come. Then I was met by a welcoming party of men in white sheets, with hoods."

"And don't tell me, a burning cross?"

"Yeah. It was all very festive, like Mardi Gras. They even insisted on carrying me to my hotel."

"In the future stay north of Seventy-second Street, okay? It's safer." She sipped, her cheeks flushed lovably from joking. "Did you see any synagogues?"

"Pardon?"

"Some of these southern towns have beautiful old ones."

"Oh. Well, but not Pikeville, that's for sure. Where'd you hear about that, anyway?"

"From Dvorah Weissbart, in my office. She's an expert on America's temples." Shelly crossed her legs and brushed a hair off her sleeve. "I went with her and her husband last night. To temple."

"You did?! What for?"

"I thought I might like it."

"And did you?"

"Very much. The congregation, the rabbi . . . the entire experience."

"Was this some hippie synagogue, with the cantor in sandals and playing guitar?"

"No. Remember, Dvorah's Orthodox? It was Orthodox." Green, speechless, stared at the room's reflection in his drink.

His parents, who before the war had attended one of Lodz's socialist-atheist schools, viewed prayer as silly, and organized prayer absurd. So he'd grown up with little connection to the faith. More: at college he'd actively avoided the observant Jews, finding them sanctimonious as well as plain nerdy. (The boys, names knitted on yarmulkes, would rush out of the dorm on Friday night to temple instead of the toga party.)

Shelly and her family were, he knew, fully assimilated. She mispronounced Jewish expressions and, until he took her down to Yonah Schimmel's, had never tasted *kasha varnishkes* or *kugel*. Not even on Yom Kippur did the Feldmans show their faces in the Winnetka *shul*. Green had been attracted to all that.

"I'm surprised at you," he said at last.

"You act like I did something wrong."

"Not wrong, just—odd. I find the Orthodox odd. Of any faith." He gulped his wine and then grinned. "Well, you've seen services. You can write home and make your old Bubbe and Zeyde happy, and be done with it."

"I was thinking I might go back next week."

He glanced down again, mumbling, "Uh-huh. So you're becoming just the religious *maydl*. Hallelujah, and whatever."

She didn't respond for a while. "Have you been to one of these new Orthodox temples? With young people and couples with babies and a young rabbi?" Green shook his head. "Then, and excuse me for saying so, you're speaking from ignorance."

"Look—!"

"Don't get mad." Her voice softened to its normal tone. "Maybe you can come and see for yourself. Dvorah says—"

"Who is this Dvorah, some Manson figure? She seems to be getting a, like, a *power* over you!"

Shelly laughed. "She's a media buyer, from New Rochelle originally. Went to Brandeis. Not exactly the Manson . . . resume. Anyway, you're overreacting wildly. *I* asked her if I could go. I thought it might enhance my life."

Green exhaled, aware that Shelly was right. What was the big deal, really? So she felt a spiritual longing—that wasn't unusual. (Why did it have to be Orthodox, though? She gets intrigued with religion and immediately plunges in the deep end; whereas with sex she wades endlessly by the baby pool.)

"Sorry," he said. "I did overreact."

"I'm not going to turn into some fanatic. Please. But I should at least give it a little chance."

"Fine. Give it a little chance. Just leave me out, okay?" She nodded, then hugged him and kissed his cheek. He closed his eyes, sensing her breasts pressing against his arm.

"Don't worry," she whispered. "Nothing'll change."

# Chapter 3

Surveying the passengers filing past into coach, Green imagined them asking, "Hey, how'd this kid get up here?" One distinguished old man who limped by made him feel especially guilty, as he felt in a Dial-Car, riding home behind someone who resembled Fievel. Maybe, he thought, this carnival world of drivers, secretaries, messengers, and receptionists would seem more fitting if he'd grown up with servants (excluding Rachel, who was unpaid). Maybe then he'd easily embrace the simple premise upon which it all rested: Life Is Unfair.

Take Baxter, snuggling into first class, his natural habitat. Accepting a fresh grapefruit juice as only his due, he slid a laptop computer from a leather case and began to work. Green watched him. He had to be forty, yet looked boyish, a lick of hair falling across his forehead. His crow's-feet seemed those of an active guy, a sailor maybe, and his Hermes tie lay on its back, as if he'd just run in from the hreezy outdoors. Every banker Green had met so far wore an Hermes, reminding him of the fad for P.F. Flyer sneakers that had swept his third-grade class.

Under a sudden compulsion to sour.d knowledgeable, Green said, "We figured a way to get rid of the union contract," then coolly sipped his Virgin Mary. Without looking up from his screen, Baxter said it was great news. "Let's just hope they don't sue," Green added.

Now Baxter was interested. "Do they have a case?"

"Well, it's hard to say. The precedents go both ways, so— But let's wait for Lou to discuss . . ." Baxter seemed dubious, and Green decided to close his mouth for the rest of the trip. He'd bought a *Sports Illustrated* at the airport but, embarrassed to read it in front of the busy banker, instead perused the entire *Journal*, even the boring commodities stuff at the back.

Outside the Pikeville terminal, Green stepped toward the taxi stand but Baxter said, "This is us," and climbed into the Lee limo, a sleek black land yacht docked along the curb. Green thrilled at the gleaming crystal wet bar and small but delightful Trinitron. There was the tiniest jolt as they pulled away.

The countryside slid past soundlessly. Green wanted very, very much to turn on the TV, but Baxter had business to transact. Clicking a lighted phone out of the center armrest, he called clients, beginning each conversation with the ebullient tale of his last golf score and only after five minutes saying something like, "Anyhow, there's been some funny trading in your stock lately . . ." Green wondered if he'd have to learn golf to succeed as a corporate lawyer. He'd played miniature golf, of course, and now imagined telling Ben Lee, "I shot a twenty-seven at Coney Island! I put one right in the clown's mouth!"

All at once he got anxious. Alone this time, he'd have to mix in with Lee and Houser, and Baxter, and everybody. He felt an impostor, a know-nothing. Then he addressed himself: You are a Harvard graduate. You make a nice appearance, slim in your suit. (Thus spake Rachel.) Just *attempt* not to be a wiseass and you'll do fine. He exhaled. Anyway, if Mandel could blend in—but they forgave everything, when you were a genius.


There was a knock, but Green, relaxing in jeans with MTV, mini-bar beer, and snacks, hadn't yet called room service. He found Bonnie out in the hall, leaning against the doorjamb. She was wearing a blue checked shirt, her hair was down, as she'd worn it the first time he saw her, and she was smiling mischievously. They stumbled into the room, kissing, and fell on the bed. He tore out of his shirt, she unhooked her bra, and they wriggled out of their pants and pressed together. She tilted her head away, gasping, "Gonna pass out."

She said he should go inside her. He asked if he needed anything and she murmured, "This time I was ready." His heart bounced, he saw white light, felt her moving, and came in a rush. He lay on her, heaving, as the room spun. He tried to speak but couldn't. Everything was too confused.

With a cigarette from her bag, Bonnie sat up against the headboard. "How did you know I was here?"

"I've still got friends at Lee reception." She blew out the match and flicked it onto the carpet. "New Yorkers coming down is the excitement of the week."

He closed his eyes, dizzy again. "I tried to call, but they said you quit."

"I couldn't take any more of the brain atrophy."

He looked up. "What happened that night?"

She shook her head slowly. "I drove home; then after my parents went to sleep I sneaked out. But my car broke down halfway, and my father had to come get me. Quite humiliating."

"Shit. And then I thought I'd see you at Lee."

"I woke up violently ill. I would've called you, but I was afraid you were mad. Also I can't get any privacy living with my fucking *parents.*" She puffed.

"I wasn't mad. Well, a little. But I wish you had called. I missed you." He paused, surprised at how much.

She was touched. "That's sweet! Because to be honest, the real reason I didn't call was I figured, Here's this big-shot lawyer with a whole life going on in Manhattan, why does he want some college dropout bothering him?"

"Big-shot lawyer," he said.

"But to hear—I know it's crazy, we just met—but I really missed you." She laid her head on his chest. "Like I kept thinking of the urine flower, remember? And every time, it made me laugh more." He felt his chest fill, as with the range of human emotions. It was truly exhausting.

They talked for hours by the diffuse orange light of a table lamp. She described growing up in "Shitholeville," where she had never fit in, reading Kerouac at home while the other kids were turning cart-wheels at football pep rallies. "I was in this James Dean stage, dressed all in black, which didn't make me the *most* popular. Fortunately, Chris transferred in, in tenth grade." Her boyfriend and fellow outcast was, she explained, an avid reader, an R.E.M. fan, a pot smoker. "And our being sexually very active together became this huge scandal! They called us the 'Erotic Neurotics.' Puritans, huh?" Green managed an ironic laugh as the phrase "sexually very active" exploded repeatedly inside his brain.

"So they thought we were nuts, but I guess I showed 'em, 'cause I won valedictorian." She averted her eyes, ashamed to brag. Green flashed with envy, still bitter about his third-place finish at Stuyvesant High, behind the ass kisser and plagiarist Steve Pintchik and the chemistry whiz Govinda Singh, who had built a robot for the sophomore-year science fair. "Half the girls in my class are already popping out babies, like they don't know, and don't wanna know, any world beyond Holeville. But the happiest day of *my* life was when I left for Vanderbilt."

"What were you majoring in there?"

She pulled the sheet up over her chest. "I don't know why, but I'm embarrassed to tell. Theater. I must admit that I ruled as Blanche in the freshman production of *Streetcar.*"

He grabbed her and said, "'We had this date from the beginning.'" Hearing his Brando aloud, he wanted to take it outside and bury it. But she kissed him anyway, saying, "You're cute." It was great to be cute. His pulse sped and then, picturing Bonnie a sexually active teenager, he made love to her as if possessed. "Go slower," she whispered once or twice.

Later, when he asked what illness had forced her to leave school, she said, "My, we are inquisitive." A cigarette end fired in the dark, not far from his face, and she said, "I was in a rear-ender. Got whiplash, which I thought only existed in sitcoms? Well, in real life it's not so funny. Just got out of a neck brace."

She asked about his youth. He described playing in Riverside Park and taking the subway to school. "Have you heard of the Upper West Side?"

"Think I'm Minnie Pearl? It's, like, capital of the liberal Jewish nation of America, right? Actually, I'm fascinated by Jewish culture."

He experienced a rush of pleasure, but then tensed. That was a strange thing for her to say. What *was* she saying? Why had she come here? "You okay?" She was eyeing him carefully.

He blinked. "Um, what makes you think I'm Jewish?"

"Wild guess," she said, embarrassed.

"Well, you were right in that I was born a Jew, but I've converted to Santeria—y'know, the whole voodoo thing. My mother still boils chicken, but now I sacrifice them, so it kind of evens out." Bonnie's merely polite laugh stunned Green, whose Woody Allen shtick invariably scored big, even when delivered on autopilot. Was she so attuned to unspontaneity?

She swung her legs out from under the sheet. "I better go." The lamp switched on again, illuminating a painting: boat in a squall, white-haired goy at the helm.

Green watched her dress, agonized. "I wish you'd stay."

She stopped with one pant leg on. "You really do? I have to admit I just feel like going to sleep. My parents, though . . . you wouldn't believe them. Very strict."

"Well, if you'll get in trouble—"

"No, it's all right." She dropped her jeans again, sighing. "I'll make up a story."

The first thing he saw when he awoke was Bonnie's hair fanned out on the pillow. Feeling lucky, he went off to the shower, sang ("Layla," of course), then stopped and leaned against the tile, water pouring over his head.

It had been nagging at him all night, and he'd ignored it, but now it was morning, and what was he going to do? The best would be to tell Bonnie that it had been great, but he already had someone. The problem was, he felt ill even thinking of that. Maybe he could keep seeing them both until he sorted it out? No, that was immoral, and he wasn't the kind of person who— Oh, shut up. He actually wanted his conscience to shut up. At that moment Bonnie stepped in and embraced him.

She offered to run him over to Lee, but he said he'd catch a cab. No reason to risk being seen together. She accepted his concern, for the present, but warned him not to start thinking of her like that.

"Like what?" he asked as they exited the lobby, into the sun.

"Y'know, the chippie you've got hidden away. 'Cause it won't fly with me. You'll be out of *my* pants, permanently." She smiled brightly, pecked his cheek, and then sashayed over to her Lebanon, leaving him dumbfounded in the driveway.

Houser's office overlooked a pond and a meadow that sloped down to a patch of woods. Among the items on his desk were a golf ball encased in Lucite (engraved "Hole-in-One! To Gilbert from the Rebs, 7/9/84") and a studio portrait of a massive white-haired woman seated between two teenage girls. His law diploma was from Tulane. Good school, Green thought.

"This is so nice, with the pond."

"Thanks. Stocked with some fish, too."

"Really? I like fish."

"Get much decent fishing up in New York?"

"Me? Oh, I haven't—I don't get to fish too often." He tittered. "I meant I like to eat fish: tuna, snapper."

With deft surgeon fingers, Houser screwed a cigarette into a black holder. Though Green assumed the extra filtering had been demanded by his doctor, the holder still made him look like a forties Hollywood queen. Lighting up, he said, "About our litigations. There's only two of consequence. One is a class action, brought by a woman who used to work here, alleging racial discrimination in promotions."

Green took notes. "Probably a nuisance suit?"

"We think so, obviously. Our society has become so litigious, it seems, that anyone who ever suffers a career setback brings a federal case. But she has won a five-million-dollar jury verdict, which we're vigorously appealing."

"Okay. Yes. What would you say your chances are?"

Houser scratched his silver hair, so gently that the gesture caught Green's attention. Then, realizing it was a toupee, he felt rattled; he'd just started losing his own hair, and this rug provided a glimpse into the bald future. He had to scrape his eyes below Houser's forehead.

"We believe there's grounds for reversal. Or we might settle. In any event, we can delay payments for years."

Green wrote. "Delay . . . payments. Okay. Yes."

"The other suit is by the state EPA, alleging that our dyeing runoff has polluted the Hecuba River, near the Pikeville plant. They're saying we ought to clean it up, and we plan to eventually, but for now we think we'll be allowed to pay a fine."

"Why do you think that?"

"We've received certain assurances from the governor, who is a friend to Lee Textiles."

"Oh." Green couldn't wait to report all this to Fievel, who'd devour it. Houser said he'd send Green the files from the routine cases, then asked if he wanted to see the fish. He nodded, as a child might have, and they strolled outside and across to the pond.

A breeze rippled the water. Houser pointed: "That's what a bass looks like before it gets in a white-wine sauce." Green glanced sharply over: the general counsel had made a joke. The truth was, it felt good to pal around with an executive. Whatever Green's pogrom-and-broken-cookie background, he'd labored to acquire skills that now gave him entree, just as Mandel had. There was no telling where he could end up.

At noon, in the company cafeteria, they encountered Baxter near the Carvery, where a hairnetted black man sliced rare roast beef. Baxter gave Green a grin and whispered, "The cocksman." Green grinned back, but inside his juices were roiling. Had Will spotted him and Bonnie at the hotel?! Cavorting with a twenty-year-old receptionist—that'd go over great with the captains of industry.

As they ate, Green mulled over Baxter's comment. First, he might've heard wrong. What sounded like cocksman? Coxswain—maybe because he was the first crew member to arrive? Very strained. Coxcomb? Not a Baxter word. Okay, say it *was* cocksman—he had no reason to assume that Will would tell anyone. This wasn't tenth grade, after all. He felt better.

After lunch, Houser drove them to the north side of town, which, by contrast to Lee's pristine neighborhood, was a sad landscape of twisted metal, burned-out appliances, and tin-roof shacks. Two barefoot black children on a sinking porch watched the car pass with uncurious eyes. Green looked at Baxter and Houser, but they were chattering about the deal and facing dead ahead.

At the mill Houser distributed hardhats and goggles, and Green almost laughed at Baxter, whose gear looked ridiculous, with his British suit and tasseled loafers. The looms droned, their noise roughly equal to that of the number 3 express rumbling through a local station. How could people work in these conditions? Green considered writing the word "Union" on a card and waving it around, but doubted that Houser would be amused.

The general counsel indicated one large loom and, over the din, shouted, "Our Jewish machine!"

"Really?!" Green called back, though it didn't make sense, unless it had been developed by Jewish engineers, maybe a team out of Emory? Then he realized it was Lee's *newest* machine. His first stop at home would be Fievel's ear, nose, and throat man.

Houser and Baxter were quiet as they drove back. When they passed the sinking shacks again, Green gestured at them, saying, "Too bad, huh?"

Houser nodded. "If you'd come just a couple weeks earlier, the magnolia would've been perfect."


Green lunged across his room for the ringing phone.

"Hey, cutie."

"Can you come over right away?"

"Check this out. I told my parents I spent last night at my friend Jen's? But it turns out she called here, so now they've grounded me, like I was fourteen. Isn't that a hoot?"

"Can you sneak away?"

"No. Wait, lemme get in the closet." A door creaked. "They claimed I was out with some 'rebel,' drunk driving around? I said far from it, I was with a gennulman lawyah." A match struck. Was she smoking in the closet? "If you came by the house for *one* minute, they'd have no excuse to lock me in."

He exhaled. This was getting too— But then, as if sent by telepathy, Bonnie flashed, naked, at the front of his forehead. He said he'd be there in an hour.

"Excellent! First, though, I have to warn you about my mother. Remember I said you wouldn't believe her? Well, she's born-again. A pain in the ass, basically."

"Oh, I can't. . . ! I mean, does she know—?"

"That you're Jewish? Yeah. She took it well. Made some reference to the Judeo-Christian tradition. She seemed to think she'd be able to discuss the Old Testament with you."

"Oh, this sounds like great, great fun."

"I'll make it up to you."

"How?"

"You know exactly how," she said, in an oddly aggressive tone.


Hyacinth Lane at twilight suggested the set of a movie promoting the goodness of small-town life. A bicycle lay on a lawn, wheels spinning in the breeze. Solid Fords and Chevrolets sat unstolen beside open garage doors. Two boys tossed football spirals. Green, still in his suit (more respectable), rang the bell and waited, thinking: I was born in America. I can be here.

Bonnie kissed him, said how grateful she was, then led him inside to a paneled living room with a real fireplace. Jesus was present in a painting above the Zenith, and also a larger work in which He berated some men holding sacks of change.

Mrs. Williams bounded off her La-Z-Boy. Youthful, brownhaired, and slim in brown knit slacks, she had a jittery manner and, when introduced to Green, nodded quickly, as if to show she understood his name. Bursts of laughter punctuated her inquiries regarding cold drinks, and then she bolted to the kitchen. Green deadpanned, "Good evening, madam. Anti-Christ at your service." Bonnie bent double, laughing.

They sat on the nubby beige couch, right under Him. Mrs. Williams returned with iced teas and a bowl containing ten potato chips. Those'll last like two minutes, Green thought, sipping. Mrs. Williams launched a weather discussion, excitedly, as if it were too important a subject to avoid any longer. Mr. Williams then entered, carrying a hammer, wiping his neck with a rag. There was a ruffling, a fluttering in the room, he stopped and stared, and Green thought: It is not impossible, or even improbable, that Mr. Williams will hit me with that hammer. Instead, he slapped it in his left palm and approached with a firm shake.

While his wife fetched him a Coke, Williams sat on Bonnie's other side. They were all facing the front window, which made Green feel they were train passengers . . . heading to a mean, primitive place where he'd be harmed. "Tough to align shelf joints," Williams opined to Green, who nodded in ignorant agreement. The father and daughter had a great resemblance in profile, except for his cracked riverbed of a face and light brown hair.

Mrs. Williams returned and perched on a hard chair opposite the couch. Riding backward, Green thought. "Well, Rick. How do you find Pikeville?"

After a beat, he said, "Turn left at Atlanta, I guess." But he hadn't gotten behind the joke, in the end, and no one even smiled. "No, it's beautiful, Mrs. . . . I could see living here easily. I—"

"Was up in New York a couple years ago," Williams said. "For a sales convention. Stayed at the Days Inn?" Green had seen the hotel, way west on a lousy street, across from a drug halfway house. Some cheap job Williams must have, to get stuck there. "Newsstand got robbed the first night."

"That's New York! Seriously, it's not as bad as you might think." He chuckled. "Hey, that'd be a good ad slogan: 'New York, not as bad as you might think.'" Silence. Green missed his mouth with the glass, and very cold tea dribbled down his jaw.

"Lotta lawyers in New York. Bonnie says you're—"

"I've only been practicing a very short time. Before that I clerked, for Leo Fineman? Have you heard of him?" Green said he was famous, a great jurist.

Bonnie and her mother were staring each other down like Ali and Frazier at a weigh-in. At last Mrs. Williams blinked, turned, and asked, "Do you belong to a—a temple?"

Bonnie exclaimed, "You promised!" and Williams said, "For Christ's sake, Linda."

Linda Williams's hands flew up like spooked pigeons. "Don, please do not blaspheme in the house."

He stood, hammer hanging. "You don't like it in the house, I'll go outside. Nice meetin' you." He left.

Green hated to cause a family fight, and thought he might smooth things over. "No, Mrs. Williams, I'm not, y'know, religious."

She was disappointed. "Hear there's some beautiful temples in New York. One in particular that I've heard about: B'nai Israel, Shalom Jerusalem, or some name that sounds like that. I'd love to see St. Patrick's, of course. My church always talks about organizing a tour."

"Oh, it's breathtaking. I went to Mass there once with a Catholic friend. Are you Catholic?"

She winced as though in physical pain. "No, Baptist. Got a nice li'l Baptist church in town, maybe you've noticed it?"

Bonnie snickered. "Jus' look for the stocks and bobwire out front." As she wrangled with her mother, her accent had kicked back in.

Mrs. Williams's face tightened to a monkey smile. "Maybe if you came to church one Sunday instead of lying in your bed smoking, you'd see how nice folks really are."

"I *went* last month, remember? First everybody makin' snide remarks 'bout 'Haven't seen you in church for a coon's age, y'been sick?' Then on the way out Reverend Bryson hugs me and cops a feel."

"You evil-speaking thing!" She rose, hands on hips, collected the glasses, and stamped into the kitchen.

Unnerved by the savage tone of the Williamses' sniping, Green released tension with a laugh, then said, "Much as I'm enjoying our get-together—"

"Yeah." Bonnie stood. "Mission's accomplished anyway. They've seen an upstanding citizen in the house." He nodded, though suspecting his real mission had been to serve as Bonnie's battering ram against her mother.

"You're not leaving already?!" Mrs. Williams wailed as they passed the kitchen. "Well, Rick, you were the sweetest thing ever for dropping by, and I surely hope that you will come and visit us again in the near future!" She had to shout the last part of this declaration, as Green had already followed Bonnie into the garage, where her father was working some sort of plane along the top of a bookcase. "I'm gonna drive Rick home." He grunted. "See you in a bit," she added, getting in the car. As she backed out, Green observed that Williams was the scrawny-with-muscular-arms type of guy.

Bonnie apologized for her parents, saying they weren't always that bad.

"Didn't you go a little rough on your mother?"

"No," she said flatly, then lit a cigarette off the dash. "She has no manners. Asking if you go to temple."

"I didn't care. Anyway, I'm the one who should apologize. I got the evening off on the wrong foot, by killing Christ and all." Bonnie laughed and he went on, "Know what was interesting? She seemed let down when I said I wasn't religious. As if she'd prefer me in a yarmulke to . . . nothing. . . ."

"She wants God-loving people around, whatever the sect. Atheists make her nervous, like they might break into sun worship or numerology, right on the couch. Leave the house all fucked up and unholy." Green nodded, having seen this before in the devout: They not only disdained, but actually feared heathens. Like Mrs. Kreindler, his Hebrew-school teacher, who'd taught the alef-bet, told Bible stories, and explained the holidays, all with joyous fervor. When he'd joined at age eleven, she'd chosen him, the round-faced offspring of unbelievers, as her pet and special project, even though she knew he was there only to train for his bar mitzvah (which his parents had felt shamed into) and that once that party/rite/fundraiser was over, he'd return to his impious life.

On graduation day, after the kids had received their embossed scrolls in the synagogue, she had pursued the Greens out to Broadway, begging them, "Don't let him go to waste!" She'd looked terrified, as if watching a jumper on a window ledge, but Fievel had brushed her off, when they got home calling her a nut case; and Ricky had agreed. Anyway, who wanted the religious kids' hassles?

But he'd never forgotten Mrs. Kreindler's tantrum, and over the years had often wondered why it had been so urgent. Had she seen in him the makings of a great rabbi? Or *was* she just a zealot? More likely the latter, he'd concluded. Occasionally, though, and on the High Holidays in particular (which he spent at the movies or playing ball), he'd get the sick feeling that he'd missed out on something worthwhile. That he had, in fact, gone to waste.

He stared out at the passing scenery, wondering what Shelly would say to— Oh. Guilt struck, sharp this time, like no more fooling around.

Bonnie idled the car in the driveway. "I wanna come in, but the KGB probably has stopwatches going. Maybe we'll meet later?"

He twisted his fingers. "I'm not sure. I'm—I might have to work. How about I call you?" Giving her hand a quick squeeze, he hopped out and across to the entrance.

Spotting Mandel and Mermelstein, bad-postured at the front desk, Green wanted to run over and kiss them. Mandel was browbeating a smooth-faced young clerk in an emerald jacket. "I have meetings! Where should I meet with people, on the toilet?!"

"I'm sorry, sir, but there are no suites *available*. As I said, we do have meeting rooms—"

"I don't want that bullshit! I need a table and speakerphone in my room!"

"Would you like to speak to the manager?"

"Damn right. Ask him, am I supposed to meet with people on the toilet." As the clerk cowered off, Mandel noticed Green and broke into a shockingly bright smile. "There he is, the leadoff hitter! How's Pikeville?"

"Great. Houser briefed me and gave me a plant tour."

"Good work. We're gonna have dinner, so you come."

When the manager—a rabbity man with corn-silk hair—arrived, Mandel took him aside. He began gesticulating, and the manager seemed to be nodding a lot. By the time they returned, Mandel had his suite.


The hotel restaurant's "motif" was Italian, which meant red, white, and green crepe tacked up everywhere and a giant vase of dirty old dried pastas. Over candlelight and a forty-dollar bottle of Barolo, Mandel explained the agenda for the board meeting. After the routine business, Lee would present his offer. "Then the board appoints a 'special committee' of all the directors who aren't Lee executives. Now these guys' job is to negotiate with Ben . . . and me, God help 'em. They'll hire their own lawyer so the record shows they had independent advice and it was all kosher. I'll recommend Paul Weinberg at Finkel, Hassler."

Green said, "You keep telling us thirty-one is a low-ball offer. What if the special committee rejects it?"

"He's opening at thirty-one knowing they'll drag him up to thirty-six. He wouldn't bid if he wasn't sure they'd sell him the company at that price."

"What about the committee's investment bankers?"

"They'll say it's a lovely price." He paused. "You look sick." Mermelstein shot Green a warning glance: Don't talk about what's "fair"; don't be a yutz.

"I just— It all seems too neat."

Mandel gave a fatherly grin. "Don't worry, everyone'll do his job. In negotiations you're expected to be a pain in the ass, to a point, past which you start to piss people off." He chomped a breadstick. "See, we work with the same guys constantly, like Weinberg. You want his reputation: tough, but won't let his ego kill a deal. You must be able to compromise, or eventually you stop getting hired."

Mandel made sense, Green thought. It'd be great if everyone could act spotlessly, but life necessitated certain . . . practicalities. He knew he should drop the subject now, yet somehow couldn't. "Do you believe Lee wants the LBO at a cheap price only to have a 'cushion,' so he won't have to fire workers and all that? Or *is* he stealing the company?"

Mermelstein hid his eyes. Mandel said, "Lemme tell you something. Ben Lee is a good man. Ninety percent of my clients are decent and honest. Some are borderline. Scumbags I don't take on. But either way, I'm just a lawyer. My clients pay me to advocate their interests, not the world's. And I fight my ass off, long as what they want is within the bounds of legality." Green nodded, feeling laughably immature. "Let's eat," said Mandel.

The waiter's accent sounded authentic, and Green wondered what twists of fate had brought him from Rome, or wherever, to the Pikeville Ramada. Mandel and Mermelstein ordered the same pasta dish, first confirming that it didn't contain ham, and Green the veal chop, the most expensive item on the menu.

After only two glasses of wine, Mandel's cheeks had turned red and his eyes shone. "Here's one. How many JAPs does it take to screw in a light bulb?" Mermelstein asked how many, Mandel informed him, they broke up, and Green worked his face into a grin. "How do you stop a Jewish girl from having sex? Marry her!" Neil howled and Lou waved, saying, "Wait, wait! Then what about the Jewish . . . some kind of JAP . . . fuck, I can't remember. Gotta take a leak." He stood abruptly, upending his chair as he went. Green noticed an elderly couple at the next table staring, and he blushed.

Mermelstein smiled over the candle and slurred, "Baxter says you had an adventure . . . with a receptionist." Green winced. Asshole Baxter! Well, Neil didn't seem mad, and in fact he was now nudging Green's arm, saying, "We need details urgently."

"Nothing to tell."

"Aw, c'mon! Lemme ask, was her body good, all undressed?" Green ached with the desire to throttle him, but then thought, The poor guy had no life—what could he expect? He refused to answer.

Mandel came back and attacked his pasta. Picking some pinkish matter from his bowl, Mermelstein sniffed it and screamed to Mandel, "Stop eating!" The waiter came running. "You said this wasn't pasta with ham!"

"Yes, so it is not." He examined the mystery substance. "Ah! That is a delicious Italian bacon."

"Bacon?!" To the tuxedoed maitre d' Mandel shouted, "He gives me bacon! I can't eat it, so I want other food!" The host bowed to show that all would be fine. Green had to smile at Mandel, who was in some ways like a gifted infant, able to convey his demands in full sentences. Later, when they received cognacs on the house, Green rolled some around his tongue (as he'd heard you should) and thought how lucky Lou was not to be shy.

Upstairs, the operator said he'd had calls from a Shelly Feldman and a Bonnie No Last Name. Shelly wouldn't have called unless it was important, and he dialed her in New York. "I'm glad I reached you! I checked, and a town, Boland, near Pikeville, does have a historic syn-agogue." Green found it disorienting, in the midst of so much activity, to be presented with a fact of such little significance. "In case you have time to visit it," she added.

"I'll be in meetings all day. But thanks for checking."

"Maybe on your next trip," she said.

"Sure," he said, and a sadness settled over the conversation.

"Sweet dreams," she said.

He called Bonnie next. "Just wanted to hear your voice before going to sleep," she explained, and whispered, "I'll think of you in bed and masturbate. Maybe you should, too."

"Okay," he said, then colored at his tone, which had been *way* off—not even vaguely romantic. She wished him sweet dreams.

He didn't masturbate (not in the mood), and for a moment felt guilty, as if he were cheating Bonnie. Then he had bad dreams.

When they arrived the next morning, the board meeting was under-way. While they awaited their cue in an anteroom, Mandel scanned the tender-offer ads in the *Journal*. "Know what, Rick? You started at the best time ever. In the seventies it was bankruptcy, busted real estate, that shit, but now we're on a nice ride, and who knows how long it'll last?" He slapped the paper. "International Shoe, sold at forty-five bucks. The stockholders must be fuckin', drinkin' D.P." Green shook his head, amazed how much money people made without doing anything at all.

Baxter appeared, and Green glared: tenth-grader! Then they all read their newspapers. Though he knew he wouldn't have to speak, Green got stage fright and ran to the bathroom with diarrhea. Soon after his sheepish return, Houser opened the door. "Ready for y'all."

The boardroom was a windowless rectangle with recessed fluo-rescent lighting that produced a sick glow. Around the table were the eight directors, seven of whom—including Lee, Houser, and McCoy—were white men between the ages of fifty and seventy, wearing full-cut suits, striped ties, and a *harvest* of toupees. Green found a seat way at the end, beside the eighth director, a shelf-bosomed black woman with relaxed hair and glasses on a chain.

Lee consulted his agenda. "Item four, a proposed acquisition by a group made up of Tate McMahon and the company's senior exec-utives." Green began taking notes for the official minutes that he would—supervised by Neil, who had already tutored him in the art of selective description—be expected to prepare.

Lee placed his palms flat on the table. "Now. We feel we've struc-tured a bid that gives stockholders a handsome current payout but still leaves the company in a position to bloom and grow. If you gentlemen, and lady, kindly turn to the materials we've circulated, you'll find a bid letter. We're offering thirty-one dollars." A few directors gasped, but Lee pressed on. "I'd like to explain how we decided a buyout was in the company's best interest."

After his presentation—an expanded version of the speech he'd made at the first meeting, but peppered with frequent references to

the "good folks of Pikeville"—Lee asked Mandel for a legal over-
view. Working a room, Mandel sounded uncannily like Jackie Mason,
so much so that Green half-expected him to start *shpritzing* on the
uproarious differences between Jews and Gentiles. Nevertheless,
accent or not, ugly tie or not, *Jew* or not, he had the directors rapt . . .
and it struck Green then that true expertise, like a great work of art,
could produce in thinking people no reaction other than admiration.
He envisioned himself twenty years hence, in Mandel's place, speaking
from wisdom and experience.

Lee invited questions, most of which were softballs, except for
those posed by one small, dyspeptic director with a white crew cut and
beady eyes. Green matched him to his photo in the annual report: he
was Otis Fairchild, seventy-one, retired CEO of an auto parts company.
His detailed inquiries about the deal and its financing finally exasper-
ated Lee, who exclaimed, "Could you please stop snappin' at my ass,
Otis? We'll have plenty of time to explore these issues!" (Green's minutes ultimately would state simply: "Discussion then terminated.")

The special committee was to consist of the independent directors: Fairchild; Penobscot Jackson, the CEO of Pikeville S&L; Rich
Spellman, a local developer; and the black woman, Ruth Royster, a
business school professor. The committee chose J. Wormer & Co. as
its financial adviser and, as Mandel had predicted, Finkel, Hassler as
counsel.

Everyone milled around after the meeting. Baxter demonstrated
a new golf swing; Fairchild, a centimillionaire, complained about
movie-ticket prices; nobody talked to Royster. Mermelstein sidled up
to Green and emitted a "We have a ton of work back home" whimper
that made his skin crawl.

When they took off that afternoon. Green searched for Bonnie's
house. But they were heading the opposite way.


Lee's stock price started creeping up the next day. Mandel, behind his
sloppy desk, puffed a cigar and said, "I expected it. All these people
know about the LBO. Somebody will always open his mouth, and
somebody else'll buy stock to make a killing. Didn't I say?" Mermelstein dutifully nodded. Mandel had indeed recommended announcing

the bid, but Ben Lee had wanted to keep it quiet so as not to disrupt business as usual. Now there was no choice.

While Mandel called Lee with the news, Mermelstein told Green, "Since we're going public, there'll be pressure to negotiate a deal fast. So don't make 'social' plans. The committee'll come to New York, and we'll sit in a room till it's done. Could be four, five days without a break." His face reflected a crow's mocking pleasure. "So don't make social plans."

"So what you're saying is, I shouldn't make plans?"

"Right."

"I was supposed to lead a quilting bee this weekend; guess that's off."

Mermelstein seemed unsure if he was joking, but just in case said, "We'll be working."

Mandel hung up. "Lee says if they have to announce, so be it. Now that we're going public, the deal has to be done *fast*. Neil, people know not to make plans?"

"They know. Negotiations start tomorrow morning."

"You'll handle it till sundown, when I can come in." Mermelstein beamed—the understudy getting his break, thanks to the Pentateuch. Mandel gazed out the window at a bleak panorama of the East River and industrial Queens. "Okay, go draft."

Green's task, assigned with great pomp by Neil, was to write "term sheets" summarizing management's and Tate McMahon's co-ownership of Lee after the LBO. Mermelstein had given him "models" to work from. Green was discovering that because every deal Crank did resembled some earlier one, a corporate associate's main job was to "mark up" old documents with the new terms. Taking his first model, he changed the name "Albany Abrasives" to "Lee Textiles," and paged through looking for names, numbers, and addresses to modify. It seemed pretty easy, and he finished in an hour . . . but when his work returned from Mermelstein, it was covered in red ink. He'd changed everything except articles like "a" and "the," drawing arrows to marginal boxes of minute lettering, a few of which ended "(Over)" and continued on the back. In order to convey all his thoughts, Neil had had to transform the simplest sentences into grotesque patchworks of clauses and subclauses. Flipping the page at an (Over), Green felt like a boy turning the corner at the playland haunted house: What terrors lurked?

The problem wasn't simply that Neil had fixed some technical omissions—if that's all it had been Green could've laughingly chalked it up to an anal lawyer's need to substitute ten words where one would do—but that Green had also missed every single substantive issue. This markup was sick, and Green felt sick reading it, as if he'd betrayed something he valued. In a minute, though, he shook off these unproductive emotions and experienced in their stead an acute fear that Neil would tell Lou, and get him in trouble. Well, probably he wouldn't . . . Mandel was too busy to be bothered with reports about the early drafts of documents. No, he concluded, only he and Neil would ever know, and then he exhaled, as relieved as if he'd gotten away with a crime.

When Rosen called, he spoke casually. "How's it hangin', man? Just got back from lunch with Alfieri.

"Hey, there's a rumor that Lee Textiles is gonna make a big announcement today. You're not on some deal for them?" He paused.

"Cause they're in Pikeville, Georgia. And you mentioned you went there."

"Aha." Careful. "No, I was—at another company."

"Not much else in town."

Green rubbed his chin. "Okay—but just for some bullshit meeting. I mean, I don't know anything. Not that there is anything to know."

"Cool. New subject. 'Member that sixteen-year-old in my building? She's comin' over tonight, and I asked did she have any friends, and she said she'd bring this girl Teri, who she swears is a major fox. Wanna come?"

Green had to smile. Now Petey was starting with eleventh-graders. God. "I'm tired. I'm breaking my ass here."

"On a deal?"

"Yeah—no, not in particular, just bullshit. Anyway, I promised I'd see Shelly, if I do have the energy to go out." Though in truth he wouldn't mind escaping that commitment. Since Pikeville II he'd been dreading her doe eyes and guileless expression.

"So you tell Shelly something came up at work."

"I don't do that, lying to people I care about."

"It's not lying. It's a kind of thing where you tell somebody only part of the truth, for their protection."

"But there's no truthful part to your story, at all!"

Rosen sighed. "Have it your way."


Green's principal pleasure during his long workday was the expectation and consumption of lunch. At noon he'd buzz Rosa, announce his hunger, and give Lee's billing number, which he'd already used so often—for meals, cabs, Xeroxing, messengers—that it seemed as much the essence of life as air or water. She'd call the local deli with his standing order of pastrami on rye and french fries, and shortly the "kitchen lady"—a white-uniformed Swede—would bring in, on a tray with plastic utensils, his food and preferred soda (Dr. Brown's cream, which she had committed to memory).

Today, as a reward for hard work, he treated himself to an appetizer of matzoh-ball soup. Just one ball plopped out of the carton, but it was the size of a shot put and perfectly round, as if punched from a die. The pastrami he ate without chewing, its hunks squeezing like stones down his esophagus, and then it was time for his greatest joy of all: a cookie run to the kitchen. Heading toward his prize, he passed the junior partner-sized office of a "Ms. Schein." A thin, birdlike woman with big glasses and a cap of auburn hair, she was on a call, but waved Green in and gestured frantically that he should sit and wait.

In one burst, suggestive of a champion speed talker, she cried into the receiver, "You can try to deduct it but we won't give a legal opinion and there's no guarantee the Service won't catch it!" She listened and then said, "That's a *brilliant* idea except we have a little problem called the tax code." Could she, Green wondered, be addressing a client in that tone—sarcasm leavened with the slightest impishness?

Hanging up, she honked merrily. "Don't get me wrong, I love our clients but sometimes they make me wanna scream! He wants to deduct bond interest when he has a 279 problem! Nutsy?" Green nodded concurrence that it was nutsy, thinking that Schein maybe got away with berating clients like that because as a tax lawyer, interpreter of the IRS hieroglyphics, she was exempt from the normal rules of civility.

She grabbed a pad with a list of names and, when she continued, had shifted to a singsong, speech-contest rhythm. "Anyway, *welcome*, Rick, great to have you. I meant to come around, because I try to get to know the new people, I like to think the firm's a *family*. So where are you from originally?"

"Upper West Side."

She was pleased. "Good, good. A real New Yorker. I'm from Long Island."

There was a news flash. "Yes."

"Are you from near Lincoln Square, the shul—temple?"

"Yes."

"Did you belong to that one, or another in the neighborhood?"

"No."

"It must be hard to get High Holiday tickets, if you don't belong..." Her voice trailing off, she tilted her head.

He shrugged, and all at once it dawned on him what she was after. He considered blurting out, "I'm a Yid, happy?" but decided not to make it easy for her, answering only, "I wouldn't know."

She lowered her eyelids as if summoning a divine inner power. "I come west to go to Zabar's. Have you tried their nova on an H&H bagel? The best, right?"

Green set his jaw. After a few moments she brightened. "Tell you what. I'll just give you this literature, and we'll talk later!" He accepted some pamphlets, but refused to acknowledge their existence until he left. As he'd expected, they described the Allied Jewish Fund and its important work, and sought donations. He dumped them all in the garbage, then after an attack of conscience retrieved them and stuck them in his bottom desk drawer.

A messenger brought in a press release headlined "Management Offers to Buy Lee Textiles," which described the bid and stated that the stock exchange had halted Lee trading. Green thrilled at the idea that he, who until a week before had lived and toiled in utter obscurity, was now making news.


He met Shelly at a cafe with brick walls and two-dollar cups of status coffee. She wore a forest green sundress that set off her eyes, and a new item of jewelry that caught his attention the moment they sat: a gold *chai*, dangling from a chain around her neck. He fingered the charm and said, "Taking a risk."

"Why?"

"Well, if the pogrom comes, this'll mark you. Otherwise you might've passed." She didn't appreciate the humor.

She looked at him and he fixed his eyes on an art poster ten yards past her shoulder, aware that his misdeeds were imprinted on his face. It had always been that way: From Rachel he could hide nothing; at poker he was a patsy. Why had other people so easily fooled him all his life, while he remained such an open book? This time his guilt was so clear, surely even Shelly would see.

"You seem out of it," she said.

"I guess I'm not used to the hours yet. The sleep deprivation."

She shook her head. "Isn't this firm a little crazy? I get the impression—" She broke off.

"What?" He waited, licking cinnamon-flecked foam off the cup rim.

"That it's already changing you."

"Not inside."

"As opposed to what, outside? Are you getting taller?"

"No, but bald."

She denied it. Then she began asking questions about Pikeville, and he began fibbing, haltingly at first, but with increasing ease. It surprised him how deception flowed, once you'd unstoppered the vessel.

Later, as they walked up First Avenue, their hands linked loosely, Green could think of nothing to say. "Wanna see a movie?" he finally asked. "I think there's a moral-choice film festival at the Loew's."

"Funny. Let's just walk."

She led him west toward Second, stopping halfway down the block, before the steps of a squat synagogue called B'nai Shalom. Green could hear chanting within. "This is the temple I told you about."

"Seems sufficiently holy."

"Would you like to go in? I said we might, if we were in the neighborhood."

"Didn't I ask you to leave me out?" She shrugged. "I'm an atheist! Or an agnostic—or, well, whatever. What would I do while everyone prays? Read the paper?"

She slipped her arm around his waist. "You can't expect it to hit you all at once. Dvorah compares religion to marathon running: You have to build up to it. Anyway, people also go to get some Jewish culture."

"If I see my parents once a month, I get enough Jewish culture to last me . . ."

"For the community, then. If you tried it you might feel so good," she added, reminding him of a pusher in an antidrug commercial. Clearly this was becoming more than a flirtation; something was happening to Shelly in here. Okay, he was overreacting again. It wasn't a witches' coven, after all, but just a shul: with long-winded sermons, and weddings, and announcements, and bake sales. And Shelly did mean well, asking him to come along. Still . . .

"Forget it," she said. "Let's find a movie."

He could tell, though: She wanted to see her new friends. "Y'know, I'm tired, and I have to work tomorrow, starting early. So why don't you go inside and I go home?"

"We should stay together," she protested, but finally agreed and, after kissing him sweetly, climbed the steps.

The singing voices and the blurred figures moving past an amber window together filled Green with a profound loneliness. He walked away, pitying himself, head down. Who could he talk to? Who'd understand? He called Rosen from the corner.

He lived just across the George Washington Bridge, in a high-rise condo whose marble lobby featured a fountain with spouting fish and nymphs. Posters announcing building events—Casino Night; Hawaiian Luau: Oh, Poi!—gave it the feel of a dorm for elderly, ostentatious students.

When Rosen opened the door, he whispered, "The blonde is Deb, she's mine, and the other is Teri. You're not gonna be disappointed." The girls were on his L-shaped black leather couch, behind which a terrace faced the river and the Upper Manhattan skyline. "This is Ricky—Rick, sorry, he's an *adult* now. My best friend since I was a kid," he added proudly.

Green sat, the leather crunching beneath him. Deb and Teri reminded him of the "hookers" in the Stuyvesant High production of *Sweet Charity*, their heavy makeup disguising childlike features. On the other hand, they had women's bodies. The style among Jersey high schoolers seemed to be Madonna-slutty-Catholic; each girl wore one crucifix earring, a lacy bustier, and a miniskirt over Lycra leggings. Their hair was upswept and tied with rags.

The fruity, fizzy, cherry-topped drinks they held appeared benign enough, though Green was certain that Rosen had spiked them mercilessly. Petey mixed him a screwdriver that was 95 percent vodka and tasted like kerosene. After downing it, Green made himself another, wondering why he was so nervous. Who were they, anyway, Charlotte and Emily Brontë?

The girls were giggling at Rosen's sexual double entendres, which were largely centered on the word "come." Green tried to join in, making a few cracks that didn't connect, and decided that if he could only start a real conversation, he'd get his bearings. When Rosen finally paused for a breath, he asked where they went to school. "Fort Lee," Deb said. "Sucks," Teri added, and they broke up at a private joke.

"So what, um, courses are you taking? Eleventh, that's, like, trigonometry in math?" Teri nodded and said she was freaking out because she had a trig final coming and wasn't ready.

"Oh, you gotta be ready for things that are coming."

They laughed, and Deb elbowed Rosen, saying, "Hey, you dumbshit!" He edged his hand beneath her skirt, but she grabbed it, dropped it on the couch, and shook a finger. Green glanced at Teri's freckled cleavage, then pretended to spot an interesting craft passing on the Hudson.

Rosen had some fun ideas for what to do, like a game of strip Scrabble, but the girls wanted to hit a bar. Green agreed, relieved to be getting out, and feeling this whole trip had been a mistake. He could never handle one female. Now he had two; he didn't need more.

Deb cried, "First we having some ganja, Rastaman!" She lit a joint and handed it to Teri, who toked and lay her head back, smoke curling from her nostrils. Green pictured Deb testifying at a Supreme Court confirmation hearing someday, but sneered at his own ego and puffed. He passed to Rosen, who waved it off, saying, "I'm cool," then put on a Bob Marley CD and gyrated his hips, singing along in a Jamaican accent that Deb found hysterical.

The condo parking lot overlooked the river. Rosen and Deb were taking his Mercedes; Green and Teri, her tiny Corolla. When she swung the keys on a finger toward Green, he recoiled as if from a Satanic talisman. "Can't drive a stick."

"It's automatic." He said he'd pass, but she insisted, shaky from whatever Pete had put in her drink. He swallowed. "The problem is, I don't have a license."

"What, they suspended it for drunk driving?"

He tried to sound jovial. "No! Never got one!" Teri gaped as at a sideshow freak ("The Amazing No-License Man"), and he explained, "See, nobody drives in . . . you don't need a car because . . ." Rosen rescued him, announcing they'd all take the Petemobile. In the back-seat Teri looked over at Green, shaking her head in amusement, and he shrugged, thinking how bad it was to be humiliated by a Fort Lee teenager.

A Bit O' Green occupied a dark, littered corner in Edgewater, the next town. The window displayed a leprechaun dancing a jig with a foamy stein in hand, but the interior was glum, reeking of beer-soaked wood and cigarettes. Torn decorations, still left from St. Patrick's Day, produced the look of a trashed apartment the morning after a violent party.

While the girls slid into a booth, Rosen and Green went to the bar. The stools were populated by mottled souses sagging over mugs, and the bartender was a pug-nosed fatso Green believed to be glaring at him with instinctive hatred. He wished he'd changed out of his pin-striped suit and Brooks Brothers tie.

Rosen supervised the bartender's preparation of a cocktail containing rum, Kahlua, and Malibu coconut liqueur. Rosen explained he'd invented it at a disco in Miami, named it Pete's Piledriver, and that no one alive could finish two without getting toasted. He ordered himself a Sprite. "That's all?" Green asked.

"I don't drink." Green couldn't believe it—a fun-loving guy? Well, he sure had back in '77 when, after Pink Floyd, high already from Rosen's Acapulco Gold, they'd gone to the Blarney Stone and gulped Tom Collinses till they'd puked.

Now they brought the drinks to the booth and slid in beside the girls. Pete's Piledriver tasted to Green like one of those fake cocktails—

grasshopper, pink lady—the mothers would give the kids at Catskills parties to make them feel grown up. Yet halfway through his second he heard a buzzing in his head and became aware that Christmas lights were strung around the room, blinking on and off.

Rosen's hand was busy under the table, and his lips were moving. His expressions looked hilarious, and Green laughed at them as Teri rubbed against his arm. Rosen and Deb walked over to a machine. Green pushed up and followed, toward the lighting bumpers and jerking flippers. The machine started to shake, and he thought, That's right, Rosen was the one who used to do that.

It would've been summer of 1972. Ricky and Petey would've been running to the casino, happy because they'd beaten Katz's Kottages 8-3, Angelo Venturino popping two homers into the woods. The Silver Glen Yankees led the Bungalow League.

They passed the pool, where Ricky's mom wore her rubber-flowers cap, then slammed open the screen door. Petey's grandma told them to hold their horses. "For you, Petey, I have a grilled cheese. Ricky, what?"

"Hamburger, please, charge Bungalow Twenty-one." This charging was great, though he now understood that it didn't mean it was all *free*. His parents paid the bill once a week, and believe me, his dad said, that Gertie Silver's giving away no food. But Petey did get everything free, even his mom's bungalow, because his grandma owned the whole colony.

Ricky had heard his parents discussing Petey's mom. The husband, Jack Rosen, was a horseplayer, a bum she threw out the year before. He gambled away all the money, and if that wasn't enough, he got Gertie in some real estate scheme. *Real* estate? Some *farkockte* land under water in Florida, try! Good riddance, but poor Petey, a boy needs his father.

Petey's mom was different from the other moms. She wore sunglasses and sat by the pool in a bikini, reading magazines. *Cosmo* she gets, hoo-ha, the other moms said. Sometimes she'd hug Petey hard, like he was going away forever. Once she hugged Ricky, too. She smelled good, and her hair tickled his face.

This year she'd only stayed at the colony till July and then left Petey with his grandma. Carmel Venturino, who had six kids, couldn't understand it. "Don't she wanna be wit her boy?" (Ricky knew that Mrs. Venturino used incorrect grammar.) Ricky's mom said, "She's going with the boyfriend to Europe—she wants him along?" Ricky was frightened by Petey's missing dad and his mom's boyfriend. It seemed a weird, whole other life for a kid.

Petey bragged that "Uncle Ray" took him to a Knick game, they met Willis Reed, then got pizza. Ricky said, "I have pizza near my house." "But you never saw the Knicks, 'cause your parents are cheap." "Who says?" "My granma says they get the cheapest bungalow every summer." Ricky wanted to say he saw the Knicks too, but Petey had that mean look in his face now and would ask things you only could know if you went, like what color were the seats.

Petey ate his grilled cheese at the machine, 8 Ball. It had a painting of a woman with big titties leaning over a pool table. Behind her was a guy with a thin mustache who smiled out, inviting you to try. Ricky hated him. Petey shoved the machine as he played, and his freckly hands worked the flippers the same way he held a softball, like the master. On the team Petey never made an error, but sometimes when Ricky was under a fly he'd see himself dropping it, and then he really would drop it.

Finally, Ricky got to shoot. The ball rolled down, lazy, like the bumpers weren't even there. Petey yelled, "Ya need to light the ten. Push it!" Ricky hated to push: it was cheating, and also you could tilt. Petey shook his fists, then knocked the machine. "Tilt" lit up on the front, and the mustache guy looked glad. "You should've let it go! Now I'm out!"

"Ya *gotta* push," Petey said, stepping in. "That's how ya get the big scores. But ya gotta have the touch."


Green took a turn. The machine showed a state trooper, with sunglasses and an evil grin, who was chasing you. The ball bounced around the bumpers, and Green flipped it onto a ramp. The ball kept going and going until a siren on top of the machine lit and spun around. People cheered. Teri hugged him and he kissed her, then danced her in a circle. He fell against a longhaired guy in filthy dirty jeans who was shooting pool.

"Watch it, asshole."

Rosen waved to come back. Teri leaned against a pole, holding her head. She had a big mop of brown curly hair.

Green said, "You're the asshole!"

The guy came at him, saying, "Look yuppie asshole, I can see you're wasted, so I won't fuck you up!" Green felt Petey's arms around him. The bartender had a gold aluminum bat and yelled something that made no sense: "Begoodorbegone!" Green told Rosen to let him go, that he wouldn't do anything.

Green walked in a circle, breathing deep, then snatched a pool stick off the wall and ran at the guy. He wanted to break it across his back, but fell in beer. There was pain on his side. The bartender yelled, "There's the door, so use it!" like he'd been waiting his whole life to throw someone out.

Rosen picked Green up, and then they were in the street, with the girls stumbling behind. Then they were in the car, and Green's face was pressed against the seat. He smelled leather. Lights shot by in streaks. Rosen asked how he felt and he said good. Rosen asked if he'd throw up in the car and he said no. Rosen asked if there were any new deals and he said, "Lotta deals," then fell asleep.

Soon Rosen was dragging him out, saying not to blow this with the girls. Upstairs he said, "We'll be in my room."

Green sat on the carpet. Teri was up on the couch. "Wanna come next to me?" she said.

"Too high." Then she was down, her tongue in his mouth. His cock pushed against his pants, hurting. He held her under her skirt and she stretched up, rubbing her hand in circles on his back. That felt fake, like something they said to do in the girl's locker. He needed to pee, and let his arms swing as he walked. He saw Petey naked in bed, moving on Deb. A rod buzzed on and he saw his face in the bathroom mirror, his jacket and tie twisted like sculpture. He tried to point his cock down but peed on the sink and Petey's toothbrush. He was sorry, and wiped up with toilet paper.

When he went back, Teri caught him; then his pants were down. Just as he felt his cock touching her, her eyes rolled up like window shades. "We shouldn't— I don't have— Can't we just—" She put her hand on him, moaned, said no, but louder, and he woke up like from a sex dream, then pulled out as she twisted away. He tried to hold it in, tried to hold it in, but came on her belly.

"That was close," she whispered, kissing his sweaty forehead. Looking at Teri's red cheeks, he remembered Bonnie's face lying on the pillow and thought he was cheating on her, even though that was stupid—if anyone it was Shelly. Still, after he closed his eyes he felt in love with Bonnie.

When he awoke, he found Teri sleeping, head on his chest. What had he done here?! He wanted to leap away but, worried he'd hurt her feelings, instead shook her gently until she made a smacking noise with her lips and said, "Hi."

"Won't you get in trouble?" She nodded and bit her lip, a girl again. "Are you straight enough to drive?"

"Live nearby. This's nothin'."

The lot was chilly, a mist coating the asphalt. Teri leaned on her fender and pulled him close. "Y'know, you're a gennleman. Not like th' Fort Lee assholes." He promised to get her number from Pete.

As she pulled away, she seemed in control, the taillights going straight and steady, but he pictured her bloody wrecked body anyhow. And it'd be his fault, for never getting his license, like every other boy in America! How could he forgive himself? Feeling wobbly, he hurried back inside, then embraced Rosen's couch.

He sensed the world moving, just turning around him in a wide, slow circle.

# Chapter 4

Roused by Rosen, Green cried, "Fuck!" and dove across the couch to call Dial-Car. Showering, he noticed a welt on his hip and flashed on the pool cue. What *had* he done last night? Other than coming all over Teri; that he remembered for sure.

He borrowed a Norelco. Rosen sat on the toilet cover watching, grinning. "Have fun?" Green shook his head. "Well, you seemed to. How d'you feel? Heard you, sounded like all your guts coming out." At around six he'd crawled to the bathroom, vomited twice, then hugged the bowl, dry-heaving.

Rosen absentmindedly flossed his teeth. "So you don't wanna tell about Teri. That's—suave." He laughed. "The best was you playing Chuck Norris, till you fell down. You showed a whole new side last night. Never thought you had so much—"

"Please can you be quiet? My head is cracking."

"Well, I hope you did have a good time—or whoever that guy was in the bar." He leaned against the tank. "I owed you, because of Lee and all."

"What do you mean?!"

"Your general, like, market advice helped us get our bets down on the LBO."

Green shut off the razor. "Look, *I* didn't tell you anything. What-ever you figured out was on your own, okay?!"

"Okay, be cool. Yes, start your tape recorder. You are right, I fig-ured everything on my own without your help."

"Thank you."

"One more thing. To thank you for your general advice on, is the market hot or cold—all of which was legal—Alfieri set aside some Lee winnings for you."

"Oh, you asshole! I don't want anything, nothing with my name! You're gonna wind up in jail!"

"No! Legal!"

"From now on we don't talk business! Actually, maybe we shouldn't see each other at all, so we don't take chances."

"You're my best friend!"

Green pushed the razor across his chin, trembling. He had to get rid of Rosen, but he looked so pathetic, crying over his best friend. And in truth Petey was, possibly, his fifth best friend. Feeling like a first-grader, he said, "We can stay friends. Let's cut it back, though. And no more—nosing around for information, or that's it!"

Green got into his wrinkled suit, still shaken. He hated to yell, but Petey deserved it. What was he thinking? Was he *so* lacking in moral-ity, not to mention practical sense?

They took coffees onto the bright terrace and looked out at the cars crossing the bridge, some sailboats on the water. Rosen said, "I'm sorry. Your friendship—it's worth more than all the money in the world." There was a catch in his voice.


Green found Mermelstein at a conference table across from a balding fortyish man he assumed was Paul Weinberg, the special committee's lawyer from the firm Finkel, Hassler. Each wore the M & A weekend work uniform: polo shirt (its chest embroidered with a mallet-toting horseman, as if this logo related somehow to the leisure-free life of the wearer), khakis, and Top-Siders. Whereas Mermelstein looked tuber-cular in his shirt, Weinberg's was too snug, emphasizing a droop of fat over his belt. Long, curly strands of hair from the fecund side of Weinberg's head were plastered across the barren top. Though uncomfortable in his suit, Green hadn't had time to go home and change. Also he was exhausted, and hoped Neil couldn't tell. *Stupid*, but at least it would never happen again. He'd worked too long and hard to get here, and he wasn't going to screw it up now, partying all night with Rosen.

Green had heard that he'd learn some lawyering, watching Mermelstein and Weinberg tangle, but in fact they spent 95 percent of the day debating whether contractual provisions should contain words like "material"; whether clauses should connect with commas or semicolons; and whether "and" or "or" was the proper conjunction. Any potentially interesting issue they tabled, pending the arrival of each side's "business people."

Mermelstein was a precedent slave. Having piled up contracts from ten previous LBOs, he addressed even the most trivial Weinberg demand by instructing Green to pick through and "see how it's done." Green would locate a few old ones that took Mermelstein's view, and these would be waved at Weinberg. But Weinberg had his own pile. After a period of form thrusting, they'd compromise on weasel words like "reasonably material," then move on. Two hours into this apparently insane process, Green was struck that it could be rationalized only if one grasped that it wasn't really about the contract, but about the men themselves. About mutual respect. Each was saying, "I'm not some WASPy lawyer who wants to finish and get to his club. I'll stay here all night for a year if I have to. I'm an animal, Paul/Neil."

As the day progressed, Green grew increasingly anxious about Rosen. It looked so fishy: Alfieri buys into Lee Textiles, makes a bundle, and suddenly there's an account set aside for Green. What if he got found out? His career could be destroyed. Worse, people went to jail! He inhaled. Calm. Because he was blameless. He wiped his neck with a tissue.

After lunch—a robust spread of triple-decker meat sandwiches and tricolor pasta salad from which Green filled two plates—Mermelstein suggested he go sit in on the negotiation between the LBO group and First Manhattan, its primary financier. Just to get the flavor.

Bankers and lawyers crammed Crank's biggest conference room. At the head of a block-long marble table sat Joe McCoy, sipping a drink that seemed at first to be milk, but was actually Maalox. Green found a chair beside Baxter, who whispered, "How's your reception-ist?" He flushed, pretending not to hear.

Down at the other end of the table, a sleek gray-haired banker in a lemon yellow polo shirt and navy blazer emerged from a huddle and said, "Prime plus five percent seems acceptable."

Eyes bugging out of his red face, McCoy yelled, "How we gonna live with that interest rate? Why don't I just lay my nuts on the table while you get the hammer?"

The banker didn't smile. "We don't want you to live with it, that's the point. We want you to pay us back."

An ugly man next to him, evidently his lawyer, made a tent of fat fingers and chortled, "The rate must cause pain—that's the only way it works. You *must* be in pain."

McCoy and Baxter rolled together. Listening in, Green got the clear impression that this dispute involved a scenario that would never occur. He counted thirty people in a room, of whom twenty must be lawyers, billing at least $250 an hour, which fees would end up paid by Lee Textiles and finally passed on to consumers in the prices of fabric and Premier sheets. The "pain" lawyer dug inside his nose, after a minute extracting something that he then inspected. A twenty-dollar booger, Green calculated.

"We'll swaller," McCoy announced. "Need I mention that after the LBO we'll all be in one boat? Strap the company and you only hurt your *selfs*. Okay, let's discuss y'all's fees, where you've really stuck your noses in the trough." The bankers' faces revealed that a topic of true importance had now been broached. It turned out that the syndicate was getting fees for funding the LBO; fees if payments were late; fees if early; fees just for deciding whether they were owed any fees. The banks, Green figured, would extend a small business loan to Al Fatah if it agreed to this fee structure.

He tried to follow the discussion, but this minuet was even worse than Mermelstein's gavotte down the hall. Eyes glazing, he imagined Bonnie entering the room, nude. He wouldn't say a word. He'd tear out of his suit, sweep the papers off the table, and they'd do it right there. She'd be rocking above him and the ceiling would open, the acoustical tile yielding to a night sky of twinkling stars, meteor show-ers, a happy-faced moon. When he came back around, the pain lawyer was droning about cash flow while rootling in his ear. Green could tolerate no more.

He left and went to the kitchen, where Murphy was chomping pizza like Jimi Hendrix with his fix. He nudged the box toward Green, who still felt full, but couldn't resist pepperoni. Josephson, across the table, tilted his slice and watched with a prince's revulsion as a strand of grease drizzled onto the plate. "The pizza in Naples is completely different," he said, nibbling.

Murphy resumed telling of a new merger he'd been assigned to. "I'd say who, but— Oh, who cares, PTR Chemicals and Bolus, they're in nuclear power. So the partner, Hal Wishner? Always ready to fuck up, and when he does, *I'll* get blamed. All I need with three months to go."

"Hi, everybody!" Schein, in a magenta sweatsuit, entered, toting an IRS Reporter with the heft of the Pelican Shakespeare. She sounded chipper, as if she could conceive of no more perfect Saturday than one spent at her desk, sheltering corporate income. "Oh, Aaron, would you be a doll and cover a meeting Monday? A hostile came in last night."

Murphy had warned Green to beware of any request to "go to a meeting." That was how they pulled you onto a deal, and next thing, you were working twenty-three hours a day. Josephson stared at the table. "I don't know. I'm already here until midnight."

"It's just a teeny strategy session."

"Barbara, I'm too busy."

She cast a look of malice so naked that it made Green gasp, then brightened. "No prob, I'll just tell Shapiro. He'll find someone! Oh, Rick, have you read those pamphlets?"

"I've been buried."

"But you *should.* The AJF's in a crisis, and Crank's associates are always so generous. Tell you what. I'll send a pledge card that says what you owe. 'Kay?" She flounced out.

"Very brave, Aaron," said Murphy. "'I'm sure our Lord Shapiro'll find someone!' What I'd do is cover the meeting, then lay the deal off on a junior guy, like Rick here."

Josephson said, "Have you heard about this new M.I.T. study? Using high-voltage currents, they've found that eighth-year associates have extraordinary pain thresholds."

"Otherwise, this might snowball, so in September one partner'll say, 'I heard he won't go to meetings,' then another will say, 'I heard he was on drugs and missed a meeting': and by the time they're done, you're a heroin addict who's too stoned to work."

Josephson's eyes closed. "A restaurant in a town, Imola, near Bologna, makes ravioli with mushrooms that grow out back. Most delicious thing I've ever tasted." He swallowed saliva.

"Sure, why not get reamed? Three months left, Aaron!"

Josephson stood. "Well, duty calls."

Murphy nodded after him. "Excellent lawyer. Pretends not to care about September, but believe me, he does. He just distances himself from the firm politics."

"He's so . . . cultivated."

"He has an art Ph.D. Taught college for five years. But had two kids, struggled—usual story—so he gave up. This he does 'cause he's good at it, and it pays. You should see his co-op. Not too happy a guy, of course."

Green pictured Josephson showing Picasso slides to a full classroom. "I think too many people go to law school."

"Now that's a truly unique observation." He stood. "Well, let's go back to our beds and lie in them."

As they headed to their offices, Green asked, "What'd Barbara mean about me 'owing' money to the AJF?"

"That's the best part of being a goy!" Murphy said, laughing. "Every Jewish associate has a mandatory contribution."

"But what if my charity is, like, the Nation of Islam? Say, because I want to *extirpate* world Jewry?"

"Then Ms. Schein will plunge you into a living hell."

"But why does she care so much? Is she some kind of Mother Teresa?"

"She wants to make division leader, this reward you get for raising a dumpster of cash. Remember how you wanted to be an Eagle Scout? Well, the AJF *is* Scouts, and who gets badges are the biggest pests, with the richest friends."

Green tuned his radio to a college station. The Sex Pistols' "Anarchy in the U.K." pulsed over his statute books, triggering nostalgia similar, he supposed, to that experienced by George Wilson hearing "The Whiffenpoof Song," or Fievel, "Tum, Balalaika." Out of respect for Sid Vicious, he cranked the volume. He was stuck on a gorgeous Saturday, and too bad if it bothered some old fart down the hall. He dug out the Elvis poster and hung it, quite proud.


Mermelstein's posttwilight update pleased Mandel: Though Weinberg had battled over details, he'd caved on the big issues. "See?" Lou said. "Paul's a good guy." Other than Ben Lee raising to thirty-six dollars under "pressure" from the special committee, which would happen Sunday, there remained one open point: the "lockup."

Mandel explained. "According to Lee, his crown jewel's the bed-and-bath division. So he got this bright idea from a CEO friend of his: to demand that when the committee agrees to sell us the company, they also give us an option to buy bed-and-bath at a cheap price. That way, if anybody shows up with a higher offer and the committee needs to break our deal, we exercise our option and walk away with Premier sheets and towels."

Mermelstein didn't get it. "Lee's happy just owning bed-and-bath?"

"Would you use your fuckin' brain for once, Neil?" Green shrank, thinking that could've been him. "If we can buy Premier whatever happens, nobody else *will* bid! Who in fuck wants Lee Textiles without its crown jewel?"

The word "brilliant" escaped Green's mouth. "Too brilliant," Mandel said. "It won't hold up in court. I told Ben, but he insists we head off other bids so he can do the deal at a good price. So we'll try. But first I gotta sell Weinberg."

It wouldn't be easy. After Mandel made his pitch, Weinberg yelled, "How can I in good conscience advise the committee to make it so no one else can bid?"

"They can bid," Mandel said.

"Yeah, but if they bid and win, Ben Lee walks away with bed-and-bath! Nobody'll want the business without it!"

"What are you, a textiles expert in your spare time?"

"I have investment bankers advising me! J. Wormer?"

Mandel swatted an imaginary fly. "First, if we do get sued, we'll be in Georgia, where everybody's Lee's 'good buddy.' But more impor-tant, Paul: We have a thirty-one-dollar bid on the table—"

"Which we both know is a low-ball joke."

"Okay, I'm not saying we *can* raise, but I will tell you: You won't get a bid near what you want without the lockup. Lee won't go for it. You tell that to the committee."

Weinberg recoiled as if punched. Green reflected a moment, then bowed his head to Mandel's genius. By conditioning the higher bid on the lockup, he'd given the committee an excuse for agreeing, a fig leaf to cover them in court. Weinberg had to know it was a bluff; there was no way Lee would stick at thirty-one dollars, and as a result blow the deal, simply because he didn't get the lockup. But it didn't matter. It was all for show, anyhow.

"I'll consider it," Weinberg said, caving. Mandel nodded, tapping his thumbs together.

They broke for the night. Beating up Weinberg had put Mandel in a good mood, and he invited his associates to dinner with Lee, who had just checked into the Palace. Before leaving, Mandel took Rick and Neil on a stroll around to see who was working, and who wasn't. The office was busy for Saturday night, a dozen lawyers grinding at their desks. Schein looked content, reading tax-court opinions while eating popcorn from a bowl. Murphy's office was empty, causing Mandel to raise his eyebrows; but a second later Jeff turned the corner, clearly relieved to have been present for inspection.

The restaurant, a steak house, had wood floors and soft lighting from lamps and sconces. Several groups were waiting, but the host waved Lee right through to a butcher-block table in a corner of the kitchen, ten feet from the ovens. The chairs were heavy and had armrests. This, Green thought, was where a CEO sat: where the meat came medium rare and fresh off the grill. There were no menus here; the waiter just assumed they'd want spinach salad, filet mignon, and a side platter weighty with piping-hot onion rings and crispy silver-dollar french fries.

Houser had been mighty happy to see Green again, as if their day together in Pikeville had established a lifelong bond. They clinked glasses, then swallowed a red wine called Cabernet that tickled the nose and left the mouth bone-dry. Houser winked, smacking his lips. There was nothing wrong with this. Here was how it could be: Rick Green, Esq., member of the firm Crank, Wilson & Shapiro. It was important to take a minute and conceive of a million dollars a year. Of how you could live.

Lee said, "Sounds like y'all did us proud. We actually may sign up tomorrow, assuming McCoy gets there. Poor Joe, stuck with a roomful of bank lawyers—don't get me wrong, y'know how I love lawyers!" He popped his eyes at Mandel, who laughed, a good sport. "I'll give him new set of clubs when we're done, as a *re*-ward." Lee was especially pleased about the lockup. "With Weinberg sayin' it's legal, anybody on the committee who causes trouble will get a nine iron wedged where the sun don't shine!"

Within thirty minutes the southerners had finished a bottle of wine apiece, plus a couple of scotches that had "started the ball rolling." Their noses were red, but otherwise they didn't seem drunk. Lee said, "Got one for y'all." He then told a joke about a man duck hunting in a blind, the punch line of which—something about shell casings—made absolutely no sense to Green. Nevertheless, he forced a smile. Mandel, however, must have created his own private joke, because he guffawed till he choked, ending with a stunning fart that may well have turned heads out by the coat check. Lee then told several ribald stories, after which Mandel's JAP repertoire finally bubbled up, like a natural humor spring beyond his control. Lee sniggered, and Green felt ashamed for Lou, but then thought, No, this was what you did. You mixed work and play and so formed a lasting, lucrative friendship. Why not forget Neil and his fun filter, take a chance, and tap into *his* infinite joke file? "How 'bout this? Moses and Jesus are playing golf." Mandel prickled. With Jesus he was starting? But Green nodded reassuringly, then went on, "So Moses is up first, swings, and the ball hooks in the water—"

"Sounds like Gilbert playin'."

"Who owes who money?"

"Then Jesus takes His swing. It starts to hook, but a dove flies over, catches it in its beak, and drops it in the hole. A hole in one."

"Down, Gilbert, you can tell your story later."

Green's face was a punch-line runway. "Moses turns and says, 'Okay, you wanna fuck around or you wanna play golf?'"

After an unnerving pause, they all began to laugh, and Lee wheezed, "Gotta remember that." Green sat back, ecstatic, then looked at Mermelstein. That's right, robot boy, the CEO loves me!

Mandel insisted on paying the check—a charade, as everyone knew it'd turn up on Lee's bill anyway—and when they stepped outside, it was past midnight. Mermelstein, confessing he finally had to have a few hours' sleep, asked Green to go proof the contract so they'd have a nice fresh draft in the morning.

A Slavic lady who was cleaning Green's office mimed completion, then dragged her vacuum away along the hall, where it produced a sound as lonesome as a train whistle. Green groaned and burped as he worked and at 2:00 A.M. dozed off, tipping forward like a drinking bird. Starting awake, he splashed his face at the water fountain. Weird life. But you had to pay your dues.

Leaving, at four, he passed the bank conference room and checked to see if anyone was still there. Incredibly, they *all* were, including the twenty lawyers with their running meters. A rank hill of cold Chinese food covered a cart near the door. Baxter then made what was, Green decided, the most astounding statement he'd heard since arriving at Crank:

"If no one has anything else, let's go on to page two."


Nobby Jackson, whose chubby bald head, round spectacles, and drooping mustache gave him a striking resemblance to the actor and oatmeal pitchman Wilford Brimley, kicked off Sunday with a stern announcement that, based on J. Wormer's valuation, the company could not be sold for less than thirty-eight dollars per share.

"I hear you," Lee said, then immediately raised to thirty-three. The committee went to another room, and upon their return Jackson announced that thirty-seven was the absolute floor. Lee sat awhile, fingers working through his straw-silver hair, before saying, "Sky-high, fellers—and lady! Even if we can get the banks on board at thirty-seven, that's some big-ass—'scuse me, ma'am— borrowing. We might have to sell assets to carry it. Who knows *what* it could mean for Pikeville?" He stared at Jackson and Spellman, the local businessmen, then with a resigned sigh took his team next door. Once there, he asked Mandel, "Should I just go to thirty-six now and get this show over with?"

Mandel lifted his palm. "Patience. We sit, *then* go in, raise to thirty-five, and say it's our final offer. And demand the lockup as a condition. But it's gotta be dragged out; we're making a record of pain. You sounded good before, by the way."

While they delayed, Mandel read the Sunday *Times*. Lee put his feet up, looking out at the East River. "You did sound good," Green ventured.

"Natural actin' talent, I guess. Next is Shakespeare."

An hour later, Lee was saying, "Nobby, I've been pickin' your pocket on the links for years, and I only hope you're enjoyin' your revenge." A pause. "Thirty-five bucks. I cannot convey the agony it took us, but we're there. There is, however, a condition: the asset option." Mandel's innocuous code name for the lockup. Jackson said it was fine, though the price remained too low. The committee was about to caucus again when a new voice was heard.

"I'd like to ask more about this asset 'option,'" said Ruth Royster. To this point, she'd been treated as if invisible—as if her main responsibility were just to *be* a black woman. She let her glasses dangle. "If I understand the law, a lockup is dubious because it impedes our ability to get the best price for Lee Textiles."

Weinberg's face widened into a lipless grin. "Ruth, why don't we discuss this in the other room?"

"Let me ask Ben something first. Are you saying if we tell you no on the lockup, you'll withdraw the whole offer?"

Lee looked for help to Mandel, who nodded. "Yes, that's what I'm saying." Royster made a noise deep in her throat. Though aware she'd become the enemy, Green found himself rooting for her, then scolded himself. He had to stop thinking like a law student and start thinking like an advocate. Like Lou.

After the committee left, Mandel asked, "Where'd she come from?"

Lee moaned. "Business-school professor. What'd she ever run? Wife talked me into puttin' her on the board. Damn! Well, Nobby'll hog-tie her." But after an hour there was no word. Lee paced, wringing his hands.

Finally, Weinberg entered, upset, and said, "We have a problem."

"Fuck-all!" Lee shouted, punching air. "What?"

"Ruth's against the lockup, and she's got Otis with her." Lee asked to meet with the two recalcitrant directors, and after he'd gone, the lawyers huddled. Mandel said, "First test of the circumference of Ben's balls."

Green found it fascinating to watch a man like Lee dig inside for strength. "I think he'll do what's necessary."

"You do," said Mandel, smiling as if Green's opinions were cute. "So, wanna know what he's telling Royster and Fairchild?" Lou then offered an impression that made Lee sound like a cross between a Cajun and a Byelorussian rebbe. "'If you-all folks don't give me the lockup, some competitor's gonna come in and bid; then they'll shut down the Pikeville plant.' I bet they cave."

Lee came back exhausted. "Otis is on board, but not Ruth. I vote we let her dissent and sign the damn thing up."

Mandel kneaded his face. "I hate a dissenter. Looks shitty." Then, giving his pockets a disappointed shake, he nodded.

"Bottom line," said Nobby Jackson when the committee returned. "You can have your asset option if you raise to thirty-six." Mandel blinked agreement at Lee, who exclaimed, "Done!" Nobby smiled. "Ben, you've bought yourself a company." The men cheered, a cart of champagne bottles clattered in, and Baxter toasted "the new, employee-owned Lee Textiles." Then everyone mingled, reminiscing about the negotiations as though they had occurred years earlier. Green noticed they were already altering the facts.

Royster was standing alone in the corner. Green grinned at her, then shrugged. She stepped forward, saying, "Mark my words, we'll regret this lockup. Do you agree?"

He sipped champagne, stalling. "No . . . well, I don't know. I'm new at this. Only been here a couple of weeks."

She studied him. "You're new? Well, here's my career advice. That little voice inside? That tells when you're crossing the line? Follow it, and don't let even your biggest client force you onto the low road."

Green nodded but found her view, though nice to hear, simplistic. First, this "low road" wasn't so easily charted. And the "little voice"? Could well be that of some inner yutz. Lee was right: what did she know about dealmaking in the trenches? He thanked her and went over to congratulate Houser.

Manuel, his downstairs neighbor, a Dominican transvestite, was on the stoop. "I hab something for ju. La señorita, she gibbing to me."

Green sat on his couch and opened the small box, tied with ribbon. It was filled with chocolate chip cookies, atop which was a note:

*Sorry about Friday. I hope at least you caught up on your sleep.*
*Well, enjoy these. I wasn't sure they were feeding you at CW & S!*
*Love, Shelly*

The cookies were crumbly and too salty. Green enjoyed milk with chocolate, but the carton in the fridge had a passé expiration. Dairy lumps and chunks poured down the sink.

Green went to the phone. When Mrs. Williams answered, he asked for Bonnie, breezily. "Is this Rick?"

"Yes! How're you?"

"Just fine and dandy, and how are you?"

"Oh, great! Working hard, though! But enjoying it, which I s'pose is the important thing."

"Well, you are certainly correct. Now Bonnie is not home, she's gone out of town a few days with her father, to a sales meetin' in New Orleans. Isn't that fun?"

"Yes, I've always wanted to—y'know, French. . . . Anyway, would you be so kind as to ask her to call me, kindly?"

"*All* right! I surely will. You take care!" She hung up.

Shelly sounded happy to hear his voice. He said the cookies were delicious, started to speak again, but stopped.

"Did you say something?"

"No, no."

"I know you're swamped, but can we go out next Saturday?" He said he'd try. Then she whispered that she missed him, missed holding him. Her words were choked and pinched, suggesting it had taken a monumental effort to be so bold, but he felt an odd lack of empathy. He said he missed her, too, and good night.


Thursday at three in the morning, he was beneath a glary fluorescent light at Triton Printers, proofing the tender offer that he'd now worked on for four consecutive days. He and Mermelstein together had turned room 5 into a trash heap, its carpet of paper reflecting their adoption of the "Hit-the-Floor Rule" (anything that did was deemed garbage). In room 6, Weinberg was laboring over his own SEC document. The two teams functioned separately, except that Paul and Neil had collaborated on the crucial passage that described the LBO negotiations. Both sides had to, in Weinberg's phrase, "get their stories straight."

The drafting process amazed Green. Every sentence was worked over and over until it conveyed the absolute minimum information required. (Extraneous statements led to lawsuits.) Green now understood what made legal writing so hard to read. It was a language, like James Joyce's, densely constructed to serve the author's purpose, without undue regard for the reader's ease. There was a key distinction, though: Whereas Joyce's goal was truth and comprehension, Mermelstein's was obfuscation.

Green again tried to focus, but couldn't. "Neil, I'm gonna nap till five. Then you'll take the cot till seven."

"No, I'm fine. Third wind." His eyes were bloodshot and round as quarters. He hadn't slept since Tuesday.

Green walked down the hall, past the antiques and shiny brass fixtures. Contrary to his expectations, Triton was luxurious, decorated in the style of a posh London club. Instead of bridge-playing Brits, however, each room here contained stubbly lawyers sweating out the papers for deals. Some of these people had been rounded up from their beds at 2:00 A.M., summoned to emergency drafting sessions. Green watched them schlep in, confused, lost, and perhaps wondering what sins of a former life had condemned them to this terrible one.

Green wriggled on the narrow cot, set up in a dark room near the bindery, his muscles aching and his breath foul. Day and night had ceased to affect him differently: He could be drowsy at noon, wide awake at midnight. It occurred to him, as the cot's ribs dug into his own, that there were clubs two blocks away where, right this minute, people his age were dancing, drinking, maybe even having sex. He felt as distant from them as if he'd been posted to an Antarctic weather station.

Where was Rosen tonight? Out cruising in Alfieri's Maserati? Their most recent—and if Green could help it, last—contact had followed Monday's announcement of the thirty-six-dollar deal. Green had called in for his messages and Rosa had said, "This guy left one that didn't make sense: 'Thanks, it's a double in the gap,' and gave his name as 'Third Base, Silver Glen Yankees'? Know who it is?"

"Yeah." A stupid, fucking idiot. With his "secret account" bullshit—putting Green in danger! But he could explain. He'd done nothing wrong. How much could there be in—? No, he could *not* let himself think that way, even for a second. He rolled over, imagining the Antarctic Ocean.

His heart jolted when Mermelstein woke him, from a nightmare. Bonnie and Shelly had been playing shuffleboard on a ship's deck. Fievel appeared, riding on a cloud and wearing a birthday hat. An atom bomb dropped toward the ship, and Green floated through the air trying to catch it, never quite reaching it. But as he got up close, he saw that it wasn't a bomb, after all, only a giant bag of broken cookies.

Back in room 5, the tender offer seemed pretty clean. Green pressed a button on the wall, and moments later Fred Rosznak hustled in. As sales rep on the Crank account, Rosznak, a handsome former tennis pro, unceasingly romanced the lawyers with sports tickets and bottles of liquor. Green told him to start assembling the SEC packages. They were required to file today, so a Triton messenger stood ready to fly to D.C., where he'd dump the boxes on the SEC's desk by 5:30 P.M. As they were already finished, that seemed a piece of cake, and Green yawned, looking out at a suspiciously orange sunrise over the toxic flats of Jersey, across the river.

At nine Baxter arrived, announced that Tate McMahon's name was printed too small on the cover, and insisted that the offer be reformatted. At ten, Mermelstein caught a misstatement in Weinberg's document and made him change it. Starting at noon, the Triton messenger waited outside the room with a handcart, and kept waiting until he'd missed the one, two and two-thirty shuttles. The lawyers ran back and forth to the production area, demanding revised pages and cursing loudly. Sheaves of paper were thrown in the air, cans were kicked, chairs overturned.

As he was awaiting the final pages in the hallway, Green's heart raced and his breathing grew labored. Suddenly he lost control, vaulted a "No Admittance" sign, and ran around screaming, "Who's helping me?" to the startled printers. Rosznak, accustomed to panicking professionals, caught his shoulder and murmured that they were almost done. Green allowed himself to be led back to room 5, thinking, This man is nice; he says they're almost done.

As the messenger at last wheeled his box-laden cart toward the elevator, Mermelstein tripped alongside, yelling, "Faster!," then threw a $100 bill. "If traffic is bad in D.C., tip the taxi to drive across the Mall!" The messenger laughed, and Mermelstein screeched, "They do it! I did it! If you pay! " The messenger, a black man in his sixties, pocketed the bill, said, "Yes, sir," then exited. The attorneys all collapsed on couches, their chests heaving.

Later, they gathered their effects, shoving the rest of their garbage onto the floor. "I am heading home," Mermelstein declared boldly, as if anticipating an accusation of sloth. "Rick, don't feel you have to go to the office this weekend. We all need a couple of days off, though I'll probably be in a while on Sunday. So rest up. Long road ahead."


When Green stepped out onto Hudson Street, he shielded his eyes, vampirelike, from the sun. The air was thick and filled with impurities; not enjoyable. He walked through the Village, staring, puzzled, at an old-timer reading an Italian newspaper, a miniskirted woman carrying a laundry bag, a young man with a spotted dog. Midafternoon, and humans everywhere were living—not in an office, not working.

Well, but who among them made a million dollars a year? Sure, his life was demanding now, but the *payoff*. And at Triton he'd sensed for the first time that he'd begun to comprehend corporate law. When people had asked questions, he'd been able to answer; that had felt great. Maybe he was a natural? Another Mandel, minus the vulgarity?

He'd had enough air, and called Dial-Car. The driver took a route that led into traffic near Herald Square. At first Green relaxed with placid thoughts, but after five minutes in one intersection, with horns going all around and bicycles zipping by, his skull began to throb. "Can't you get out?"

"Sorry, sir! Is some kind of accident!"

Studying the driver, Green felt at once contemptuous of his white hair fringe, bumpy nose, and veiny hands clutching the wheel. "Get *out* of this shit! "

"Sir, I—"

"Right away! Can't you do your fucking job? I haven't slept in a week! I do my job, why can't you?" The driver maneuvered across lanes but got cut off, and the light again turned red. "Is something wrong with your goddamn fucking brain?" They escaped, then got stalled again up at Seventy-second. Green kept yelling that he needed sleep, and had just begun threatening to get the driver thrown off the Crank account when they pulled up to the building.

Green's apartment was dark and hollow-quiet, as if its tenant had passed away. What could he *do* here for a full weekend? Maybe he'd call a friend, but who? Most of them lived in other cities, and Rosen was off limits. There was Shelly, of course, but she'd start with synagogue, and whatever . . .

He undressed as he played his messages: Fievel inviting him to a Workmen's Circle lecture; Shelly asking if they were on for tomorrow night. He stood at the mirror, shocked by the stomach he saw bulging from his underpants, which suggested that of a woman in her second trimester of pregnancy. He must've gained fifteen pounds since starting at Crank! How was it possible?

The machine reached the last message, and Green instantly recognized that lilting voice, like honey in his ear. "It's Friday at oh, 'bout six. You won't believe where I am! A place called the Pizza Joint! I know I should've called first, but I was afraid you'd say don't come, and I needed to escape Pikeville so bad! I have a lot to tell you, so I hope you come and get me soon. 'Bye, sweetie!"

He hopped around searching for a clean shirt, upended a lamp and left it. Not bothering to lock the door, he flung himself down the stairs, crashed into Manuel on the first-floor landing, and stood in his arms, enveloped in a coconut musk. *"Bailamos,"* Manuel said, smiling. Green had no idea what he was talking about, but gave him a squeeze anyway and ran past, out into the twilight. A warm breeze dusted his hair.

He spotted Bonnie at a back booth, sipping a mug of beer, smoking, reading the *Voice*. She fell into his arms, saying, "Now everything's gonna be all right," and he kissed her, his whole being filled with uncontrollable, limitless love.

# Chapter 5

Bonnie sat up in bed and lit a cigarette. "It started with this New Orleans trip. Twice a year my father has these sales meetings, and since I was twelve I've gone along, when they're to fun places. Also I go because, frankly, I pity him; he's lonely and he has a shit marriage. So in my mother's sick mind I'm her 'competition.'"

Green raised up on an elbow. "When did she start with that?" Bonnie flicked her ash into a Knicks mug on the nightstand. "I had the misfortune of developing young—and take it from me, it is one. Anyway, at thirteen, made up. . . . On the trips, we'd go to restaurants, and the waiters assumed we were married. We'd correct 'em, of course."

"He's a handsome man." Green had the odd sense of chivalrously praising a rival.

"Used to be. But now—did you see him, beaten down? That's her doing."

Green laid his arm across Bonnie's shoulders, gingerly, as if she were made of sand or sugar. Though it had been hours, he still couldn't grasp the reality of her presence in his bed. It was easier when he thought: The molecules that comprise "Bonnie Williams" were now contained within the space called "360 West End Avenue," in turn owned by the assortment of atoms labeled "Gruber Realty."

"Why doesn't he divorce her?"

"She has him by the balls, financially."

"So what?"

"How'd *you* feel workin' your butt off for years, then starting over from scratch? So what. Thank you, Mr. . . . ." She puffed.

"Okay, sorry." He filled a glass from the kitchenette tap, vowing to avoid criticizing Williams in the future. Too many layers. "But you still haven't told what happened to you."

"Right, so when we came back from New Orleans, my mother went after us with her sarcastic tongue. She and my father were screaming, and I couldn't stand it, so I hid in my room, thinking of you and how we laugh together. Then I saw in the paper this PBS show on Jewish humor. But I can't get the station too well, so I strung the antenna on the roof. I was stretching it to the gutter, and I lost my balance and rolled off!"

He sank onto the bed. Off a roof? "Wild shit like that always happens to me." She laughed. "I fell on a lawn sprinkler. Here—" Lifting her nightie, she revealed a latke-sized, borscht-colored bruise. "Doctor says there was internal bleeding, and I need to rest. Gotta take my pills. I couldn't be stuck in that house, so— I knew it was risky to just descend on your life. But sometimes you have to do the unexpected."

Later, after her Valium, she curled up against his chest. "I'm glad you did the unexpected," he said, stroking her hair. "The week at the printer, I kept remembering you, and the more I did, I realized I—*love* you." The words stuck, then escaped inside a croak.

She let out a joyous cry. "I truly believe two people can have such chemistry that it EXPLODES, the first second. I felt it the last time, in Pikeville, but I was afraid to scare you, saying so." They kissed, and soon she whispered, "Sweetie, taking these drugs I can't, y'know, feel anything." She studied his face. "Please don't be upset! We'll make love the moment I'm well. Isn't that better, if we both can enjoy it?" He nodded, ashamed of his selfishness. Here sat the girl he loved, she'd fallen off the roof, and all he could think about was getting laid.

On Saturday he picked up videos and Chinese lunch. He found himself eating dumplings while watching *The Apartment* with an angel, certain that life could not be better. His fortune read: "A thrilling time is in your immediate future." He snorted. "My *immediate* future? They don't usually go out on such a limb. Maybe they put ground-up glass in the cookie."

"Oh, I'll liven things up for you," she said, and he giggled. "I will," she promised, but he couldn't stop giggling.

She disdained the Beatles-Stones conservatism of his CDs, preferring the old records he had stowed in a closet, by such shameful artists as The Carpenters and Chicago. Her most prized discovery was a warped copy of the *Shaft* soundtrack, the front of which showed the Afroed detective in a shiny leather jacket and flare slacks. She kissed the picture on the lips, held it beside Green's face, and said, "You *are* Shaft. The coolness, the platform shoes, the mastery of the art of love." He felt he was being mocked, also a momentary jealousy of Shaft, but then shook it off. Bonnie sang along, changing the words: "He's a complicated man, and no one understands him but his woman—Rick Green."

Becoming highly excited, she broke into a funky dance around the room, while Green watched, conscious that a beautiful woman can act spontaneously, whereas he'd seem an idiot if he joined in. He had a sudden desire not just to be with her, but to *be* her. He'd felt this before, when he and Fievel used to watch Miss Teenage America on TV. They'd laugh at the contestants' inane self-descriptions, but Green secretly envied them and their uncomplicated lives ahead. Did any Jewish girls get in the pageants? Or were they excluded for fear their multipart answers to the questions would show up the smile-faced shiksas? (There was Bess Myerson, of course, but she had her own tsuris.)

As the day progressed, there was more music and dance, animated discussions of sixties sitcoms, popcorn making, debates on current events (which failed to generate much heat, as they were equally liberal), some kissing and hugging. The apartment seemed too small, by half, to accommodate Bonnie's energy—and she was sick, and on tranquilizers! Around nightfall she ran out of gas, slipping under the covers for a nap, while Green collapsed in a chair, exhausted.

Then the phone rang. He ran the cord into the bathroom.

"Oh!" Shelly cried, "I thought maybe you'd slipped off the earth."

He spoke softly. "I meant to call, but the printer—"

"Crazy. I know. So are you awake enough to go out?"

"Tonight? Well, I'm still recovering. Tired."

"Then how about I come and we rent a movie?"

"I'm not sure. I'm not sure I'm up to it yet."

She sighed and asked, "When will you?" as if haranguing the super about an overdue repair. He paused, despising his failure to prepare when this had so obviously been coming. If only he could stall . . . but why? It seemed clear now: He loved Bonnie, and the more things dragged out, the worse it'd be for Shelly. Still, breaking up here, sitting on the toilet? The way you did it was in a cafe, with tears and a last embrace. Then you walked away in the rain. Something like that.

"Rick? Are you alive?"

"We have to talk, though maybe in person. . . ."

"I knew it! That something was going on!" Green chewed the cord, which had a satisfying rubbery texture. "Whatever it is, just tell me. I have to get on with my life." She paused. "Come on, don't be an asshole."

He fell back against the tank, thinking how much more effective curses were when saved for special occasions. "Okay. I'm seeing someone else . . . okay? I'm sorry, it just happened."

"Someone you knew before me?"

"No, no."

"Really?" That seemed to have upset her even more, and he pondered.

"In fact, yes, I dated her last year. I thought it was over, but now I've realized we hadn't worked it out. I should've told you at the beginning."

"My luck," she said, almost relieved: He hadn't met someone new and better, after all.

"I feel awful. But we were nearly engaged—" He stopped. No reason to overdo it. "Maybe I'll call when this situation gets resolved."

She sniffled. "Don't do me any favors. 'Bye," she said, but it came out as a sob. He heard a click, then let the receiver fall and covered his face.


With the tender offer running, the Lee LBO had hit a lull that was opportune for Green, who thought of nothing all day but getting home to Bonnie. He feared squandering Mandel's good will, however, and devised tricks to make it appear that he hadn't left before eight. He'd slip away in shirtsleeves, jacket draped over his chair, cup of hot coffee on his desk, and an uncapped pen lying beside a half sentence, as if the author were taking an emergency leak. Sometimes he'd spot another escaping associate down in the lobby, and they'd exchange guilty looks before vanishing into the night.

It felt incredible to find her, napping or reading magazines or watching TV. She had to rest, so he'd pick up the items she needed: Evian, *Backstage* (she wanted to check out the audition notices), and Tampax. Unashamed to buy the tampons—and having cheered inside at her first request—he'd toss them on the drugstore counter, thinking suave thoughts. Sometimes he'd bring a surprise, like a single red rose (seventy-nine cents at the Koreans). Then they'd talk all evening, holding hands. She was like a beautiful friend he could kiss; in his mind they were Hansel and Gretel or the Bobbsey Twins.

He got off half of the July Fourth weekend. Jubilant, he stopped on the way home to pick up two cooked lobsters and a dozen oysters. He found Bonnie still in bed and handed her the fishbag, beaming. "My favorites! You sweet!"

They sat on the floor among lit candles, and she slurped an oyster from its shell, the ecstasy weighting her eyelids. Green, never having tried one, copied her, gagging as it slithered down his throat. She asked if anything was wrong. "No, just the concept of the nervous and reproductive systems, all in one swallow."

"Very romantic." She put her mouth on another, tilted her head, and the glistening matter disappeared. "Aphrodisiac, y'know." In fact he didn't, and could see absolutely no reason why. Still, there was a tickling in his loins.

Locating a nutcracker in the toolbox, she crunched the lobster ferociously, wrenching off the claws and sucking at the feeble legs. Green envisioned his frolicking along the seabed just a day before, and covered its accusatory head with a napkin. Bonnie offered to help and, with a few deft twists, laid the unlucky crustacean open. "The tail meat's the best. Don't eat the green stuff, though."

"Why? What is it?"

"Something you don't want. Forget about it!" He lost his appetite, which seemed to annoy her. She ate the second lobster, then lay in the candlelight, wineglass balanced on her belly. "I'm stuffed." Green considered ordering Chinese for himself, but decided it'd spoil the mood, probably.

"Think I'm well again," she murmured, glancing over.

That's good, he said, and sipped, his sudden tension a strange counterpart to his erect penis, suggesting some mixup along the neural pathways.

Don't you want to come down here?" Lying beside her, he watched shadows flicker across the ceiling. "Don't you want to kiss me?" He touched his lips to hers. She moved his hand under her nightgown, then wrapped her arms around him.

He entered her, his eyes squeezed shut. She began to shift gently, and he said, "Wait . . . don't," but then came as if exploding. He rolled onto his back, thinking maybe they'd do it again. The wine had made him very drowsy, though.

By Sunday, Bonnie was itching to get out of the house. "Is that okay? I've been cooped up for a week, and it's making me dizzy. Also, I'm getting paranoid from the Kafka." She'd found *The Metamorphosis* among his college paperbacks, and said that reading it in his apartment was the total experience. "Roach surround," she called it.

Green had the *Times* crossword in his lap, defiantly red-inked. "Wanna see the World Trade Center?"

"You must be confusing me with Tammy Tourist. What I would like is to go hear some cool music." Green hadn't been to a club in years, and in retrospect it seemed a singularly uncomfortable way to spend an evening. On the other hand, he didn't want to seem stuck-up or old.

Watching her dress, he felt he was in the presence of a craftsman. After trying three hairstyles, she said, "Screw it," and combed it straight down. She applied her makeup precisely, as if etching glass. Prince was her special "getting ready" music; she danced into a minidress and then, satisfied at last, shook her hips at the mirror, singing into a hairbrush-microphone: "Tonight we're gonna party like it's 1999. . . ."

On Broadway, men stopped to stare. A Spanish guy cried, "Ai!" as if she'd stabbed him. She caused another commotion in the subway: Businessmen peeked over newspapers, while teenage boys ogled openly. Unsure at first how to react, Green decided simply to ignore them, as she did, but this course worked only to the point when the eyes traveled to him, frankly questioning his right to accompany beauty. If only he were very handsome!

As they exited at Astor Place, he said, "Men look at you a lot, have you noticed?"

She flashed a smile. "I don't think so, but it's sweet of you to say." He sensed she was reciting a charm-school phrase.

The "club," occupying the ground floor of a ramshackle building on Bowery, was really just a narrow room, at the back of which stood a "stage"—really a balsa platform two feet high. Absolutely nothing would've prevented a displeased audience member from striking any member of the speed-metal band that was now performing. Green led Bonnie through the churning, slam-dancing crowd, then anchored himself to the bar. She wanted a Jack Daniel's and, when he asked if that was wise, gave the okay sign.

To his relief, she didn't seem to be attracting much attention here, her dress prim in comparison to the underwear worn by women all around. A man passed, his ring-pierced nipple wounding Green in the vicinity of his rectum. The music abruptly stopped, the dancers staggered about, dazed, and the song "Pride" pumped out of the speakers. Bonnie took a swallow of bourbon, then whispered, "Here's a secret. I like to make love to this. My boyfriend Eric at college is a U2 fanatic." She swayed, eyes closed, a dreamy smile on her lips.

Green paled. "I didn't know you had a boyfriend."

She looked at him. "Obviously we're not seeing each other now, since I'm with you." He collected himself. She was a beautiful woman—did he think he was the first to notice? And after all, he'd had Shelly. Whatever.

"Wish I had a joint," Bonnie said, glancing around as if a dealer in a generous mood might materialize. A millisecond later a young beanpole with a straw buzz cut pushed off the bar and asked in a Cockney accent, "Someone in need of the wackiest weed?"

She giggled. "I can't listen to live music straight."

"And why should you," he said, patting his breast pocket, "when nature's been so kind? To you, especially." Bonnie smiled at that, and Green felt extremely angry. "I'm Keith."

"Bonnie. This is Rick, my honey."

"Pleasure," Keith said, then let loose a stream of chatter concerning New York, London, the London tube, the Moscow metro, Stalin, Yalta, on and on. He was impossible to interrupt, and when the next group began, continued by shouting his monologue toward Bonnie. Green leaned over, couldn't make out what he said, and finally gave up to watch the band. Out of the corner of his eye he saw Keith's mouth moving and Bonnie laughing. He'd touch her arm to emphasize a point.

Green finished his beer. "You guys need anything?"

"A Guinness would be appreciated! And the lady seems to be drinking J.D.!" Green nodded: I know. She's here with *me*, schmuck. What did you do in *this* situation?

Upon his return, Green was pleased to find that Bonnie and Keith's tete-a-tete had been invaded by a stumpy, middle-aged man wearing a metallic jacket with "GBR Records" embroidered on the back. The man was evidently telling a joke, because Bonnie's face wore the fixed grin of someone awaiting a payoff. "'Tacks? I thought you rolled 'em on!'" She howled, head flying back as if snapped at the neck. Green wedged between her and Keith, extending the bouquet of drinks.

Bonnie pried hers loose, crying, "There you are! Meet Al." Green nodded collegially, enlisting him in the struggle against Keith.

Slurping the head off his Guinness, Keith said, "Then we have the Irishman who visits the eye doctor, carryin' a violin case. 'What seems the problem?' He opens the case, and inside is a turd about, well, size of a violin!" Bonnie and Al were laughing already, satisfied, but Green knew that Keith had more. "Doc says, 'Why come to me?' Irishman says, 'Doc, when I made that me eyes watered!'" During the subsequent hilarity. Green maintained a grin while combing his memory for any topper that didn't involve an old Jew—or worse, a rabbi.

"What's the longest turd you ever made, then, eh, Bon?" Shocked by Keith's vulgarity, Green braced excitedly for a slap to his pallid, snaggle-toothed face but watched in wonder as Bonnie, with a boastful nod, held her hands a foot apart. Green flooded with envy over the deeply, almost sexually, intimate moment that Keith and Bonnie had just shared.

She whispered to Green, "I feel like dancing. Just burning off excess energy. Want to?" He shook his head, believing himself the world's worst dancer.

"Mind if I dance with Keith?" He frowned, then felt prudish and shrugged. They slipped into the maelstrom. Chugging his Corona, he smacked the bottle on the bar.

Al appraised him over shades. "Never had a fox before, huh? Lose your cool and she'll walk. She's young—she wants to have fun."

This guy's nerve was unbelievable. Green changed the subject. "So you're in the music business?"

"You could put it that way."

"That's interesting." Green got on his toes to search but, unable to spot them, leaned against the bar, trying to reconcile this new Bonnie with the nightgown magnolia he'd been coming home to. Though he'd thought of her as honest, tonight she was exaggerating every smile and laugh as if overplaying to salvage a lame comedy. And—it couldn't be, there was no *reason*—she seemed to wish he were gone. Al smirked at him.

Bonnie and Keith came back sweaty and red-eyed. "Whoa, full-contact karate out there."

"In London they'd get their faces smashed."

The next band, The French Are From Hell, stank despite their witty name. Al suggested they all go score some coke, and Bonnie's face lit up like a child's. Green checked his watch: one o'clock, and work tomorrow. "We should go home, honey."

"I'm not tired at all," she pouted, then whispered, "I have a reason for staying out that I can't explain now. But don't feel you have to come along."

After a glance at Keith, whose innocent expression struck him as utterly fake, Green said, "No, it's cool. Now I'm in the mood for some coke myself." Outside, a teenage girl with a powdered face and dyed black hair hung on a car hood, vomiting.

They trooped down Bowery, past vagrants, rubble, and junk. Though he tried, Green just couldn't fathom that Bonnie preferred this journey to their nice warm bed. He took her hand, but it was lifeless, and soon he let it drop. On Delancey Street, Al slithered inside a dark, spooky brownstone while the others waited outside. A Rastafarian appeared. "Need somethin' nice? Senss?" Green wanted to answer, "Thanks, we're already being helped," but you could get shot making jokes down here.

A police car sped toward them, siren screaming, and Green's scrotum tightened. How could he be so *stupid?* Buying cocaine on Delancey Street. He'd get arrested! Disbarred! He began inventing a story, but the cops tore past and around the corner. "Hey," he said in mock outrage, "we're committing a perfectly good crime right here!"

"Chill out," Bonnie said, unamused.

"Fag?" asked Keith, producing a strange European pack from the pocket of his tattered, red-checked sports jacket. While he cupped a light for her, she made some remark about the tobacco that Green didn't catch.

Time passed, and he was thinking, *Nu?* Where's the drugs already? when Al emerged and pulled them into a huddle. "My connection's dry, but he gave me another address."

"Allonzey," Keith said with a waiterly gesture.

In six hours, Green thought, he'd be dealing with L. H. Mandel and N. R. Mermelstein, attorneys-at-law. Why wasn't Bonnie mature enough to understand that he had a job? Well, as Al said, she was twenty. If he wanted her, he'd have to accept this kind of thing. He told her to go on, and she kissed his cheek, promising she wouldn't be too late. He waved frantically at a cab.

Al held the car door open, whispering, "That's it. Cool, like you don't give a shit."

"Thanks," Green said sarcastically, then added, "Don't let her do too much drugs, okay? She's on medication." Al put his hand to his heart.

As Green rode away, he looked back and saw them striding off to the next brownstone, linked arm in arm in arm.


Green managed to get to work on time the next morning and was at his desk, gulping coffee and rubbing his eyes, when Mandel called. "Guess what? The Lee stockholders filed a class action against the LBO." Green cursed, but Mandel explained that it was standard practice. "We'll settle with 'em. Just gotta pay fees to the plaintiffs' lawyers."

"What's the claim?"

Lou said the usual crap, that the deal had been rigged to hand the company to its CEO without an auction. "Anyway, it's better. If we settle this case now, we bar future ones. So if it ever turns out that Lee was really worth, say, fifty bucks a share, nobody can sue that we screwed 'em in the LBO. Understand?

"But why I called, they'll subpoena our papers. At the first meeting, Baxter made some remark about paying forty dollars. You don't have any notes of that, right?" Green thought a moment, said right, then hung up and took them to the shredder.

Bonnie called soon after he returned. "You sneaked out. You should've woken me." She'd crawled in bed at six, bringing a pot-and-booze smell, and was still comatose when he left.

"So what happened?"

"Oh, Al's such a loser. We hit two more places and never even scored any coke. I said good night to him and Keith—who went back to England this morning, by the way—but I forgot to bring any money! So I had to walk all the way home."

"From the Lower East Side?"

"It was nice. We should go walking at dawn sometime." She paused. "Anyway, I wanted to explain why I stayed out. Jerk though he is, Al has tons of entertainment contacts, and I thought he might help me get a first break in acting. I'm just being realistic."

"He seemed like a lowlife to me. A drug dealer."

"No, he's a manager for musicians. And he has to score drugs for 'em once in a while, to keep 'em out of trouble. But the main thing is I *love* you. Can you get home early? I think we need to be together tonight. Also I have something to show you."

Green had promised Mermelstein he'd work late; but what could she have to show? Lingerie? "I'll try." There was a coolness, he thought, in partying half the night with a beautiful girlfriend, then being a skilled, suited professional the next morning. "I love you too, Bonnie."

He spent the rest of the day in a Crank conference room, staring at the top of Neil's head, willing him to write faster so they could finish and leave. But he just churned at his usual pace, one that implied that the hours of life were infinite. By early evening Green's frustration had grown so wild that he had to grip his own arms to keep from lunging and strangling the senior associate. When would Neil be satisfied? When was a contract exact enough? If it took twenty more hours of work to improve the document a tenth of a percent, would Neil stay? Green knew that he would; of course he would. It was that policy of perfection, set at the top by Bernie Shapiro, that justified Crank's enormous fees. The clients paid the Crank lawyers to live like lunatics, so they didn't have to.

"I just caught something," Mermelstein declared. "On page twenty-seven. See how it cross-references Section 3.2(b)? But that's circular, because the formula in 3.2(b) references back. Right?" Green nodded, a sick ache in his chest as he realized Neil was right. "We'll have to revise the whole thing," Mermelstein said with glee. "Go get the first draft and we can work from that." Green dragged himself down the hall, feeling like crying.

"Freeze!" It was Barbara Schein, behind him with a maniacal gleam. "Plans for tonight must be canceled. We bought a table for the AJF dinner at the Pierre but Lou was called to a meeting, which leaves us empty seats, which would be humiliating for the firm." Green said he had to stay with Mermelstein, but Schein said she'd pull rank on poor old Neil. He began to argue, then stopped: Why wasn't he jumping at this chance? He'd go, then quickly smuggle himself out under a giant chafing dish!

"Great! Chicken's at seven-thirty, drinks are before."

He called Bonnie and said he'd put in an appearance, then hurry home for her surprise. "It's an open bar?" she asked.

"Hm? Sure . . . why?"

"Why don't I come? It'll be fun! We'll goof on—!"

"Oh, I don't know." Bad enough to pick up a Pikeville receptionist, but to bring her to New York like a white slaver, then parade her in front of the firm? Certain disaster.

She made a hissing noise. "Ashamed of me?"

"No!"

"Bullshit. Make me feel . . . great. Y'know, just *stay* at your stupid dinner, okay? Al invited me to a party."

"Wait!" That hurt; no parties with Al! He was shocked she cared so much—but with her he could never tell. Anyway, who'd know her?

Lou was the only one and he'd be elsewhere. He sighed. "Wanna subject yourself to this? Be my guest. But if anyone asks where we met, say, '*No hablo Ingles.*'"


Cocktails were served in a marble foyer just off the hotel lobby. Green hugged the bar, looking out over the Jewhive, and suddenly felt a hand on his arm: It was Schein, the queen bee. "Till your date comes I want you to meet some AJF Young Leaders. Maybe you'll see why your contribution is important." So she hadn't forgotten; but then again, it was her business to remember. "Why don't you have a tag?" she asked, pulling a "Hello, My Name Is . . ." sticker from her pocket. (Did she carry them around, in case she wandered into an occasion?) She shoved him toward a cluster of workers.

He read their tags: all lawyers and bankers—no mercenaries or performance artists today. From their eye pouches, he guessed most were in M & A. Ellen Fiddelman said, "Were you on the mission to Israel in April?"

Rusty Schulman said, "You're thinking of Ron Bruch from Cahill Gordon. They're similar."

Green said, "We were both poured from Jewish male mold number three: lawyer with bad posture." He'd expected laughs, but instead got falling faces. The Young Leaders, a proud bunch, clearly did not appreciate Jewish minstrelsy.

The "mission," despite its lofty name, seemed to have been primarily a singles tour of Israel. "So it was good?" Green asked, building bridges.

"All except the West Bank part," said Fiddelman, exchanging a glance with Schulman. "Some Palestinians threw rocks at the tour bus."

"Just kids," Schulman added. "Y'know, like we used to throw water balloons?" The Young Leaders all coughed.

Green wound up alone with Fiddelman. She moved in close, spoke animatedly, and all at once he realized she was flirting, which still took him by surprise. For most of his life, the opposite sex had ignored him—"Nice guy," they'd said in a tone that implied "leprosy"; the confidant type, to be played in the movie version by Tony Randall—but in the last year, things had changed. In stores, subways, elevators, etc., women now tried to pick him up. It appeared that twenty-five was the age in the men market when the bottom fell out of Abusive Asshole and Nebbishy Good Provider soared.

Though attractive, Fiddelman was not, for example, in Shelly's league. And *Bonnie* . . . where was Bonnie? Now, of course, he'd seen her painstaking artistic methods. "Waiting for my girlfriend," he explained, and Fiddelman's smile scattered. At that moment Bonnie entered, her hair piled up, wearing one of his white shirts and a gray skirt, the first he'd seen with a hemline below mid-thigh. The crowd seemed to part for her, heads of both genders turning. When Fiddelman saw what was coming, she gave Green a look of betrayal, then stepped away.

Bonnie hugged him, and he inhaled her Chanel No. 5 (from a bottle bought, she'd explained, with her entire first week's salary at Lee). "Almost as crowded as last night," she said.

"Fewer nipple rings, though."

"Ah, but who knows what's under the suits?"

Soon some AJF whips herded everyone into the vast ballroom, jammed with a hundred tables. Green spotted Crank's, which had two vacant seats. Beside Lou! Okay, concentrate. What did he know? Did Neil tell about the sex? Maybe not; maybe he'd shown some restraint. And Lou might not even recognize Bonnie. The working class was invisible to him.

"You okay?" she asked. Anyway, there was no choice. If he tried to leave, she'd flip out.

"Remember my boss? Just don't say where we met. I don't want him to think I pick up our clients' receptionists." He sat on Mandel's right, putting Bonnie next to Barbara Schein. Mandel stared at Bonnie, reflecting; but it was too disconnected, and he finally grunted, then chomped a roll.

Their arrival had interrupted Schein's description of an AJF project in Tel Aviv that was short of completion funds. "So we're trying Deutsche Bank. I mean, if they don't owe us, who does? The frustrating part is we broke ground a year ago, and the people have been waiting and waiting."

"Low-income housing?" Green asked.

"No, a tennis complex. Clay courts. All they have now is crappy rubber ones." Bonnie looked puzzled. Green nodded, as if in wholehearted support. Schein, however, highly attuned to skepticism, exclaimed, "They live in constant danger! Shouldn't they have a little fun?" Green nodded again, munching his field salad.

After a shy microphone tap, the emcee began to heap praise upon the night's honoree, Joe Blau, and his fund-raising work. Green had heard of Blau, a powerhouse investment banker. (Well, what bus-driver or sewer-worker honoree could assure the sale of a $10,000 table to every law firm in the city?)

"So, what do you do?" Schein was addressing Bonnie.

"I'm a student at Vanderbilt."

"Good school."

Mandel perked up. Green watched him watch Bonnie. This blondie with the accent. Hmm. And the tits I know I've seen. Comprehension then filled his Flintstone face. Green arranged his Brussels sprouts into a football formation, aware what Lou was thinking: His lust-crazed associate had not only brought the sex-receptionist to New York, but had found the chutzpah to flaunt her to the AJF. Bad boy. Stop your penis.

It struck Green that until two weeks ago he'd had the perfect escort. They'd have adored Shelly, and word would've gone around Crank (maybe even up to Shapiro) that he had a lovely girlfriend. A partner's-wife-one-day kind of girlfriend. When Green tuned back in, he heard Bonnie chattering to Schein with the same peppy charm she'd turned on Al and Keith the night before. Now, of course, she was feigning interest in AJF activities, rather than coke connections.

"So," Schein said, "it's an irrigation project—"

Bonnie nodded. "It's incredible how they've made the desert bloom!" Green felt a burst of annoyance at the way she was kissing Israel's ass.

To the podium stepped a Knesset member from the Labour party, whose lecture took the view that Israel would eventually have to negotiate with the Palestinians. Though his tone was measured, he'd set the ballroom to bristling. "Jews historically have found it in their interest to make peace, even if they give something up." Mild gasps. "Even land." Muffled groans, sharp intakes of breath. The peroration was inaudible as each table became an ad hoc discussion group of his crackpot errors.

Schein said, "I can't believe, with the money we raise, this guy comes here and tells Israel to give land." She shoved her plate away, too disgusted even to eat her capon.

Mandel agreed. "I don't want him here. He sounds like a yutz."

"What do you think?" Schein was again addressing Bonnie, which caused an instant sweat to break on Green's neck.

"After what the Jews have been through? Israel's survival is *crucial!*"

Schein folded her arms, satisfied, but Mandel had apparently heard a hollow ring, because he eyed her and asked, "So in no event should Israel be required to give land?"

She thought; Green hadn't the vaguest idea what she'd say. "Required? No. I do believe that in territorial disputes a negotiated peace is best." Green chewed his lip. What was she, taking Modern European History before she dropped out?

Mandel said, "You don't know what you're talking about. The Palestinians have no *claim*. They're descended from nomads!" Bonnie sipped her wine and smiled slightly, which angered him. "You disagree? Let's hear, since you're an expert."

"I pray for Israel as much as you! But I think the speaker has a point. The Palestinians must be dealt with."

Mandel shooed her. Droplets trickled down Green's spine, he squeezed Bonnie's leg, and Schein spoke patronizingly. "If you want *historical* evidence, *Bonnie*, you can stop with the Bible, which says Judea and Samaria belong to the Jews."

Bonnie didn't like Barbara's tone—not in the slightest. Clicking her thumbnail and pinky nail together, she mumbled, "There's an Arab Bible, too."

Mandel went red. "Pardon? No, what did you say? Something with an Arab Bible?"

Green whispered that he needed air. "What're you doing?" Bonnie cried as he led her out. In the foyer, behind the abandoned bar, he said, "Protecting you. Because in two seconds Barbara would've stabbed you with the butter knife."

"Y'think so? Well, I didn't like her *fucking* attitude. Talk to me like I'm some bimbo. I'll stab her bony fucking ass!"

Astonished by Bonnie's fury, Green tried to calm her. "Listen, it's not you, it's the subject. You can't discuss Israel rationally here. There's too much . . . emotion."

"And I'll make you look bad, right?"

"That's not it at all."

"The dumb receptionist." Jabbing an olive sword into her palm repeatedly, she said, "I'm not an—asset." She brushed stray hairs off her forehead, and he caressed her shoulder. When upset, Bonnie was exquisite to look at.

"You are." He embraced her, but she let her arms hang. "You're the most beautiful woman in the room."

"So you see me as some ornament."

His heart hurt. "You're intelligent and classy. You were very, very charming. Lou isn't fit to share a table with you."

Now she hugged him. "Mean it? 'Cause if I thought you were ashamed of me, I don't know what—I couldn't bear that." Liquid filled her eyes.

"I do," he said, kissing her. She slid her hand down his back, whispered, "Let's go home," then reached around to his groin, causing him to buckle. "We haven't . . . *you* know, since Friday. Three days is long, for me." He chuckled nervously, aware that most men would find her frankness thrilling, and that he was in a lucky, enviable position.

At that moment a horrifying apparition entered the lobby: Mermelstein, jogging jerkily toward the ballroom. Green shrank into the drapery, but too late. "Take me to Lou!" Neil called to him across the checkerboard patch of marble. "The shit has hit the fan!" Bonnie looked Neil over with a swift, merciless acuity, and the smirk she flashed at Green embarrassed him: This being was his teacher and commander.

Saying he'd be right back, Green led Mermelstein across the ballroom, where Blau was delivering an ignored speech whose gist seemed to be that every Jew who'd attended CCNY in the fifties was now rich. Mandel was puffing a cigar, his eyes glazed, but snuffed it when he saw the associates approaching. Neil whispered, "Bill LaCroix from Country Home Textiles called Lee to discuss 'participating' in our LBO."

"Damn. What'd Lee say?"

"Brushed him off."

Mandel nodded. "That was right. But I know about LaCroix. He won't just walk away. We'll have to deal with him or he'll go hostile for sure." Mermelstein looked frantic, but Mandel was relaxed. "Go to the office and pull everything on Country Home. If you need library staff, call 'em at home and drag 'em the fuck in. I'll see you tomorrow morning, and we'll plan our defense." Mermelstein nodded crisply, as if he might salute, then hustled off, with Green trailing behind.

Green veered off toward Bonnie, who was waiting on a gold satin bench. "Ready?"

"I have to go back to the office."

"You're kidding. I wanted to be with you tonight!"

"I'm sorry. But what choice do I have?"

Her head lolled against the wall. "Okay. If that's what you think you have to do."

"I do." He gave her fifty dollars. "Here, for a cab and whatever else you need. And there's more cash in—"

"In the dresser? Top drawer?" She smiled. "How do you think I got down here?"

"I've gotta run," he said, and ran. After a last glance back, he revolved outside, pumped. So they'd mobilize all night, while at some still-unidentified firm their adversaries would be assembling an attack plan. He was making news again.

He caught Neil halfway up the block.

# Chapter 6

As Mandel had predicted, LaCroix wasn't going away. The morning after his rejection, Country Home Textiles delivered a letter to the Lee special committee requesting a chance to bid and saying its offer would likely he in the forty-two-dollar range. They were given two days to respond.

Green found his colleagues hunched over Lou's speakerphone. Lee was screaming, "I mean, shit, what's LaCroix doin'? He knows we have a contract!"

Mandel said, "He's telling the committee, 'You were naughty, and slipped the company to your buddy Ben at a cheap price. But I caught you, and it's a new ball game. I'm in.'"

"Well, a deal's a deal! I won't let the committee out of it! Anyway, we have the lockup. LaCroix's all hot on bed-and-bath, so even if they could weasel out, it'd be useless."

"Okay, but if he doesn't get what he wants, he'll be in court, suing against the contract *and* the lockup."

"What're his chances?"

"Between you, me, and the mezuzah, if the case was up here, we'd be in trouble. But in Georgia? You tell me."

"Hard to see a court ruling for LaCroix. He's a Yank—from New Hampshire—and if he bought the company he might shut down the Pikeville plant." Lee sighed. "I'll get back with y'all later. I'm gonna call around to the committee and throw some fear into 'em."

Mandel grabbed the speaker as if collaring him. "You can't! Everything we do now ends up in court transcripts. Just stay calm and we'll win this!" He disconnected. "I knew Lee was fucking himself, going out at thirty-six. Well, Weinberg better tell the committee they have a binding deal with us and to blow LaCroix away. Thing about him is he's weak, but he's also scared of pissing me off."

Mermelstein asked, "Should we get Baxter's input?"

"His input?" Mandel sneered. "Don't you know investment bankers are incapable of thought? What Will's contributed, I could've gotten five monkeys with calculators. . . . Sure, I'll call him. You two can go back to work," he added, meaning they must go back to work. "By the way, this is top secret for the next forty-eight hours." He gave Green a long, piercing stare.

Green's desk was a disaster. In the middle of the paper, like a pink flower in snow, lay a phone message from Bonnie. When he called, she asked, "Did you come home at all?"

"At six. Then I had to go in again at nine."

"You should've woken me. We could've had coffee at least."

"You were too peaceful." She'd been lying face in her palm, angelic. "So what's on your schedule today?"

"Don't know. Check the calls in *Backstage*. Guess when I tell 'em I played Blanche DuBois freshman year, the doors'll come crashing down. Or maybe I'll stay in bed all day, being lonely."

She was lonely, he thought, but what had she expected, coming there? Did she want him to wreck his chances at the firm, babysitting her? "I'm sorry you're lonely, and for last night. But in this business you have to be ready to—"

"I think you should quit."

"Excuse me?"

"You heard. You've changed for the worse, even just since we met. That job's for assholes."

"Look, last I checked nobody was paying money to sit and sniff the goddamn . . . daisies."

"Startin' to sound a little like Lou Mandel there, Rick. So everything's about money, huh?" Now he was getting mad. Who was she to talk to him that way? "Not what you were saying when we met. Or were you just trying to get laid?"

"This isn't the *time* for this! I'm very, very busy!"

There was a pause. "Sorry. Tell you what, if you get home early, I'll make dinner. Cooking's one of my hidden talents, the rest being sex-related." As if checking in from another state, Green's penis stirred. Then he felt bad for criticizing her, thinking that a million guys would gladly change places with him. He said he'd try to escape and that he loved her.

Rosa buzzed him. "Rosen's holding on your second line." Instant shrinkage.

"I'm not here." In a moment she buzzed again. "He said it's urgent and he'll hold. He's a—persistent guy."

Green tried to ignore Rosen blinking, but then worried it might relate to the bank account. The fucking bank account. He picked up. "What?!"

"We gotta meet, today."

"Impossible. And you have to stop calling me!"

"It's not about the Lee deal. It's about you personally. It'll only take five minutes, but I can't tell it on the phone. Can't you trust me?"

"No." But he had to find out. One of his faults, he knew. He always had to find out.


He spotted Rosen loitering on a sunny Lexington corner, wearing a striped double-breasted suit that made him resemble a boy gangster. He also had on gray calfskin loafers, a gold collar bar, and black Ray-Bans. Green approached, checking his watch. "Okay, you've got five minutes. Go!"

Ignoring him, Rosen turned and walked into a deli. Green caught up to him at the counter, ordering a roast beef hero. "We gotta eat lunch, right? You know, you're very tense."

They sat on a bench in a small park wedged between two skyscrapers. Carefully landscaped by the Rockefeller Foundation, the park could have made you feel you were in the country, if not for the trucks spewing smoke as they passed, the homeless rooting through the garbage, and the building across that blocked all but a narrow shaft of sunlight.

Green had no appetite, and just watched Rosen. A dollop of Russian dressing dribbled onto his chin, but Green lacked the energy to mention it. "So. What did you want to tell me?"

He took a last bite and swallowed. "Get ready. You remember Teri? You got her pregnant."

Green leaned back, hands on his face. "I can't—! I only went inside her for a—for less than a second!"

"Guess you got industrial-strength jizz. Wouldn't think it to look at you, but hey."

"How does she know it's even me?"

"She's a nice girl!" Rosen cried, offended.

"I don't know what she does out there in New Jersey!"

"What, you think Jersey's some big orgy? You're really a snob sometimes."

"Okay, I apologize. Anyway, what am I supposed to do?"

"Take it easy. I'm just telling you because you should know. I'm gonna take care of everything, so don't worry."

"You mean she'll—?"

"Yeah, we don't want any half-Italian Ricky Green Juniors running around Bergen County."

He sighed. "Thanks. God. Should I—call her?"

"Nah. Frankly, she's upset and she doesn't— It'd be worse if she talked to you. You know?"

"Fine. I owe you big." Green wished he could suck the words back the moment they passed his lips.

Rosen opened an orange bag of Lay's Bar-B-Q chips and ate one, checking around. "Funny you should say that. Rumor is a new bidder's gonna come after Lee and break up the LBO. Some arbs are buyin', and they've pushed the stock up to thirty-eight. Vince has to decide if we should sell our stake—or buy more. It's a tough call."

Green stared into a waterfall of sculpted stone, framed by vines and bushes. "Petey, why is it the only favors you ever ask me are against the law?"

Rosen shook his head. "Law. When're you gonna grow up? This world is about grabbing, and there's no rules. Do you have any idea how rich people are getting? Right now, while we're eating our fuckin' sandwiches? And how many of them play by the rules?" His fingers formed a zero. "You wanna schlep along forever, breakin' your ass at that firm? What do they pay you, eighty thousand a year? You think that's a lot? It's chickenshit! Alfieri makes that every *day*, and he leaves work at three. Then he's on his yacht, in the sun. By the time Crank is finished with you, you'll be an old man!"

"I'm not a lucky person. We'd get caught."

"Believe me, we wouldn't. We know how to do this."

Green looked at the pavement. "I can't. It's too dangerous, and it's not right. I can't."

Rosen removed his sunglasses. "I see. Okay, I'll leave you alone. We'll just hold on to our stock for now, all right?" Green nodded and then, suddenly conscious of hunger pains, unwrapped his sandwich and swallowed it.

"New subject. I called last night, and Elly Mae Clampett answered the phone. What's that about?" Green told the story, producing from his wallet a picture of Bonnie, unable to conceal his pride.

Rosen glanced from the photo to Green. "She's too pretty." Green was uncomprehending. "She's too *pretty*. A guy should date someone as good-lookin' as him, or maybe a notch better. But she's in another class. I mean, you're a handsome guy, but let's face it, George Michael you're not. Me either, and that's how I pick my women. Ones who don't think they're doin' me some favor goin' out with me. Because, fuck that shit."

He reexamined the picture. "Funny. She's pretty, but not as nice as I thought at first. What it is, she has some monster sex appeal happening. Still too nice for you, though."

"Life's not just looks. We have something deeper."

Rosen grinned sadly. "The way you talk, I know you'll get hurt. She comes to the big city, where there's millions of guys. One day she meets one handsomer than you, richer, bigger *dick*, and the last time you see her butt is when it wiggles out the door. I'm speaking from experience." He stared into space.

"Girl I met on the beach in Miami. High school senior, but she was modeling already. Sex with her was like—heaven. So she moved in. I gave her money, bought her stuff. Then of course she meets some

*producer*, guy says he's makin' a movie with Gene Hackman, he's sucking Gene Hackman's dick, I can't even remember. Anyway, soon she's
out all night, comin' home with stories. Which I believe, 'cause you
have to, right? But one night I, like, wake up, throw her shit in a bag
and leave it outside for her to find. Next morning she yells up at the
window, 'Gimme a chance!' and I put my Walkman on, not to hear.
Hardest thing I ever had to do." He sipped a Sprite.

"What happened after?"

"Oh, I was so messed up I got back on coke—" He stopped.

Green blinked. "Did you have a drug problem?"

"Did I?" He grinned. "My man, you got one, you *always* got one.
Where'd you think all my money went, from commercials? I did coke
all through high school, though it only got really bad in Miami. Then
I got off it, but after Tanya I started again. Lost my job. Came back up
here to get my shit together. I've been clean a year."

"I didn't— Wow. I didn't know."

Rosen crumpled his bag. "So. It'll be a long time before I let a
woman get to me again. I mean, I wanna fall in love and have a family.
I just can't go through the shit again yet. And that's *my* fox story. What
does it tell you?"

Green pitied him, but what could he expect, picking up teenagers
on the beach? "Sounds terrible, though I don't think it has a lot to do
with me and Bonnie."

Rosen patted his back. "Okay, you're different." They took their
trash to a modernist can. Rosen held up his Lay's bag and said, "I ate
one chip. Not bad for an addict."


Everything about Rosen made more sense now. Why he'd quit college. How he'd wasted his early twenties. Why he always drank soda.
Poor Petey, with his gambler dad and *Cosmo* mom. It'd be nice to
spend time with him, to help him stay clean, but it'd be too risky.
Because he'd already crossed the line. His values had come unstuck,
and he was . . .

Mermelstein appeared in Green's doorway. "Thought we'd leave
around five. You did remember the printer is tonight?"

"Yeah, of course." His heart sank; he'd forgotten.

By seven they were down at Triton, proofing the same document simultaneously, to be doubly sure of catching a scandalous typo. As Green read, he scooped honey-roasted peanuts robotically from bowl to mouth. He'd called Bonnie earlier, promising he'd figure a way out, but the session was dragging on and on. Just as he was picturing Neil impaled on a long spike, blood gushing from the consumptive frame, he looked up with a comradely grin. That was sad.

When the phone rang, Green snatched it. "Guess what? I'm at a bar on Hudson and Vandam! I had to be near you." He flooded with love. "Can you escape?"

"I don't know."

"Can't talk? That wienerwald's in the room?"

"That's correct."

"I'll wait, and if you don't come in an hour, I'll call back. But you'll try?"

"Yes." Mermelstein looked over curiously as he hung up, and he shrugged. "My mother. Thinks my father's having a heart attack. Worrier." Green fixed his eyes on the document, waiting. But Neil simply resumed work, which he found infuriating. This was how the bastard reacted to a family tragedy, albeit a fake one? He cleared his throat. "Shooting pains in the left arm, then constriction in the chest. Just gas, you think?"

"Actually they should call a doctor, to be safe. You ready to turn to page seven?"

When Green went down the hall for his next pee, he stopped with his hand on the bathroom door, overcome by a prickly warmth and a sense that nothing mattered. Was this what it felt like to lose control? He ducked into the stairwell, descended as if pursued by a maniac, then burst into the cool evening.

Finding Bonnie on a stool drinking a margarita, he kissed the nape of her neck. As she swiveled to hug him, a middle-aged man rose and nodded goodbye. "Who was he?"

"Oh, some old jerk comin' on, as usual. Good news is I got my drink free. So how'd you break out?"

"I just left! It was easy." He shook his head, marveling at *how* easy. He'd had a choice between misery with Mermelstein and bliss with Bonnie; of course he'd chosen bliss.

"That's what I like to hear."

He ordered a bottle of wine and toasted Neil, feeling festive. Bonnie matched him glass for glass, then pulled ahead, pouring for herself when he was too slow, saying, "Granny needs another bit of her rheumatism med-i-cine."

His tongue felt thick. How would he proofread? Well, coffee. His life was coffee. "I should get back."

"You're fuckin' kidding me!"

"I can't just not go back! I'd get in trouble."

She hooted. "Trouble. What're you, five years old? Be a man, okay?" There were red circles on her cheeks, and her eyebrows tilted at a vicious angle. She looked as if she could kill him. Then she softened, like a layer of wax melting off her face. "Sorry. I just *can't* be alone tonight! Aren't you ever scared to be alone?" Her face changing again, she rubbed her leg against his. "Come with me, y'won't be sorry." He gulped wine. Another hour, who cared? He'd make up some excuse.

She began to strip as they entered the apartment, and was naked within seconds. He stumbled over his pants, thinking how everything physical came easier to her. They unfolded the couch and she shoved him onto his back, then straddled him. He closed his eyes, feeling somehow disconnected.

When he looked again, she was deep in concentration, as if taking the math SAT. He flashed back to her father, working the plane up and down his shelf. She was even making noises like Williams's labored grunts. Green's mind wandered, snagging on an image of Neil twirling his hair as he proofread. That was crazy, having such a repugnant vision while making love to a beautiful woman! He willed it to vanish.

They turned over, and he shifted down her body, his head between her thighs, his legs jutting off the bed. This time, when he closed his eyes, Shelly appeared. How would she be, sexually? She'd been evasive about her experience, though he knew she'd had a college boyfriend. Could she be a *virgin?* He got excited, thinking how everything would be new to her. In fact, she might turn out a dynamo . . . they said it happened that way sometimes. He glanced up at Bonnie, staring at the ceiling; quiet. Unexcited. Okay. He crawled up and entered her again.

She rolled him on his back, then lay forward, moving and focusing. "Do you like my ass?"

"Hm? Yes."

"Then why don't you touch it?" Did she—? Oh. He slipped a finger in, uncertain how long she'd want it After a minute he felt as if he were taking her temperature. The length of her body pressed against his, she ground her pelvis and finally stiffened, then relaxed on his chest. He hadn't come yet and sensed he wouldn't be able to; his erection subsided.

Having an orgasm, Bonnie reminded him of Diane Perchik, from college. Diane used to get there pretty quickly. She was a premed, so she needed the release. A chem major. Or was it bio? Why did he keep drifting?! he wondered, and hoped Bonnie hadn't noticed.

She lay on her side, breathing evenly, staring at him. He kissed her forehead, feeling like a liar.


An hour later, they were in a punctured vinyl booth at the Shamrock, a dimly lamplit bar off Amsterdam. She'd wanted to get out for a while. He had planned to return to Triton, but it seemed rude right after sex. Also, he'd been gone so long now, all his prepared stories were obsolete, and he'd need a new one, tailored to all-night AWOL. Maybe he'd say his father *had* had a heart attack! Ghoulish, but it might work.

Green liked this place. In high school, when he and his friends had devoted much of their energies to finding bars that served youth, the Shamrock had always come through. But tonight the bartender was carding a kid who looked fifteen. Things had sure toughened since the seventies, Green thought; of course, back then they'd needed the business, their clientele being a sparse gathering of drunks and boarding-school boys home in disgrace, whereas now the yuppies had discovered it. New York was so hot, nothing was allowed to stay shitty anymore.

While Green sipped at a bottle of beer, Bonnie went to buy her second Jack Daniel's. She put alcohol away like Ben Lee, he thought. What was it with southerners? Unlike Lee, however, she showed the effects, eyeing him through the glass and slurring, "You're funny. Not ha-ha, though y'are that. I mean queer." She tapped her temple.

"Lemme ask, do you enjoy making love to me?"

He was thrown. "I . . . yes! More than anything!"

"Tough to tell. You're a quiet lover, y'know." He blushed, wondering what other guys did. Howl and bellow like grizzlies? "When they're with me, most men—" He raised his palm to stop her. "Y'act like you wish I was a nun before we met. Even though you wouldn't've wanted me then."

"Sure I would." She shook her head so hard her hair whipped horizontal. "I *would*," he repeated, sounding to himself like a boy negotiating with his mother.

"No you wouldn't. You responded to me *because* I'm free. See, mos' people have sexual hang-ups. Reading *Playboy*, you'd think guys all want a woman without 'em, but give 'em one in real life and they freak. Of the lovers I've had, I'd say—"

"Can we—? I don't want to hear any more."

"See? You can't handle it because I'm a woman! But I bet *you've* had dozens of girls." She extended her glass. "Am I right?" He nodded, though she was quite wrong.

"So if I've had experience too, what's the difference? You're a sexisss. Could you get me one more Jack Dannels?"

"You've had enough."

"Can hold my liquor with anybody. Drink you under the table, Poindexter, that's for sure. If you don't wanna go, I will." She rose, then sank back onto the vinyl.

"All right!" Squeezing in beside the fifteen-year-old—who'd finally gotten his gin and seemed in pain from the taste—Green ordered a beer and, under silent protest, a J.D. He hoped she wasn't— Shit, all he needed was a live-in drunk.

When he returned, he was not at all surprised to find a hardhaired guy in a track suit standing over Bonnie, making time. He was informing her of the astounding weight he could bench-press, as if she could possibly care about such a thing. Still, she was smiling at him, eyes twinkly; the look she'd given Green at Lee reception. Now, seeing it again, he realized that something in her expression screamed, "Sex!" like a fire alarm. He shoved past. "Excuse me, we were having a private conversation."

The guy studied him, then backed away, giving Bonnie one last grin. "Enjoy New York, now, hear?"

"Why were you being so nice to that scumball?"

"Politeness."

"Listen. You have to just blow *off* men like that." She smiled. "It's not a joke. This isn't Pikeville. People get raped and killed here!"

"I can handle myself. I know aikido, okay? Get tough with me. I'll kick you right in the balls." Her leg flying out of the booth, she emitted a martial-arts cry.

"Yes, that was bloodcurdling."

She fumbled for a cigarette. "I can't just shut off the—*life* inside me, Rick! Tell you, New York would be a lot happier if people were more . . . southern."

Green set down his bottle. "Yup, the South's the friendliest ol' place. Slavery? Just neighborliness. Lynching? Practical jokes that got out of hand." He sat back.

"You through? Then do me a favor and wipe that shit-eatin' grin off your face. Nothing offends me more than racism. But maybe you could learn a thing or two from a southern gennulman."

"Like what? How to beat my wife? Screw my sister? What?"

She caught her breath and said, "You do have a small fucking mind! For an intelligent guy, you're *so*—! Like you could learn how to treat a woman. I mean, pull out a chair, open a door for once, for God's sake!"

His grin fled. "I open a chair."

"You pull out a door." She laughed. "I'm sorry, you're cute."

She sipped. "See, women're simple. We jus' wanna feel pretty, and special. It wouldn't hurt if you'd compliment me occasionally." She inspected her fingernails. "Like when we make love, you never say if I have a nice body." He blushed. True, but he found that kind of talk embarrassing, like dialogue out of soft-core porn. "We're in the most intimate situation, but still there's all these barriers."

"You know how . . . beautiful I think you are."

"Well, I need to hear it, especially in bed. Now I've hurt you." She moved to his side of the booth, hugged his shoulders, and they leaned their heads together. All at once he was filled with sorrow, like a drafty hole through his chest.

"I jus' wanna be loved." He closed his eyes, saying he did love her, he'd never loved anybody like he loved her, he was literally crazy over her. She kissed him a hundred times.

It was past three when they left. Bonnie had trouble walking, and he counted her drinks: many. She stopped, facing him in an angled wash of streetlight. "No one's ever said the beautiful stuff you just did. I'm so happy." He said he was too, though he couldn't shake the sorrowful feeling. They walked again, she began mouthing words, and a diamondlike tear welled in each of her eyes. "What's wrong?"

"I'm afraid that—"

"What?" She shook her head, refusing to answer. He led her across Broadway, misty and creepy-quiet, then half-dragged her up the building stairs. Inside the apartment, she sagged forward over his shoulder. Supporting her with both arms, he couldn't reach the light switch. "I'm afraid," she sobbed.

"What of?"

"That people will turn you against me."

"What people?"

"Like my mother."

"Your mother? What's she—I don't give a shit about her!" He pulled Bonnie up, her tears running hot inside his collar.

"She's a sick woman. Promise you won't let her come between us? Do you promise?"

Green filled with a raging desire to strangle that tight-cheeked, Bible-kissing hypocrite for having driven her own daughter to such a state. But for right now, Bonnie needed comforting. "I promise," he said, into the darkness.


At four he sat up sweating. Had he simply walked out of the printer? For all he knew he'd committed a Class A law-firm felony. And he'd only just hit his stride at Crank. "You're fired!," heretofore a cartoon phrase preceded by the name "Jetson," would soon be heard in actual life.

He started to dress, but stopped, wondering if Bonnie would be okay alone. Though she'd calmed down before going to sleep, he remained disturbed by the emotion that had poured from her. She must've had some awful childhood, but they'd talk it out. He just knew if he loved her enough, she'd get free of her past. Slipping her Valium in his pocket—a precaution that felt fairly debonair—he left a note and tiptoed out.

Downtown, he told Mermelstein that he'd become ill in the bathroom and had run home with diarrhea. "It was grayish green—" Mermelstein waved off further details, appraised him briefly, then turned inward. Green sensed that he was struggling to believe the story; more, he was grappling with his faith in humanity. Finally he said, "Okay, but you've fallen way behind me." Green exhaled, glad he'd chosen diarrhea, the little black dress, over Dad's heart attack, the sequined gown. And the color thing was good; you had to make your lies visual.

When they returned to the office at noon, Mandel was just getting a call from Lee. "Great news, boys! Committee sent a quick 'fuck you' to LaCroix! 'Thanks, but we're bound by a contract.' Can't wait till the Textile Association dinner next month. I'm gonna laugh right in his ugly New Hampshire face!"

Lee's thickheadedness pained Mandel. "Before you start laughing, Ben—like I said, my bet? In court by five today."

Lee sighed. "Can't you let me enjoy myself even for a minute? Naw, you're right to say it. Wait 'n' see." The speaker went dead.

"You both look like shit," Mandel said. "Gonna sleep?"

"Feel good," Mermelstein said, lids flickering. Green had seen him, on several occasions, experience rapid-eye movements while awake.

"All right. Don't kill yourself, though. You too, Rick. Save some strength for fucking." Green jumped. He knew! What? Mandel grinned and winked. He knew, but it was okay.

Save strength for fucking, Green kept thinking as he stumbled back downstairs. A colleague's jest. He had *not* blown his assignment to Mandel. On the contrary, when he came up for partner, Lou would say that it was incredible how a young man could be so red-blooded and frisky, and at the same time so capable.

On Green's desk was a memo from the pro bono coordinator, whom he'd been ducking for weeks. She needed a volunteer to handle an eviction case in housing court, if he had extra time. He made a crazed noise similar to a laugh, tossed the memo and then called to check on Bonnie, expecting misery and a hangover. Instead, she sounded elated. "Al knows someone at *Endless Night,* the soap? They need a southern blonde for a bit part, so he's getting me an audition!"

"That's wonderful," Green said with faint enthusiasm.

"You bring me luck!" She whispered, "Maybe because you love me so much. You do love me, don't you?" He swore he did, and she blew a kiss through the phone. Bonnie had mood swings, he was thinking as he hung up.

A messenger brought in a press release: "Country Home Sues Lee Textiles in New Hampshire." So Mandel was right again. The release stated that Country Home would, if allowed to bid, offer at least forty-two dollars per share. Green pictured Rosen and Alfieri uncorking champagne.

Upstairs, Mandel already had Lee on the speaker, shouting about New Hampshire, New Hampshire, fuck New Hampshire. "Calm yourself. Paul Weinberg's gonna file a transfer motion saying the case belongs in Georgia."

"All right, but he better win!"

"He will. But let's step back a minute and I'll explain where you're at."

Mandel fingered his tie. "Your stock's up to thirty-nine. That means the arbs saw LaCroix's willing to pay forty-two and have been buying, betting thirty-six isn't the final price. You've got a whole new set of greedy stockholders, bad guys like Vince Alfieri, who'll do anything to get you to raise."

"Never thought you'd be the one to lose his nerve, Lou. I still aim to do this deal at a sane price. I told you—"

"I know, cushion. I support you, Ben! All I'm saying is, thirty-six bucks is dreamland now!"

"I will not throw more money on the table until we see how the litigation turns out."

"I'm not sure he has the balls for this part," Mandel said after Lee disconnected. "See, Rick, it's like war: When the shit flies, some men turn out strong and others weak, and you can never tell who's gonna be which. What's coming here is, will Ben stick to this 'cushion' idea till he loses to LaCroix? Or will he be strong and say, 'I'm not Pikeville's Santa Claus.'"

"We make more if the LBO happens, right?"

He eyed Green. "Don't worry, Rabbi, I don't push my clients into deals. I can live without the fee. What I will do is help Ben find the guts to reach for what he really wants."

Green noticed a pleasing absence of Neil and was struck that he had a fine opportunity to get in good, maybe by expressing amazement at Mandel's prescience. "You know, Lou—" he began, but no more words would come. He'd always had a block against ass-kissing, and could be nice to those in positions of power only if it was clear that he stood to gain nothing by it. He suspected that if he'd been born in an earlier time he'd have ended up like his great-uncle Pinchas, beaten nearly to death for cursing a Cossack.

Bonnie greeted him that night with a bear hug, then pranced around, saying, "Your father's the cutest! He is so sweet!"

Green sagged onto the couch. "You spoke." He'd been dreading this, though aware it had to happen eventually.

"He called, and we had a long talk. I made plans for us to go over there for dinner Friday."

Green moaned. "Okay. I'll get us out of it."

She stopped in the center of the room, hands on hips. "Why? *Again*, are you hiding me for some reason? Frankly, I was shocked you hadn't told your parents about us."

He loosened his tie to ease the flow of words. "My father. My father talks nice—I mean, he is nice. But he's incredibly complex. If you think your mother's manipulative, well, now you're dealing with the master. And the other thing is, my parents aren't *quite* as provincial as yours, but—"

"You said they were atheists."

"You're expecting logic. But see, the decision-making process of a Jewish parent is the ultimate black box.'

She clasped his neck. "You're sweet to be so sensitive to my feelings. But don't worry, I can handle them."

He agreed, though he still felt she underestimated the forces in opposition. Divorced from religion though Fievel and Rachel might be, they'd never confronted a full-size goya in the apartment. He wouldn't be at all surprised if they circled the wagons, as Jews had done since the day Moses' family hocked him for marrying an Egyptian Cushite.

·   ·   ·

Green's sense of impending calamity grew sharper as the week passed, and by Friday evening he'd whipped himself into an anxious frenzy over the dinner. Bonnie, too, continued to worry him. It made him nervous, leaving her all day. A recurring image: returning to find her white body in a bloody pool, razor lying nearby. Though in truth she was on an upswing, thrilled for some unfathomable reason to be meeting his parents and also about the *Endless Night* audition. He expected a major letdown on the latter front—Al, yeah right—but didn't want to deflate her, saying so.

Her good moods also worried him, in a different way. When she went out with that fire-alarm smile, men hit on her everywhere. He didn't need to see it happen, to know. Not that she'd cheat, but . . . maybe he'd feel less insecure if they had sex more often. They *were* living together, after all. Plus he was paying her expenses. No, that sounded awful, as if they had a business arrangement. Anyhow, she called it "loans" and kept a running tab, taped to the refrigerator and entitled "Bonnie's Debt to 'The Man.'"

Arriving home, he gasped at her transformation. Her hair was neat, gripped with a blue velvet band, and she wore a starched white blouse, pearls, and a knee-length blue skirt. Clasping her hands before her, she resembled a model in the kind of WASPy catalog, filled with horses and sailboats, that his parents periodically, and pointlessly, received. "You look beautiful," he said, kissing her.

"Thought I'd give 'em the full shiksa experience," she explained.

"Fort Knox?" she asked at the Green door, indicating the three pick-, shotgun- and bazooka-resistant locks. Fievel opened up, wearing a jacket and—wonder of wonders—a tie.

"*Hell*-lo. You must be Bonnie."

"Pleased to meet you," she said, exaggerating her accent. As they entered, Fievel's eyes had a conversation with Green's. Green took his father's popping and rolling to mean "Some tomato!" while his own were trying to convey "Watch your step, you old bastard." Rachel emerged from the kitchen, wearing a flowered muumuu and a necklace ending in a lapis chunk the size of a Ping-Pong ball.

The hallway amazed Bonnie. "Lotta books." She took one off the shelf. "Isaac Bashevis Singer. I've been wanting to read something by him. Can I borrow it?"

Fievel and Rachel exchanged a confused look. "Of course!" he cried. "By Singer I have plenty!" He reached in and pulled out ten, squeezed to his chest like an accordion.

"Just this one's okay."

"But why not more?" He shoved them at her with his torso. Green felt his temper working loose.

"She just wants one!"

"Okay, fine. You know he lives on Eighty-sixth, on the other side Broadway." Two of the books separated from their bindings and fell in a crumbling, dusty pile. "Shit!" Fievel yelled, then smiled apologetically at Bonnie.

She turned down his offer of a cocktail, opting instead for a ginger ale. "I'm not much for alcohol." Green snorted, then covered by hacking into a tissue.

Fievel brought shots of vodka for Green and himself and Sabra—an Israeli chocolate liqueur with the consistency of hot butter—for Rachel. Green's parents gaped silently from their chairs, as if awaiting the overture of a musical. Green opened his mouth, nothing came out, and he gulped his drink.

Finally Bonnie said, "It was so kind of y'all to invite me! This is the first real New York apartment I've been to."

Fievel smiled. "What's your town like?"

"Pikeville's a . . . sleepy place." She described it, making it sound like some antebellum hamlet, not at all the glass-office-and-strip-mall sprawl that Green had visited. He was sure Fievel would see through her bullshit, but on the contrary he appeared enchanted.

"What's there, a general store, they sell everything?"

"Dad, it's not Tobacco Road! There's a department store with as much space as Gimbel's, all on one floor. Groceries on the left and guns on the right, okay?"

Rachel, sliding a bowl of raisins and nuts along the coffee table, asked Bonnie's impression of New York. She smiled. "Hope I don't sound too much of a hick—it's hard to adjust to the pace." But the coke *is* better up here, Green thought, then swallowed and poured another vodka.

Fievel leaned over, as if to tell a secret. "Livin' in Georgia, did you see *racism* against the blacks?" (He pronounced it "blocks.")

She sipped her soda demurely. "That's what I like least about the South, though it was never tolerated in my home." Green snickered: total crap. Linda Williams would *anchor* the fire hose.

"We're so cut off here," Fievel said, gesturing out the window at the world of Seventy-second Street. "But you're from real America. If you could change one thing about it, what would it be?" Green had to laugh: Fievel thought he was Bert Parks; Bonnie, that Miss Teenage America they used to watch, grown into lovely young womanhood.

"There's some dirt-poor people in Pikeville. All over the South, really. I just wish the government took responsibility. It feels like Reagan's almost trying to starve 'em out."

Fievel smacked his hands together. "Let me tell you some things about *his* Reagan."

Lacking patience for the coming avalanche of conspiracy theories, Green followed Rachel to the kitchen. "Bonnie is cute as a button," she said, chopping up a block of frozen peas. "She's really winning Daddy over."

"He likes anybody who'll sit still for his spiel."

She glanced up. "Are we doing something wrong?"

Green waved. "No, it's just, she's not the queen of Sweden, you know, that's all I'm saying."

Rachel placed the peas on a low flame. "So Shelly's finished?"

"I mean she's not dead . . ."

"Daddy predicted it. He said she was too . . . sweet. We loved her, don't misunderstand, but we expected you'd get tired of her." Green was stunned, then angry. Where did they come off criticizing Shelly?

He watched his mother tend four bubbling pots like a plate spinner at the circus. How could she, who had rarely, if ever, raised her voice, have reached the conclusion that *Shelly* was too mild? In fact, in fact—it had never occurred to him before—she and Shelly had a lot in common. The placid surface, rippling eyes, and submerged but stealthy will. Her opinion smelled of Fievel.

"What did *you* think of her?" he asked in a low voice, as if to imply that dissent would be kept secret. She shrugged, and suddenly seemed a stranger, maybe a soup-taster acquaintance. While Fievel pestered, argued—made his living presence felt always—Rachel went about her business quietly, saving energy for occasional forays into family real-politik. Maybe it was only through open conflict that you got to know people at all.

At last she answered, "I loved her, like I said. But I know you, too, and I had to agree with Daddy." Too strong. The old man was too fucking strong for her.

Back at the couch, Bonnie was telling a PG-rated version of their meeting. "So, even on our first date we knew we had something special." Green closed his eyes, picturing their very, very special first date. "Right?"

He opened his eyes. "Mm-hmm. Mom says go to the table." When they turned, he produced one of Bonnie's Valium from his pocket and took it with the remains of his vodka.

During dinner he felt as if his head were swaddled in pillows. He saw Bonnie and Fievel talking and wondered why the old man was being so nice to her. What was his game? Chewing mechanically, he remembered his last dinner there, with Shelly. No matter what they said about her now, he'd been so comfortable. They'd even had an argument in front of her, but so what? She was like his cousin or something, none of this royalty business. Was she at B'nai Shalom tonight? Or had that faded yet? Did she have a new boyfriend, some paleface from shul or, God forbid, an Uzi-carrying soldier in the JDL?

He became aware of Rachel addressing him; it felt like surfacing in the Silver Glen pool. "Bonnie's asking about that African mask you bought for me." She pointed at the hanging football-shaped face that he'd found at a Columbia crafts fair, with its slits for eyes and painted red nose holes.

"You know," he said, "it's really ugly."

Rachel's face fell. She clearly wanted to defend the mask, but how? Fievel knew how. "Why ugly, because it's made by blocks?"

"I'm sorry, but it looks like a day camper did it."

"So who's good? Norman Rockwell, that fake?"

Green nodded, enjoying himself. "Rockwell had more talent in his pinky than all the tribesmen put together."

Fievel gestured dismissively. "I apologize for him, Bonnie. He was dropped on his head as a baby. Doctors tried, but . . ."

After an awkward silence, Bonnie spoke up. "So you were both born in Poland?" She asked about Lodz.

"Americans don't know what really means poor," said Fievel. "We lived in one room my parents, my sister, and me, and a grandmother, *and* a uncle who stayed by us sometimes. He slept across three chairs in the kitchen. Now he was a real Communist, a organizer from the union of Jewish . . . guys who carry? On their backs—?"

"Stevedores?" Bonnie offered.

"Right. Funny, because you wouldn't think, but Jews did *everything* in Poland. Heavy laborers, you name. The streets were full with Jewish prostitutes. I still can't figure where the Poles got the idea Jews were rich. Were a couple, but—"

"Times were bad for everyone," Rachel said. "People look for someone to blame."

"That's why Jews must pray for prosperity wherever they live. Including here, believe you me. Anyway, if my uncle didn't stay, it was another relative. And if not a relative, my father brought in people from the street. Homeless? There was no such thing! Do you understand? You took people *in*.

"And no food stamps. If you had soup or a piece of bread, you were happy."

"There was no word 'eating,' " Rachel said.

"True. The word we used, *iberbaysn*, meant oc-tually 'grab a bite.' In our language was no concept of sittin' down to a big meal."

"What'd your father do?"

"Had a agency that distributed newspapers to kiosks. But he was learned enough to be a rabbi, all from reading. Was a atheist, though. Too many terrible things happened to him in life, so he couldn't believe. And me the same. I *wish* I could, but when I go to temple, like for a bar mitzvah, I sit and think, Who is this God? They say, 'Thanks for your blessings. Thanks.' What're they thanking for, for the Holocaust?"

"That's so interesting!" Bonnie exclaimed. "I've been around religious people a lot, and I've always wanted to ask them, 'Don't you see the suffering in the world? How could God allow it?'"

So fucking neat, Green thought. He recalled something he'd read in college, to the effect of: "Dabbling in philosophy brings a man to atheism, but depth brings him back to religion." So here was the junior-class dabbler mouthing off, just as she'd mouthed off on the Palestinians at the AJF dinner. Whatever made the best drama. Bonnie's life was a string of dramatic scenes.

Fievel said, "Eggs-actly my point. I got away from the subject, though, which was poverty. See, when you grow up poor, you never forget. That's why I believe in social justice."

"Me too," Rachel said, but her eyes were on her son. "Are you okay?" she whispered. He didn't answer

Fievel suggested that Bonnie come downtown and visit the Labor Bund, where she'd find a few people left in New York who care about the poor, the blocks. Green pictured the Bund's creaky wood floors, clattering fans, and autographed photo of Paul Robeson. All over, books from the thirties, pamphlets from the fifties, calendars from the seventies. Junk and shit. In every corner, junk and shit.

Bonnie was asking how Fievel escaped Poland. Green watched him cast his eyes down, knocking a potato with his fork. Green had been meaning to tell Bonnie the story, but it wasn't the kind you just launched into, and the moment had never seemed right. "That's some involved thing. For another time. Which I hope there'll be." She said she did, too, and they smiled at each other for a good three seconds.

Green felt all at once repulsed by the falsity of this. Because Fievel was a scene player as well, and tonight he and Bonnie shared top billing in the Yiddish drama *My Daughter-in-Law*, in which stern Papa banishes young couple in act 1, but by the end everyone's embracing, shedding buckets of brine. "Sure you're okay, Ricky?" Rachel's face was twisted with concern. Bonnie gave him a baffled stare.

"Actually I am feeling a little—I should go."

Bonnie insisted on helping Rachel with the dishes first. Fievel fetched a bag of prunes and, storing one in his cheek like a chipmunk, said he needed legal advice. Green tried to focus. "I told you I manage a investment club? Well, I made investments—did I make! In some lousy bonds. Of good companies! But my luck, whatever I buy, the company goes in Chapter Eleven! And then the bonds are worth sssheet. So the question, can the club sue me?"

"They're your friends! They'd sue you?"

"Nah, not really. Though even not, it's bad. I feel humiliated, making such—idiotic decisions." His fist dropped on the table. "See, it's not me—I have enough to retire on—but the other investors depend on this money. Mrs. Ekstein, Zweig. Working people. *Fershteyst?*"

"Yes, but I don't know what to tell you."

Fievel examined the prunes. "The best would be if I made back some. So you'll keep in mind—if you hear anything, a deal, a LBO, you'll let me know." He looked up, anguished. "*Not* to break the law. It's not illegal, but it's a—leg up." He liked the term. "*Ja*, a leg up, like the executives get on the golf course." He exhaled, winked, chewed, spit out his pit, and then, when the women returned, put a sly finger to his lips.

At the door, Bonnie thanked her hosts profusely. She was silent as they walked up West End, and finally Green ventured, "Sorry I got sick. My mother cooks the meat in heavy water, like they use in the nuclear . . ." His voice trailed off. The joke was forced, and she wasn't interested, anyway.

Manuel, at his usual post on the stoop, raised a Heineken in greeting to the young lovers. "*Hola,*" Bonnie said, "*como está?*"

"*Bien, gracias,*" he answered, delighted. They seemed fast friends.

Upstairs, Bonnie threw on her nightie. Because the building's antique wiring couldn't tolerate air conditioning, Green had stuck a fan in the window. He started it, but all it did was blow more heat into the room. He went to the toilet and rested on the lid, looking at the wall. What's wrong with me? he kept asking.

Then he sat beside Bonnie on the couch. "I was thinking, the other day you said you had something to show me."

She stared blankly at the TV news. "Unimportant."

"Come on, now I'm curious."

She was bitterly amused. "Wanna see? Over by the closet."

Inside a plastic bag was a book entitled *Conversion to Judaism*. His stomach dropped. No, she was not planning to marry him! He looked at her, but she wouldn't meet his eyes.

The book cover featured improbable illustrations of harmonious family life. He turned it over, then flipped pages, thinking, Well, why not marry her? She was beautiful and intelligent; and she'd convert, though who cared about that anyhow? He envisioned them walking their blond children along a foamy catalog beach.

"I'm—touched you'd do this for me."

Her eyes flashed. "Who says it's for you? Maybe I was gonna do it anyway! I told you I like Jewish culture."

"Sorry. You're right. Whatever the reason, I think it's great. You—" But she wouldn't discuss it anymore.

They stayed up watching some seventies movie with Desi Arnaz, Jr. After they shut it off. Green lay on his back, feeling that it wasn't too late to say something comforting or wise. He saw her shoulder shaking and stroked her arm, going "Shh," then rolled her over. "It's okay," was all he could think to add.

She sniffled. "It's not! You were, *I* don't know—" She lacked the word. "Terrible!" He whispered that he was sorry, he'd felt sick and then held her awhile. At some point he touched her breast, which made her sit up, emitting an angry sigh. She lay at the foot of the bed.

He felt truly ashamed. Why had he done that? It was so unlike him. He took a deep breath and said, "We should get married," his voice quavering. She didn't answer.

# Chapter 7

Bonnie spent the rest of the weekend smoking in bed, reading fashion magazines, and listening to R.E.M. through headphones. A few times Green tried to apologize for his parents, but she shrugged him off. He hid out at the office each day and, by the time he summoned the nerve to face her at night, found her half asleep, an empty wine bottle on the floor. Discussion would be futile.

On Monday he took a garment bag to work. The New Hampshire judge had transferred the Lee litigation to Boland, a town near Pikeville, and Mandel was bringing him down for the injunction hearing. In his hotel room that night he grew melancholy, thinking that he and Bonnie had somehow gone off track. What had happened? He'd expended all his energy, and still she seemed unsatisfied. Well, cohabitation required adjustment even in the easiest cases, and their lives diverged radically. But they had been reaching an accommodation—he saw that now. If only Fievel hadn't chosen that fragile moment to interfere.

He called her at home. "I've been worrying. Because I hope the dinner at my parents' didn't—"

"We had the whole weekend to discuss it! Can we not do it now, on the phone?"

"I tried to, but you—"

"No! All you tried was to blame them for—"

"I wanted to explain that the Jewish parent is in many ways a psychotic who—"

"Oh, stop it! When'll you be back?" The hearing was expected to take all day Tuesday, and he'd have to stay over again. Saying they'd talk Wednesday at home, she told him to sleep tight. He recalled that instruction as he wedged under the bedcovers, made up snug as a mummy's wrapper. He lay anxiously awake and then had to masturbate, picturing her, to fall asleep at all.

In the miserably humid morning he accompanied Mandel down Main Street, sweating copiously in his wool suit. He noticed that all the other men around wore seersucker, like blue pajamas.

The federal court, an incongruous hunk of stone in the middle of Boland's brown-glass business district, had a deliciously cool lobby with a floor mosaic that resembled a terrorist victim but was actually Justice blindfolded. Whereas the entry to Judge Fineman's building featured armed guards and a metal detector, here there was only a lethargic fellow reading the *Boland Gazette* and saying, "How'd you do?" over half-glasses.

They found Lee and Houser fidgeting in an anteroom. Mandel asked after Weinberg, and Lee said, "He and his litigator are prepping Nobby one last time."

"Jackson'll do fine. It's Ruth Royster who worries me. What've you found out about this judge . . . Tranh—whatever?"

"Tranh Dinh," Lee enunciated. "Tell him, Gilbert."

"As it's July, many of the judges are gone fishing. Of those left we drew Judge Dinh, a recent appointee; of Vietnamese descent, I believe. Grew up in Savannah, went to Emory Law. His family became wealthy in real estate, it seems, and are well connected politically."

Lee grinned. "Two of the judges I went to college with, two I know from my club, and I get Tranh Dinh! If it wasn't so damn funny, I'd be cryin'! "

"Don't go berserk," Mandel said. "He's as much a Georgian as the others."

"Tranh . . . Dinh," Lee repeated ruefully.

Calling the hearing to order, Dinh thanked the lawyers for preparing on short notice. "Y'all ready?" He wore tinted aviator glasses, like Houser's, and a red bow tie beneath his robes. At one counsel table sat Weinberg's partner Nick Themopoulos, fiftyish and burly, with a thick head of wiry black hair. Hair, in fact, sprouted from every visible part of the man's body; it crept from his cuffs over his hands and from his collar over his neck. At the other table sat Cletus Tilford, a Boland lawyer hired by Country Home. White-haired and imposing, he looked exactly right in seersucker and white bucks.

The gallery was packed with the Lee directors, curious Bolanders (including ladies dressed for a matinee) and, clustered in the back rows, some spiffy types whose presence puzzled Green until he realized they must be scouts for the arbs, eager to see how this turned out. And sure enough, there he sat, chewing gum in the corner; Rosen waggled his eyebrows, but Green frowned, snapping front.

Tilford called Jackson to the stand. While he was sworn in, the lawyer slouched, thumbs hooked in suspenders as if he might start reciting from *Inherit the Wind*. When the questions began, Green watched Mandel to see how *his* brain processed the testimony. For Mandel, this hearing wasn't an isolated legal event, but a point along a continuum. How had earlier decisions shaped this moment? And how would today's developments be addressed? If you wanted to become Mandel, these were your issues.

Tilford promptly established that the committee had sold Lee Textiles to management without seeking a better price, though Jackson, well coached, cast it differently. "If you read the bid letter, it was contingent on confidentiality." That was right; Green recalled Mandel adding that sentence at midnight. Tilford kept hammering, but Jackson stuck to his story: It had been either work with Lee exclusively, or nothing.

When Tilford shifted to the lockup, Jackson was again ready, saying Lee had made it a condition of raising to thirty-six. Also staged by Mandel, Green recalled. It seemed there was no reality here except that which he had constructed.

"I'd like a sense of the relationship between 'Mr. Lee' and the committee members. You, for example, are close friends with him, aren't you?"

Jackson smoothed his mustache. "We occasionally play golf. Pikeville's a small town."

"Gettin' smaller—" Tilford held his arms in a circle. "And isn't Rich Spellman the third in your foursome?" (And are *you*, perhaps, the fourth, Cletus? Green wondered.) Tilford tightened the circle. "Mrs. Royster attended college with Mr. Lee's wife, did she not? Quite a coincidence!" He closed the circle until he was hugging himself, then sat.

Themopoulos rose. "Before I start, Judge, I want to apologize for my New York accent. If you can't understand what I'm saying, lemme know." Stiff, Green thought. Very schmaltzy.

Under Themopoulos's questioning, Jackson confirmed that the committee had had independent financial advice throughout the LBO, then went on to describe the negotiations, which sounded so arduous that Green would've pitied him if he hadn't been there and didn't know he was exaggerating wildly. When Jackson finished, Themopoulos shrugged toward the judge: See? All kosher.

Tilford's next witness was Royster. She said, "Your Honor, I'd like to note that I resent the implication that my friendship with Virginia Shaw Lee tainted my independence." Tilford "humbly apologized," with a flourish.

"Now, you voted against the lockup, did you not, ma'am? May I ask what you found . . . inappropriate?"

She ignored him, speaking directly to Dinh. "I thought the board should keep an escape hatch in case someone came along at a higher price. Unlike Nobby, I never believed we needed to agree to the lockup, to get the thirty-six-dollar bid I know Ben Lee, and he finishes what he starts."

Tilford smiled. "Thank you ma'am, that's all I have."

Lee cursed softly. An arb ran out, dialing his mobile phone. Green looked to see Rosen's reaction, but he'd dozed off. *Putz.* Themopoulos didn't ask Royster any questions, obviously convinced she'd just do additional damage.

Tilford's last witness, Bill LaCroix, took the stand with boneless grace, a dapper purple handkerchief peeping from the breast pocket of his suit. He caressed the Bible and, when asked if he'd tell the truth, reflected a moment before saying he would, with unquestionable sincerity.

LaCroix, his prep-school accent an obvious irritant to Lee, explained that the lockup impeded the offer. "The bed-and-bath division contains much of Lee's growth potential." Tilford asked if Country Home had the financing to acquire the company. He smiled, saying, "That would not be a problem." Lee, who'd had to battle with the banks, looked furious.

Themopoulos cross-examined. "Does your company have manufacturing plants?"

LaCroix was confused. "Of course."

"Where are they, sir?"

"The flagship's in Manchester, and we have four more."

"Including one as far south as North Carolina. So it'd be fair to say that if you bought Lee, you could do without some—maybe all—of its plants in Georgia?"

Tilford objected. "This is irrelevant!"

"Your Honor, his intentions for plants and so forth are factors the board may consider in selling the company."

Dinh overruled. LaCroix said, "Well, it's hard to tell, in advance of . . ."

Themopoulos lumbered forward. "But in coming up with your bid, you must've considered how plant closings and mass layoffs could add to the bottom line?"

LaCroix began to glisten. "We've considered cost-efficiencies, yes, but no . . . no firm—"

"Of the three Georgia plants, wouldn't you close two?"

After a glance toward Tilford, LaCroix nodded. Themopoulos thanked him, and Lee seemed pleased: LaCroix spelled disaster for the state economy.

Tilford's summation denounced the lockup with such vitriol that it might've been the Hitler-Stalin nonaggression pact. He urged Dinh not to be influenced by layoffs, characterizing them as a "red herring designed to becloud the real issue, which is—" his finger stuck in the air—"whether the process was rigged to hand the company to its CEO on the cheap, and whether this court may countenance such chicanery!" He dropped in his chair, shrugging toward Lee: Sorry, my job. See you at tee-off.

By the time Themopoulos concluded, it was after one, and the spectators gathered their effects for the lunch break. But Dinh said, "I'm aware there's a tender offer runnin', so I'm gonna decide right away."

The judge continued: "Now, I live in Boland, and I'm very concerned about plant closings. I hope any owner'd think long and hard before mass layoffs. Nonetheless, I agree with Mr. Tilford that my task is to ensure the process complied with the law, which is: Once a company's for sale, the board's main duty is to the stockholders, and it is to get the best price, period."

Lee went pale. "And the facts show this wasn't done here. The lockup stops an auction, so I'm issuin' an order restraining it. And because the contract was signed without shopping the company, that's out too."

The arbs cheered and poured into the hall. Green spotted Rosen's carrot top bobbing in the pack. Mandel was concentrating, his eyes closed. Green tried to act upset, but couldn't help feeling admiration for Dinh.

Ruth Royster and Otis Fairchild caught Lee on the courthouse steps. Royster, huffing from the effort of running, called, "I want to talk to you, Ben!" He tilted his head in her direction. "Otis and I are taking control of the sale process. We don't want any more embarrassments."

Fairchild spoke in a clipped tone. "We've reopened the bidding. We're coming to New York, and anyone who wants in has to deliver their best offer to us by 0900 Friday."

"Fine," Lee said. "Hope y'all enjcy runnin' the show." They began to respond, but he marched down the steps to his limo. Mandel accepted a ride to the hotel; Green said he'd walk.

He called Bonnie from a booth. "The bad news is the court took about two minutes to decide against us, but the good news is I'll be home tonight, after all. Maybe we can have a late dinner or something." He hoped candlelight and wine might patch things up.

"Well, since you said you wouldn't be back . . . Al invited me to this *Endless Night* party. I'd meet the writers. It could help my career."

Green watched the state flag droop off the courthouse pediment into the breezeless heat. "Obviously you should go."

"It's a dinner thing, so I may even be back and fast asleep in my p.j.'s by the time you get home."

"Obviously you should go. The writers of *Endless Night*, that's exciting. Chekhov'll be there, and I'm—I'm sure Sam Beckett'll show, once the Yankee game lets out."

She sighed. "See, that's exactly—What do you want me to be, totally dependent on you?"

"I want you to be happy."

"I just wish you'd decide. Have a safe trip," she added, and left him staring, confused, at the flag of Georgia.


Main Street looked frozen in the fifties. Green passed a Kress and a cigar store with a wooden Indian, and was enjoying the tinted photos of DA's and crew cuts in a barbershop window when a pair of arms grabbed him from behind. "Howdy, pardner." He struggled loose. "Big day for the home team," Rosen said. "Bye-bye, thirty-six."

"I don't want to be seen with you." Green walked on.

Rosen hurried after. "I know, that's why I waited till everybody was gone."

"Listen. Go away!"

"You know, I'm incredulous at your bellicosity."

Green had to laugh. "What are you, taking Word Power?"

"I meet executives now, and Alfieri says it helps. I just wanted to tell you about Teri."

"Yes!" he exclaimed, feeling like a cad—he'd forgotten. "How is she?"

"Okay. Like gettin' a tooth pulled."

Green was relieved, thinking he should send her a card. Sympathy? No, he knew: Get well. "Thanks again, really. And sorry if I was nasty."

"Forget it. Let's have sushi sometime. But I guess you'll be busy the next few days, workin' up a new bid."

Green wanted to explain that their relationship was over, but pictured Petey on the floor, coked up and bleeding from the nose, all because his best friend had dumped him. "Maybe when the deal's done."

"So how's Elly Mae?" His lip curled. "Any mysterious all-night disappearances yet?"

"No."

"What's she planning to do in the city, anyway? Just as long as she doesn't wanna be an actress." Spying Green's wince, Rosen groaned. "Oh, God. Did she have any 'auditions' yet? 'Cause when she does, she may not get a part, but she is gonna find out the dick sizes of a lotta guys."

"See ya," Green said, and stalked off. Listening to Petey's embittered view of women, he thought, you might as well be taking in the street-corner ravings of a Times Square degenerate.

"Ask her whose is the biggest!" Rosen called after him.

Green continued on Main and turned on Magnolia, just liking the name. The street was a tree tunnel, lined with historic houses. He envisioned life here, married to Bonnie, leaving for work in his seersucker. Maybe Tilford could use an associate? If he met Bonnie, he'd see that Green—he'd definitely offer a job. And everything was so close together, you didn't need a driver's license.

He passed a church, but stopped, his eye caught by something bizarre. It couldn't be, yet when he turned, he saw that it was, in fact, a synagogue: Beth Israel of Boland. A beauty, too, of bricks and wood, and then he remembered: Boland was the town Shelly had discovered. Hard as it'd be, when he got home he had to call and tell her.

The wooden door creaked heavily open. The interior was dark except for light filtering through stained glass along the sides, and candle-shaped bulbs that illuminated the engraved rolls of dead congregants. Green read the names, hoping to spot a funny one like Bubba Weinblatt; but most were standard Jewish except for a few, like LaMotta and Mendosa, that sounded Italian or Puerto Rican.

The pews were covered in burgundy velvet. It could easily have been a church, if not for the floodlit ark at the end where the cross should hang. He peered through blue glass at the Torah—a glorious old one, with intricate embroidery and silver scroll handles. Alone in this cool darkened shul, looking at a holy book, he felt peaceful, almost spiritual.

"Can I he'p you?" He leaped as if he'd been vandalizing the place. Standing over him was a man wearing an ill-fitting suit and a striped tie with a clip. "I was about to lock up." Green assumed he must be the caretaker—the *shammes*.

"I'm just snooping around. I'm from out of town."

"You'd be surprised how many visitors we get. We're in a coupla guide books. Come on if you want and I'll show you some things." Green followed the man to a room in the back with a display case. "S'ere kiddush cup's Civil War era."

The Hebrew words sounded great in a southern accent, and Green wanted to hear more. "When was this synagogue built?"

"In 1870. By a wealthy planter named Mermelstein."

Green laughed: Life had no end of surprises. The *shammes* seemed offended. "Sorry. I work with someone by that name." He then explained what had brought him to Boland.

"Never been to New York. Hear it's a little wild." He indicated a colorful platter that depicted bearded Jews involved in some sort of agriculture. "That Seder plate was used by our earliest Jewish settlers, around 1740."

"1740?"

"The southern Jews were some of the first: Spaniards who fled the Inquisition, then later wound up here. Lotta families trace to 'em. Like my last name's Mendosa," he said humbly. Green was surprised, having always imagined the South a wasteland where Jews might stop a few years before expulsion. Trailing Mendosa around, Green began to sense about him something strange, something hard to identify. When they exited out into the sun and heat, Mendosa asked where he was headed. "Oh, I'll run y'over! Right on my way." Green waited for him to unlock the car door, but he smiled and said, "Open."

A foam Georgia bulldog hung from the rearview, and a Braves head on a spring hobbled in the back window. They turned onto Main, where the speed limit was twenty, but Mendosa drove so slowly he could chat with pedestrians. One obvious Christian yelled, "Hey, Bobby! Be at Little League?"

Mendosa nodded and explained to Green, "My son's pitchin' tonight? Goin' for his third win."

"Hunh. So you take care of the synagogue?"

Mendosa was amused. "Naw, I jus' volunteer? It's a small congregation. Actually I own a sportin' goods store." He greeted more people. Green observed him . . . and then realized what was so odd about him: Though Jewish, he was not in a hurry to get somewhere, not working an angle, not even thinking much. His face was a relaxed, contented blank.

A man who had a house. "Do you own a house?"

He was stumped. Where else would a family live? "Huh, a Victorian. Been in the family a hundred years." Green thought about Fievel and Rachel, who had no house, no car—nothing but a few rent-control regulations. They seemed so rootless, a strong wind could blow them away.

Swinging into the hotel drive, Mendosa said, "Gonna be in town tonight? 'Cause if you were, I'd be glad to have you for dinner. Then you could see the baseball game."

This act of simple kindness left Green speechless for a second and then, like a gust rising up out of nowhere, whipping papers and grit along the street, proud to be a Jew. "I'd honestly love to, but I have a flight later."

Mendosa handed him a business card, saying that if he found himself coming down again he should call, so they could plan something fun. Green promised he would and then watched him drive off, the Braves head bobbling.

On the plane he thought about Judge Dinh, who right now was probably having "Go Home, Gook" painted on his garage, and about Mendosa and his kid. Imagine that: a Jewish boy notching his third Little League victory. At one point Mandel asked if he'd seen anything interesting, walking around town. "No," he said.

The firm had arranged for cars to meet them. Riding across the Triboro Bridge, Green resolved to take it slower, like Mendosa; to enjoy life. He'd do his work with utmost efficiency, then tell Neil he was finished and leave. Because it seemed clear now: His problems with Bonnie had been caused mainly by his office stress. He'd give her a big kiss the moment he came in.

But she wasn't there. She'd left a message that a group was going out after the party and she'd be back by one at the latest. Green opened the refrigerator, empty except for condiments and a couple of her lidless, half-eaten yogurts. The sink was piled with dishes, a roach cowering under a coffee-stained spoon. In fact, the entire apartment had become a pigsty. He couldn't believe he hadn't noticed Bonnie's dirty ashtrays, her clothes strewn across the floor, her magazines and Evian bottles. To have created this mess in three weeks she must never once have picked up after herself, much less lifted a broom or sponge. If Rachel saw what was happening here, it could actually kill her.

He pictured Shelly's neat apartment, then remembered about the Boland shul. He called, but froze, receiver in hand. "Is anyone there?" she asked. He hung up, vowing to apologize someday.

He couldn't sleep, worrying about Bonnie. What if she wandered into a bad neighborhood? Horrifying scenes of violence infested his imagination. He moved the phone to the bed in case she should call, injured, from a Harlem street corner. By three he felt sure she was in danger. Could she have accepted a ride from some lunatic? Was she *that* trusting? Either she was in danger, or—the alternative was even worse, and he put it out of his mind.

At six he called admissions at a few hospitals, but no luck. He called police precincts, unsure what to ask, and settling on "Would you know if a Bonnie Williams was the victim of a crime tonight?" Finally he lay down again, the phone cradled in his arms, a congestion of sobs in his throat.

When the alarm rang, she still hadn't come home. He dressed, experiencing a new anguish that burrowed inside him like a plague of termites, and before leaving, he taped up a note: "Please call me at work! I'm afraid you're dead!"

He stepped out into the morning sun with a complicated emotion that, if he could've expressed it, might have been: "Here I am, stepping into the morning sun, filled with the sweet agony of love."

"*Endless Night.*"

"Yes, hello. My fiancée went to the party last night and never came home, and I'm worried. I'm worried there may've been an accident. And I thought someone might've seen her go?"

"I can give you to Mary Jo in casting. She threw it."

"Terrif." Green's stomach was jittery, and he needed to use the toilet.

"This is Mary Jo."

"Hi, Mary Jo, how are you?! I'm—there's a problem." He repeated his story, asking if she'd met a Bonnie.

"Can you describe her? Age? Height, weight, eye and hair color?" He gave an impassioned description that made Bonnie sound like Venus incarnate. "Oh! I saw her with Chip Slaney."

"Ah. Who's that?"

She was put off. "He plays Larry. On the *show.*"

"Sorry, I work. Did you see her leave?"

"Well, a bunch of us went out after, and—sure! Oh, she got really . . . Well, Larry—Chip—took her home."

Green was so livid that to avoid smashing something he had to pace the length of his office, muttering. He hated himself for his naïveté; how long until he learned what people were about? When his hand had steadied sufficiently, he tried home again, and this time she answered. "Where the fuck have you been?"

"Just stay calm. I'm really sorry! We went to a bar, and I ordered ice tea! I kept drinkin' ice teas!"

"So?"

"*So* this jerk writer got the bartender to spike 'em—you know, they call it 'Long Island Ice Tea?' And I got trashed beyond belief. There was no way I could make it anywhere on my own, so someone took me to sleep it off."

"Chip Slaney?"

"How—?"

"I called the show, that's how worried I got! It was—humiliating. I called hospitals—" He broke off, heaving.

"I'm sorry."

"Did you have sex with him?" He had to wrench the word out of his chest.

"No, I did not. How could you think that? Am I so . . . horrible?" She sounded on the verge of tears. "Why does everyone hate me?" Now she was crying.

"What could I think? You're out all right with some actor. . . . I'm sorry. Don't cry."

She sniffled. "For your information, Chip's gay. Happy?" Green felt angry, guilty, and in love all at once. It was not an enjoyable feeling.

"I'm sorry to accuse, but . . ."

She blew her nose, saying at least she'd seemed to click with the writers. Green congratulated her, unsurprised. He'd seen her operating the charm steamroller. They agreed to talk it all out that night, and he hung up, physically weakened by rage.

.   .   .

There was a TV in the Crank library. Green's first observation about soaps was that they wrote the dialogue so you could follow the intricate plotline even if, like him, you were a new viewer. Two women sat at a kitchen table, and one said, "You're my sister-in-law. I'm obligated to tell you about the cheating of Frank—your husband, my brother, police chief!" Though it was supposed to be early morning, their faces were slathered with makeup. The second woman's eyes rolled around like marbles, and soon the scene changed to a hospital, where some nurses chatted across a plywood counter so flimsy it could be demolished, with a single karate kick, by *Rachel.* Enter Larry the intern, in scrubs. Larry had a jaw sharp enough to cut cantaloupe, his eyes gray gems set in a large head of coiffed hair. A nurse with lashes as long as spider legs contrived to get him alone in a supply closet, where they kissed, faces turned so all America could get a good view. He glued his lips to hers with such ardor it was hard to believe he could really be gay. But, Green thought, that was acting for you.

That evening, Green sat on the couch waiting until he heard Bonnie's key. "Were you out? Obviously," he answered himself. Trying to look stern, he went on: "About last night—"

"I gotta tinkle," she said, wobbling to the bathroom on heels. Could she be drunk again? She talked through the open door. "I 'pologize one more time. What I did showed no class."

"I just—I was afraid you were in danger."

"Well, I won't ever do it again!"

He felt disappointed. This was the "talk" he had rushed home for? A few words while she peed? He'd expected her to collapse in his arms, begging forgiveness. But she didn't seem up for drama tonight.

"So I'm gettin' closer to this audition! I had drinks with Mary Jo from casting!" Green fiddled with the TV antenna, surging with jealousy—but against whom? Mary Jo? Chip? Al? No—more likely his rival was unknown to him, creeping and insidious, with sweaty palms and greasy hair. Hearing the flush, he entered and found Bonnie removing her makeup. "Yeah, Mary Jo's hot on me. Think she's *got* the hots for me, too. She's into that."

"Why do you think so? Did she make eyes at you?" *Make eyes?* Why, when upset, did he lapse into Fievel-speak?

"I can tell. Flattering, really." She rinsed her face and squeezed past him into the other room.

"Was Chip around?" Let's pin down all the players.

She unhooked her bra, but held it in place. "If you're gonna stay in here, maybe I'll change in there."

He was astonished. "I've seen you without clothes."

"Jus' feel a little funny tonight." She squeezed past again, back to the bathroom. He felt like a clumsy dog, always underfoot. She emerged in her nightie and got in bed, then assumed her sleeping position: on her side, facing the wall. He slid in behind her. "You asleep?"

"Mm-hmm."

He kissed her ear, bending at the waist so his erection wouldn't rudely poke her. "Do you want to make love?" he whispered, thinking how ridiculous he sounded.

She reached up and touched his cheek. "Can't we just go to sleep?" He exhaled. Weird, weird. Everything was weird.

He lay back. As she had the night before, Shelly entered his head. He compared the way she and Bonnie kissed, then wondered if Bonnie compared sex with him to all her other men. He hoped he was in the top quartile, at least. She'd never seemed to have any complaints, though he had to admit he'd always felt a bit—tense. Why, he couldn't say.

Actually, for all her talk of talent, Bonnie was a quiet lover— never mind him. Sometimes he wondered if she was even there, mentally. Not like that docket clerk he'd met in the courthouse just before he'd begun dating Shelly. He'd found her attractive—well, not much—but they'd copulated like wild animals, anyway. He'd never seen her again, after, and remembered their drunken encounter only hazily.

Once, he'd asked Petey if he compared women sexually. "No," he'd said firmly. "The only important one is who you're doin' *today.*" Like most of his advice, it had sounded dumb at the time, but now Green felt certain it was correct, though difficult to follow. The problem was that everyone came to bed with so much . . . history. Look at Bonnie.

·    ·    ·

The following night, Ben Lee stood in a Crank conference room, glancing at his watch. "Thirteen hours left. Time to talk turkey, my buddies. I'm gonna ask you each for a final bid, and then we'll decide." He pointed at Baxter. "You first, money man."

"Okay." After some final clicks on his laptop, he looked up. "I'm at fifty-four." With a red marker, Lee wrote his name, then "54," on a white pad set on an easel near the window.

"Reason?"

"Start with the forty-two LaCroix's already offered. Add his savings from shutting the Pikeville plant. That translates to eleven dollars more he can pay: fifty-three. So fifty-four is the least we can bid to win."

Mandel swallowed cold pizza. "Sorry, Will, but you're wrong." He wiped his mouth. "LaCroix likes to win. That's the bad news. But he'd rather lose than pay so much he breaks Country Home's back with debt. That's the good news, and it's very good." He rubbed his belly with both hands. "So he'll bid around fifty-six: a manly price, but sane. That means if we're lower than fifty-eight, the committee may decide it's too close to call and ask for another round."

McCoy moaned. "That's too damn much! If we miss our earnings targets by a hair, we'd have trouble makin' the debt payments."

"Joe, face reality! Even if you win now, you'll own a leveraged company. You should start figuring ways to cut costs."

"Whoa!" Lee shouted. "All this talk about 'cutting costs.' You think we live like pashas? We're the only company our size I know of that doesn't have a jet! Okay, I got a limo, big effing deal. How'd you all go home, on the subway?"

"Please, I wasn't suggesting that."

"Just wanna get it in the open. One more thing. My salary's $650,000 a year. That's below market, okay? Heaven knows what *you* make." He looked at Mandel, who looked back, unashamed.

"Ben," he said, "I'm talking costs on a macro basis. Like plant consolidation."

"Plant—! Told you before. I'm not doin' mass layoffs!"

"I understand, but if you lose, LaCroix'll close *all* the plants. Somebody's gonna cut this company's operating costs, so it might as well be you, who gives a shit how it's done!"

Lee sagged slightly, rubbing his face "You make a point. But I have to try it my way first."

"All right." Mandel thought. "Then I have a different suggestion. How 'bout we meet with LaCroix tonight, head off this auction and sell him a piece of the company?"

Lee shook his body like a witch doctor, warding off Mandel's idea. "I'd rather be boned up the butt by a baboon than split my company with that Ivy League snotnose."

McCoy and Houser whispered, and McCoy said, "Gilbert and I think it's worth meetin', seein' if there's a way—"

"I will not!"

Mandel raised his arms. "Let's stay rational. Maybe—"

"No means no! Now, you gonna tell me your bid, Lou?"

Mandel gave up. "Fine. Fifty-eight."

"Okay, more bids. Who else? Rick?" Green shook his head, but Lee said, "C'mon, I'm payin' for a Harvard brainiac, lemme get my money's worth."

Green glanced around as if the solution might appear etched on a forehead. Strategically, he knew Lou was right. The way to win was to blow LaCroix away. But looking at Lee, nervously scratching his neck, Green had a premonition: The LBO would end in disaster for Lee and everyone else involved. Retreat was the only answer.

He'd sound a stone yutz if he advised that, though, so he just said, "I agree with Lou." Mandel sat back, satisfied.

Lee said, "Appreciate your all's input. I wanna bid fifty-five, a buck and a half over where *I* think LaCroix is. If that's not enough spread for the committee to name us winner, I'll kick Fairchild's skinny ass all the way to Pikeville. Okay at fifty-five, Will?" Baxter nodded, and Lee clapped his hands.

Mandel stood, seething. "So you've decided? Because in that case I'm going."

Lee said, "It'll work out, Lou, trust me."

Mandel nodded. "Yeah. Neil, fill fifty-five into the letter and deliver it, personally, to Finkel, Hassler by eight A.M. Then we'll meet back here to wait for the committee's decision."

"Good luck, everybody!" Lee exclaimed. But he no longer sounded so confident. Mandel had him rattled.

.   .   .

Bonnie lay on her back, a wineglass in her hand and music crunching from a speaker into her ear. She wore only a bra and panties, which surprised Green until he realized that it was about ninety degrees in the apartment. Her eyes were closed and her cheeks flushed, as if—really, as if she'd just had an orgasm. Could she have been—? He said her name, but she didn't hear. Kneeling, he touched her arm, and she looked up, vacant: plastered again. "You okay?" She nodded, shutting her eyes.

"I was gonna order Chinese. Do you want in?" He wasn't sure she'd heard, so he repeated, "I was gonna—"

"I'm fasting. Gotta clean the poisons out."

"Uh-huh. We could just get moo shu vegetable; that doesn't have too much poison." She didn't respond, so he stood and removed his suit. She was acting crazy, though she did look luscious in her underwear. Her breasts, waist, legs, made him weak with desire, and he lay beside her in his briefs, then placed his fingertips on her stomach. "You awake?" But she'd drifted off.

Why was she such a lush? Unable even to converse like a human being. He stopped the CD, causing her to whine and grope toward the buttons. He caught her hand. "I don't want this shit on! I wanna talk!"

"Talk then," she said, abruptly sitting up. She waited; he had nothing to say. She reached for her cigarettes.

"Don't smoke now," he said, arms going around her. She tried again, but he locked his hands.

"Let me up, please." He shook his head, feeling he had to take control of her for once. "We need to go to bed together." She wriggled, then suddenly thrashed, got a hand loose, and punched his chest. He fell on his back, winded, and she ran behind a chair. He began to rise.

"Don't come near me! I'll kick you in the balls!"

"You think I'd hurt you? I love you," he gasped. "I just wanted to sleep with you. What's so wrong with that?"

She leaned against the chair back, heaving. "I think it'd be better if we didn't. It makes things too confusing."

"What do you mean?"

Bonnie stepped forward tentatively and, seeing him immobilized, grabbed a cigarette, then lit it and sat on the couch. "It obscures reality. You may not realize it, but I'm trying to save our relationship."

"Don't you love me anymore?"

She nodded. "And I want to stay with you, but it'd have to be non-sexual for a while. Can you deal with that?"

"For how long?"

"I don't know."

He looked at her, and everything came clear. Out all night, auditions, and now a platonic arrangement. How could he have been so blind? Well, as Petey said, you believe whatever you have to. "Look," he said, "if you wanna fuck Chip Slaney, that's up to you. But don't expect to live here while you do. I'm not some—"

She snuffed her cigarette, saying, "I'm gone," in a businesslike tone. "Since that's what you think of me." She picked a black dress off the floor and pulled it on.

Green sensed that he'd misread the situation; she reflected the regal composure of a woman wronged, not the shame of one exposed. He scrambled to his feet. "I didn't mean tonight! I meant maybe in a few weeks."

"No. You were right the first time. It's not fair to ask you to live together as friends. I'll see if I can crash with Chip again."

His dry mouth formed the words, "You coming back?"

"I don't know. He's sweet, but I'm not sure he'll let me stay past tonight—because, despite your fantasies, he is gay and has a sort of boyfriend." Green's nails dug into his palms. She had said it simply, like a baseball score, the plain truth. But what if he was, again, swallowing any lies she threw him? "I'll take my stuff anyway."

"Wait, why shouldn't you leave it? Until you know where—what the whole thing will be?" He could keep a link in case he was wrong. He needed time to figure. His lip bled.

She said she would, and thanks, then put on makeup and brushed her hair slowly. He watched her, antsy, thinking she looked especially beautiful tonight. Of course. Women must be at their best for the move-out. Was it to give you an extra dig? Or to boost their confidence? Whichever, in Bonnie's case it seemed overkill all around.

It hurt terribly to watch her leave. Was he so sad a weakling that he'd surrender his lover with barely a moment's resistance? He touched her arm and she jumped back as if from an electric man. "You don't have to go!" he cried, like a brainstorm. She waited to hear it. "I can handle platonic for a while."

She shook her head. He moved toward her, and she stepped back. "Really, I can! I'd miss you and I'd rather you stay here. I love you!"

"What you *have* is a strong physical attraction to me." She'd said this drily, like an observer, but now her emotions rose again. "I wish you'd see that I'm protecting myself! Things aren't as simple as you make 'em. I should go."

"Wait, let me tell you a point!" He raised his finger, Tilford style. "If not for my stress at work lately, we have no problems! And I'm going to change how—"

"We have big problems."

"What problems? We had a fight because of my parents? We don't ever have to see them again!"

"Let's stop and not hurt each other more. Please!"

He exhaled. "Okay. That's how you want it." He'd tried to sound tough, but it was hard when you were in pain. Looking away, he noticed her cigarette burning down. He stubbed it, then on an impulse flung the ashtray against the wall. Ashes floated to the floor.

Bonnie recoiled when the tray hit. "I really have to go."

At the door, he opened his mouth as if to initiate a memorable exchange, but she just kissed him quickly on the lips and ran. He watched her disappear down the stairs, feeling she'd been right not to drag out the goodbyes, after all.

# Chapter 8

The next morning the team waited, anxiously encircling the speak-erphone, and Green felt it again: impending disaster. He closed his eyes, letting his mind float.

He'd lain awake all night and then, the minute a purple glow rendered it arguably dawn, began to shuffle around the apartment. After a fruitless attempt at cleaning, he wound up slumped on the couch, which was permeated with Bonnie's smell: a blend of soap, per-fume, and cigarettes. He tortured himself, imagining her lying at that moment beneath Chip's perfect frame, tousling his mammoth hair. Surging with desire for her, he became so agitated that he paced the floor, wishing he could shed his skin. If only he'd thought to refill the Valium! Maybe some pot? He could breeze into the Delancey brown-stone, down a dim corridor with sweating walls, and up to a drug mer-chant, clear-eyed and competent as a Zabar's counterman. (He'd have to be, if they cared about repeat business.) "Al sent me," he'd say. No, too movieish. Why not just "I'm a friend of Al's"? Pithy and confident.

He dressed, as if to execute this plan immediately, but sagged back onto the couch. What was he thinking? Wreck though his personal life might be, at least he was on track at Crank. Should he ruin that too, going in stoned? He had to get control, to remember who he was.

Now McCoy was biting at his cuticle, Baxter tapping a pen on his laptop. Lee stood at the window, watching the rain. Only Mandel appeared calm, eating a bagel while reading the newspaper. A front-page headline caught Green's eye: "How Luck and Brains Made Alfieri Rich." Bullshit "luck and brains," he thought.

Lee snatched up the ringing phone. "Ruth? Mind if I put you on the box? I'm with a roomful o' curious folks."

She said, "We're not yet in a position to pick a winner."

Lee toppled into a chair. Mandel nodded. He'd told everybody so. Baxter said, "Can you tell us if we're ahead . . . or behind?"

"I'm not at liberty to divulge that," she responded in a stilted tone. "It is close, though. We're asking all bidders to come back with their best offer by Monday. Sorry to destroy your weekends, but the longer this drags out, the more we risk leaks. Well, we're busy so— Oh, hold on. Weinberg says I should tell you, you were behind. Best offer by nine A.M. Monday, okay?"

After she disconnected, Lee cried, "The snotnose bid more than me, for my own company?!"

McCoy ventured, "Maybe she's lyin' about t'other bid."

Mandel shook his head, and Baxter said, "Okay, what do we do?" They all turned to Mandel, ignoring Lee, who seemed shellshocked.

"Now I definitely think we should try and meet with LaCroix. Otherwise, we have to raise to at least fifty-nine or sixty."

McCoy cringed at those numbers, then said, "I agree." Houser did too, glancing at Lee as if expecting an outburst.

But he just nodded. "Get him over here." Lee looked almost pathetic, then winked and said, "*Yeah*. I can hardly wait to stick my foot in his ass."


During the delay, Green read the article about Alfieri. It said he'd grown up in Hoboken and had never graduated college. Starting as a messenger at a brokerage, he talked his way into a job on the trading floor, where he showed a talent for arbitrage. At twenty-five, already rich, he opened his own shop. Ten years later, he was worth around a hundred million.

The article noted his "uncanny knack for betting on companies that became takeover targets." Green frowned, thinking the only uncanny thing was that no one had caught him yet. But the article contained not a suggestion, not a glimmer, that Vince was insider trading. Instead, it gushed over his cars, houses, and yacht, the *Ashley II*, on which the reporter seemed to have spent a fun-filled day.

Green slapped the paper down. He'd always hated it when cheaters prospered. Still, he had to admit Petey was right: this guy obviously knew what he was doing. Reopening the paper, he saw that Lee's stock price had risen in anticipation of the new bids, but was still well below what he knew the company must sell for now. With that information Alfieri could make enough to christen *Ashleys* from *III* all the way to *L*.

LaCroix and Lee shook hands, exchanged some insincere pleasantries, and then made introductions all around. Lee's team occupied one side of the conference table, backs to the wall, while LaCroix's filled the other side, backs to the window. LaCroix directly faced Lee, who affected a serene look, as if he'd love to spend the day simply admiring the handsome, younger man.

"Ben, why don't you start, since you called us over."

He nodded. "As is obvious, we both want to acquire Lee Textiles." Green noticed that he had adopted the courtly tone he used in meetings, until he got excited. "My concern is, if we keep bidding, the price will run up to a level that'll prove onerous to whoever wins. Now." He slid a piece of paper across the table. "We've considered which of our assets would be most valuable to Country Home and, of those, which ones we're prepared to do without."

"So you're suggesting we stand back and let you do your LBO and then you'll sell us the assets that are listed here? That's possible, depending on what they are." He read the list, muttering, "Good, good." Houser and McCoy were holding their breath; Lee was grinning confidently.

LaCroix put the sheet down. "This looks generally okay." Mass exhalations. "But one thing's missing. As I testified, the bed-and-bath division is crucial to me."

Lee's face hardened. "See, Bill, now there we have a problem. I built that division outta shit, *nurtured* it. . . ." He mimed a gardener's loving work. "Now it's just starting to blossom. How could I live, lettin' you take it from me?"

"I sympathize. But I want bed-and-bath, and I intend to buy it, one way or another."

Lee didn't like his tone. Mandel reached over to forestall an eruption, but without success. "Oh, you 'intend to buy it'? Well, I don't intend to sell it!"

"I figured as much, and that's why I'm bidding to buy the whole company, from the stockholders! This is pointless," he said, rising. "Good luck Monday."

"Good luck to you too. I been whippin' your butt for years in business. It'll be a pleasure to whip it again in the bidding!"

"Maybe it's your butt that'll get whipped."

Mandel was holding Lee, but he had to get the last word. "Great comeback! Work on that all day?!" LaCroix slid out, effortless as a stream.

Once Lee cooled off, the team discussed their final bid. Clearly they'd need to raise to fifty-nine even to have a shot, but McCoy kept shaking his head. "We can't carry that much debt."

As if awaiting this cue, Baxter produced a sheaf of papers. "We ran the deal at fifty-nine in case it came to this. And it's eminently doable, but you'd have to restructure the company."

Lee examined the run. "I can't read this shit. Just tell me in plain English. What's assumed here?"

"Right after the LBO closes you'd pay off part of the debt by selling assets: the industrial textiles division, your foreign operations—"

"Hey, we need to go global!"

"You can live without foreign. Also it assumes you'd close one or two plants."

"I told you I'm not closing plants!"

Baxter went on calmly. "The workforce is a huge expense, and if you automate—"

"No way, José. I won't go down in history as the man who screwed Boland County just to do a deal."

Baxter made eye contact with Mandel, who said, "Know what? We're all tired, and we've got till Monday. So why don't you guys go to your hotel, watch a porno movie; then tomorrow you'll spend downtown with Will. See if you can make the numbers work. Sunday we'll meet back here and decide."

After Lee left, Baxter unburdened himself. "I'm afraid Ben doesn't have the spine to finish this. We could wind up with nothing after all our effort. A million plus expenses."

Mandel comforted him. "I know. But what I realized, watching Ben with LaCroix? He must beat that guy now. Remember, though, he's a god in Pikeville. He just has to get used to the idea of downsizing. And he will."

So Mandel had at last concluded that Lee *was* the kind of man who, when the shit flew, would do what was necessary to prevail. Green sensed that this time, for once, Lou was wrong. In the crunch Ben would not betray his town, even if it meant losing to LaCroix. He'd rather walk away.

All Green could do Saturday morning was mope around the apartment, which felt vast and empty without Bonnie. Heading over to Big Nick's for lunch he passed, in the gutter out front of the Monroe Hotel—a fleabag where prostitutes and junkies congregated—a man asleep under a cardboard box. He had the strawberry face of a hopeless drunk and wore a Crazy Eddie T-shirt. (Their new store had had a grand opening the previous Sunday morning, with gifts; but the only people out at that hour were the homeless, and now the neighborhood was filled with walking, vomiting, dying billboards for discount electronics.) Things could be a lot worse, Green thought, and resolved to cut the melodrama. Maybe he'd even find a way to take advantage of his new freedom.

In the afternoon he called Shelly, began to leave a message on her machine, but then worried she might not return it and hung up. He kept calling every half hour, disconnecting when the tape started. Finally, just after sunset, he reached her. "I was trying you all day."

"I was here."

"Then why wouldn't you pick up?" She didn't say. "Anyway, I wasn't sure you'd be home tonight."

"Well, I am."

"Um," he said, thrown by her honesty. "Um, I wanted to tell you, remember that temple in Boland, Georgia? I saw it! They had a Seder plate from the 1700s, and the *shammes* . . ." He trailed off.

"That's nice." Green could hear, in the background, Bea Arthur yelling at the other "Golden Girls." The studio audience sounded like they were being tortured.

"I know this is last-minute, but do you think I could take you to dinner tonight? I'll come crosstown. I have some things to say, though not on the phone."

She moaned. "Can't you leave me alone?"

"See, this other relationship, I don't know where it's going, and I thought. . . . Maybe you're right, it's not a good idea."

"You sound awful."

"I'm sort of down. No, I am down. Way down."

She sighed. "All right, give me an hour."

He waited for her at the Negev, a brightly lit Israeli restaurant near her building. (He'd suggested Szechuan Kitchen, but she said she didn't go there anymore. Had it gotten lousy? he wondered.) He sat on a wobbly chair, facing a Jerusalem travel poster that depicted a gold-domed mosque. The walls were covered with chipped fake wood and the floor with grimy linoleum; the ceiling was leak-damaged. This hole was her new hangout?

He considered how to act when she arrived. Despite what he'd said, he had nothing in particular to tell her, and decided to keep it light: two old friends out for an evening.

His heart bounced as she entered. Though he'd planned to keep a physical distance, he couldn't help but hug her. She seemed to be trembling. "You look great." Which she did, pretty as ever; but when she smiled, he saw she had changed, after all. A depth in her eyes, maybe a curve at the corners of her mouth, suggested someone who'd been through the mill . . . and then he realized that it had been unfair to call. What *did* he want from her?

The waiter, an unshaven Sephardi in a frayed black vest, filled their water glasses from a dented pitcher. "You've become a fan of Middle Eastern food?"

Shelly paused and then, with a curious mixture of shame and defiance, said, "I keep kosher now."

"Aha."

"I've also started to keep Shabbes. That's why I didn't answer the phone until dark."

"And shul, I guess . . ."

"I belong to B'nai Shalom." Her expression was guarded; clearly she expected derision. But Green had no intention of passing judgment. She'd been seeking meaning, and if she'd found it in temple, he was glad. He'd certainly done his part to fuck up her life. "If it makes you happy, mazel tov. I mean it." She smiled tentatively.

They shared a falafel platter. Shelly ate in her usual dainty, furtive manner, and consumed much less than half the platter, which Green found wonderful. (Bonnie insisted on an equal share, even busting him if he tried to sneak some extra.) He recounted his tale of Boland, featuring a broad impression of Mendosa. "'S'ere's our *kidd*-ush cup.' Slowest-talking Jew ever. You could take a shower and read the *Forward* by the time he finishes a sentence." When Shelly laughed, he realized, happily, that she was free of grudges.

He probed into her social life. A few guys at shul had asked her out, all nebbishes. Yeah, he wanted to say, and at the beach you find lifeguards; but he had resolved not to sneer. It wasn't long before he got the sense, distressing as well as flattering, that she'd take him back, or some religious version of him, anyway.

After tea and halvah, Shelly said she ought to go home. "But first—" She swallowed. "You said you had things to tell me. Just about Boland?"

He feigned confusion at the check, and finally looked up. "I wanted to apologize for our whole . . . business."

"It's okay," she said quickly. "It wasn't your fault."

"How could I know I'd meet—I mean—"

"You mean, how could you know your old girlfriend would turn up? I have to apologize, too," she added. "For pushing Judaism on you. It was just . . . let me explain how I see it." She sipped her water. "You know I come from an assimilated family.

"I've thought about you a lot since we split, and what I've realized is that being from New York, you can't understand what assimilation means. Because here everything's Jewish, anyway! But in Chicago, assimilation means you lose your Jewish identity completely. And what you get in return is—what? The Bears? What is that? It's not real.

"If you have no identity, you have no code to live by. I know you think of me as little miss sweet, but there's parts of me you haven't seen. Like in college . . ." She stopped.

"What? What. Really, what? Tell me. What?!"

She shook her head. "It's not important. That was somebody else."
What could it be? Drugs?

"The point is, for me Torah's a way of living. It's given depth to my existence. And I thought . . ."

"What?"

"I thought maybe you needed something like that, too. Also I thought it'd bring us closer together. I was wrong, but I meant well." She blew out a long breath.

"I know," he said, squeezing her wrist.

"So what do you think? About what I said?"

He considered. "Maybe I'm lucky, but I don't feel I need a Torah to tell me what to do. I have my own code."

"You are lucky, then."

He wondered, while walking her home, what she had meant about college. Could she possibly have been some wild coed, with sex and drugs? No, not her. Probably she just egged a frat house on Halloween. Whatever—he'd almost forgotten how happy he felt around her. Why was he putting himself through hell, trying to hang on to Bonnie?

Outside her building he stared at the pavement, twisting his feet around. "I'm glad we're friends again. And maybe—" Before he could finish, she touched her lips to his and hurried inside.


The next morning, Lee and Baxter were acting like grade-school buddies, tapping each other's arms and sharing private jokes. What had happened during their Saturday together? Lee ended the mystery, saying, "Will and I had a real productive time, figurin' ways to squeeze more juice from the lemon."

Though Mandel grinned only mildly, Green could tell he was elated. "How're the numbers?"

Lee brushed crumbs off his golf pants. "We're talkin' fifty-nine, maybe even sixty, waste that fucker LaCroix. And I'll explain how we got there, 'cause it was a logical process."

He counted the stages of logic on his fingers. "First we ID'd the assets to unload. Industrial, dump that sucker for two hundred mill or so; foreign, should get a hundred from the frogs." He glanced around the room as if expecting an objection. "Y'all know at first I didn't wanna sell anything. But once I thought it over, the LBO's an *opportunity* to clean out the crap and make ourselves a lean, mean textile machine." He smiled gamely and bobbed his head like a shadowboxer.

Houser picked lint off his polo shirt, and McCoy looked out the window. "Okay," Lee admitted, "losin' foreign does hurt. But if it turns out we missed the boat in a few years, we can start again. Always can go global . . ." He drifted.

"Anything else?" Mandel asked.

Baxter said, "Um, to reach fifty-nine we had to find a way to—rationalize operations." His computer screen lit up, orange and watery. "Once we sell industrial, the Marietta plant's superfluous." He clicked keys.

"So you'll just close Marietta?" Mandel asked. "That's not too bad." Lee aimed his eyes at a point on the wall. McCoy kept staring out the window, Houser at his shirt.

Baxter coughed. "Well, but we had to analyze whether any other high-cost facilities could be eliminated. And the Pikeville plant . . . it's a dinosaur. The efficiencies just don't permit keeping it going. Um, um . . ."

The room was quiet until Lee said, "Let's face it. If I don't do it, LaCroix will. Least I care how it's done."

Baxter said, "We'll relocate some workforce to the Louisiana mill. For the rest, we'll offer early retirement."

Lee nodded vigorously. "A good package!"

"Also we've considered ways of cutting overhead."

"Yeah. Despite my tantrum yesterday, there is some fat. Like they're makin' me sell my gold-plated urinal!" Lee pinched out a weak laugh. "Seriously. We subsidize our cafeteria? Okay, so the employees won't get roast beef for a dollar anymore, they'll live. Or another *perfect* example: the employee bowlin' alley. That's twenty thousand square feet we can rent, then folks can bowl at Dixie's on Route 29—more fun anyway. Point is, it's easy to cut if you try. Right?" Houser and McCoy couldn't meet his eyes.

"Right," Mandel said. "You all know how I feel about LBOs. I've sure bent your ears enough. But put on your shit hats, 'cause here it comes again." He bit a cranberry walnut muffin. "An LBO is like buying a house with a mortgage. It makes you live honest. But y'know what? In the nineties only the lean companies are gonna survive. Because we're in a global economy now and the fuckers in Sri Lanka or wherever will underprice and outcompete you. Clear out the shit, like Ben says—streamline—and you'll be doing Lee Textiles a favor in the long run."

Mandel looked from McCoy to Houser. "I understand there's pain. And we'll all respect you if you decide you can't, and wanna walk away." He faced Lee. "It's not too late, Ben! We can bow out!"

Lee shook his head sadly. "Not an option anymore. If LaCroix wins, he'll gut the whole business."

Mandel smacked the table. "Okay then. We go strong and bid sixty. And we always remember tomorrow as the day we sent LaCroix back to New Hampshire with his dick in his hand." Green half-expected the room to erupt in shouts of "Hurrah! On to Agincourt!" but instead Lee and his men shrank, stunned to hear, aloud, what they had committed to.

Lee's eyes glazed. "Long way from thirty-one bucks, tell you that." Finally he blurted, "Oh, hell, let's finish this! Sixty it is." Green felt disappointed in Ben, but once again amazed at Lou. He was never wrong. Because he really did see people as they were. If Green could pick up any skill in his two-year rotation, that was the one he wanted.


Mermelstein handed the revised bid-letter to Green. "Have Lou sign off."

Mandel's floor was dark; even the worst workaholics slept late on Sunday. Through the door, open a crack, Green was surprised to see George Wilson sitting on Mandel's couch. He backed away, but when he heard the topic, froze, hugging the wall.

"You know that partnership decisions are by consensus, Lou."

Mandel, though clearly angry, kept his voice down. "The M and A group's separate. Once he's a partner you'll never have to work with him again."

"That's not how I see the firm. Each of our partners should be prepared to work gladly with any of the others. I know Jeff is a good lawyer, but the role of partner also requires great interpersonal skills. And he's never smoothed his rough edges."

"I know what you have against him. That he went to Hofstra! Bunch of snobs."

"Certainly not," said Wilson with a betraying pompous sniff. "He just doesn't project . . . presence."

"So you're dead set?" Mandel sighed. "Jeff and Aaron shouldered a lot of our group's work. We'll be shorthanded. Hey George, get that door." It clicked shut. Green remained against the wall, stunned that this was all it had come down to for Murphy after eight excruciating years: an asshole in a room announcing he lacked "presence," as if a Crank partner must be a cross between Einstein and John Barrymore.

He knocked and entered. Wilson's expression suggested that of a goat boy caught plotting the ascendancy of Satan. Green desperately wanted to say, "You should be ashamed," but what good would it do? He gave Mandel the letter, spun on his heel, and headed downstairs, thinking how lucky he'd been to get into Harvard. He was a smooth-coated, bright-eyed Weimaraner.

Murphy was already at his desk, editing a prospectus while eating scrambled eggs from a Styrofoam box. He was getting ever fatter, his hair was thinning, his eyes squinted, and he'd also developed a hacking cough. Green tried to slip past, but Murphy waved him in. "How's it going with Lee Textiles? How's Sigmund Mandel, lawyer-psychologist?"

Green looked away. "You're here early for a Sunday."

"Home stretch, y'know. Pouring it on." He aped a sprinter's pumping arms.

"If I were you, I'd take a vacation."

Murphy, whose radar system was now on constant alert, asked in an alarmed tone, "Why do you say that?"

"No reason. I just hate to see you living this way."

"I've been doing it eight years, and this isn't the *best* time for me to ease up. Thanks, though."

Green ached to tell what he knew, but it just wasn't his place. He moved to go. "Um, wait a minute," Murphy said, seeming conflicted himself. "Close the door, and sit." Green sat.

"I was at dinner the other night, and Neil and Lou were there. So someone asked how you were doing." Green blushed; praise embarrassed him. "And they said not well. You seemed not to understand what was even going on. They said you showed poor judgment in handling people, and had done some offensive things."

"*I!*"

"Basically, you were a 'disaster,' that was their word. Also you weren't willing to work hard enough." Something burst inside Green's head. How did a stroke feel? "I'm only telling you this because I want you to succeed. One thing: You should kiss Lou's ass a little. And Neil, too. They think he's a superstar."

Green tried to respond, but could not. "Now, maybe you don't *wanna* make partner. A lot of people jerk off a few years, get the Crank name on their resume, and leave. Of course, then they'll move you out of Shapiro's group, which is only for top-track people. It's a matter of what you want from life."

"I thought I was doing well. I did work hard!"

"Maybe it's just presenting yourself differently. They were saying you like to joke around, but you're working with serious people on serious shit, and million-dollar legal fees at stake. People don't take it lightly at all."

"I was just trying to—"

"You don't have to convince me. I know you're a good guy." He examined his eggs. "Another thing, and make of it what you want. This Lee receptionist has become a big deal. The story is you're up late getting laid, then coming to work zonked. Now, as far as I'm concerned, people can screw all night, then do a great job the next day. But the partners frown on it. And there's also jealousy, because they see the receptionist and say, 'I'd like to screw her.' But of course they couldn't even talk to a woman about anything but law, so instead they say, 'I *could* screw her, but I don't mess up my work with that.' Then you come along and ruin their excuse.

"I hope you're not too upset. I thought it was better you heard now, before any irreparable damage was done. But I should really get to work."

Next door, Green stared at Elvis's tongue, then covered his eyes and reclined in his Swedish chair, which molded to his back as if mocking him. He thought, I'm a disaster, over and over. He considered the word's etymology (from the Italian *disastro)* and, noting the connection to "asteroid," wondered if it had been coined in Roman times to describe wreckage caused by space debris they didn't understand. He pictured himself a chunk of debris, crashing down into 349 Park: a human disaster.

He paced, saying, "What do they want?" kicked a metal cabinet, causing a spectacular pain in his toe, then thought, Fuck them anyway. He'd quit. Tomorrow he'd tell Mandel, quite calmly, that he found the work uninspiring at best, unethical at worst, and in any event not how he envisioned wasting his life. He'd collect his last paycheck, which would cover his loans until he found another job. But what should he do? Whichever firm he chose, it'd end up the same shit. He closed his eyes, trying to visualize himself involved in some life that was happy and worthy and good. Varied images flew past, and then he realized what connected them all: Bonnie, by his side, loving him.

He'd do Legal Aid and they'd live in the East Village, where she'd act in experimental theater. Or they'd relocate to Boland, where he'd work with Tilford and she'd stay home with the kids. Or—wait, this was it, this was great: They'd move to Vermont, open a general store, and no TV, not a single TV in the house! (Okay, maybe a small one, which they'd keep in the attic and only bring down for the Oscars.)

He just had to get her back. Starting today he'd make courting her his full-time job—his shift was twilight to dawn, his supplies flowers and champagne. He almost laughed, picturing Chip's square face as he struggled to grasp the notion that Bonnie had been lost back to the man who offered not glamour or male beauty, but love and friendship.

He ran out into the sunshine, thinking, Fuck you, Lou, Neil, and your bid-letter! I'm free!


Rosen had left a message. "It's Sunday morning. You can't be so sick a fuck that you're working now. I wanna meet for sushi dinner, and I'm tired of your bullshit. So I'll be at Yokohama at seven, and if you don't show, I'll come and pull you over by the dick. *Ciao.*"

Green moved into the living room. It was all wrong: Bonnie's stuff was gone. He flung his clothes out of the closet, thinking hers might be hidden underneath. But nothing. How could she, without a word? He slid down the wall as if shot by firing squad.

Then he noticed, on the coffee table, a page torn from a yellow legal pad. He read the small, looping script:

> *Chip is being sweet enough to let me crash with him a while. It's honestly better this way, for you even more than I, though I know you probably don't believe it.*
>
> *I have to write something, that I didn't have the heart to say in person. We have deep sexual problems. I'm not placing blame. I'm just saying it's a fact, that in all the times we've slept together, I've had approximately one orgasm. This is coming as a surprise to you. I think that because, when we make love I feel like you're on another PLANET.*
>
> *You don't have to be a genius, to figure out that our lack of sexual chemistry is a symbol of the fact that we're deeply incompatable. I don't know why. Maybe a shrink could explain.*
>
> *I do love you and hope and pray you still love me and aren't too hurt. Maybe we'll "meet again someday on the avenue," as Dylan says.*
>
> *Bonnie*

The liquid was getting in Green's nose and stung, but he couldn't seem to lift his head. The bartender said, Need help, and Green wanted to help him, but how could he when his own head was so heavy? Then the bartender pulled him up, still talking about help. How can I help you? he tried to ask, but it came out a tangle of words. At least he was sitting up now. Things were better when you were up, your face dry.

He raised his finger and said, One beer.

But the bartender said, Have to go home. All right, go home and let another man serve me, Green thought, annoyed. He smiled, though—no sense getting in a punching-fight. Anyway he'd already had about ten beers, plus scotches and other. He stared at himself in the mirror, then tried to see how long he could go without blinking. After sixty seconds he decided blinking was stupid, and this way no one could sneak shit by you, like card cheats waiting for that blink to deal off the bottom.

Now here was Petey, pulling at him. Then they were on the street, going like pals with their arms around each other. Keep walking, Petey said. One foot in front of the other.

I know how to walk, penis brain, Green wanted to say. Broadway was dark. When he went in the Shamrock, it was day. Maybe a total eclipse, but you couldn't look; you had to cut a hole in cardboard. He said, Don't look up, you burn the retina. Petey said, What? Baretta, the detective from TV? No the retina—oh, forget it. Here was his friend Manuel, with gold earrings. Petey spoke, and Manuel laughed, his head back, gold in his teeth.

Inside, Petey would push him and he'd fall up a few steps, then catch the rail. Soon he was tired, and sat. Everywhere smelled like pee. Petey yanked his arm. You could separate a shoulder, end up like Seaver, miss a season. Then they trade you to the White Sox. Why do people trade you? You try your best, but nobody cares. They send you to Chicago or Louisiana. All they care is themself. No—all they care is for theirselves. So important to have grammar.

Next he was falling through darkness, falling and wondering when he'd ever land. His face went in the couch, his knees on the floor like he was praying to the couch. To the smell in the couch. Lights came on. Something was happening in his chest. Things had to go out of there.

He crawled with dust in his mouth, saw the toilet, raised up on his elbows, and just when he got his face over the rim, a wave covered everything, like the end of the world.

He closed his eyes and saw dancing pin lights in the dark. He was on the couch, and Rosen was pouring coffee in him, saying, "I have never observed one so inebriated." Rosen started to stand.

"Wanna tell you," Green said, tugging his sleeve.

"All right, you're not gonna get weird on me now?"

"No, listen. What'd Lee close at Friday? "

"Forty-five," Rosen said, surprised. "Why? Wait, you're drunk—"

"Jus' listen. Buy, buy, buy. Gonna be deal—" Rosen tried to stand, but Green grabbed him again. "Gonna be deal at sixty t'morrow!" He sank back, his head drawn to the couch-magnet. He heard a hissing noise, then Petey's voice in his ear.

"Want me to buy for you too? Roll your account?"

He nodded and passed out.

When he woke again, it was dark. He had no idea how, but Petey had gotten his clothes off and the bed opened. One-thirty and his head was throbbing, his mouth terrible.

The toilet was a tragedy. He brushed his teeth but stopped, his mouth full of minty water, remembering what he'd told Rosen. Adrenaline, liquid terror, coursed through him. He spit, then grabbed his head, frantically figuring how to undo it. He could call Petey at home now and insist he not trade, but he'd do it anyway. Or he could say he'd been lying, but Petey wouldn't believe it. At least he'd say not to buy for him.

After listening to the dial tone for a few seconds, he hung up. On the other hand, he thought, why should he? There was probably enough in the account to repay all his student loans. He might even have some left over to take his first vacation in years. And it wasn't as if he'd get caught: Alfieri knew how it was done.

Plus, who was he hurting? Not Ben Lee, who was paying sixty anyway; not the company; not Crank, though too bad if he was, the bastards. No, the only "victims" would be the arbs who'd sell blocks to Alfieri at forty-five, then miss the pop; and most of them were criminals themselves, low characters from Hoboken or Hempstead.

He lay in the dark, trying to find a reason to cancel the trade; but he couldn't, and closed his eyes to sleep. For an hour his mind churned with images of everyone he knew and everywhere he'd ever been. One image that kept recurring was of his father's agonized face, telling how he'd fucked up the investment club. Fievel—he'd never caught a break in his life. And these Bund zhlubs, who'd slaved forty years as tailors or shoemakers and now were relying on measly nest eggs. Why *not* take from the rich and give to the poor?

The machine answered: "*Hell*-lo, we are not home. . . ." Then the real, sleepy Fievel picked up, saying, "*Ja?*"

There was piercing feedback. "Turn off the machine."

"What? Who's there?"

"It's me. Turn off the machine!"

"How?" Green had bought it for Fievel's last birthday, and he still hadn't mastered the three rules of working it.

"For Christ's sake!"

They waited until the beep sounded. "What's wrong?! "

"Nothing. Listen. Tomorrow morning first thing, the club should buy Lee stock."

Fievel didn't speak for a while, but when he did, he sounded wide awake. "Is it legal? I don't want anybody to get in trouble! Your job . . ."

Green exhaled. The big shot—begs for information, and when you give it he chickens out. "No, it's fine. Just don't buy a huge number of shares. So you don't attract attention."

"Huge. Where would the club get that kind of money, anyway?" He paused. "And it's safe?"

"Yes!" They couldn't even break the law, Green thought, without driving each other crazy.

It was morning. "I'm not coming in, Rosa. I'm sick."

"You got people lookin' for you. Mandel—"

"I don't care. Tell 'em I'm dead."

He woke again when his machine answered a call. Though he pressed the pillow over his face, he couldn't block out Mermelstein's whiny voice. "I know you're sick, but I thought you'd want to hear. The committee came back before and said we had the winning bid at sixty! And guess what? We blew LaCroix away! If you turn on FNN, you should see Ben Lee with a big smile. So get well, because we still have a ton of work to finish this damn deal!" Green curled into the fetal position, wanting desperately to sleep.

# Part Two

Mischief is how some Jews get involved in living.
—PHILIP ROTH, *OPERATION SHYLOCK*

# Chapter 9

*June 1988*

Mandel smiled when he saw Green in the doorway. "There he is! How are you?"

He entered, sat, and leaned back, crossing his legs. "Recovered, basically. The closing was a bitch."

"So, did the buyer ever figure out your little trick with the eyeliner inventory?"

"We certified there was a million dollars' worth of eyeliner in the warehouse. But they never asked if we had any at the dock, ready for lading."

Mandel clapped. "You got 'em! That mistake cost 'em two-hundred thousand." He chose a cigar from his humidor, snipped the end with a device that resembled a guillotine, then slid the box across the desk. Green took one, circumcised it, and lit it while sucking.

Mandel blew a stream of smoke and, looking mischievous, said, "Oh! This came." It was a note on the stationery of Eastview Inc.— Office of the General Counsel:

> *Dear Lou,*
> *I am happy to enclose a check for $1,000,000 in connection with the divestiture of Angel Face Cosmetics. We appreciated*

> *your firm's efforts and in particular, Rick Green did a terrific job.*
>
> > *—Best personal regards,*
> > *Jim Hall*

Green grinned, glad Hall had gotten around to the note so soon. He'd been gushing at the closing, and Green had suggested he shoot a line to Mandel, Nothing grabbed the partners' attention more than written praise from clients.

"I sent a copy to Bernie Shapiro. He was impressed." Green puffed, his cheeks warm with pleasure at the thought of Shapiro's important eyes reading this. "He may let you handle a new deal he's got. You realize what it means, after only a year, working directly for him?" Green nodded. It meant he was on a fast, fast track at Crank.

And why not? He'd hit nothing but home runs, starting with his solo completion of the Lee LBO after Mermelstein contracted hepatitis A from a bad salmon steak, following which he'd helped defend Orem Petroleum against a raid. His responsibility had increased all year, culminating in Angel Face, which he'd run under Mandel's loose supervision.

The phone rang: Baxter. "Six o'clock," Mandel said. "When's Shabbes?"

"Seven thirty-five," said Green.

"I'll keep it short." He switched on the box. "Willie, what's doing?"

"It's about Lee Textiles."

"Yeah, how's their business?"

"Aha. Not too good. Second-quarter earnings are going to be way off target . . . even after all the cost cuts. I admit the projections we used to justify the last bid were optimistic, but this is ice water down the shorts."

Mandel nodded. "Same thing's happening to some of our other clients that leveraged up. Is it temporary, you think?"

"Let's hope. If not—if it's the economy, slowing down? Lee won't have a prayer of carrying its debt. Which brings me to why I called. You know the bank loan requires a big payment in August . . . so we need a slug of cash urgently."

"But you were shopping the industrial textiles division, and foreign. They were gonna use the money—"

"The problem is, since the crash, potential buyers are all shell-shocked." He coughed. "We have no offers."

Mandel tilted back his head while exhaling a plume of smoke; he looked like an active volcano. "So, in other words, Lee can't even make its first loan payment."

"Not in other words, Lou. Those are the exact words."

"Shit." He muted the speaker. "Rick, five monkeys with calculators, okay?" He hit the button again. "So what'll they do?"

"Well, Ben wants to ask First Manhattan to reschedule the payment."

"Which they must. All we've gotta do is threaten the officers who approved this loan that we're gonna go bankrupt. Like they say: If I owe the bank a thousand and can't pay, I've got a problem. But if I owe a billion and can't pay, the *bank's* got a problem.'"

"Right, ha, but see, at Tate we don't want Ben to even know that. If he did, he'd say great! But he'd just be putting off the day of reckoning. And what we've realized is there's a fundamental problem we have to address now: We overpaid for the company. By five dollars, at least."

"So what do you want the company to do?"

"Pay down a significant chunk of the loan, which we can only do if we raise a lot of cash. Like, even in this market we're sure we could get a quarter billion for bed-and-bath."

Green looked quizzically at Mandel, who shook his head and said, "Ben'll never agree. He loves bed-and-bath."

"I admit it's sexy, but it isn't the core business. And Ben will agree if he thinks his alternative is the b-word. Anyway, I'm making my pitch at a meeting Monday in Pikeville. You free?" Mandel was booked, but offered Green.

"Great. Looking forward to seeing you again, Rick."

"Me too. How're Nancy and the kids?"

"Fine, thanks. By the way, Lou, I may have a new deal for you. I'll call next week. Okay, gotta hop."

After Baxter had hopped, Green said, "I don't get him. He knows the battle we had with LaCroix over bed-and-bath. Why would he want to sell it?"

"You heard, he wants to face reality. So back him up."

"And this idea of hiding things from Lee—"

"It's not! What it is, we don't give him hopes of a quick fix from the banks, 'cause then he says yippee! and gets addicted to loan extensions. Meanwhile the interest compounds up the wazoo, and in a year his hole's too deep to dig out of."

Mandel slipped his jacket off the chair back, saying, "No, Will's right. If it's a structural problem, Ben should confront it now. But it's tough medicine, so you have to maybe play down the alternatives. See?" Green nodded; he had found, this past year, that Lou was right occasionally to treat clients like children. As Mandel screwed on his fedora, he asked himself, "Sell bed-and-bath for two fifty, what fee could I charge?"

"If I have to do the deal, charge a million."

"Yeah, because you're fuckin'—you're *valuable*, your time." He smiled, shook Green's hand, then said, "*Shabbat shalom,*" and left, trailing smoke. Green stubbed his cigar. He still hated the taste, though he did enjoy the ceremony.

Murphy was out in the hall. "Any news?" Green asked.

"Walk with me. I have offers from two small firms and one branch office of an L.A. firm."

"That's good!" Hal Wishner passed, flipping Green a warm wave and ignoring Murphy.

"See that?" Murphy said. "After you get dicked, the partners act like you're dead." Closing his office door, he went on: "I need to make a decision, but I don't know. I'm not really eager to live through all the making-partner bullshit again in a new place. I'm actually thinking of leaving law."

"Completely?"

"There *are* other occupations. Speaking of which, I heard from Aaron." Soon after being passed over for partner, Josephson had dusted off his art degree and landed a curator job in a Boston museum. He'd sold his co-op just before the crash, rolling the proceeds into a house in Brookline and two Volvos. "Says he feels like he's been paroled. Now he's taking sailing lessons." Murphy chuckled at the image. "So I thought I might try something else, too."

"Like what?"

He looked down, cracking his knuckles. "I love guitars. In college I played in a southern rock band, which was amusing since we were all from Queens, but there you have it. So I had an idea to buy a grove of spruce trees and use the wood for special, virtuoso guitars. I'd have a, a sort of guitar-making business and all." He glanced up, prepared for Green's mockery. "I'd live near the grove. It could be in Vermont."

"Mm-hmm. Interesting. *Different,* for sure. But maybe you should take more time. I'm sure the firm'll let you stay—"

"Oh, they won't push me out. Not after what I went through. Though I don't want to end up like Riggs, either." Riggs, a fifteenth-year associate, had never been told to leave—as was the custom with passed-over lawyers—and now inhabited a kind of purgatory in which he was rarely seen, except as a flash of suspender rounding a corner. Some said Crank kept him on out of guilt for destroying his nervous system. Whether or not this was true, his very existence gave Green the creeps.

"So how's life as Lou's boy? Poor Neil is jealous, but he should've considered that before deciding to get hepatitis."

"Now Shapiro wants to work with me," Green said, lifting off Murphy's shelf a two-pound memento of the PTR/Bolus merger: two pewter nuclear reactors set on a wooden base engraved with the Goldman, Sachs logo.

"The rising star," Murphy said, grinning. "Know who you remind me of? Me, at your age. You're even starting to look like me." Green winced. Had he gotten that fat?

"Yeah," Murphy said, "right in my path. Just watch out when you rotate to George Wilson. Don't expect Lou to protect you. That was my fatal mistake." Murphy swung his jacket on with a triumphant flourish. "One bright side to the dicking: I go home when I want."

Next door, Green found a note on his chair:

*AJF Young Leaders mtg. a week from Weds, at my house.*
*Can you come?*

*Barbara S.*

He marked it in his calendar.

Packing up his briefcase, he considered Murphy's guitar-tree idea, which seemed the product of an addled mind. But Green felt certain he'd eventually come to his senses and pick one of the smaller firms.

And he'd be better off, somewhere they didn't care that he was a Hofstra grad. As for his following in Murphy's—or, God forbid, Riggs's—path, he knew it wasn't true. He'd known it ever since Crank's election day, when Lou had come by to make sure he wasn't discouraged by the senior lawyers' bad fortune. "Jeff and Aaron were good, but between us? Neither of 'em had the 'something extra' you need to make partner. But you do, I can tell already. You just have to work hard and achieve your potential." Well, nobody could accuse him of slacking off in the months since. He'd billed thirty-five hundred hours this year, which meant a seventy-hour workweek with no vacations. He'd given up trying to explain—to friends, relatives, whoever asked—the level of endurance it required. You had to live it to comprehend. The weird part was that he hadn't really minded; he liked to keep busy.

Nodding to the doorman, Green crossed the lobby to the elevator bank, a gold and chrome vault with ceiling mirrors that afforded a dispiriting view of his distinct bald spot. Upstairs, halfway down a carpeted hall, he stopped before a brown metal door emblazoned with the logo of the Guardian Alarm Co., Bronx, N.Y.: a helmeted colossus astride the globe. He turned the two dead-bolt locks and entered.

The small foyer led into the living room, a narrow rectangle with bare white walls, a parquet floor, low plaster-caked ceilings, and a sooty window that faced the snarled, honking Second Avenue traffic. He dropped into the wicker chair that was the room's only piece of furniture. He'd never had time off to buy a couch, though he had, in one mad lunch-hour sweep through Macy's, gotten a bed, a dresser, and two excellent TVs. He aimed a remote at the 25-inch Mitsubishi, grazed channels too fast to see what anything was, then shut it off and went into the bedroom, which was square, with a smoke-gray pile carpet.

Removing his shirt, he stood before the mirrored closet door. Murphy was right, he thought: He must weigh near 190. He knew he should cut back on his eating, especially those damn cookies; also, he'd done not a second's exercise since starting at Crank. At sixteen he could run the Central Park reservoir in ten minutes, but now the slightest exertion, like bending to tie his shoes, winded him. A fat boy, breathing hard.

He put on a clean shirt, then a blue knit yarmulke, positioned to cover his disc of denuded scalp. He programmed the bedroom TV and in the kitchen lit a burner, laying an aluminum sheet over the stove top. Making sure the wall timer was set, he headed out and down one flight of stairs. He knocked, and in a moment Shelly appeared.

They held hands up Second Avenue, past the dozen bars with names like Mingles and Chuckles. TGIFers were pressed together inside, guzzling daiquiris and seabreezes. Through one window Green saw a girl shimmying to the music, which gave her an excuse to shake her breasts at three simian-jawed, fist-pumping men. "The mating dance," he said.

"I must admit I'm glad to be out of it," Shelly said. "Not that I ever went to bars, anyway."

"Yeah, you cruised the shuls. 'Pray here often?'"

"You can laugh, but lots of matches are made there."

"I thought people went to shul to get religion, not picked up. That's why I go."

"Well I know you're a holy man, but not everybody's so pure. Anyway, it's more complex than you make it. These *shiddachs* are a part of Judaism. If people didn't meet in temple, they might wind up marrying out."

"Bite your tongue," he said. Shelly, like most of their friends, thought intermarriage a tragedy, a creeping Holocaust. Dvorah Weissbart once told Green that, starting in college, she'd never accepted so much as a friendly lunch invitation from a Gentile man. She'd been afraid of falling in love.

"That reminds me. I spoke to my mother, and the temple near their house is available Labor Day weekend."

He frowned. "I hate to mess up people's holiday."

"But a lot of my relatives aren't from Chicago, so it makes it easier for them to travel."

"In the summer, though, people have things planned on the weekends. I was thinking maybe we'd wait till fall."

"I want to get settled! I can't stay in that apartment much longer, especially now that I'm back in the living room."

"So move in with me," he said, aware it was useless.

They'd reached the synagogue steps. He watched Shelly chew her lip for a few seconds, then finally he nodded and said, "Okay. It's probably better that it's a holiday, since I'll have an easier time getting off work."

She smiled and kissed him.

They'd been engaged a month now, back together eight. After the split with Bonnie he'd avoided social contact, immersing himself in work. Sometimes, though, usually at his desk at 2:00 A.M., he'd think of Shelly. But he was afraid to call; at least until he'd sorted out his feelings for her. He couldn't bear another emotional catastrophe.

The October 19 stock market crash derailed all pending deals and that night, for the first time in years, the M & A industry went home early—without a clue what you did there. (Shapiro's group seemed to have figured it out, as it was expecting a miniboom of babies in July.) Coming to his hovel and finding no mail except monetary solicitations and not a single phone message, Green felt friendless. The abrupt suspension of crazed work, like the lights popping on at a dance, had clarified his situation brutally: He lacked a life.

He lay in bed, thinking of Shelly. He pictured her going to work in the morning—straphanging, maybe buying bitter coffee at the Greek diner—and returning to her drab room at night. Then he saw himself reentering her world, making her happy . . . and suddenly it seemed so obvious: She was the one all along! So she was sweet, what was wrong with that? He'd tried the other kind, and had found misery. As it used to, his mind filled with vivid images of their wedding (her big family embracing him); a suburban house (him licensed, in a Volvo); a brown-haired boy and girl kicking through fallen leaves toward a yellow school bus; him in a tux, hosting a charity dinner arranged by Shelly, beautiful in a black dress and diamond bracelet. This future seemed so *good*, it left him breathless.

Though it was past midnight, he called and asked to see her, explaining that Crank had turned his head, but now he'd rediscovered his priorities. She was wary, only agreeing to meet after a week of wooing. When they did, he overwhelmed her with affection, begging for another chance. She struggled, saying she was twenty-five and couldn't risk a long relationship with no future. She wanted a family. So did he.

He admitted having done some awful things before, but swore he'd always loved her. "Maybe I loved you a little, too," she said, with a teary stab in her throat.

After that, they were happy. Things deepened over the winter, and in December, when an apartment above her vacated, he shocked his parents by making the move crosstown. Shelly began to spend several nights a week upstairs. Sometimes he'd come home from work late, find her asleep in his bed, and kiss her hair. If she woke, she'd rub his head, saying, "Poor baby." She sympathized with, but never complained about, his hours.

Sunday mornings she'd make challah French toast with berries, and they'd read the *Times* while listening to classical music. He wouldn't go into the office till about noon. She understood how hard it was for a Crank associate to manage life's necessities and gradually, without being asked, started to buy his groceries and even his clothes.

One night, while they were eating kosher Chinese in front of the TV, he looked over at her, filled with love, and proposed. They kissed, chopsticks clicking to the floor.


As they entered the temple, Shelly said, "You'll see, it'll be good. We'll have activities. Like my parents'll do cocktails Friday to welcome people, and my Aunt Marge wants to make a brunch in Evanston, but it depends what happens with my uncle's prostate operation."

"Yeah, let's see what'll be with that first. I don't want him losing bladder control all over his own brunch."

She laughed and slapped his arm, saying, "You're bad."

An hour later they were standing in their usual pew, thanking God for Shabbat, the day of rest. The tune always lifted Green's spirits, and he sang out in Hebrew. Past Shelly, Dvorah rested her prayer book on a pregnant belly; her husband, Larry, a roly-poly Paul, Weiss litigator, worshipped nasally in his Queens accent; and Michael and Wendy Kogen, both radiologists, harmonized sweetly. Across the aisle were Max and Ida Perl, the shul's greatest benefactors. Ida rested her hand on Max's aged curved back, and Green's eyes moistened: to share such a love, coming here every Friday for fifty years—it was beautiful. It meant something.

Rabbi Leventhal told the congregation to sit, then leaned over his lectern, hands grabbing the sides. He was a fortyish skinny with a majestic nose and thinning hair in a shade that Fievel would call Kiev red. *"Trust,"* he said dramatically, then paused, looking around. "Society depends on our ability to trust each other. If I write a check, you have to trust I can cover it, right? If not, everybody'd demand cash! Or a money order or bank check!

"So our business dealings are built on trust, as, of course, are our social relations. But people being people, they don't always live up to the trust placed in them. They may cheat in business—even commit crimes. Or they may cheat on their spouses. Yes," he assured the congregation, nodding. "And the Torah instructs us to forgive. So my question is: 'How can we find it in our hearts to trust another after they've wronged us once already?'" Guilt, like ants in his pants, made Green squirm. Shelly squeezed his hand.

"For example, the Arabs ask Israel to trade land for peace. They say, *'Trust* us. We know, the last time we attacked you on Yom Kippur. But this time is different. If you give us the West Bank, we'll be satisfied.' And maybe Israel answers, 'We can't risk trusting you! From there your tanks can roll into Tel Aviv in twenty minutes!'"

Leventhal stared right at Shelly. "The distance is shorter than from here to Jericho, Long Island. Did you know that?" He faced a few others to see if they knew that, and shouted, "Who can blame Israel for refusing to put the Arabs like a knife to their throat?" He took a breath. "But I won't discuss the Middle East tonight. Let's stick closer to home.

"I guess you're all familiar with Richfield's, who make the nondairy creamer we put in our coffee? Our observance of kashrut depends on our ability to *trust* companies like them. Now, they have a line of parève desserts, including a nondairy eclair." There was murmuring. "It's good, right? Well, this week my family was having a *milchik* dinner, fettuccine Alfredo, and for a treat I'd brought home Richfield's eclairs. So we're eating, we're eating, and suddenly I notice the ingredients. Who can guess what they use as an emulsifier?" He straightened up, swept back his *tallis,* and hooked his thumbs in his belt.

"Nobody? Gelatin!" Dvorah gasped. "Which is . . . ?" Like a schoolteacher, he waited for the congregation to answer.

*"Fleyshik,"* they said in unison.

"Correct—a meat derivative. That's their parève eclair. So we'd inadvertently mixed milk and meat, and I had to take the eclairs away from my kids in the middle, which, believe me, was no fun. So, next day I call Richfield's and reach an executive by the name of Gianelli. Okay? He says they'll change the recipe. They ask, just trust them. And what should we do? We need them for our coffee, but *can* we trust Mr. Gianelli?"

Green tuned out, wishing the rabbi hadn't gone off on the intricacies of kashrut, as the sermon had begun well, with the part about cheating. Leventhal was at his best when he stayed abstract and metaphoric; it was when he sank into this kind of technical bog, or shoveled up his shallow political opinions, that Green grew restless.

After the sermon's close, which linked Richfield's, the West Bank, and marital infidelity all in one homily, they sang "Sholom Aleichem," then filed out. Green, Shelly, the Weissbarts, and the Kogens joined the crowd outside. It had grown chilly, so Green draped his jacket over Shelly's shoulders. "Good sermon," said Dvorah, who was short, dark, and FFB (or *Frum* from Birth, as the lifelong orthodox called themselves). Wendy Kogen nodded in agreement, but Green made a slight honking sound.

"You didn't like it?" Dvorah asked.

"I don't know, it's just some gelatin in the eclairs. . . . It's not like Richfield's is Union Carbide, poisoning babies."

Dvorah emitted a wave of intensity. "But people expect when something's labeled, it'll be parève! You have a right to that, and it matters a lot!"

Green's mouth opened, then closed. "Whatever. I can't get too worked up." He sensed them all looking at him.

Wendy changed the subject, inviting everyone to dinner next weekend. Green said he had to check his calendar at home. In fact he knew they were free, but didn't relish dinner at the Kogens. Their five-year-old, Jason, was a brat who'd greet guests joyously, golden ringlets bouncing and a new toy on display in his arms, but would invariably end up crying piteously over some mild parental decree.

Michael Kogen was approached by a swarthy man in a beige felt yarmulke and wrinkled suit. Michael himself was fair, slim, and together with Wendy, a willowy blonde, made a handsome couple (a cover for *Radiology Today*? Green wondered). After exchanging a few private words with the disheveled man, Michael explained to the group: "That's Jess Berkman. Went to Penn with me. Just got laid off from Merrill Lynch. But it gets worse." He leaned forward. "I've heard he's under investigation for insider trading."

"*Wow*," Larry said. Green glanced over as if he might recognize Berkman, though there was no reason he should. Berkman stood at the curb shuffling his feet, hands in pockets and eyes on the gutter. That guy, Green thought, is guilty as sin.

Dvorah said, "I can't see why someone like him would throw it all away for a quick buck. You, for example." She swung toward Green. "You must get information constantly. Could you imagine endangering your career?"

"Of course not. Shel, we should get home because—"

"Wait, lemme make it tougher." Dvorah's eyes locked on his. "Say you were guaranteed to get away with it."

"That would be no—it wouldn't matter. 'Thou Shalt Not Steal.' I believe in the Torah."

"Dvorah, you're interrogating again," said Larry, chuckling. Every statement he delivered, whether intended to be funny or not, came wrapped in a laugh.

Taking Shelly's arm, Green said, "Sorry, guys, but I'm tired. *Shabbat shalom.*" They headed off. He felt jumpy, a patina of sweat on his forehead. All he needed to hear were the words "insider" and "trading," in the same paragraph even, and his systems crashed. Also, Berkman's gutter-fixed eyes and shuffling feet had been merciless.

"Are you okay, sweetie?"

"Oh, oh—I just find Dvorah annoying. When she gets her teeth into an issue, she's a pit bull. And Larry . . . he stands there, like a statue honoring *nebbishkeit.*"

"Don't be mean. They're nice. I was hoping we could get even friendlier with them. So what about the Kogens' dinner?"

"Only if they're serving Jason."

She grinned. "He *was* a pest last time. But he's cute, really." She hugged Green's waist and said, "Has anyone ever told you, you always see people's bad side?"

"No I don't. It's just—I mean, there's a lot of horrible people in the world, and rotten kids." He stopped abruptly and held her by the arms. "Listen, Shelly. Horrible things happen in life, for no reason."

She was uncomfortable. "What's that got to do with anything? Anyway, even things that seem horrible at the time may turn out fine. God works in mysterious ways."

"God. Maybe what's mysterious is that He doesn't give a—doesn't care *what* happens to people."

"I hate when you get into this mood. And I don't especially feel like standing in the middle of Second Avenue debating God's methods." He agreed. A bum was listening.

After they'd resumed walking, she said, "Want an example of how God works? When we broke up, I was miserable. But we got together again, and now it's better than it ever was before." She threw her arms around him. "And now I love you," she whispered.

"I love you too." Face in her hair, pressed to that familiar smell, his anxiety eased. "Very much, Shelly."

They continued home. He kept thinking of Dvorah, who embodied the qualities he most disliked in the FFBs: their sanctimony and certainty. Their Torquemada relentlessness.


He'd met Dvorah just after New Year's, when he'd finally agreed to attend services with Shelly. That first time he hadn't known any of the prayers, so he just listened, following in the book, his finger tracing the Hebrew letters he'd learned long ago. And he felt serene, as he had months before, in the dark Boland synagogue.

He bought a shul membership and by March had become semi-observant, for reasons he didn't fully understand. Was it to please Shelly? Guilt toward his ancestors? Or just to fit in, in temple? His choices as to which rituals he'd obey and which he'd let slide were subjective; mainly he balanced his personal assessment of the significance of each against the hassle involved. The Sabbath and kashrut were in; morning prayers and constant head covering out. (The last was actually the subject of some controversy at Crank. Shapiro, an assimilated German Jew, had suggested that the Orthodox lawyers leave their hats home when visiting clients. Though they had obviously hired Yids, he felt for their good money they shouldn't be slapped in the face with it.)

The rituals, far from being the burden Green had expected, comforted him by creating structure. No matter how crazy work got, he knew, come Saturday, he'd be in synagogue, praying. When he first announced his "conversion," Mandel was suspicious; associates had been known to fake piety to escape weekend duty. But once he realized that Green was in earnest, a new bond was created between them. He had at last become a person with a definition, instead of a wisecracking oddball with an Elvis poster.

A lifetime's skepticism wasn't so easily cast aside, however, and during his religious ascent Green found himself nagged by doubts about, say, the logic of the kosher laws. At those times he envied FFBs like Dvorah, whose faith was so strong that they'd no more consider ingesting pork than a rock. Ultimately he silenced his doubts and accepted the Torah as his basic guide to life; once he did, he couldn't imagine another way. He knew, from personal experience, that without religion a person banged and floated around like a boat released from . . . those ropes.

They sat on his bed eating turkey sandwiches, watching *Dallas*. Shelly was still concerned about his outburst on the street. "Did something happen at shul to upset you?"

"No. I had a hard week . . . I'm just on edge."

"Because you know—could you look at me instead of Sue Ellen?— you know you can tell me anything. Whenever you get this way, I feel you're hiding stuff. And we shouldn't have secrets, especially now."

He did want to tell; sometimes he felt ready to explode. But it was too big. Anyway, despite what Shelly said, he wasn't at all sure she could handle it. Why should they both have to live under a swollen cloud? He swore he was just tired, and they concentrated on the program.

Shelly asked if J.R. was Jewish. "Hagman? No. His mother's Mary Martin."

"He has a Jewish feel."

"Sorry. Tell you what, I'll check with my father." Fievel collected surprising Jews the way other dads did stamps.

Green went to make tea. It was forbidden to light a fire on Shabbes, but the aluminum sheet having warmed  he set the kettle on the area directly over the lit burner. It would take half an hour. Back in the bedroom he unclipped his yarmulke, then stripped to his boxers and lay down. On TV, Jane Wyman was arguing, though her face remained impassive as a closed door. Reagan, Green thought, must have a taste for the inhuman.

"Don't you want to get comfortable?" he said into Shelly's ear. She rubbed her nose against his, then took off her blouse and skirt. She turned away before unhooking her bra . . . still modest. Out of the corner of his eye he glimpsed her slim, lovely body in the mirror. Only three months left to wait.

She dove onto the bed, her nightgown billowing. He yelled, "You'll break my box spring!" Scrambling to her feet, she started bouncing it like a trampoline. He bounced beside her, shouting, "No jumping, you kids! You'll never have a sleepover again!" When his head grazed the ceiling, he stopped, panting, then pulled her down. "We'll never have a sleepover again," he said, and kissed her.

He left his arms around her, hands on her shoulder blades, until she raised the gown and pressed against him. Eyes shut, she held her lips to his for some time, moving gently. When her face grew too red and her breath too short, she rolled away, without opening her eyes. He stroked her hair and touched his mouth to her forehead, whispering nice words.

After their tea, she went to sleep. Green flipped through the newspaper, which was dull today, describing jitters in the junk-bond market and potential problems in the thrift industry. Shelly's breathing had become soft and even, and he felt compelled to kiss her face one more time.

He slid out the business section. A front-page headline caused his heart to palpitate—"SEC Investigating Arb Trading." The story began:

> *In its first assault since the Ivan Boesky settlement, the SEC has been investigating trading by several prominent arbitrageurs. According to sources familiar with the investigation, several takeovers are involved, including Grant Industries' hostile bid for Willis-Cross, and two leveraged buyouts. . . .*

The article continued on another page, and Green almost tore the paper in half, turning.

> *. . . from 1987, Diamond Supermarkets and Lee Textiles.*
> *In each case, heavy arb trading preceded major announcements*
> *regarding the transaction.*
> *Among the arbs said to be under investigation are . . .*

At that point, all the lights shut off. "Shit. Oh, shit."

The TV was still on, so he leaped out of bed and tilted the newspaper to it:

> *. . . Allan McCann, Abraham Schneidman , . . .*

Then the TV clicked off.

Green said, "Fucking timers," then stumbled out to the living-room window, but he was able to discern by Second Avenue's glow only the shapes of words. He ran to the front door and, holding it open with his leg, read by the hallway's dim light:

> *. . . and Vincent Alfieri. All three refused to comment on the*
> *reports.*
> *In 1986, Boesky settled SEC charges . . .*

There was nothing more about the new investigation or Alfieri.

An old man from down the hall passed with his terrier, and they both stared at Green. Realizing he was wearing just his shorts, he closed the door and dropped into the wicker chair, shaking with terror. This was bad. *Bad.* What if he got caught? It'd be so unfair! After all, when he'd been tipping Petey, he hadn't been in his right mind: despairing over Bonnie, drinking heavily, planning to quit the firm. It all seemed another lifetime now.

He hadn't spoken to Rosen since the preceding October, when he dropped out of the scheme, telling him he didn't want the money in the account. He'd never even known how much it contained. He deserved forgiveness, if anyone did, but the SEC, he knew, wouldn't see it that way.

He paced in the dark, trying to form a strategy. Petey! He needed to speak to Petey, to confirm that Alfieri was untouchable. He lifted the phone but then remembered, no calls till sundown tomorrow, and sank to the floor. Hold on, he had it! You could use electricity in a health crisis, which this arguably was, since, if he waited, the suspense might give him a heart attack. Okay, good, but not from there. The SEC might be logging Petey's calls. He crept into the bedroom for his clothes, then dressed in the dark foyer, finding the buttons by feel.

From a booth down on Second he dialed Rosen in Fort Lee, but a recording gave a new, local number. A woman answered, saying, in an unfamiliar foreign accent, that she'd get Pete. In the background, disco music pounded through a system as loud as a dance club's. When Rosen heard Green's voice, he sounded delighted, then concerned. "Where you callin' from?"

"Phone booth."

"Good. How you been, man?"

"I *was* fine till today. Now I'm going crazy! About this article, what're we gonna do? I'm—"

"I know, pissing in your pants. You have to learn to relax. You heard of Sri Chinmoy? It's this meditation thing—"

"Uh-huh. Listen, I'm very upset! "

"Do not worry. It's all bullshit. You can't prove an arb used inside information, because his *business* is trading takeover stocks, right? So they're investigating Lee, but we were already in Lee from the beginning, right? Of course—because we're arbs! And it doesn't look like they spotted the others. Even if they did, same answer: It's our job to buy into takeover stocks."

"But what about Boesky?" A woman appeared behind Green, awaiting the phone. Ten empty booths between there and Seventy-second, he thought, and she needed this one. He waved her away angrily and continued in a whisper: "They caught Boesky."

"Only because his partner turned him in. But we don't have to worry about that. Who's gonna inform on Alfieri? You? You'd just be fucking yourself, because it's the only way you'd ever get caught! Even you're not that dumb."

Green scratched his head. "Yeah, yeah. Fuck you. I still can't believe—fuck. I can't believe I let you use me. Nice friend, taking advantage at the lowest point of my life."

"Bullshit! You gave me the information. I didn't even want it the first time! Then, okay, after that I admit I encouraged you a little."

"'Encouraged'! You—!" He was too mad to finish.

The truth was that Rosen had kept after him constantly, until, just to get him off his back, he'd told about the PTR/Bolus merger. As for the tip on Orem Petroleum, it had been one more bout of temporary insanity, simple as that. "'Encouraged,' sure."

"All right, don't get so—don't be like Mr. Innocent over there. Because you knew what you were doing."

"Again with—!"

"Anyway, that's all the past. *Today* the SEC is just jerkin' off. If we stick together, there's nothing they can do. Please promise you'll keep your mouth shut! Will you?" He waited, and Green heard a bass thump shaking the loft.

"No. I mean yes. I'll keep my mouth shut."

"All right, good call. Hey, your account's still sittin' there, anytime you're ready to—"

"Dammit! I told you I didn't want it! Why do you keep on with this?!" He paused. "Oh, I see. You want something hanging over me, evidence. To be sure I'll—"

"That's not it at all! You're some paranoid, *God*. Sri Chinmoy teaches that placid thoughts can—"

"Petey, would you shut up with that bullshit?! Anyway, you don't have to worry. I'm scared enough already. You can give the money—give it to the AJF, okay? Anonymously."

"Oh, yeah, I saw your name on a thing lyin' around the office. A 'Young Leader.' Mazel tov to you." Green didn't respond. "So how's Shelly?"

"Fine," he said sullenly. "We're getting married."

"Mazel tov again." He whispered, "The girl who answered, she's livin' with me. You should see her. Runway model, fuckin' gorgeous. . . . Eurasian, like eleven feet tall. My face comes up to about her snatch."

Green had to laugh. "What happened to your rule? Don't go out with girls better-looking than you?"

"But now I've got the bucks, that's the difference. I moved to SoHo, y'know. Bought a loft, two thousand square feet. I got all designer shit."

"You must be up to your ass in debt."

"Leverage—that what it be all about, my man. I traded in the Petemobile for a Porsche. Tell you what. I'll come take you for a drive sometime."

"Thanks, but we'd better not." It wasn't only the risk; their friendship had always been thin as powder. A gust blew up Second, making Green shiver. "I've gotta go."

"Hey, while you're here, you know of any new deals?"

"Jesus Christ! Don't you ever—?"

"Kidding, Ricky. You used to have a good sense of humor till that firm zombied you up. So go home now, and remember—"

"Stick together. Mouths shut?"

"Exactamundo."

Green hung up, relieved, though still rubber-kneed. Three young men in Brooks Brothers suits staggered toward him, and he side-stepped to avert a collision. They looked fresh from college, come to New York to seek their fortunes. Two had arms on each other's shoulders and were singing, "Louie, Louie," as if in denial that the frat party had ended. Watching them, Green wondered what ethical standards they'd learned at Sigma Chi. Which of them would break the law if—if he could make a killing without risk of capture? They *all* would, Green decided.

He climbed the stairs, resolving not to think about the arb investigation again until morning; it'd all seem clearer then, and there might even be something helpful in services. When he snuck under the covers, Shelly moaned, nuzzling against his chest. "I dreamt you went out, and it wasn't safe. You got mugged. Did you go out?"

"Go back to sleep, sweetie."

"I love you."

"Sleep," he said, laying her head softly on the pillow.

# Chapter 10

At the airport monday morning, when Green received his ticket—for coach—he made a small noise. "With Lee's cash situation," Baxter said, "I can't justify charging them first-class." More to the point, Green thought: Expenses the company reimbursed now came half from Tate McMahon, and so indirectly out of Baxter's pocket. People got positively frugal when they were spending their own money.

After a year up front, coach seemed a miserable comedown. Green felt like an animal, squeezed into a middle seat once again, eating the canary yellow omelet and battling his neighbor for dominion over the armrest. Was he supposed to just forget about the tablecloths and fresh fruit going on beyond the curtain?

Outside the Pikeville terminal, Baxter stepped to the taxi stand. "No limo?" Green asked, and Will explained as the spring-busted Chevy pulled into traffic. "We sent a couple of our consultant types down, and they decided it was too expensive to keep a full-time chauffeur. So now Ben mainly uses his own car. Even takes a regular cab sometimes." Baxter turned to the driver, a grizzled seventy-year-old in a golf hat. "*You* don't mind."

"Nossir. It's my pleasure to drive Mr. Lee. Especially lately, I'm happy for the business." He glanced in the rearview, his crusted milky eyes moving from banker to lawyer. "If I may ask, were y'all involved with the LBO?"

When they didn't answer, he continued: "Been some interesting changes since then. Did you know the mill closed last month? My son was a supervisor, worked there twenty years. They said there's a chance he could transfer to Louisiana, but he'd be back on the floor. Anyway, he and his family like it here pretty well. Yeah, it's all been kinda interesting." He began whistling, off-key.

Baxter raised his *Journal*—not to read, but to hide. (Green sometimes thought the *Journal's* ubiquity in the business world stemmed less from its content than its convenience as a shield.) Soon Baxter said, "See that story about the arbs trading in Lee stock? I knew there was something funny at the time. We have a Chinese Wall between my group and our arbitrage department," he added defensively.

"It seemed funny to me too," Green said, unfolding his own *Journal* with a snap. After two days of worry, he'd almost forced the investigation from his mind, having convinced himself that Rosen was right and that, despite its saber-rattling, the SEC could not prove a thing. But now fear had again gripped his intestines, producing, first, an urgent need to defecate.

Baxter paid the taxi, tipping big. The driver said, "Thanks. Say, if you want later, I'll ride y'over to the old mill, then around town. Show you some changes. No charge." Baxter appreciated the offer but said they'd be busy.

At Lee reception sat a resentful gray-haired woman whom Green recognized as one of Ben's two secretaries. She must've been demoted in the layoffs. She was droning, "Lee Textiles, may I help you," into the headset in a tone that suggested not help but obstruction, and Green flashed on his first glimpse of Bonnie, speaking this same phrase—with vitality, as if any call could lead to a new adventure. What had become of her?

Walking the halls, Green noticed that the carpet had worn thin in spots, the windows were dirty, even the water-cooler was empty. He passed McCoy's secretary, struggling to write with a pencil stub. Lee Textiles was becoming shabby.

No one brought coffee while they waited. When Lee entered the conference room, he cried, "My buddy!" and shook Green's hand with genuine gladness. He'd aged tremendously, his hair now more silver than blond, his eyes pouched and shoulders rounded. He looked, in fact, exactly like what he was: a businessman beset by difficulties. Green had expected, in the serious circumstances, that he'd dispense with pleasantries; but as always he inquired into their flight down, health, and feelings about the weather. Breeding, Green thought—or foolishness—he couldn't decide which.

When Lee noticed the absence of coffee, he shouted, "Belt tightening's one thing! But I'd rather liquidate than allow downright rudeness!" Within a minute he'd organized a pot and a pillar of Styrofoam cups. He held one up, said, "Hope you don't mind—cheaper than plastic," then grinned sheepishly.

They sipped and chatted until McCoy appeared, apologetic. "I was on with the banks, holdin' their hands. They're a mite nervous, as you can imagine."

Lee turned to Baxter. "Okay, Doc, give it to us straight. Any takers for industrial textiles?" Baxter shook his head. "And foreign?"

"Not a nibble."

"I mean, what the hell's goin' on?"

"You said we'd have tons of offers," McCoy added.

Baxter showed his pink palms to the disappointed men. "That was last year. It was a . . . euphoric time. But the crash reminded people there's a downside. Buyers are afraid the minute they spend money there'll be an economic collapse." He smoothed his suspenders. "The deals that are getting done are all at bargain-basement prices."

Lee lifted his wrist. "How 'bout my watch? It's got some *gold* in it." Baxter laughed warily, unsure whether Lee was about to scream. Then, seeing it was safe, he continued: "I know how you feel. Don't forget, Tate McMahon owns fifty percent of the company. It hurts us, too."

Green found Will's empathy disingenuous. After all, Tate had collected a $40 million fee for acting as financial adviser to the LBO, and had funded its half ownership by just plowing back a portion of that sum—giving it a perspective different from that of management, many of whom had sunk their life savings into the deal.

"So what're we gonna do?" Lee said, stroking his jowl.

Baxter simpered like a boy about to ask, for the hundredth time, to play a forbidden game. "There's always bed-and-bath. If we shopped that, I'm sure—"

"No," Lee said, then grunted and folded his arms like a movie Indian.

"If you'd just hear me out—!"

"I didn't go through all this to lose the part of the business I have the biggest plans for. If we can't come up with enough cash to pay the banks, we'll have to work 'em for an extension. Joe, what's your read on that?"

McCoy grimaced. "Well, they sound pretty hard-ass. I don't know. Maybe they're bluffin'."

Baxter shook his head. "No bluff. It's principle with them. Why should they delay the payment when they know we can sell bed-and-bath easily? Also they know if they call the loan, the company goes in Chapter Eleven. And believe me, bankruptcy's no picnic, either. Our stock would be wiped out. So the banks have all the leverage, excuse the pun."

He continued in the tone of a man courageous enough to confront reality. "Look. Even if First Manhattan somehow let us slide in August, they'd just give a six-month extension, max. Come year-end we'll be right back where we are today. Then we'll wind up selling bed-and-bath anyway, but at a distressed price." He paused. "Let's face brutal facts. Paying sixty dollars a share—"

"And whose fault was that?!"

"Partly ours—but how does finger-pointing help?"

"Makes me feel good," Lee said. "That's how."

"Anyway, paying sixty one week before a market crash, we have to think about survival now. And in Tate McMahon's view, downsizing is the only solution." Lee and McCoy exhaled. Green averted his eyes, unable to watch Baxter misleading his partners.

For days he'd been puzzling over Will's eagerness to unload the crown jewel. One answer he'd come up with rested on a simple proposition: Tate's interests were now diverging from Ben Lee's. For Lee and the other management investors, the hoped-for bonanza was five years off, when they took the company public again. If they ran it well until then, they could reap five, ten, even a hundred times what they had invested. And pending that happy day, they didn't anticipate drawing any money out except their normal salaries. Tate, on the other hand, could get big cash from Lee now, through investment-banking fees—like the millions it would get for selling bed-and-bath. Seen this way, it made sense for Will to push the deal; if the company went bankrupt, at least he'd have squeezed out some more money first.

But this was, admittedly, the cynical view. The trusting view, which Lou had espoused, began by accepting Baxter's sincerity. (There was, after all, little doubt that Lee Textiles faced financial calamity, as he claimed.) Maybe Will honestly believed that the bed-and-bath sale was the company's best available course. Unfortunately, even his short experience had taught Green to assign the cynical view a robust eighty percent accuracy rate.

Baxter was about to repeat his argument when Lee said, "I've heard you once. It's all pretty confusing, though, and I need time to think."

"That's fine. I wanted to go over the earnings reports with Joe for a while, anyway."

"Rick, why don't we leave the nerds to their math? I've been promising you lunch at Twin Pines for a year now. But we gotta go Dutch, 'cause I'm on a budget." When Green blanched, Lee smiled. "Pullin' your leg. It's my pleasure to treat after all the work you've done." He patted Green's back. "Let's go."


Breezing along Route 29 in his Cadillac Seville, Lee tuned the radio to an oldies station and, when "How Much Is That Doggie in the Window?" came on, began to sing along lustily. Green didn't know whether to join in, or clap his hands, so he just stared ahead as if nothing unusual were happening. After Lee had sung the entire number (even barking where appropriate), he explained, "Lost my cherry to that." Green felt he should offer a reciprocal confession, but there'd be no point. He was completely, absolutely sure that Bennett Lee, the CEO of Lee Textiles, was not familiar with the song "Dreamweaver."

They passed a two-story red-brick building, separated from the highway by a long stretch of grass and surrounded by a wire fence. Could this modest structure, Green wondered, be a so-called country-club prison? The kind that he would go to? And were these prisons really like clubs inside, with cabana boys and pinochle and whatnot? He grinned at the thought, then told himself: You should be crying, not smiling; you are a stupid, stupid person.

A two-lane road, thick with foliage, led to a long driveway, at the end of which was Twin Pines's main house, which resembled Tara. The Seville crunched across gravel into a space marked with Lee's name. Several fellows, all comfortable in seersucker and white bucks, stood on the veranda smoking pipes or cheroots. Inside, the club was pretty much what Green had expected: antique guns, animal heads, and sports trophies, all together comprising a cornucopia of goyim naches.

To everyone he passed Lee said, "My buddy!" followed by some remark that elicited a chuckle. Then he added, "And this is my buddy Rick Green," so fast it sounded like "McGreen." Green preferred it: Let 'em think he was Irish. In the dining room, which overlooked the first golf tee and the immaculate course beyond, the maitre d' showed them to a spacious table near some open French doors, through which wafted the smell of freshly cut grass. Each setting included a tumbler of iced tea decorated with a mint sprig; water was not life's basic liquid here.

In this club, Green noticed, the members were all white males and the servants all black males. One said, "Sho' happy to see you, Mr. Lee. Got some warm buttermilk biscuits," he added, putting one on each bread plate. He avoided eye contact, instead fixing his gaze on the table, an untroubled smile playing over his lips. His attitude, indeed his very existence in 1988, disturbed Green. In his excitable law school days he might even have walked out, but after a year at Crank he saw things differently. Everyone had his job, he had no right to judge, and disturbance, if not indulged, passed quickly.

There was no written menu, only oral history. Green shrugged off the waiter's blithely trayf recommendations of shrimp cocktail and smothered pork chops, instead extricating a green salad and poached salmon. Awaiting the food, they reminisced about the LBO's characters and its crises, such as the injunction. "The judge cleaned our clock pretty good," Lee said, and added, "Tranh Dinh," just liking the sound of it. "How's Neil?"

"Better. Kind of slacks off now, though. Leaves the office at midnight."

"Tell you, while he was in the hospital, they should've given him a personality transplant. Boy was dull."

Lee suddenly turned serious. "Lemme ask, do *you* think we should sell bed-and-bath?"

Though Green normally enjoyed advising clients, this time he wished he could abstain. Lee deserved an honest opinion, but if he gave it, Baxter would be furious and get him in trouble with Mandel. He stalled by eating his biscuit, meanwhile wondering whether anything in the Torah was relevant. Since becoming religious, he had often sought solutions to ethical dilemmas in the holy law; but except for the Ten Commandments, he found the Bible too vague. On the other hand, the Talmud was too specific, its examples involving shtetl disputes that could be applied only by the wildest analogy. (Was the bed-and-bath division more like a cow or a cartful of wheat?)

The fact was that Green's problems, unlike the straw men set up and toppled by Rabbi Leventhal each week in his sermons, rarely reduced to clear questions of right and wrong. They were more about minimizing the damage. Like now: was it proper to impugn Will's motives when he might be telling the exact truth as he saw it? No, he decided, the course of least harm to everyone involved—including, yes, to himself—required him to give the benefit of the doubt.

But before he could answer, Lee said, "I see you don't wanna crap on Will. It's just, I know he's my financial guru and I should trust his judgment, but I feel he's up to something. Even got suspicious he's advisin' me to sell bed-and-bath just so he can collect a sale fee and get s'more cash out in case we go in the tank. But he'd have to be lower than a snake's belly to do that." Green aligned the edges of his napkin.

Lee dipped a shrimp in sauce, saying, "And he does have a point. If we don't sell bed-and-bath now, we *may* wind up unloading it later, for less." He sighed. "It's a pickle."

Cletus Tilford appeared at tableside. Lee, evidently having forgiven all the courtroom rhetoric about "chicanery" and "mendacity," exclaimed, "My buddy! How're you?"

"Fine, fine. Thanks again for dinner—nobody cooks sole meuniere like Antoinette. I'd love to steal her away!"

"You 'n' everyone else."

Tilford paused. "Have a message for you from, I won't call him a mutual friend—Bill LaCroix."

Lee's smile froze over. "Yes?"

"Says he heard you may be sellin' bed-and-bath and he'd still like to buy it. Says he'll beat any offer." Tilford looked at the floor, embarrassed to deliver discourteous news.

"I don't know where he'd have heard such a thing, because bed-and-bath is most assuredly not for sale."

"I thought so, and that's what I told him. But he insisted I pass on the word, anyway."

"Mm-hmm, 'the word.' Well I have a word for him, too. Starts with 'f,' ends with 'k,' and it ain't 'firetruck.'"

"I'll tell him," said Tilford, grinning.

"No, what you *do* say. I'd be happy to work a deal with him on our industrial textiles division. Bygones and all that."

"I will, Bennett. Regards to Virginia "

Lee watched him walk away. "Vultures. Circling already. But where'd LaCroix hear about bed-and-bath? We didn't even decide to sell it yet."

Green stared at the network of veins on a lettuce leaf, and all at once comprehension flooded his mind, like a pipe bursting. He couldn't believe no one had ever figured it out. Maybe it had been *too* obvious. "He was probably expecting it all along."

"What do you mean?" Lee's eyes widened.

"Look at what LaCroix did. Remember when we tried to settle with him? He said, I plan to buy bed-and-bath one way or the other. Then he put in this really high bid for the company. Maybe he went so high because—"

"He knew I'd chase him into the stratosphere. He'd watched me at the meetin' and knew I'd never let him win."

"Right, and then in the last round he raised his bid only five dollars, and you won by a mile."

Lee sipped iced tea, his cheeks coloring. "And at the time I'd bragged, 'The snotnose lost his nerve.' But that wasn't it. He figured if he let me win, payin' that kinda price, I'd be crippled as a competitor. And he was right: We got no cash for capital improvements, no cash for advertising."

"Plus, if things got desperate enough, you'd have to sell assets to stay out of bankruptcy, like bed-and-bath."

"And he'd be waitin'. So he *did* mean to buy it one way or t'other, and the little shit outfoxed me." Lee slapped the table. Then he reflected. "Guess I screwed up."

"You couldn't know there'd be a crash."

"Doesn't matter. We'd had problems anyway, overpayin' the way we did. I wanted to win so bad I swallered whatever Tate McMahon fed me."

Lee drifted, his eyes glazing. Then he blurted out, "See that fat guy?" He was indicating, among the portraits of whiskered nine-teenth-century men that ringed the room, one of a stern fellow with muttonchops and a stiff collar. Green knew from the jowls that he must be a Lee ancestor.

"My grandfather, Lucius Lee. He founded Lee Textiles in its current form, in the 1880s. Took *his* father's cotton business and industrialized it. Created thousands of jobs. Built Pikeville . . . and this club we're sittin' in." The waiter set a steaming plate of chops before Lee. Fork and knife poised for action, he went on: "Lemme give you a history lesson.

"Long as my grandfather ran the company, he had offers to sell it, or interests in it. But he'd always refuse, sayin' Lee is a family business. In his view, once you let outsiders buy in, you have nothing but trouble. So he kept the company private.

"But after my father took over, in the early forties, his advisers started pressurin' him to go public. Said he needed the capital to expand. Said if he didn't, the business'd get left behind. Then, when the economy started boomin', they told him he had a window of opportunity to cash in big. And unlike my grandfather, you could wear my father down. So finally, right after the war, he agreed. And he did make a fortune—millions on the one day he sold off half the stock. And that was when a million *meant* something." Lee dragged a square of pork through gravy.

"And at first," he continued, chewing, "it was fine. The company grew as planned. And in those days the stockholders were a quiet sort. So whenever someone in the family needed money, it seemed easy enough: Just go public with some of your stock. My father had a good-for-nothin' brother who sold all his shares. I have a vain, silly sister who sold off hers. So the family's ownership dribbled away."

Green ate a flaky, juicy piece of salmon, and the waiter poured hot coffee. Lee sipped. "By the time my father retired in '75, Lee was ninety-five percent publicly held. And it was still okay. We'd send the stockholders a slick annual report every year with my picture in it, and hold a meetin' where I'd make a speech. Running the business, though, we'd do basically what we wanted."

Green ate a few more bites. Outside, an old man in red pants sliced a drive into the woods, flung his club to the ground, then kicked it. "But things changed in the eighties. Guys like Boone Pickens came along preachin' this idea that stockholders should be 'active.' What happened, mine started tryin' to 'advise' me. They'd say we should automate faster, close Pikeville and expand Louisiana, lay off, lay off, cut, cut, cut! And I'd say, You don't understand; we're committed to Georgia. Even if it costs more in the short run, eventually we come out ahead, 'cause if you fire your workers, and so does every other industry, who'll be left to *buy* our textiles? But they just didn't get it." He pushed away his plate and wiped his mouth with a napkin.

"So I became obsessed with getting the stockholders off my back, and that's when Baxter suggested an LBO. It seemed perfect. We could return Lee Textiles to family ownership, and by the way, I include the executives who invested, like Gilbert and Joe, in my definition of family. But the key was doin' it at a sane price. Remember I kept sayin' 'cushion' over and over? You prob'ly thought I wanted to steal the company cheap and get megarich, right?"

Green shrugged, ashamed. "That's all right," Lee said. That's what everyone thought—includin' Tranh Dinh, I might add, 'cause people want the world in a neat little package. But in my case, I promise you it wasn't about money. It was about *destiny*. I believed my destiny was to reclaim Lee Textiles for the family and to do it at a price that wouldn't wreck it along the way. I could almost hear him tellin' me so." He indicated the portrait.

"But, unhappily, LaCroix got us in an auction. And then I confess it became me against him, win at any cost. Every time I thought of him takin' over, I saw red. Even when I knew I'd have to close the Pikeville plant, I pressed on."

"That's not fair. You were—"

The waiter approached. "Can I tempt you with dessert, Mr. Lee? Got a numptious Key lime pie." Lee cradled his belly. "Sorry, Raymond."

Green continued: "You knew he'd shut the plant, too. All the plants!"

Lee seemed grateful. "That is true. Also, everyone—Will, and your boss, Mandel, was pushin' for the LBO. 'Just a buck more! You're so close!' And guess what, their advice always turned out to be whatever'd earn them the most fees. Funny coincidence, huh?" He frowned. "No, I can't blame 'em. Down at the wire, Lou was still tellin' me I could back out. I made the final calls. I thought I was doing right."

He looked out, across the fairway. "Saw this article last week, title was somethin' like, 'Decade of Greed.' Had this section on LBOs, and I will tell you, Rick, *the* most simplistic shit I ever read since kindy-garten. Greed. Kiss my ass."

He pressed his palms down on the table and said, "Shall we?" Passing beneath his iron-willed grandfather, he threw up a brisk salute.

Here's the point, Green thought on the ride back from Twin Pines: Nearly everyone alive acted on the basis of "good" intentions, falla-cious, delusional, or insane though they might be. Ben Lee had meant well; as had LaCroix, as had Baxter, Mandel, Ruth Royster, and Tranh Dinh. Take your Decade of Greed—take, in fact, all categories into which human decision making might be grouped—and throw them overboard. The moral history of mankind was, after all, about mini-mizing the damage.

McCoy and Baxter were still at work, big green sails of computer paper covering the conference table. McCoy lifted a stack and said, "Gotta admit, Will makes a strong case. With the cash, we could get out from under the banks. Without it, they'll just choke us slowly."

Lee sank in a chair, rested his chin on his fist, then let out the low growl of a dog too old even to bark at a passing rival. "Kills me, that's all. Can't we press the bankers some more? Maybe we can get a real extension, one that'd give us time to fix things."

Baxter clicked on his computer. "As I told you, it's principle with them. If we play chicken, we'll end up in bankruptcy. Rick, do you agree?"

"I can't say."

Baxter glared. "Well, *I'm* telling you that's how it is. We have no choice."

Lee sighed. "Tell you what. I won't commit now, but why don't you and Crank put together a book on bed-and-bath—"

"Already working on our part," Baxter said. His clicking had become joyful.

"We can at least have a buyer in place if we don't scare up any other money before the payment's due. By the way, I know of one buyer who's hot to trot. Shitbird LaCroix." Lee eyed Baxter sternly. "But try hard to shop industrial. Maybe we'll get an offer in time." Baxter nodded.

Soon Green had to leave. On the way out he stopped in to see Houser, who was reading something and looking distressed. "Hello there! Heard you had lunch at Twin Pines."

"Yeah. In fact, we sat right by the Gilbert Houser memorial hole-in-one tee."

"It was the eleventh, but you're kind to remind me of pleasant matters. Actually, I'm a bit troubled. Got this before." Green's stomach turned when he saw a letter on SEC stationery, captioned *In the Matter of Trading in the Securities of Lee Textiles, Inc.* It directed Houser to provide a chronology of the LBO, as well as drafts and final versions of all the key documents. "Obviously," he said, "there's nothing to worry about. But it'll still be burdensome to comply."

"I'll have a litigator call you," Green said, and gave back the letter, which quaked as if in the grip of a Parkinson's victim.

"You okay?"

"Yes."

Out in the reception area Green sank onto the couch, trying to relax and telling himself, the world is good, things will be good. He had already known about the SEC investigation, and nothing Lee might have in its files could get the prosecutors any closer to catching Alfieri. The trick was to act completely normal, as if he were guilt-free. And the normal thing would be to call Lou.

When Mandel came on the line, Green assumed the tone of a lawyer whose client had a problem: concerned, but with no personal stake. "Hey, just finishing down here."

"How'd it go?"

"Kind of interesting. I'll tell you later."

"Can't talk? Willie the Trained Chimp around?"

"No, ha. Um, Houser got an SEC letter—"

"About trading? I know, I got one too."

"You?"

"They also send it to the lawyers on the deal. It's a pain in the ass, because we have to dig through all our papers."

"Pain," Green repeated, then abruptly called out, "What?" to no one. "Sorry, they want me here. See you tomorrow."

"See you," Mandel said, then hung up.

Again Green's mind raced. What if there were incriminating documents in his file? He'd have to destroy them. Great—he could add obstruction of justice to his other crimes. He was becoming Clyde Barrow! When he felt sufficiently composed, he walked out to the waiting cab. In the backseat he reclined, then resumed his mantra: The world is good, things will be good.

At the terminal, he phoned Rosa. "I'm glad you checked in! Your father called a few minutes ago. Said it was urgent."

"Urgent?" That wasn't Fievel's style at all. His messages were usually "Not important. I'm insignificant, sorry I bothered you." There must be a death.

He dialed home. Fievel cried, "Thank God it's you!"

"Is someone dead?"

"No! Worse than that!"

"Jesus, what?"

"I got from the SEC a subpoena! Says I have to come testify wit' a whole thing about Lee Textiles!"

Green was astonished. They must have spotted the investment club's trading, but how? He'd never asked the exact amount of Lee stock Fievel had bought—figuring the less he knew about it, the better—but it couldn't have been large, because the club lacked the money. He dropped to a whisper, as if the SEC might overhear through some global listening apparatus. "How many shares did you get, anyway?"

"Shares?! I didn't buy shares. Call options I bought. Lots and lots of them!"

Now Green needed to vomit. "Options? How could you be so stupid? That sticks out like a sore, a sore—!"

"A t'umb?" Fievel sounded tormented. "After you told, I was just gonna buy a bissel stock. But then I figured, why not take the same money and *once* make a killing, for the pishers in the club! And I said, how would anyone ever catch it?"

Green gave his forehead a savage scratch, drawing blood. "You idiot. You complete—Oh, God!" He wanted to curse long and loud, but there was no point.

"I'm sorry!"

"Forget it! It's done. So what, what—what's this subpoena?"

"First at the top is some Latin: 'Subpoena duches tuches,' I can't even read—"

"*Duces tecum?* You have to bring your papers?"

"*Ja*, there's a whole list of shit, account statements, bank records . . . goes on two pages typed, attached to a fancy printed paper. Says I am hereby required to come to the New York office to appear before Gerald Byrne! I am hereby required to testify! Involving a 'investigation pursuant to the Exchange Act of 1934'! Came certified mail!"

Green feverishly organized his alternatives. He could continue to cover up, maybe devise a strategy to throw the SEC off his track. Or he could call them right now, tell the truth, then beg for mercy and offer whatever information they wanted.

For the second time in a day, he wondered what the Torah required him to do. He pictured approaching Leventhal for advice; pictured that smug expression, and the rabbi acting as if he were an expert on securities fraud. He'd say Green's duty as a Jew was to come forward and, to the extent possible, make amends to those he had wronged. But this view seemed naive to the point of childishness. To confess meant to lose his job, maybe go to jail; and then he'd always be remembered at B'nai Shalom as the zhlub who'd had such potential, but ruined himself. If, on the other hand, he used his brain to survive this, he'd probably end up a rich Crank partner, a respected congregant. Someday the shul might even honor his philanthropy. And an AJF dinner—he'd get one because he could sell tables. . . .

"Are you still there?" Fievel asked, and Green floated back down to reality.

"Yes." His nausea had passed, and he was now oddly calm. It felt like entering a new zone where there was no fear or guilt, only alertness and cunning; it felt, he imagined, like becoming a criminal. "Are you going to go see the SEC?"

"What *can* I do, say, 'No, thanks?' I'll say I'd *love* to."

"Okay. Just don't do anything till I've figured how to play this. Also we may want to hire you a lawyer."

"But then it looks like I have something to hide."

"You may be right." There was a boarding announcement. "I have to go. I'll think on the flight and call you from home."

"Okay, but first let me read you what it says at the bottom of the subpoena: 'Fail not at your peril.'"

"Oh, that's just the old legal language."

"But I figured out why the SEC leaves it—and it's not for tradition. It's because it makes a point, more subtle than the KGB used to make, but almost as scary: '*We* are the government, *we* have the power, and you my friend are now at our mercy.'"

# Chapter 11

Green entered the parklet off Lexington and spotted his father waiting, old and puny—too negligible, really, to be anyone's legal target—on the bench near the waterfall. He was wearing his best suit, a gray pinstripe with seventies-width lapels.

"Good afternoon, Rabbi," said Fievel. He'd been using that nickname lately.

Green had no patience for joking. "How'd it go?"

"I lied, to save you. That's how it went."

Fievel had that morning visited the SEC, unaccompanied by a lawyer, he and Green having agreed that he should just stick to his story: His hunch about Lee Textiles had turned out an incredible stroke of luck. Why hire a lawyer if you have nothing to hide? Also Fievel preferred not to be clipped, a hundred or whatever dollars an hour.

"Thank you so much, Dad. I—appreciate it."

"I hope so. You have no idea what this means . . . how terrified I was! I almost cracked. You have no idea," he repeated, shaking his head.

"So what happened, exactly?"

"I come into the room, there's a table with all microphones, and he—"

"Who's 'he'?"

"Byrne. A middle-aged guy, a Irish I would assume from the name. He says I'm under oath, I say of course, and he tells this block guy, like a reporter, to turn on the tape player.

"I try to seem relaxed. I suck a Velamint to keep my mouth wet. I offer him one, but he shakes with his head.

"He says they're investigating unusual trading in Lee, 'specially on July twentieth, the day I bought the options. By a computer the stock exchange found my trades! Byrne asks how I came to buy so much, just a few hours before the announcement? And I answer that morning was a guy on FNN sayin' Lee should wind up selling for a high price."

"FNN?! They can check the tapes!"

"So let 'em! There *was* a guy. Would I be so idiotic to make that up? Then he asks did I have any other sources of information, and I say, 'Not that I know of.'"

"Not that you 'know of'? What does that mean? You were supposed to just say no!"

Fievel's eyes flashed. "Isn't it bad enough I had to lie? So I made it a little better." Green bit at his fingers. This sounded awful.

"So then he's lookin' at me, thinking. Finally he asks, 'Do you have any children?' I say, 'I have a son, yes.' 'And what is his profession?' 'A lawyer at Crank, Wilson,' I say—proud, nothing to hide."

Green nodded. "Right, right."

"'And did your son work on the Lee transaction?' I say, 'I think so.' Then I say, 'He's very successful, all the partners at the firm want him on their deals.' I'm acting like a real stereotypical Jewish parent—shepping naches—but in a *ignorant* way, like one who doesn't really understand his kid's work, just knows it's wonderful.

"I go on: 'Of course, he never told me what was happening with his deals.'"

"What'd he say to that?"

"Nothing. Just stares a while. Asks for the papers I brought along, then thanks me for comin' in. Congratulates me on my stock picking, though obviously that was meant sarcastic."

Green nodded, gauging Fievel's performance and deciding it had been awful. He'd convinced himself that the SEC would listen to the story, then give up, and now he couldn't imagine how he had reached that silly conclusion. Had he really thought Fievel was such a good liar? "They'll call me," Green said. "But I'll keep saying it's a . . . a—" He couldn't recall the word.

"A coincidence? Yeah. Because they won't be able to prove you told me something." Fievel grinned; he seemed to be having fun, in a way. Suddenly he became angry, muttering, "Fuck 'em! The big *investigators*. You should've seen Byrne, sittin' there, so serious, and I wanted to ask, Why don't you go after the CEOs from Exxon and IBM? Make 'em wear microphones on the golf course!" He wrung his hands as if twisting a chicken's neck.

"No, only the pisher—be honest, the Jewish pisher! No, when *he* gets a leg up, then the sky's falling down. You know why? Because he doesn't know how to cheat *right*. He's too greedy, and winds up spoiling for everyone!" Green nodded, accustomed to his father's claims of Jew persecution by varied government agencies and bureaus.

"Or maybe," Fievel said, "they want to get even for this Joel Steinberg case." Green smiled, but saw that his father was quite sincere. "A Jewish couple beats to death a Christian child? You realize in Poland or Russia would've been immediate a pogrom! If all they'll do here is oppress a little with the SEC, then we'll be very good off."

Green found it difficult, today, to dismiss his father's paranoia. Who could dispute that the passage of information was a tradition, a foundation even, of American business? Who could doubt that it went on every day in the yacht clubs, the steam rooms, the boardrooms? And yet, reading the newspaper you'd think the Jews invented it, in 1986. Bullshit!

Fievel licked at his dry, chapped lips. Green offered a soda. "Maybe a ginger ale: my stomach's shitty from this morning." When Green returned from the nearby kiosk, he found Fievel admiring the surroundings. "Landscaping. I saw a sign that the Rockefellers built. What's it called, the 'Exploitation of Labor Park'? ' Fievel rubbed his abdomen to distribute the healing ginger ale. In a minute his mouth curved downward, his cheeks sagged, and a careworn look spread over his whole face.

"Are you okay?"

"I'm gettin' nervous." He gripped his scalp. "Was it a dream, or did I *lie* to the SEC? Soon I'll be retired, and tsuris with the government I don't need. They'll get Social Security to make my life a hell!" Then his face lightened, shedding years again, as he formed a notion.

"Maybe I'll call back and tell the truth. And you will, too. They'd probably give a slap on the wrist. This was nothing—one deal, you made a mistake?"

"No, no, it's dumb."

"Easy for you to say. I'm the one who had to lie."

Green jabbed his finger. "Look, it's your fault I got caught! Begging for information. I should've never felt sorry for you and all the Bund *shmendricks*. And then your stupid, stupid shit with the options! Dammit!"

Fievel's face was tortured. "I'm sorry! I was a idiot! How many times would you like me to say it? But now I'm just asking, isn't it better to turn yourself in?"

"Listen. The SEC would bankrupt me and you both! Also, at the *best*, my legal career would be over."

Fievel grinned gamely. "It wouldn't be the end of the world. Maybe you'll write a autobiography. About a boy who grew up watching all day the TV, then had to face real life!"

"That's a great idea, but it's like you said: They can't prove anything if we stick to our story. Please, Dad." Fievel rubbed his chin, and Green went on: "Do you want me in jail? Haven't you lost enough family already?" That was vicious, he knew, but it had just flowed out.

Fievel's eyes slid shut. "What can I say, no to my child? You make me feel like my heart's splittin'." Opening his eyes, he cried, "Okay! That's how it'll be. Stick. We stick, and fuck 'em.

"Know why? Because until they make the CEOs play golf wearing microphones, the stock market is a rigged game anyway." He thumbed his chest. "Wasn't I on the other side of the game—screwed—for as long as you remember? Wasn't I?"

"Yes," Green said. He was.

He'd bend over the kitchen table like a man praying, run his finger down the line of numbers in the newspaper, then stop. "Now you're talking," he sometimes said, but mostly he made noises of pain. Ricky, maybe nine years old, didn't know what the market was, except you could make a million dollars. He dreamed of living in a mansion like Richie Rich, with an indoor pool and a bowling alley.

He helped. "Let's see how fast you can find Eastern Microsystems and Mustang Oil. Maybe we'll have some mazel today." Ricky would find them, but they never went up. They stayed the same or went down. His dad would run to the phone, make a call, scream "Sell!" then listen and say, sounding very tired, "All right. But put a stop loss."

One time, though, Gartner Stores said "+6," and Ricky's eyes got big. He'd never seen a stock go up that much. His dad hopped up and down, slapped his belly, then called his mom in to see. "Okay? The options cost next to nothin', and now they're worth a thousand. How many weeks would I have to work?"

But she just said, *"Gantzer knocker."* That meant big shot. "Tomorrow it goes back down." He got mad, wiggling his fingers at her. Who was she? he wanted to know.

For days after, he was happy. He took Ricky to the ninety-nine-cent movies at Times Square, a double feature of *Butch Cassidy* and *The Prime of Miss Jean Brodie*. They were great, except a big stain on the screen made it hard to see. Later, they had Nathan's hot dogs, then went to a bookstore. His dad said Ricky was too old for the Hardy Boys and bought him *The Count of Monte Cristo*. It was the first book his dad loved as a kid.

One morning a few weeks later they were checking the stock numbers, and his dad yelled, "Oy!" His mom ran in and made him tell. "Mustang might go bankrupt, okay?" Then he pointed. "Don't say nothing or I'll . . . I don't know what." They sat at the kitchen table, sad, and sent Ricky to his room. But he listened from the hallway, scared. They talked in Yiddish, though his mom said the word "margin," and his dad said "broker" a few times.

That night, his dad came to sit on Ricky's bed. "I wanna tell about stocks. Maybe I made it sound like you can get rich quick, but you don't need to take all kinds of risks, because you'll get rich just with your brain. The important thing, after healthy, is to be secure. Secure means you go slow, make money by working."

On TV, Darrin Stephens turned into a donkey. Ricky had a scary question. "Are we going to be poor?"

His dad smiled with sad eyes, then hugged him. "Nah! We'll be okay. *Schayn yingl.*" That meant beautiful child.

. . .

"One more thing," Fievel said. "Maybe till this is over you'll move back by us. So you won't have to think about cooking and cleaning."

"Don't worry. Dad. I don't cook or clean in my own place, anyway. Besides, we probably want to downplay our relationship right now."

Fievel waved. "All right, stay on the East Side with the fancy Republicans. I don't see how you can stand it."

"It's cleaner and safer."

"But it has no—soul. Let's face it: The whole Second Avenue is now for people who come from Iowa to live."

"I don't care; I like it. And I wanna be near Shelly."

"*Ja*, what does the *rebbitzin* think of all this?"

"I haven't told her. She's emotionally—fragile, you know? I don't think she could bear the stress."

Fievel shook his head. "There you're wrong, my friend. She *could* bear, better than you—because she expects God to fix things. You, on the other hand, deep down you know there's no God, so you'll have to get *yourself* out of trouble."

"There is a God," Green responded, without enthusiasm.

Fievel snorted, sipped his ginger ale, and chuckled guiltily. "I told your mother I was going to Orchard Street today to buy pants."

"She still doesn't know?"

"Nah. She'll commit suicide if she thinks her baby might have some problems. Or worse, she'll give me that guilt of hers until *I* commit suicide. She has that sheep's way of thinking, you know—following along, baa-ing, afraid for any little angle."

There was silence, out of which rose the faint vibrato of Fievel's humming. "Know that tune? It's a Yiddish folk song, from the Lower East Side immigrants. About a father that works in a sweatshop. By the time he comes home at night, his child, a beautiful son, is asleep. The father stands over the bed and hears the son ask in his sleep, 'Oh, where's my papa?' And the father sings that one day the answer'll be 'Your papa is gone.' Means dead from work.

"Sad. But it doesn't translate, so you'll have to learn Yiddish to appreciate. There's classes by the Ninety-second Street Y, which I've told you I'll gladly pay."

Green hung his head, exhausted. Fievel touched his hair, saying, "You'll be okay." Green watched water collect in the Rockefeller pool, then swirl down the drain.


Two days later he was at his desk studying the annual report of Madison Materials, Inc. Madison's CEO, having learned about Shapiro in *Business Week*, had contacted him with visions of an LBO. Shapiro had routed the background documents to Green with a note that said: "Read carefully. Then see me." Though aware that this was a career-making assignment, Green now found himself unable to focus on the hundred-page saga of an Alabama concrete and aggregates company. His eyes kept drifting to the phone. When it rang, he jumped, as he had after every call this week. But this was the one. He sensed it.

"It's a Mr. Byrne, with the SEC."

Cold and numb, he activated the blinking line. "This is Gerry Byrne . . . from the SEC?" Yes, Green thought, I've heard of it. "How are you?" Byrne continued.

Sick, he wanted to answer. Dying inside, but thanks for asking. "Fine," he said.

Byrne had a kind of Brooklyn-Irish accent that sounded strangely effete. "Under the Privacy Act I'm required to give you notice that I'm calling about a securities investigation. You're not required to answer any questions right now. Are you willing to continue?"

"Sure. Why not," Green added, then regretted the last fragment, which was nervous overkill.

"Of course you know we met with your father about his trading in Lee Textiles stock. I understand your firm worked on the LBO."

"Could you hold a sec?" Green closed his office door, then spoke slowly, conscious of taking a giant, irrevocable step. "I know it looks funny that my father bought options. It was just a wild coincidence."

"Sure, no, I understand. Um, did you work on Lee personally?" Green hesitated, but Byrne could find out easily.

"Again, it's a—"

"A funny coincidence. Another funny thing: When I met your father, I asked if you'd been involved in Lee, and he said he *thought* so. Weird thing to say, considering he'd taken a big position in Lee options. Like it was a secret."

"He thought it would look bad. See, he gets frightened of the authorities. He barely escaped the Holocaust, and his entire family perished." Byrne was quiet then, which gave Green time to hate himself for mentioning the Holocaust, and to wonder why he had. As a ploy for sympathy, it had been too heavy-handed. Maybe he'd been sending the message that the Greens had withstood peril far beyond any the SEC could administer.

Finally Byrne said, "You've probably heard that three arbs, McCann, Schneidman, and Alfieri, are targets of our investigation. Would you have any contacts with any of these men?"

"I've *heard* of them."

"But you don't know them, or anybody who works for them?"

"Not really."

"Okay, well then. Anyway, we sent your firm a request for documents relating to Lee, so I assume you're keeping an eye on your files. Nothing should be lost or destroyed."

"We'll also be getting your phone logs from last year."

Green squeezed his temples, concentrating. "Oh! You mentioned Alfieri, right? I just remembered I have an old friend who works for him, though I'm not sure his job. His exact job." There was a sharp sucking sound from Byrne's end. Green went on: "We haven't spoken in a while, but we may have once or twice last year. I don't recall when that was precisely."

"What's his name?"

"Petey—Peter Rosen. An old friend."

Byrne could not hide the excitement in his voice. "You know Rosen? From school?"

"No, from the summers. We went to the same bungalow colony," he explained, embarrassed by the term, which sounded old-fashioned and Jewish. "We were maybe twelve. I think I'd spoken to him five times in the next ten years. But then he moved to New York and got in touch, a little." Though conscious he should stop blabbering, he continued: "Spoke on the phone a couple times. Really not much to tell."

Byrne waited, allowing him to finish, then said, "Well, thanks for your time. I may call again to arrange a meeting. In case you remember anything else, let me give you my number." He did and then added, with chilling nonchalance, "You probably ought to talk to a lawyer."

After hanging up. Green laid his head on the desk, tears forming as he silently repeated Byrne's awful last remark. What agony, to *need* a lawyer! It was, in fact, unendurable; he decided to call back and confess. But, hand in the air, he stopped—because even if he could cut a deal, he'd be ruined. Who'd give him a job (maybe a Bund tailor, as an apprentice)? And he had to keep reminding himself that the SEC had some circumstantial evidence, true, but as far as he knew no *proof*. He and Fievel would stick together down the line, and Alfieri's end was airtight.

The first thing was to warn Petey. Down in the 349 Park lobby, from a booth behind the newsstand, he dialed. "It's Donn Clendenon." They both hung up, and two minutes later—the time it took Rosen to reach his own lobby—Green's phone rang.

"What is it? And I hope it's not about what I think it's about."

"Listen. The night I told you about Lee, I did a stupid thing. I also told my father, and he bought call options."

"Fuck-piss," said Rosen without inflection, as though it were a noun in common usage.

"I'm sorry. Remember how wasted I was?!"

"I knew I should've stayed and watched you. Go on."

Green described Fievel's meeting with the SEC, and his own conversation with Byrne. "I had to give your name! He'd have seen your number on my logs, anyway, and we'd have looked guilty!"

Rosen was calm. "You did right. Just stay with that you didn't tell me anything. And make sure your father keeps to his same story. Is he—I don't really remember him from Silver Glen—is he . . . cool?"

"Yes," Green said, though the adjective "cool" seemed one of the least applicable to Fievel, a man prone to wild mood swings and obsessive, crippling guilt. A man who badly needed therapy but refused, claiming to be his own analyst. If Rosen knew the real Fievel, Green thought, he'd be on the next flight to Mexico. "What about Alfieri?"

"Totally secure. So relax, and call me again in a day or two so I'll know you're okay. Always from a booth, now."

Before hanging up, Green mimed chatting and laughing into the phone, all for the benefit of any possible witnesses to his distress. Then, resuming the role of innocent, he headed straight to Mandel's office.

Lou was on a call, so Green sat on his couch and looked out at the bridge, jammed with cars heading to Long Island—commuters leaving early for the weekend. He imagined them singing along with the radio, worrying about nothing but the traffic and weather, and tried to remember the feeling of life free of fear, free of this constant clenching in the intestines. One thing was certain: He had never appreciated it.

Mandel hung up. "Glad you came by. I'm irritated with you." Green gaped. "Willie called me to complain you didn't back him strong enough on bed-and-bath, that day in Pikeville."

At first Green was puzzled, but when it came clear, said, "Bullshit," angered less by the substance of Baxter's charge than its sheer pettiness. "I just shut my mouth instead of joining his lying! He's supposed to be advising Lee, but all he really wants is to suck out another fee before they go in Chapter Eleven!"

Mandel was taken aback. "You shouldn't write Baxter's ideas off so fast. He knows what he's doing."

"You're the one who says how incompetent he is! The Trained Chimp, you call—!" He broke off, feeling he shouldn't be alienating Lou, whom he needed now more than ever.

"I know, I say a lot of things. But I have an open mind, all right? I listen to people. And this time he makes a lot of sense. You think Ben Lee's such a genius, either?"

"I see your point. I'll support Will from now on."

"Okay." His jaw hardening, Mandel said, "I don't like to be accused, especially of screwing a client. I bend over backwards for my clients, like Lee. So don't take that fuckin' tone with me."

Green swallowed, trembling. "Sorry. I didn't mean it. Actually, I'm upset about something else, which I wanted to discuss." He took a breath. "It's about the Lee investigation." Mandel's eyebrows rose as if pulled by little strings. "There's these, um, weird coincidences that have gotten the SEC on my back."

He then told his story, from the perspective of a blameless person caught in a nightmare scenario, his voice even breaking once or twice at the injustice of it all. As he spoke, Mandel's expression alternated between horror and suspicion, but by the time he'd finished, Lou seemed nearly won over. Waving, he said, "Wait, now. What I hear from you is: Your friend works for an arb—well, we all know bankers, arbs, whatever, but we're careful not to say even a word about pending deals."

"Of course—" Green began, but Mandel cut him off, excited, flailing his arms.

"You're careful, but arbs have twenty ways to find out about deals. It's not—you can't go after people based on a coincidence." Mandel paused, thinking, scraping a finger along the side of his nose. Finally he said, "That's the whole truth?" Green nodded.

"Then listen, the firm's behind you one hundred percent. Anything you need . . ."

"Well, the SEC suggested I get a lawyer."

"Right. Even though you're innocent, you must deal through a lawyer. Tell you what. Let's go see Bernie Shapiro. He'll make two calls and you'll have the best." Green opened his mouth to object. He hated for his first substantive meeting with Shapiro to concern something so unpleasant, but then he realized there was no choice. On any truly important matter, no Crank partner would make a move before consulting him.

Hands jammed in his pockets, Green followed Mandel up the internal stairway to the building's top floor, home to George Wilson and the other senior partners. Associates were supposed to don their jackets when they visited this corridor, also referred to as "Olympus." Green wondered if he'd get in trouble, but then thought: How much more trouble could he be in, anyway?

Shapiro was at the square oak table in the center of his corner office, skimming a law review article on golden parachutes. The blinds were, as always, down—a seemingly odd preference, since a sweeping city view lay blocked out behind. The reason, Green had learned, was not some optical sensitivity to sunlight but rather Shapiro's fear that arbs, positioned across the street with high-powered binoculars, might be able to read the secret documents constantly passing through his hands. That's how fanatical he was about confidentiality.

Mandel knocked on the open door. "Got a minute? It's important." Shapiro waved them in, and they dropped into leather swivel chairs, facing the great man. He had black-streaked silver hair combed shiny off his high forehead, a long, though bump-free, nose, and full rosy lips. Altogether his effect was not handsome, exactly, but so powerful and wise as to be almost dashingly magnetic. A cross between Kissinger and Errol Flynn.

"How are you, Rick? I've been hearing terrific things about your work, lately." Green thanked him, his heart pounding. "Get that stuff about our friends in Alabama?"

Green whimpered, "Yes," like a shy toddler, his terror now surpassing any previously known level. Shapiro gazed at him with incisive hazel eyes, forcing him to look down at the table, which was empty except for a Quotron inches from Shapiro's fingertips. Like some corporate fireman, he kept watch over the screen all day, monitoring the stock prices of the companies that had him on retainer for takeover defense. If he noticed any suspicious pops or crackles, he'd immediately sound the alarm.

Shapiro leaned forward on his elbows, fingers steepled, ready. "Here's the problem," Mandel said with a crispness that showed he'd take not one second more of his leader's time than absolutely necessary. "You know the SEC's going after the arbs for insider trading. One of the deals—"

"Lee. Yours."

Clearly, Green thought, you had to assume Shapiro already knew everything about his business that was knowable. All he needed to hear was the brand-new stuff. "Right, well through some crazy coincidences the SEC's gotten the idea that *Rick* may've been involved. Rick, why don't you go over it for Bernie?"

At first Green's voice faltered, but soon he found his rhythm. In the retelling he highlighted the parts Mandel had reacted best to earlier and exaggerated his facial expressions in the manner of a hammy child actor. Shapiro nodded as he spoke and, when he finished, said, "What a mess. Let's get you counsel."

Green exhaled, wondering when he'd developed this talent for performance. Or maybe . . . maybe there really *was* a lot of truth to the story? Shapiro buzzed his secretary, said, "Helen Swensen," then explained, "She's a partner at Thomas, Peel who does white-collar defense." Green experienced a fleeting, perverse thrill at being a "white-collar criminal."

Within seconds Swensen was on the speaker, listening as Shapiro summarized Green's predicament. "So we're in your hands, Helen."

She spoke with a Midwestern accent reminiscent of Shelly's, but broader, her O's egg-shaped, her A's flat as a pasture. "In dealing with the SEC it's important to move fast. Rick, I'd like you to come downtown to our office tonight. I have a dinner, but I can meet you back here at eight."

"That'd be very—no problem. I'll be there, thanks. No problem. I will see you then."

After they'd disconnected, Mandel thanked Shapiro for his help. "Not at all. These are the things that happen," he added obscurely. As Mandel and Green were about to leave, Shapiro spoke after them. "One obvious question I forgot to ask specifically, Rick. *You* didn't buy any Lee stock?"

Green felt for the doorknob, stunned that Shapiro still needed to ask. But he'd spoken casually, implying that he'd had no choice, as head of the firm, but to pose this awkward and essential question to his employee. "Absolutely not," Green said. "In fact I've never bought a stock in my life," he went on, thinking what a delicious pleasure it was to say something true. "I wouldn't even know what to buy," he threw in, then cursed his inability ever to let the air go dead.

"Do yourself a favor," Shapiro said. "Stick with mutual funds."

Out in the hall, Mandel patted Green's shoulder and said, "I'm sure everything'll be fine." Green was amazed by the compassion he felt flowing from Mandel. Lou must've become personally fond of him over the last year, though with Mandel it was hard to tell, busy as he was screaming and pounding tables all day for a living. Now the thought of misleading him punctured Green's conscience, but he shrugged it off as unavoidable.

Anyway, the more he considered it, the more he had to question his culpability. Things could be seen from many angles, and it was the jury's function to choose among versions of the truth. But self-judgment was a trap, guilt often a form of vanity. Why? Because you always placed yourself at the center of events. In Green's mind he was never a supporting player, but always the star, the catalyst.

And how else could it be—what other attitude was possible—in the only son of a Jewish mother?

.   .   .

Helen Swensen stood behind her desk, extending her hand. She was in her forties, six feet tall, thin and bony, with frizzy brown hair that looked like solid cigarette smoke. When she spoke, she revealed the edges of stained teeth. She sat, stubbing a smoldering butt, and Green perched on the edge of a bucket chair facing her.

On the wall hung a Yale Law diploma, magna cum laude, and beside it an autographed photo of Thurgood Marshall. There was a plaque that congratulated her for completing her service as an Assistant U.S. Attorney, and various other medallions and scrolls attesting to a distinguished legal career.

Green nodded toward Marshall. "What an honor. I clerked too, for Leo Fineman." She grinned, and he grinned back. She knew about the judge; no more need be said.

"Mind if I smoke?" she asked, a pack already in her hand and a Marlboro sliding out. While lighting it, she appraised Green. "I made notes when Bernie was talking," she said, flipping pages in a pad, "but I'd like your version." Hearing her accent, he thought again of Shelly and then gasped, checking his watch. In all the excitement he'd forgotten that Shabbes had begun. Shelly was at this moment waiting to be picked up for shul, sitting on the couch, her hands folded patiently in her lap. And he couldn't call; she'd shun the ringing phone. Well, soon enough she'd realize he wasn't coming, and go on alone. Later, of course, she'd give him that hurt, disappointed look.

Now for the third time, Green repeated his story. What happened was: Peter Rosen, an old friend, had gone to work for Vince Alfieri in June 1987. After that Green had been careful whenever they spoke, and in October, concerned about the very same appearances that had now caused all the controversy, had decided to end their relationship entirely. They had discussed neither the Lee LBO nor any other deal, though it was within the realm of possibility that he'd let something slip. Beyond that, Green couldn't say where Alfieri got his intelligence.

As for Frank (Fievel's alias to Social Security and the other Gentiles), obviously he had known that Green was working on the LBO. But they had never discussed it. If he bought Lee options, it was probably for the reason he said: A man on FNN had recommended them. He believed whatever he heard on FNN. And who knew? Maybe his decision to invest had been part irrational. Filled with pride over his son's career, he had wanted to participate in it somehow. Parents were crazy that way, he added, grinning as if Swensen must herself have a worshipful set, out in Minneapolis.

As Green spoke, he decided this was his best telling so far; nevertheless, Swensen listened impassively, without a nod or wink that might suggest predisposition toward one conclusion. A cigarette dangled continuously from the corner of her mouth, and Green let out a violent cough at the end. "Too smoky?" she asked, waving at the cloud. But the fumes just curled around her fingers like gaudy, complicated rings and re-formed.

Green then told about his conversation with Byrne and the investigator's jubilance at the Rosen connection. "Yeah," Swensen said. "Obviously, that's what he needed."

"He gave me his phone number and said I should call if I remembered anything else. He told me to hire a lawyer. And that was it."

"Okay. First some news. I called over to my friends at the U.S. Attorney's, and I found out the SEC's now working with the criminal division on Alfieri. The fact that they've turned the case over to the prosecutors means it's gotten big. And now that the SEC has established this—this link between you, Rosen, and Alfieri, they'll probably incorporate your case into the big one. Do you understand?" Green nodded.

Swensen eyed him. "The other thing about this being a criminal investigation is they'll want prison for anyone they catch." Green felt faint, imagining Attica, imagining—oh, no!—a muscular, unreasoning cellmate; but he calmed himself. He wouldn't go there; he'd go to the country-club prison that looks like Twin Pines, where they have tennis, TV . . .

"I used to be a prosecutor," Swensen was saying while lighting a fresh cigarette. "Which helps me to see things from their viewpoint. Let's consider a hypothetical case. Or rather, I mean, let's cut through the crap. If you did this—"

"I don't—!"

"Hear me out." She puffed. "We know they're after bigger fish than you or Rosen. They're after Alfieri. But it's hard as heck to nail an arb for insider trading unless someone testifies.

"If you testify that you passed Rosen information, you'd help the government squeeze him. Then they might be able to turn him, too.

So your testimony could be crucial to their building a case against Alf-ieri, and we might swing a good deal for it. But that's if we act imme-diately, while they're searching for a way at him."

Green had been shaking his head vigorously throughout her speech and now looked out at the sunset, painting the harbor in pink and blue. The Staten Island Ferry was loading some delayed commut-ers, and Green wished he could go away somewhere, like Tahiti. He pictured himself in a hut, drinking from a coconut shell, then bit his lip, trying to concentrate. He knew the longer he reflected, the guiltier he'd seem, and he desperately wanted Helen to believe in his inno-cence. But he felt hypnotized, unable to focus his eyes.

She was speaking his name. He apologized. "Out of it. Nerves." There was some meager sympathy in her face.

"Here's the most important advice I'll ever give as long as I'm repre-senting you: Do not lie. Obviously don't lie to me; everything you tell me is privileged. And even more, don't lie to the government, because they will almost certainly find out. Tell the truth, right from the beginning."

Tell the truth, he thought. Easy for her to say—a partner at Thomas, Peel. But what would she do, really, facing a wrecked career and a dis-graced life? It was too important. He needed time to decide. For now he'd keep on. "I wish," he said sincerely, "I had something to give the SEC, but my story is true. I can tell them what I've heard about Alfieri from Rosen, but it's secondhand and it's not much anyway. Maybe . . . I don't know what else to say."

She nodded. "Okay. You're a fool if you're lying, but if that's what it is, okay." She slapped her pad on the desk. "We'll play hardball. I'll tell the government to stop harassing you, that you have a hard job and don't need it. The U.S. Attorney's office may still want to meet with you."

"Be happy to. Tell you what, we'll all go to Rumpelmayer's for ice-cream sodas, my treat." He'd thought humor would demonstrate his innocence, but Swensen stared as if he were insane, and could he really be surprised? She was used to representing serious people, usually in the most serious trouble of their lives.

"As to my fees. I'll need a ten-thousand-dollar retainer against three hundred an hour. The ten assumes you're just a witness in the case. If it goes beyond that, it'll be twenty-five at least. Ordinarily I'd charge more, but since Bernie Shapiro sent you . . ." Green nodded, grinning dumbly. Ten thousand! He hadn't considered who would pay her; he had semiconsciously thought that Crank would. But after all, this was his problem. Three hundred an hour, though. If she put in any real time, he'd end up broke. He stood immediately and, to stop her meter, said he'd find his own way out. She insisted on showing him to the elevator, where she left him with the promise "We'll get through this." Her confidence brought a lump to his throat.

State Street was dark, though the sky over the water remained lit with colors. Taxis whizzed by, some slowing to entice Green, and drained as he was, he almost hailed one. But he didn't ride on Shabbes; he'd walk home, even though he lived halfway up Manhattan Island. Facing disaster, he felt it crucial to observe the rituals, which, symbolizing commitment to the eternal, would keep his troubles in perspective. Plus they might bring good luck with the government.

He passed the deserted office buildings, assessing Swensen. Initially he'd wanted a male Jewish defense lawyer, a Dershowitz type—in fact, the bigger the nose and curlier the hair, the better— but thoughts of Helen, savvy and connected, made him increasingly optimistic, and he slowed to a stroll. Trinity Church was on his left, a moldering remnant of old New York in whose spooky graveyard reposed the dust of Alexander Hamilton. Though darkened now, the church was open during stock exchange hours, allowing traders to run over for, say, a quick prayer to cover their short positions at a profit.

Green passed streets with solid American names—Pine, Cedar, Liberty—and then City Hall Park, where bums slept: dark, rag-wound shapes on benches and in the grass. More and more of the homeless appeared uptown, wedged in the crevices between buildings, searching the garbage for bottles and objects with any conceivable use. Though he had trained himself to see through them, like grimy transparencies, tonight he was overcome with pity, and with the knowledge of how feather light was the motion that could set a life spinning out of control. A few mistakes had brought him to the edge, a few more now separated him from an irreversible descent, and the solution appeared in no guide or manual, not even the Torah, but instead had to be created out of intuition and experience. It was funny—the lessons that seemed most applicable to this process were those he had learned, not from Rabbi Leventhal, but from Louis Mandel:

"Don't judge, advocate."

"Legal truth can, and must, be controlled."

"When the shit flies, some men will be strong, others weak, and it is impossible to say who will be who. Keep your head."

He didn't reach home till eleven-thirty, but he wasn't tired. Actually he was wide awake, apprehending the world with a new clarity, as if danger had sharpened his perceptions. He groped along the wall to the kitchen, then in the cupboard for a Shabbes candle that lit his way toward the bedroom. He noticed the flashing message machine, reached for the button, but stopped: electricity, Shabbes—why did everything worth doing in life run on a current? Screw it, he thought, then rewound and heard his father's voice. "Call! It's urgent!"

Fievel spoke in an agonized whisper. "It's a disaster! I looked better at the subpoena, and it asks for 'all records of incoming or outgoing telephone calls.' Includes tapes from the answering machine, right?"

"I don't understand. Who cares about that?"

"When you called that night to tell about the deal, remember I couldn't turn off, so the machine taped us. I checked, and our talking is still on the end from the tape."

"Oh, just erase the fucking thing!"

"*Pssh.* But then I'm really gettin' in trouble!"

"You're in trouble already!"

"Lying," Fievel whined, "then destroying evidence. *Vey iz mir*"

"I can't believe we're even discussing this. Erase the fucking shitty motherfucker!"

"I don't think I can. . . ."

Green pinched his nostrils, ordering his thoughts. "Let me explain. I've realized that I did nothing inherently wrong, and the only reason the SEC is after me is I'm smarter than them and I make more money. Who wrote the insider trading laws? People who can't get *access* to information.

"It's that whole—that Communist ideology, you know? Because some guys in the race are faster than others, we make them wear leg weights. Instead of the American way, which is to tell the slow runners, 'We'll train you, but if you still lose, well, life is unfair.' The same with this tape. It's my leg weight, which the SEC would use to make it appear I did wrong." He paused. "Did you follow what I said?"

"*Ja.* Something about a race, and leg weights, and Communism. Frankly, you sound like this crackpot who hangs around by Lincoln Tzenter."

"Anyway you should erase it now, before the SEC calls again. Because they might ask about the subpoena, and you don't want to lie that there is or isn't a tape."

"Like Nixon."

"Huh?"

"He should of gone on TV right after the break-in, made up some bullsheet about Communists in the Democratic party, and *announced* he'd be burning the tapes. The American people prefer a Fascist, a criminal even, to a sneak."

"That's interesting. Please do it right now."

Fievel didn't respond. Sensing a presence behind him, Green turned to find Shelly in her nightgown. He ignored her, focusing on the candlelit phone and on his father, whom he imagined an elf cowering within. "Will you?"

"Who are you talking to?" Shelly asked. "It's Shabbes," she scolded.

"Leave me alone!" he screamed, and she stomped to the bedroom. "Please, Dad."

Fievel sighed. "Okay, stay on. Then you can listen to me break yet another law, which seems to make you quite happy." There was a sound of mechanical fumbling. "One button says ERASE, but when I press, nothing happens."

"The ERASE switch moves sideways."

"I'm pressing, but nothing happens."

"Wait a minute—"

"If you press, usually it—"

"Would you fucking wait a minute! Move the ERASE switch from left to right."

"Oh! I figured it out. It goes to the side!"

In the background Green heard the smooth swishing of erasure, and closed his eyes, envisioning the little gap teeth clamping the spools. Soon he heard the click that signaled the process had ended, and the machine had destroyed its memory. The past had disappeared.

# Chapter 12

Green awoke on the living-room floor, wearing only socks and underwear, his face pressed against the answering machine. It had been a sleep made fitful by SEC monsters, and Mandels and Shapiros the size of dinosaurs. Shelly was crouching in her nightgown, touching his arm. "Why did you stay out here?"

"Couldn't sleep." He'd been up till three, pacing by Shabbes candlelight, then had lain on his back and soothed his brain by picturing a Shea day game, box seats behind the dugout.

"Was that your father you were yelling at last night? I thought you were having a seizure."

"Yeah. A money problem. Private family stuff."

She stroked his back. "I've told you a thousand times, if you're in some kind of trouble, I want to know. So I can help. We shouldn't have secrets."

He propped himself against the wall. Shelly remained in a crouch, her expression open, nonjudgmental. "Okay, but don't overreact." She nodded. "The SEC's investigating insider trading in Lee Textiles. I didn't do anything wrong, but they're suspicious because Rosen's an arb. It's just a matter of clearing up a misunderstanding."

She thought. "That doesn't sound so bad."

"Well, but once the government starts with you—"

"You'll just tell the truth, and everything'll be fine."

Her blind confidence bothered him. "There's another complication. My father invested in Lee right before the final deal was announced. So you have both facts, and it looks funny."

She stared. He stared back, unabashed. "Are you saying—? What *are* you saying?"

"I'm saying I'm innocent, but everything's closing in on me, anyway."

"Have you seen a lawyer?"

"That's where I was last night. Her office is by the South Ferry. I walked home," he added with a martyr's subtle pride.

"What does she think? I mean, it's not like you'll go to *jail* . . . ?"

"That is possible," he said, watching her face.

She sank to the floor, hugging her knees. His eyes closing, he flashed back to himself after a playground fall, faking injury to see how upset Rachel got. Outside, in the lavender light, a garbage truck huffed and crunched. Shelly started to speak, stopped and then, her eyes distant, asked, "What about the wedding? Maybe we should hold off."

"No. At *worst*, I'll just have to get a prison furlough." She stood, sighing with frustration. "I was kidding."

"It doesn't seem funny to me. I'm getting ready for shul." He followed her into the bathroom and embraced her over the sink, feeling, now that he'd frightened her, like comforting her again.

"Sorry I joked. I just wanted to show you it'll be all right."

"I understand. You're not a hundred percent yourself." She hugged him back, still holding her toothbrush, dabbed with a blue line of paste. "You're not going to jail—but anyway, I was in myself once, so I know what it's about."

"What?" He glanced at her in the mirror, as if the reflected Shelly might be a less preposterous convict.

"Only for one night. It was Chris's fault, of course." She had told stories about her college boyfriend Chris Duval, a blond-haired skier and drinker who had often gotten her in trouble. Green, hearing about Duval's behavior, wanted to track him down and punch him, then walk away before he could punch back.

"We were at a party, and he was so bombed I had to drive his car back to campus. But a trooper stopped us, and it turned out I was over the limit, too. My parents were in Hawaii, and I couldn't find anyone to bail me out till morning. Later, my dad's lawyer pleaded guilty and got me just four points on my license."

"How come you never told me?"

"I was embarrassed. Because I was so stupid."

"So what was jail like? Were you scared?"

"No. There was one prostitute who'd already passed out, and another drunk driver. I wasn't scared because I spent the whole night furious, planning to dump Chris once and for all. Which I did, the next day.

"After that I was happier, and my grades improved. I swore I'd only go out with nice, stable guys from then on."

"And look what happened." He grinned bitterly, tapping his razor on the sink.

"You are nice. Stable, I'm not as sure," she said, and kissed him. "I was thinking maybe we should cancel dinner at the Kogens tonight."

"No. We have to go about our lives as usual. Y'know, so if you have any banks to knock over, you should go ahead." She laughed. "Jailbird," he said.

He squeezed her hard. "I promise by September we'll be on our honeymoon and all these little problems will be forgotten. As Maimonides said, 'Without problems, the day would be over by eleven o'clock in the morning.'"


Green swayed over his book and sang out loud, especially the prayers that thanked God for vanquishing the Jews' enemies. ("Thou hast made the [SEC's] plots against us come to nothing and hast foiled the [U.S. Attorney, Southern District, Criminal Division].") To the other congregants he must've seemed pumped up with piety, but in reality his mind was far away, rearranging Byrne, Rosen, and Fievel into multiple geometries. Leventhal's sermon concerned Job, whose story Green felt he was hearing for the first time. The truth was, until a week ago his life had been a cakewalk, free of affliction. Job, however, offered little in the way of helpful hints, being a bit of a yutz.

Drinking Manischewitz and eating *ruggelech* in the temple basement with Shelly and the Weissbarts, Green spotted Berkman, the accused inside trader, pale-faced and hacking into a hankie, skulking along the wall. Though loathing him, Green was riveted by Berkman's jerky movements, reminiscent of a whipped dog's, and by his quick, mirthless smiles. Finally, unable to stand any more, Green said he was exhausted, but that Shelly should stay. Following his eyes to Berkman, she rubbed his neck and whispered, "Go rest and you'll feel better."

He walked down Second, rattled. What if Berkman had been sent as a bad omen? Supposedly they came in threes, and now he looked around for the others. An eagle atop an ATM? A limited-stops 15 bus draped in black cloth? Wait! For all he knew, Berkman was an SEC plant, intended by his broken figure to illustrate what became of non-settlers. At home, Green collapsed on the bed, still wearing his shoes, tie, and yarmulke.

He was awakened by a voice in the living room. ". . . calling because I spoke to Stuart Sterling. He's the Assistant U.S. Attorney who's running the Alfieri case. He wants you to come down and meet with him. It's not a subpoena, you don't have to go, and in fact I told him basically get lost." Green was now standing over the machine, watching Swensen turn the tape. "But then I got a call from a prosecutor friend of mine—"

He lifted the receiver. "I'm here." Feedback pierced his eardrum. "Sorry. So what did your friend say?"

"He knows about the investigation. He wouldn't tell me much, but he did advise that we'd be making a mistake if we didn't meet with Sterling soon."

"Maybe a bluff. Is it mind games?"

"Not with my friend. But of course what the government thinks or claims it has, and what it actually has, are different things." Green paced, swinging the cord. "What if we say no?"

"They might subpoena you."

"But I want to be cooperative. Because why shouldn't I be?" He'd almost forgotten; he was innocent. And consistency was key. "So we should go down and talk to them."

"Yeah . . . this way, we'll see what they've got. And if it gets too rough, you can just stop answering questions."

"Good."

"I'll see if I can get us in on Monday. But Rick, one thing: You must be completely truthful. I mean, if you go in and lie—"

"Why are you starting again with that? I told you—"

"I'm just saying that the consequences of lying would be very serious now. This is no fooling around."

"I'm not fooling around. Please arrange the meeting."

He hung up and leaned against the wall. If the government meant to psych him out, it was succeeding. But fuck them! Because he'd go in on Monday and recount his (largely true) story so brilliantly—with such poise—that they'd see no alternative but to fold their tent and leave him alone.

He noticed that his feet hurt, having during his nap swollen inside his shoes, as often occurred when he worked all night. He kept a pair of sneakers at the office, to change into when the pain got unbearable. Once, at 4:00 A.M., he'd put them on and run a lap around the deserted fortieth floor, feeling wild and free.

Now he pulled off his shoes and lay back down, thinking about his many all-nighters, and his thirty-five hundred hours. It was crazy! Just once he wanted a sympathetic word from Fievel instead of sarcastic comparisons to Lodz poverty. "So quit if it's that bad," he'd say. "Go to the coal mines." What a pain in the ass!

But, pain or not, they had to stick together now. Rosen, too. It was the three of them against Byrne and Sterling. Jews versus Gentiles— there was a matchup about as novel as "Shirts" against "Skins."


Shelly approached a York Avenue doorman wearing a military-style uniform complete with epaulets and braided cap and said, "Kogen," which word apparently had the magical power of "Alakazam," for they were waved past instantly.

The apartment seemed poured from the same plaster-and-parquet mold as Green's. The living room featured a huge black-lacquer cabinet in which the Kogens displayed a large collection of Judaica (including their *ketubah*, hand-lettered in Aramaic and decorated with fruits and a lemon yellow sunrise over Jerusalem). One shelf contained a photographic tribute to little Jason in various costumes.

After the Weissbarts arrived, the three couples enjoyed Baron Herzog kosher chardonnay and crudites on the sectional. While the women discussed Dvorah's Lamaze, Michael lamented to Larry an investment he and a few other doctors had made in some Holsteins that had contracted an incurable hoof disease. Green quietly drank, envisioning himself, on Monday, confronting Byrne's pug face, which would no doubt feature that burst-capillary nose and be framed by that lank blond hair. At least Swensen would be there to translate Green's tale into the special goy language.

"To the table!" Wendy announced. The dining alcove was lit by candelabras. After Michael said the *motzei*, Green bit a roll, staring into the flame. Here was the key question, he thought, the answer to which might explain all his troubles: What was it about Jews that everyone hated so much? Why not Hindus or Slavs? Oh, and the Irish, the Irish! Byrne would *love* to polish him off! He—

"How about you, Rick? Anybody home?" Green raised his eyes. Larry said, "Michael and his doctor friends are voting Republican. And my point is, Reagan has wrecked the economy with his defense spending."

"Not to mention his social policies," Dvorah added.

"The Democrats," said the male radiologist, "have been an economic disaster every time they've gotten the White House. As for the Republican social policies, I don't agree with them, but they're all hot air anyway, to please the right wing."

Larry waved his fork. "Why don't you admit it? The only reason you're voting Republican is you're afraid Dukakis and his pal Jesse Jackson will tax the wealthy. Rick, do you agree?"

Green spoke, though his eyes remained unfocused. "Michael reminds me of the rich Weimar Jews. They helped bring Hitler to power, you know—to keep out the socialists. And they dismissed his rantings, saying, 'Oh, that's all hot air.'"

Michael snorted. "You're comparing Reagan to Hitler?"

"He's in bed with the Moral Majority. Don't you think if they had a chance they'd round up the Jews? Do you seriously believe a pogrom is impossible in this country?"

"I'm sorry," said Michael, grinning, "but you're nuts."

"Let's continue this chat when they're loading us onto the railcar." Larry giggled nervously. Michael was still grinning, and Green went on: "Smile, but I've experienced this government's anti-Semitism, firsthand." Shelly squeezed his knee, and he revealed the roll he had crushed in his fist.

There was silence. Wendy glanced around, seeking a way to salvage her party. "Talk about happier subjects," she implored, then collected the salad plates. Green felt annoyed at Michael's smugness. In fact, he thought, the Kogens would be taken in the first wave; they were too conspicuously well off, with their Saab and their Berkshires condo. Green, by contrast, had few possessions, though he'd received a staggering $35,000 bonus for his seven months' work in 1987—a banner year for Crank. (While other associates had thrown their bonus money around, he had gleefully repaid his student loans and squirreled the rest away in a bank CD.)

He sipped his wine. It would happen in the next depression, when an uneasy alliance of white supremacists, Black Muslims, and fundamentalists would begin armed protests against Jew wealth, complete with window smashing and random killing. In a so-called protective action, groups of Jews would be rounded up into army barracks.

The protests and roundups would continue amid media outrage, which would die down after a month or two, eclipsed by hotter stories: a war somewhere, a movie star's love baby. The Jews left in prominent positions either would stop complaining or would disappear. Legal actions would be brought, but the courts would cave as they had in 1942, when the Nisei were encamped. (If still alive, Fineman—to prove his patriotism one last time—would collaborate meekly.)

After a year, the barracks overcrowded, the "residents" would be given a choice of moving to larger "safety areas" (walled ghettos) or "extraterritorial relocation" (deportation). Many would flee to Europe, many more to Israel, if it hadn't yet been leveled by nuclear strikes. Then there'd be those who would refuse to go, insisting that sanity must return. And for them, the consequences . . .

Green's reverie was interrupted by the arrival of the main course: prime rib, new potatoes, and baby vegetables. His appetite stimulated by visions of persecution, he attacked the food, then sensed Michael watching him. "You okay, Rick? Still worried about the pogrom?"

He put down his fork and turned to Michael, happily slicing his beef. "I understand your scoffing. Your father grew up where?"

"Shaker Heights."

"Sure. But see, my father was from Lodz. So we have a whole different perspective on things, I guess."

Dvorah was interested. "Lodz, really? When did he get out?" Green had forgotten she'd majored in Holocaust Studies.

"In '39, after the Nazi invasion. He didn't want to leave, even then, but he was beaten up by some Germans, so his parents begged him to." Green pictured Fievel's face as he told this same story, misting up at every mention of his mother, her endless labors and acts of charity, and of the last time he'd seen her, sobbing at the window as he vanished into the night.

"The idea was he'd go on ahead and they'd follow. He made it to eastern Poland—"

"Which the Russians controlled?"

"Right, and Russian anti-Semitism was sort of a known quantity, unlike the Nazis', though of course no one had a clue what the Nazis would end up doing to the Jews. The other thing was, my father had been educated in socialist schools, and believed the Soviet Union was a workers' paradise. Well, when he saw the actual—the *degradation*, he decided to go back home.

"But the Russian side of the border was impenetrable. Try to imagine it, really try: Sixteen years old, alone in a strange place, no money, and you can't get home. What you also have to imagine is a boy who's been raised on the brotherhood of man, and ideals of social justice. And now he's thrown into a maniacal state of nature where the goal is to avoid starvation."

"God," Dvorah said. "How did he make it?"

"Well, that's the ironic part. Once he'd accepted his situation, he found he had an incredible instinct for survival. And there were ways. Like one store had an oversupply of vodka, so he'd fight his way through the crowd, buy a bottle, and trade it for food. Then he'd sell the food, and so on. That worked awhile, until the police arrested him for speculating and threw him in the gulag."

Michael shook his head. "Speculating."

"Yeah. They called him an 'enemy of the people.' After he got released from prison, he spent the rest of the war dodging the police, getting caught, in and out of prison . . . the basic stuff. 'Let's Go—Stalinist Russia,' you might call it."

Everyone laughed guiltily. "What about his family?" Dvorah asked.

"The ones who survived the Lodz Ghetto died at Auschwitz. When my father came home in '46, he found everyone and everything he ever knew just . . . obliterated. Also the culture, the language even. So."

Larry said, "How does he deal with what happened?"

"Well, as you'd expect, some days he's okay, and other days he gets horribly depressed. He feels guilty for leaving home—like, if he'd stayed he might've saved them. Though he knows, rationally, that he'd just be dead, too. But it's tough to forgive yourself."

The table was quiet for some time. "What," Green said, "were we discussing originally? Oh, my point was, you should fear a government that promotes intolerance. Because history shows it eventually turns on us."

Though they looked compassionate, Green knew that these Shaker Heights and Winnetka Jews couldn't understand. Different from him as they were, they might've been Pilgrims.

Later, in bed in the dark, Shelly said, "If you're so afraid of American anti-Semitism, maybe you should consider making aliyah."

He wheezed. Not this again! "I don't want to leave this country. I just want a decent government for once." He paused, then asked whether he'd ruined the party. There had been little gaiety after his speech.

"Not really. It's just—"

"What?"

"Don't be offended, but when you discuss your family, you can take a . . . superior attitude. As if you're a Holocaust survivor yourself."

"I do not!"

"Or as if to say, Nobody whose parents didn't suffer in the Holocaust can understand what it was."

"I don't believe that. Or—well, maybe to an extent. But you wanna know what I do believe? That there are aspects of my upbringing only a first-generation American will comprehend."

"Such as?"

"Oh, what about my father changing the prices in stores?" Green had to smile, recalling how Fievel would mutilate a $29.99 tag to make it read $9.99, then boldly bring the item up to the register, where he'd pick the dumbest-looking clerk. It worked about half the time. (It was his rule only to pull this on the big department stores, which deserved it for routinely clipping the workingman by raising prices. He seemed to regard Gimbel's as a branch of government, and the crime therefore victimless.)

"And then of course there's also the weirder stuff, like the way he's always trying to get me to move back in. You laugh, you think he's funny. . . ."

"I think he's sweet."

"Sweet isn't the point. It's a psychological— Look, I'm tired. Let's not get into this."

He made out the shapes of a shirt over a chair, a yarmulke, a briefcase. "The thing is, sometimes I feel I don't fit with people like the Kogens. Because their values—they're all about money and possessions."

"Who are you, *Gandhi* with your bonus?"

"Well, soon enough I may be broke again." His voice cracked. "I'm finished, let's face it."

She hugged him. "No you're not! You're innocent. They'll have to see that."

"I should just be dead, that'd be better."

"Oh, stop! It's not funny. Even if the worst happens, we'll have each other, right? Anyway, have a little faith in God." Green exhaled. There was God again, ending all inquiry. He was in some ways becoming a source of confusion, not clarity. Worse, like a nudge you wanted off your back.

Shelly continued in a small voice. "What do you think of my values? While we're discussing values."

"That's a bizarre—I love your values. What else?"

"Just sometimes I—oh, never mind. Let's sleep."

He stared into the gloom, then said, "I love you." She touched his head and rolled over.


There was another war story, a favorite of Fievel's that he'd first told when Ricky was no more than seven or eight and that now ran through his head as he lay trying to sleep.

Fievel had been sentenced to hard labor in an Arctic logging camp. The prisoners were fed only bread and watery soup, in amounts proportionate to their production, so if one got sick, he cut fewer logs, received less food, and got sicker until he died. They slept in an unheated tent, on a floor swarming with bedbugs. Their clothing was rags, and rags were wound around their feet, then covered with "boots" that were really fragments of rubber tires.

After Fievel's release, he arrived, bedraggled and penniless, at a town called Kaluga, where he sought refuge in a synagogue and was found by a Jewish family. They nursed him, cleaned him up, even got him work in a local printing plant.

"Was pretty good," Fievel would explain. "The head from the plant, a Russian—big like a bear!—he took a liking to me. He told me to register with the NKVD, that was the KGB then, but said he'd protect me from them.

"Bein' from a modern city, I knew things. I taught to the boys jujitsu; to the girls dancing. I was a tzelebrity among the Jews. I had food, clothes, a job—after the camp, this was for me heaven! Well, every week more Polish refugees came to this little town, also city boys like me. And immediate they started complaining about there's no food in Russia, it's dirty, and so on. I, of course, knew already that you never complained! But anyhow, we refugees all got close. They hung on me for some reason, like a leader.

"One day I was in the print shop, and a man walks in, sayin' the KGB wants me. Well, everybody starts crying, because this can mean only one thing! And the bear is crying, too, hugs me goodbye. But I was lucky. At the KGB office are two men, and one says, 'We hear there's a lotta complaints among your Poles about the living conditions. Is this true?' I pretend I'm offended: 'If I'd heard something like that, I would of come in and told you on my own! Everyone *loves* it in Russia!' They look me over and say, 'Fine, from now on you'll report to us once a week, tell what you hear.' They even gave me a code name. Vladimir, I think it was.

"Well, my friends keep complaining, but every week I tell the KGB how happy everyone is, what a incredible workers' paradise is the Soviet Union! This continues awhile, till one day I'm called to the *home* from one of the KGB, taken in a nice den, and there I meet a high-up KGB official, come all the way from Moscow! The local officers then ask the usual questions, I give the usual answers, and finally this official says, 'We have a match factory outside town.' He points to a enormous box of matches on a shelf, and I see, inside it, a camera! Then he says, 'You know, I look at you while you talk and I see that simultaneous your mind works, like you're thinkin' of something else. Why is that?'

"I say, 'To be honest, I was thinkin' about my plant, that they're late payin' me my salary, and I have no money.' So he calls the plant, screams they should pay me, then hands me extra rubles. And now I realize I'm cooked. On the KGB payroll? Or I inform next time, or I'm dead. Well, what am I gonna do? I have it there good, and if I leave I could be arrested for vagrancy, returned to the camps, and who knew if next time I'll get out? But if I inform, I'm sentencing my friends maybe to death! Well, what I did was pack my belongings and run away from Kaluga. And for three years after, I was in awful danger!"

Fievel would pause then. "So what's the point of the story? I was a survivor, but some things I was not capable of, no matter my position. Happened a few times during the war that I couldn't get down to that real level of a animal, and I suffered as a result. Most people, I think, have many layers, like a onion. There's layers of humanity, then layers of animal, but then, if you keep peeling, you find the human again. The mensch.

"I think that's true. Though I don't know. Maybe it's just what I *hope* is true."

Green and Swensen were greeted by two men in blue suits. The one who introduced himself as Gerry Byrne looked athletic, with graying blow-dried hair and gray eyes—not at all the Tip O'Neill figure Green had envisioned. The other shook Green's hand warmly and said, "Stu Sterling." Sterling was barely thirty, and resembled Green: tall, with a stoop at the shoulders; thin frame but flabby; brown eyes. Glancing at his crown, Green was glad to discover signs of male pattern baldness, as if this somehow placed them on an equal footing.

The room was windowless, jammed with cardboard boxes, metal carts, charts, and easels. The walls were bare except for a photo of

Reagan (iron-haired, insouciant, and so utterly unlike Green) and a travel poster of Puerto Rico taped up at the corners. "Thanks for coming down," Sterling said, then continued in a relaxed tone. "I'm sure Ms. Swensen has advised you of your rights, but anyhow you have the right to remain silent, and your statements can be used against you in court. So we appreciate your willingness to answer questions voluntarily, though of course we could subpoena you."

Green said, "I want to be helpful." He measured out his words, having been warned by Swensen—aware that she had in him a dangerously garrulous client—to speak only in response to specific questions, and then as precisely as possible.

"Great, thanks. So . . . we've gotten your story in bits and pieces and thought we should hear it through. This meeting is not on the record." Green cleared his throat; he had rehearsed several times in front of the mirror on Sunday.

"But first," Sterling went on, "let me bring you up to date. We've found some new sources, including one who's told us that Alfieri received information on July twentieth—just before he bought a big block of Lee stock—from a lawyer working on the deal. Now it's a matter of finding out who."

Green felt himself redden to the hairline, and noticed Byrne eyeing him. Swensen said, "I don't suppose you'd like to tell us who this source is?"

"You know we can't," Sterling said. "But take our word, it's well placed and highly reliable." He faced Green. "I'll be honest. Alfieri's going down in the near future. We're building a major case against him, and Lee's just the start. We know he inside-traded in a few other deals, including PTR's merger with Bolus. Which your firm also worked on." Green was boiling hot and chafing at the collar. So they had picked up Bolus! "There's also stock parking, 13D violations . . . a list of felonies as long as this table."

"He's going to prison," Byrne added.

"But I admit we could nail him quicker if we had corroborating witnesses who could appear before the grand jury. Also people who could help us gather more evidence."

Byrne leaned forward on his elbows. "What we're telling you is we'll get there anyway, though we could save time and effort if you came on board now. But we mean *now*. In a month the situation may be very different."

Sterling held up a finger. "I'll tell you one thing that'll be different in a month. Your friend Rosen will be cooperating. He's in serious trouble. And no matter what he says to you today, when he's looking at ten years in prison, you know what he'll do."

Green held his face impassive, though it weighed a ton. Swensen came to his rescue. "Can we caucus a minute? You've hit us with a lot of stuff." The prosecutors leaned back, two bullies interrupted by a teacher, then nodded and left.

Already Green's back and neck were drenched. Despite a No Smoking card screwed to the wall, Swensen lit up, then said, "You're aware that what you tell me is privileged?" He nodded. "Because these guys obviously know what they're talking about, and I want you to tell me the truth now. I promise you, from long experience, a case based on lies will fall apart!"

Green didn't respond. "Here's the options," she continued. "One: Give me a straight story and I can negotiate a proffer for you. Meaning you tell them the truth and they can't use it against you. Because that's what they're dying for. This claim about a 'source' sounds to me like bullshit, which would mean they may need your testimony bad enough to get you off completely."

"What's the other option?"

"We walk out of here. Remember, you have rights. Their evidence is all circumstantial." She took a drag. "The one option *not* available is bringing them back in, then lying. Lies *can* be used against you."

Green rubbed his face. "Let me ask this. If I were to tell them something they want to hear, would—"

"Not a made-up confession, either! Truth only."

"Wait! I mean, hypothetically, would a lawyer who confessed to something like this be disbarred?"

"It'd depend on the SEC. That's usually a condition of your deal, but they might make an exception." Green pictured Byrne's coiffed hair and freezing wolf eyes. To Byrne, he was nothing: a roach or worm to be squashed. And Swensen couldn't seem to grasp the significance of professional ruin! Someone like her, she could go back to Minnesota, open some general store or whatever, but what would he do? It was no good.

If only he could talk to Petey! To get some reassurance that Alf-ieri's side was holding together. Then, if he didn't like what he heard, he could always call the SEC back. Until he did, it was important to stick with their story. But should he speak or walk out? If he walked out he'd look guilty, and this agony would drag on. Swensen had said not to lie, but she was required to deter perjury, right? And the fact was, everybody lied, everywhere, and usually got away with it. It was the confessors—the yutzes, with their stupid, sad faces, silently, uselessly begging for mercy—that you read about in the paper, in some item at the back of the business section. "Lawyer, Dad Accused," Green's headline would say. But fuck that!

He exhaled. "I see they want information, Helen. It's just, I'm not the one. Let's get 'em in here so I can say what happened."

"I'm warning you. Don't expose yourself to additional charges!"

"All I can do is tell the truth. Bring 'em back."

"I'm against it. I *feel* you messing up." She thumped her chest.

"Well, I mean, what'd you bring me down here for, then? To get scared? So I'd sign any confession they gave me?"

She grimaced, and it struck Green that that was what she'd thought might happen. He squeezed his forehead between two fingers. "I'm innocent and I won't do that!"

Swensen stubbed out her illegal cigarette, fanning at the smoke ineffectually. "Okay. I believe you. I'm calling them back. But say the minimum for now."

When the men returned, she explained, "We don't have anything like what you're after."

Byrne frowned almost imperceptibly at Sterling, who said, "In that case, why don't you tell us the facts."

Green knew the story so well by now that his mouth worked with-out conscious effort. As he spoke, a feeling passed over him of calm, of surrender to fate, like the moment when he had—a chubby, chuckling boy with bangs, shouting "Geronimo!"—finally run off the high diving board at Brown's Hotel in the Catskills. Sterling took copious notes, though Byrne seemed bored, drumming his fingers with his head down.

When Green finished, Byrne stood abruptly. "I'd love to chat more, but I've got a lot on my plate. Thanks for coming in," he added, and left without a handshake.

"I'll show you out," Sterling said, then led them down a hallway. Passing the men's room, Green became aware of an urgent bodily need. Sterling followed him in and stepped up to the next urinal, then let loose a loud, almost equine stream. Green, however, couldn't pee with the law at his side. "So, Rick, where you from originally?"

"New York. Manhattan."

Sterling grinned. "Thought so. I grew up on Eighty-sixth and Central Park West."

"Seventy-second and Riverside," Green replied, delighted. A fellow Manhattan boy might go easier on him. "Where'd you go to school, um . . . Stu?"

"Horace Mann." A prep school on a lush Riverdale campus. "You?"

"Stuyvesant." A public school downtown; Fievel and Rachel couldn't afford, and in any case opposed on principle, private high schooling. "But I knew some Horace Mann kids. David Schwartz?"

Sterling laughed. "I know three David Schwartzes."

"This is the one who went to Harvard."

"Oh, yeah, he was—he's a real—"

"Yeah, a total asshole. Works for *NEC News* now."

Sterling shook his penis. Green gave up, zipped his fly and then flushed, hoping Sterling hadn't noticed his failure to urinate. Why would he? Who cared?

After three squirts from a dispenser filled with pink liquid, Green soaped his hands thoroughly, as if to say, I'm a very very clean person. Please let me go.

"So you're from Seventy-second," Sterling said. "There was a place that had backgammon and—"

"Ping-Pong, upstairs! I used to play all the time. There's nowhere for Ping-Pong now."

"The city's not what it used to be. First they traded Seaver, then it's the homeless, then it's no Ping-Pong." Green laughed—too loud, too gregariously—and there was a pause as Sterling caught his eye in the mirror.

"Listen, I know how upset you must be about all this. I know how I'd feel. Obviously, any dealings with me should be through your lawyer, but I just want you to be aware that . . . well." He flipped his hand as if thinking better of his remark. Green was suspicious, having watched more than enough TV to know the "good cop" routine intimately, but thanked him anyway.

When Green and Swensen left Sterling at the elevator, he was greeted by several other young prosecutors. Green envied their camaraderie—that of soldiers fighting for justice. And it hurt, too, because he could've been alongside them. Instead he was the enemy. Or . . . maybe it wasn't too late? Maybe, when the trouble blew over, Stu would consider putting in a good word at the U.S. Attorney's?

Swensen and Green crossed the lobby. "Sterling didn't say anything in the bathroom, did he? I hated to leave you two alone, but . . ." She indicated her genitals.

"No, just chatter."

She stopped. "What exactly did he say?"

Green sighed. "We're both from Manhattan, so he asked where I went to school. I asked if he knew David Schwartz, and he said he knew three. We talked about a Ping-Pong place on Seventy-second, and then—" Green paused, reluctant for some reason to recount Sterling's statement of compassion, which Helen would only twist into something malicious and unethical. "That was it, basically. We washed our hands."

"Only deal through me," Swensen said.

"Of course."

"I'm serious, Rick. I'm . . ." She nodded.

They exited out onto Foley Square. The courthouse was ahead, and Green had an urge to drop in on Judge Fineman; it had been a while since he'd been treated to some good old-fashioned verbal abuse, and there was a lack of subtlety to the judge's ill will that he might find refreshing. But time was short. Opening a taxi door, Swensen said, "Overall it went okay. Byrne seemed fine. The one who may give us trouble is Sterling, the men's room man. He's an ambitious young fellow."

Green stood for a minute after the cab peeled out, surprised at Helen's assessment of Byrne and Sterling. She had them backward.

When Green had worked on his first hostile takeover, Mandel had, to illustrate a stratagem, told him the tale of the "prisoners' dilemma."

Two men committed a crime together. Because the prosecutors had no evidence, the prisoners would go free if they both denied it. What the prosecutors did was separate the men and tell each of them that if one confessed and the other didn't, the one who confessed would get a year in prison, and the one who didn't would get twenty years. If they both confessed, they'd both get five years. Each prisoner, distrustful of the other, confessed and got five years.

Green had enjoyed the prisoners' dilemma as an abstract logic problem, but he could never have imagined that just months later he'd be walking the streets of Chinatown at midday, living it.

After Swensen had ridden off, he'd gone right to a booth to call Rosen. He had lifted the receiver but then stood, figuring. His ability to hand Rosen to the SEC was his only bargaining chip, and it might be worth enough to free him completely. If he told Petey what was happening, *Petey* could run to the SEC to save his skin. If he did, Green's usefulness would be at an end, and then he really would be cooked. It seemed unfair: The less involved you were, the fewer people you had to rat on, and the more you were at risk.

He had hung up and now was heading east on Worth Street, burdened by the unfairness of it all. The Chinese children skipping around a schoolyard seemed unfair. Even the dazzling spring sun seemed unfair. On Mott he stopped to look in the window of a souvenir shop, at the flimsy, gold-sprayed trinkets with no apparent use, and the red-tasseled lucky-character medallions. (Here they pretended that luck, like any commodity, was available for purchase. If only that were true!)

Down a flight of metal stairs, in a dank basement, was a Chinese restaurant that Green and his co-clerks used to like. Unkosher, of course, but he'd just order vegetarian. He sat beneath a stained, curling calendar from a pagoda-shaped bank, eating hot-and-sour soup. The steam cleared his sinuses, and his eyes glazed as he thought about Rosen, with whom his future was now linked. Who was he anyway? Grew up in Brooklyn, broken home; good third baseman; cheated at pinball. Star of commercials for Alpha-Bits cereal and Bactine spray. Later, an angry adolescent with violent flashes (mostly during sports); got laid at fourteen; enjoyed Pink Floyd and pot. After the eight-year gap, a recovering addict who dressed flashy and liked disco music; still a Yankee fan; still obsessed with sex. Confident at all times, as if blind to his own limitations. Worked for an arb and finagled secret information from a friend.

Those were the facts. But what was his essence? What choices would he make? Point one: As far as Green knew, since rehab he'd never touched drugs or alcohol, which demonstrated his toughness. Then there was his help with the Teri abortion, which demonstrated his responsibility. One more, crucial point: during their years of friendship, Green had never considered Petey a fink. On the other hand, who knew how much Rosen might have changed since the last time he'd seen him?

It had been a night in late October, during Green's reconciliation with Shelly. That morning Mandel had received a letter from Houser praising Green's work on the LBO, and Green had spent the day elated, feeling his luck was finally turning around. But every few minutes he'd remember Rosen and slide back into misery. In the afternoon, his brain in a fever, he ran to the lobby phone to call Petey.

They'd met for sushi dinner down on University Place, where there'd be just NYU students around. Green begged: "I can't sleep at night. The guilt is destroying me."

"You want out, fine. I never forced you. Did I ever, or blackmail you?" Green shook his head. That was true—but there were subtler ways of bending a person's will. "So you're out. I don't know why, though. We have a good thing goin'."

"Maybe good for you and Alfieri."

"Quiet down."

"Maybe for you," he whispered, "but not me. I'm not the kind of person—I have to make money legally, by working for it, or forget it."

Rosen appraised him. "How *are* you doin' at work? Pretty well these days, I'm betting."

"They say my judgment and strategy—"

"Stratego. Remember we'd play? Sorry to remind you of the drubbings."

"But it isn't Stratego anymore."

"Sure it is. Movin' your pieces, bombs everywhere. You know how I always knew where your general was? I'd watch your eyes to see where you looked." He lost his grin. "What about your account?"

"I can't take loot from crimes."

"*Now* you're being an asshole."

"I'm doing the right thing, finally." Green felt proud, though he couldn't deny a selfish motive as well: If they ever got caught, it might look better.

What would Rosen, after a year of criminal or near-criminal activity, be willing to do to preserve his leveraged-up loft, Porsche, and model girlfriend?

Green had been shoveling food from plate to face in a continuous motion and now paused, his mouth full. The brown shreds that covered the mound before him—might they be pork? He examined one, drooping from the chopsticks. No doubt: a Leviticus-violating quid of pig meat. He swallowed, then shoved the rest aside. The pork had been moist, flavored with ginger, and what, precisely, did God find so offensive about little Rick Green's eating it? He wanted, just once, to hear an argument for kashrut that didn't end with the sentence "Anyway, the Bible says so."

His fortune read: "You are very popular."

Walking down the hall at Crank, he glanced nervously at the other lawyers. It appeared, however, that Shapiro and Mandel had kept his secret, because nobody gave him a distrustful fish-eye, or worse, a sympathetic nod. Nevertheless, some sixth sense, felt as a prickling along his spine, told him that more was going on, that somewhere— maybe not here, but *somewhere*—people were talking about him, even plotting his downfall.

A pile of messages awaited him, including one from "Richie Hebner." (Rosen's alias, adopted when Green began to feed information, came from a Pittsburgh Pirate of the Silver Glen era. For Green he had selected a Met outfielder.) The message was marked "ASAP," but Green couldn't call back—not until he'd chosen a course of action.

Instead, he reached Shelly at work. "So I told them my story— I mean the truth—my story that's the truth. And they seemed, you know, pretty satisfied."

"Good. How're your spirits?"

"Fine. I'd still rather be dead, but otherwise—"

"Oh, please! Why do you keep trying to scare me?"

"I'm not. I'm just saying death is better in some ways, that's all. Because you just lie there. Listen, I should work now. . . ." She made him promise to call the minute he got home. Then he tried to bear down, to clear away the backlog that began mounting the moment a Crank associate slowed, even slightly, his pace of output, but everything—all the memos, contracts, letters—was baffling, as if he'd sat at the wrong desk.

The phone rang. It was Norman Bluestein, one of the firm's senior litigators. "Bernie and Lou told me what was happening and asked me to keep up with you. To help if I can. Could you meet with me and go through the whole story?"

"Of course, but can we maybe do it tomorrow? I'm kind of jammed up this afternoon."

"Sure, tomorrow morning is also good. Around ten?"

"See you then," Green said, though he had no intention of keeping this engagement, which would require him to expand his circle of inquisitors to include yet another sharp-witted, probing, hectoring, arrogant lawyer. Another goddamn lawyer!

Heading toward his lobby that evening, he stopped, nauseated all at once by the prospect of seeing Shelly. He was facing the most important decision of his life, and felt that her presence would only make it tougher. What he needed, instead, was a drink. One ancient people, he recalled, used to make crucial decisions at night, drunk, and reconsider them, hung over, the next morning. At a singles' bar just up Second, Green took a stool, ordered a martini—served in a festive Y-shaped glass—and gulped it, the liquor blooming down his chest like a burning flower. He ordered another.

Though he was there to make a final judgment on Rosen, he found himself preoccupied by his odd feelings toward Shelly. Since the SEC had surfaced, he'd grown increasingly uncomfortable around her, and had just experienced an aversion—that was the only word for it. She was intelligent and kind, and he loved her, so why did it seem essential that he exclude her from this crisis? Was she playing Rachel to his Fievel, judging him, dragging him down? Would he always see her this way, even after marriage? These questions, and the many others they raised, felt far too complex to address right now. Right now it was time to decode Petey.

He finished his third drink, searching his memory for any scrap that might reveal Rosen's character, and so predict his actions. And there was something, just beyond his consciousness, buried beneath fifteen years of debris. It involved Silver Glen, of course. A ball crashing through a window . . .

They were playing grounders inside the casino, which Petey's grandmother had forbidden. But he said it was okay, that she was a battle-ax. He played for the Pirates and Ricky for the Mets. Fielding a two-hopper, Ricky winged it back, too high. The spaldeen sailed past Petey's hand and broke the window over the jukebox, playing "It's Too Late," H3. When the wart-nosed old lady came running in, Petey said, "I did it. You gonna hit me?" So Ricky wouldn't get in trouble! She raised her bony hand and gave him a shaky slap that just made him smile.

They went outside to the swings and pumped standing up, then timed their fly-off to go together. Petey—windmilling his arms, pedaling his little legs in the air—got the better distance, as usual, and rolled across the grass. Ricky rolled up next to him. "Sorry about the throw. And thanks for saying you broke the window."

Petey answered, "It was fair, 'cause the game was my idea."

That was it! Green's gut said that his essence hadn't changed. He'd never snitch on a friend for messing up in *his* game.

Light-headed now, Green probed clumsily through his wallet, then lay down some money and slid off the stool. At home he needed both hands to insert his key into the lock. There were two messages, the first from Rosen. "You were supposed to let me know how you're doin'. So I called you at work, but you don't call back. You're makin' me worried that you might do something stupid. So call me *right* when you get this."

Shelly was concerned. "Where are you? Please call so I'll know you're safe."

He leaned over to unplug the phone. Blood rushed to his head, and he collapsed in the one wicker chair.

# Chapter 13

When reconsidered the next morning, Green's decision seemed foolish. First, it was a long, long leap from a broken window in 1972 to criminal securities fraud in 1988. More important, he'd over-simplified. Rosen might well keep silent stretched on an SEC rack, but even that didn't ensure Green's safety, because there was also the "source." What if Sterling were working on Alfieri's accountant, or head trader, and this person beat him to the confession? He'd be screwed. Knotting his tie in the bathroom mirror, he wondered: If the prosecutors did have a source, would he or she know Green's identity? Petey was smart enough not to tell anyone. Nonetheless, with an insider's help they could assemble a solid circumstantial case. And it was so unfair.

Shelly was still asleep, an arm flung across her eyes. She had let herself in at one o'clock, afraid because he hadn't called, especially after the comments he'd been making about death and how pleasant it seemed in comparison to his current life. He'd apologized and said, "Don't worry, I won't commit suicide without taking you along." She hadn't laughed. Now he wished he could just slip out, but she'd give him the hurt look, later. He touched her shoulder. "I'm going."

"Huh? I overslept. Wait, can't we have coffee?"

"I'm late."

"Okay, but can you try to get home early? I want to help you." She pulled his head down. "I love you, you know."

He kissed her cheek. "Me too."

As soon as he stepped outside, he got the spine prickles that told him he was being watched, followed, or talked about or something. He looked up and down Seventy-fourth but saw nothing unusual. Downtown he felt safer, chameleon-like in his suit and wing tips, and purposely merged into every pedestrian cluster. Approaching 349 Park, he heard a quick tap on a car horn, then experienced a flash of red hair. It was Rosen, at the curb in a royal blue Porsche. When Green shook his head angrily, Rosen moved as if to climb out and come after him. Then Barbara Schein passed, glancing back from the revolving door. Green hurried to Petey.

The car's interior was like a NASA capsule, and low—the lowest Green had ever been in, excluding go-carts. Rosen headed east, adjusting knobs and switches. "I'm like Top Gun over here. How's the climate? Radio too loud?"

"Everything's perfect. I'm very very impressed. Now can you take me—Turn on Lex, please. Turn! Shit. Now you have to go to Second."

Rosen kept straight on. "I only need an hour of your time. We'll take a ride." Green squealed, but soon Rosen was angling toward the entrance to the FDR. "If you returned my calls, I wouldn't have to kidnap you."

"I'm busy. I can't be on the phone all day."

"A one-minute conversation? To tell me how your head is, so I don't get scared?"

He was scared. That meant Green would have to be *so* cool. To keep him, at all costs, from running to the SEC first.

Now they were on the highway, breezing down toward Wall Street. They swooped in a long curve along the East River, which glittered almost attractively in the sun. "Are you gonna tell me where we're going?"

"I thought Japonica, like the old days. Had breakfast yet?" Green held up a paper bag stained with muffin grease. "Japanese is better. Soba noodles have the carbos that give you energy for the day. Easy to digest. Not like that butter and shortening and shit." He patted Green's stomach. "Why you're a chub" Rosen himself was trim and tanned. And being in his car felt like riding a tiger. Maybe there was something to the arb life, after all.

Though the restaurant was empty, they were careful to take a back table behind a paper screen. While Japanese banjo music played faintly, Rosen ate his noodle soup with deft chopstick snips. "Well," Green said, "as you can see, my head is all together."

"Is it. That's good, 'cause I know you get excited." He inspected a snow pea. "Had any more discussions with the SEC?" He glanced up.

Green fiddled in his soup, stalling. "I hired a lawyer, but I told her the same thing I told the SEC on the phone. It was all a coincidence."

"And how's your father?"

"I have him totally in control."

"So we're all being smart for once. Because when you're smart, you got a whole smart thing happening." With chopsticks, Rosen described a circle of cleverness in the air. Then his face changed. "Ready for the wedding?"

Green was stumped. "Oh! We're just starting to. It's still a few months off." Rosen lowered his head shyly, and Green realized: He wanted an invitation! With the SEC on their asses, with their lives on the line, he was worried about his stupid invitation. Green began to respond, but Rosen's eyes shifted front, registered a presence, and in a second Alfieri slipped in beside them.

He was dark and much handsomer than in news photos—like a movie star. He even had that shiny appearance celebrities did in person, as if his face gave off light. His suit was British, his shirt bold-striped with a sharp collar, and his cuff links resembled gold candy. He reached across the table to shake. (When Green next touched his mouth, he smelled cologne on his hand. It stayed a full day despite repeated washings.)

A bizarre notion then struck Green: His entire future depended on the words he chose, and his demeanor, in the next five minutes. He took a breath and said, "I've read a lot about you."

"Don't believe any of it," replied the arb. The waitress brought him a rough clay cup and a pot of tea, batting her lashes. Green sensed that if Alfieri gave the signal she'd go somewhere with him and have sex. Why did some men have so much of this . . . essence, while others had not even the slightest bit of—?

"I won't keep you long, Rick, since I'm sure as a Crank lawyer you're perpetually swamped. I just felt—in some ways we know each other already—that we should meet." Green tried, but couldn't make out even a hint of Hoboken; Alfieri sounded like George Plimpton. "Also I'm aware that we're all going through a stressful time, and I wanted to address any concerns you might have."

Green assumed the firm, serious tone, alien to his real self, that he'd developed for negotiations. "Actually, I'm very confident. I agree with Pete. Everything will be fine as long as we keep our heads. I mean, what's their case? It's bullshit."

Rosen gave Green a satisfied blink, and Alfieri nodded. "Right, when the situation's considered rationally, but of course there's always the psychological element." He paused. "Have you ever heard of the prisoners' dilemma?" Green shook his head.

Alfieri told the story, then said, "The SEC operates the same way: by turning people against each other. Planting doubts about your colleagues. Or by claiming to have a 'source'—which they never identify, naturally—so you begin to feel your friends' trustworthiness is irrelevant. Mind games."

"Well," Green said, "I strategize for a living, so I know all the tricks."

Alfieri displayed a mouth of polished ivory. "I can see." He sipped tea. "In fact, Pete's told me something about your career—that you've had a meteoric rise." Green shrugged. "I'm always looking for new legal talent. How does Crank feel about associates bringing in business?"

"They feel fine."

"Obviously not now, but when things cool off, in a few years." When he'd be coming up for partner, Green understood. Oh, this guy was good.

"One thing they write about me that *is* true: I never forget a favor." All at once Alfieri's eyes narrowed inside a hard crease, so they suggested a credit card peeping out of a leather wallet. "Conversely, when someone wrongs me, I remember that too." Green's throat tightened, shutting off airflow. Rosen was calmly eating noodles.

Pinching the bridge of his nose, Alfieri continued: "The first man I worked for used to say, 'Life is long.' He meant that in the course of a normal career you'll deal with the same people many times. I think in the M and A world you need about five powerful friends to counter-balance one powerful enemy." He downed his tea. "See what I mean?"

"Mm-hmm."

"What's the word in Italian? *Vendetta?*" He laughed. "God, I've gotten rusty. I was over there in April and couldn't even put together a whole sentence."

Alfieri didn't speak for a while, but instead kept shaking his head, grinning at his rusty Italian. Finally he said, "We should let you go. I don't want to get you in trouble with your firm." He signaled for the tab, checked the addition, then left exactly sixteen dollars and some coins.

While Alfieri led the way out, Rosen whispered to Green, "He likes you, I can tell. This is very lucky. For once we're all being smart." He massaged Green's shoulder blade.

On University Place, buttoning his jacket, Alfieri said, "George Wilson's a friend, by the way. We're on two charity boards together."


Green managed to get uptown and to his desk before collapsing. His legs felt like assorted cold cuts—prosciutto, mortadella—but nothing a person could *walk* on. He'd been poised and glib with Alfieri, but the question remained: Had the arb threatened him with violence? Was he, despite his smooth veneer, a mobster? It felt dizzying, like looking over a cliff's edge, to consider whether your life was in danger. You had to step back, touch everything solid, and tell yourself, "Don't be silly."

But the fact was, accidents were arranged. Every day people flew out of windows, fell under subway cars, got stabbed or shot during "robberies." And beneath it all, unknown to John Q. Mermelstein, ran an underground river of crimes, favors, and vendettas. How much could it cost to buy a hit: fifty, even a hundred thousand dollars?

Alfieri had a hundred million.


There was a message from Norm Bluestein that just said: "Meeting?" Green had forgotten about it completely. He'd have to duck the litigator for a while, maybe by spending a lot of time in the toilet. That seemed quite attractive all of a sudden: a job where you could come in, go to the toilet, sit all day, and then leave at 5:00 P.M., never having interacted with anyone. He went there now, to his favorite stall, a marble vault down at the end with a cozy curved seat and a shiny metal coat hook.

As the morning passed, he grew calmer about Alfieri. He'd been agonizing over a decision that now had been made for him. He wanted to live! The idea of his brain not functioning struck him as intolerable. Alfieri might have mob connections, or he might not; but either way, Green was unwilling to run the risk. So he'd keep his mouth shut, the SEC could masturbate forever, and then, come September 1994, the rainmaking associate would rise to partnership at Crank, Wilson & Shapiro. End of story.

Moreover, he felt surer now that they were a solid front, cool-headed businessmen all. Well, except for one weak link: Fievel Isaac Green, who may have had amazing survival skills as a boy, but at present was a panicky loose cannon. He needed soothing, and Green returned to his desk to call.

"How am I? What should I say, I'm *lighthearted?* I don't sleep, all food comes up on me, and I spend half the day on the toilet."

"Me too. So what?"

"I'm nervous. Nervous!"

"But you shouldn't be. I had my meeting at the SEC."

"What happened?"

"I told my story."

"The fake?"

"I told the story, and that was it. They have nothing. And Alfieri's side is holding."

"Who?" Green cursed himself. *That's* why he was a lousy liar; he had a short memory. Fievel didn't, and couldn't, know about Alfieri! If he thought it went beyond the two of them, he'd crack instantly. "Alfieri, the arb? What's he got to do?"

"Nothing, I just—"

"Don't tell me it's some *ring*, with him and you and me!"

"No! I just mention him because he's also being investigated for Lee trading, and the SEC seems to be getting nowhere with him either. The point is, they're not too bright."

"Don't underestimate them just because they're Gentiles, believe me. They can be pretty smart. I'll ask once more: Shouldn't you confess? Because I'd like to. And I'm considering it every day. I can't live, nauseous all the time."

"You're overdramatizing. Just relax and it'll all fade away."

"How will it fade? It'll hang over us!"

"Well, I don't care. I'd rather that than it destroy me now. My future's at stake!"

"Mine too!"

"Yours? How long are you planning to *live* anyway, to a hundred? You're already retired! But I'm just starting out! For me this is survival. Don't you understand I'm talking about survival? You of all people should understand."

"Are you seriously comparing what I went through to—?"

"I have to compare! This is as serious to me as—!"

"Is your life in danger?"

"What do you call prison? A fucking—a party? With a rapist in my cell! And there's other things you don't know about, too."

"What things?"

"Forget about it. Just do what I'm telling you, all right? Just listen to me."

Fievel wheezed for a few seconds, then said, "I'll go along. But I don't agree it compares. Think about and you'll see. That it doesn't compare."

Green sagged over the phone, composing himself, and decided that everything was in hand, now that he'd put down Fievel's rebellion. What he needed to do was resume his life as usual, and then it all would fade away.

He was just setting to work on the prospectus describing bed-and-bath, due by week's end to be sent to all potential buyers, when the phone rang. He started—ringing telephones, he'd found, generally brought bad news—but it was only Mandel, checking his progress. "I know your mind's on the SEC, but this must be done on schedule. Maybe I'll get Neil."

Green was repulsed by the thought of that crow-face pushing back into Lee. "I'll finish. Anyway, Ben wants me. I shouldn't say, but he's not big on Mermelstein." There. A nice jab, and fuck you, Neil. "You can do one thing to help me, though: Get Bluestein off my back. I just don't have time to deal with a litigator right now." Green assumed a contemptuous tone, figuring it would appeal to Mandel, who viewed most litigators as gnats buzzing around the hides of the corporate lawyers.

"Well, you will have to talk to him soon. But I'll get it delayed a couple days." Green thanked him.

Despite his assurances to Lou, Green spent the next several hours staring at the document's words—"sheet assets," "towel cash flow"— without comprehension. Even when he wasn't actively sweating over the investigation, it occupied part of his consciousness, like a radio playing in the next room.

He was still distracted, picturing Alfieri's savage expression as he described his lust for revenge, when a messenger brought in the afternoon mail. Atop the pile was a postcard of James Dean walking through Times Square, hunched against the rain like an idiot, without an umbrella.

> *Dear Rick,*
>
> *Guess you thought I dropped off the earth. Well I've been around it since I saw you last, but I just couldn't escape its gravitational pull. Anyway, I'm back, living in New York's fabulous Greenwich Village!*
>
> *Many strange things have happened to me in the last year, and I've understood a lot about our relationship. I'd truly appreciate it, if you could spare an hour to talk.*
>
> *Pls. call me 555-2158.*
>
> *Love,*
> *Bonnie*

Green read the card over three times, certain that the biggest favor he could do himself was to throw it away and pretend he'd never received it. Things were complicated enough without Bonnie back in his life . . . but this message was absolutely fucking intriguing. What "strange things" had befallen her? What had she understood about them? At least they could talk on the phone.

"I'm so glad you called! I was afraid you despised me. We parted in a sort of—"

"Yeah, I have to apologize."

"Me too, but let's forget it. It's aeons ago. So how are you?"

"You know. Life goes along. Pretty dull. So your card worried me. Are you okay?"

"It's a long story. But I can't, on the phone. . . ."

He thought. "Did you want to meet for a drink tonight, near my office?" One hour at the Waldorf bar, then back to work.

"I do want to see you, but I can't face midtown right now. Remember Chip from *Endless Night*? I'm house-sitting his mom's apartment on Grove Street, and I was hoping maybe you could come down." He didn't answer. "C'mon, play hooky a little while!"

She imitated a Gypsy. "I see in my ball a handsome man; he is bent over a desk, marking on paper. Now he sits up, filling with the desire to run free in Greenwich Village and let the wind blow through . . . what is left of his hair."

"I wish I could, but I'm on a deadline." She wasn't surprised. He promised to call again when he had more time.

He disconnected, picturing Bonnie in a cozy Village apartment, smoking a clove cigarette and drinking wine from a gourd. Then he remembered their candlelit dinner, wine and lobster on the floor of his old apartment. They'd been happy, dizzy with love. And he'd changed—aged, really—so much in . . . Could it be just eleven months? Maybe lawyers' years were like dog years, seven for one. That meant he wasn't twenty-six, but thirty-two. In about 1991 he'd turn fifty; in 1998, a hundred.

Bonnie. Their split had been for the best, he knew. She was wild and unpredictable, whereas he preferred a quieter life. What a thrilling few weeks she'd given him, though! And there had been so much more to her than anyone could grasp in such a short time . . . well, than he could, because he'd been a baby, unprepared for an affair so intense. For months afterward he'd hated her, but in retrospect the events were blurry, and the fault harder to assign. Maybe, now that he'd lived a tiny bit, he could read Bonnie?

And, well, why not get out into the sun? Clear his head of the shit for an hour or two?

. . .

Grove Street was so quiet at midday, Green could distinguish the songs of individual birds and the rustle of leaves lifted on a slight current of air. He stopped halfway up the brownstone steps, suddenly aware that this excursion made no sense. Under pressure at work, engaged to be wed, and, incidentally, target of a major criminal investigation, the last thing he needed was to visit a crazy woman in Greenwich Village. He descended but, hearing his name called, spotted Bonnie in a fourth-floor window, her face washed out by a halo of glare. "It's the right building!" Now he had no choice.

The foyer could have served as a turn-of-the-century stage set. There was an antique mail table, over it a gilded mirror, and a banister that began with a carved eagle and then curved upstairs, wide and smooth. "You can do it!" Bonnie yelled when he reached the second-floor landing. "Crank up your pacemaker!" Now that he was so close to seeing her again, his stomach fluttered. He pictured her the night she'd come to New York. Catching her in his arms, he'd thought he might burst with love. But that was long past, and first off he'd tell her about Shelly, to avoid any misunderstandings. He reached the top, panting, his legs tired.

In the doorway was a woman he hardly knew. "Hey, sweetie." She now had big, black-rimmed glasses and chin-length light brown hair. His lips parted—it had never once occurred to him that she'd dyed it blond. Though she wore a baggy sweatshirt, it was obvious she'd gained at least twenty pounds. She smiled tentatively, and the expression behind her glasses made her seem sad, vulnerable, and years older. She wouldn't be stopping any more Broadway traffic.

"I know. I've changed."

He nodded. But the truth was, he felt the same stirrings as before. "You look . . . beautiful. More like your real self, you know?"

She hugged his neck. "Thanks for saying that. And for coming down."

"It's okay," he said, arms limp at his sides. When she stepped back, he saw she was crying a little. Then she laughed, flicking at her eye. "*Homo Suitus*, the suited man. Bringing bad karma to the Village. Well, c'mon in anyway. You won't believe this place." Inside, there was a brown couch, a yellow rug, and a kidney-shaped coffee table. Mexican and African knickknacks cluttered the shelves, next to tattered paperbacks like *Lolita* and *On the Road*. "Isn't it great? Around this stuff I feel I could walk over and hear Dylan playing at Folk City."

"It really does have that kind of beatnik feel. And Chip's parents live here?"

"His mom does, but she's in Paris. His dad's dead." She gestured at one wall, covered with Pablo Casals concert posters. "He used to play oboe for Casals. Howard Slatkin."

"Chip Slaney's real name is Slatkin? The brick-jawed wonder?"

"Thought you'd like that."

"I love it," he said, smacking his hands together.

"Don't get too excited, though. His mother was a shiksa—an English war bride. So Chip doesn't count, right? Learned that from the conversion book. 'Member?" He blushed. That was the night of Bonnie's dinner with his parents, which they had made such a disaster.

She put a Pete Seeger record on the dusty, scratchy player, then sat on the couch. Green sat at the opposite end, near an open window. From a branch outside a bird called, "Chip, Chip, Chip," as if pining for the handsome half-Jew. Bonnie seemed to be reading his face, like the history of his year apart from her. He felt transparent, and spoke to deflect attention from himself. "Did you really go around the world?"

"Want the story of my travels? Okay. Last I saw you I was leaving to stay with Chip. Then I got a job as a P.A. on *Endless Night*. In December, Chip's boyfriend moved in, and he kicked me out. All I could afford was a room in the Monroe Hotel, on your old street? Which was scummy, with like, whores shooting up in the halls. I was surprised I never ran into you."

She took her cigarettes off the kidney table. "To be honest, I picked the Monroe *because* I thought I'd see you. I missed you. So I called information and found out you'd moved to the East Side— shocker—and when I finally got the nerve to call, a chick answered. So I left you alone."

Lighting up, she continued: "I had a tough period then, so bad I wanted to get out of New York. So I moved to the Virgin Islands, where I got work as a waitress at a beach bar. Wore a bikini all day, chilled out with the staff. I loved it."

"Why did you leave?"

"The owner—this really sweet, older guy—he and I became involved, which turned into my usual fiasco. So he booted my ass out, right? So I figured nothing was working for me in the U.S. or its territories, might as well try another continent. I found a cheap fare to Paris and borrowed some money from Chip." She paused. "Why are we sitting so far apart? It makes me uncomfortable." She shifted toward him.

"I ought to tell you I'm engaged."

"Not surprised. Probably the one I talked to. A nice Jewish girl?"

"Nice is too mild a word. So is Jewish."

"Good for you," she said, blowing out smoke. "You're an up-and-coming young professional. You should have a wife who's an asset. What's her name?"

"Shelly."

"I'm sure Shelly'll be a good mommy, throw a suave dinner party. Not like me, right? I was just a pain in the butt."

"That's not true. You made me very happy for a while."

"Yeah, absolutely." She stubbed out the cigarette. In an exaggerated drawl she exclaimed, "Where *are* my manners?! Might I offer you a beverage? Beer? Ice tea? Sarsaparilla?"

"Beer would be good."

"Back in a jiffy!" She flounced to the refrigerator and fetched a Heineken and an Evian for herself. "Sorry I cain't join you, but I've got a li'l ol' drinkin' problem."

He sipped. Eyes glinting, she said, "Tell me more 'bout *Shelly*. Bet she's a whiz at Scrabble. May I ask, she a good fuck? Moves? Or just kinda lays there?"

He began to rise. "Look, maybe this wasn't such a great idea." He *was* curious to hear the rest of her story, but things were getting too tense. Suddenly he longed for his desk and his document.

"No! Don't go. Sorry I was nasty." She picked at the Evian label. "When you said you were engaged, I guess I got upset. I really am sorry."

"It's all right. It's just, I'm surprised you care, the way you dumped me."

"I dumped *you!* After all this time you still think—? Wow." Pointing at him, she said, "You dumped *me*, babe. It was just hard to tell, 'cause you were doing it in slow motion. I was just smart enough to get out before you hurt me too much."

Green tilted back his bottle, wondering how she could possibly have concocted such a false history. "I didn't dump you," he said at last.

She mussed his hair. "Y'know, for a smart guy you can be pretty naive. Take a minute and really think about our relationship. Especially the night at your parents, and what happened after."

"You don't think they could've made me break up—!"

"It wasn't them! It was you. I knew what was going on in your head, even if you didn't. On the other hand, I can't say I blame you. I would've gotten rid of me, too."

"You're confusing me. I feel like you're showing a half picture. Maybe if you told me more . . ."

She stared past him, out the window, and brightened. "Y'know, it's a great day, and I bet you're always cooped up. Wanna take a walk? But leave your jacket and tie or I won't be seen with you."

They headed west toward the river, into the part of the Village whose narrow, labyrinthine streets had always perplexed Green. Pigeons skittered about and, when a car occasionally came along, flapped up at the last moment, more irritated than frightened. New Yorkers.

At the corner of Christopher was a gay bar, the last in a long strip, with a cowboy theme. Green recalled the first time he'd ventured this way, searching for a cabaret where a Stuyvesant classmate was singing. He'd gawked at the scores of men milling in Stetsons and chaps, laughing, bursting into show tunes, just having a lot of fun. Of course that was '77 or '78, and now the place resembled an abandoned saloon in some shot-up, tumbleweed town.

They crossed West Street toward the Hudson, then walked onto a long cement pier. A man passed, checking Green out, grinning as if to say, I love the office-boy look. He was a muscled specimen in Lycra shorts and a net T-shirt; his hair was close-cropped, his face smooth-shaven. Why, Green wondered, had this man lived—even thrived—while so many others had died? Maybe he hadn't been promiscuous, or had always used condoms. Or maybe there was such a thing as a survivor's genetic code, part physical and part mental, but innate, like the gift for music or languages.

At the end of the pier Bonnie sat, her legs dangling over the water. "I can tell about my year," she said, "but it won't make sense if I just give dates and places. I have to tell you where my head was.

"First, after we broke up. That killed me."

"So why did you go, then?"

She sighed. "You remember I used to say, all I wanted was to be loved? But you didn't love me."

"I . . . !"

"You *didn't*. Maybe I wasn't smart enough, or I was too wild, or maybe you had issues with me being a shiksa."

"My parents—"

"Not them! You! You. Well, if you know me at all, you know I can't bear emotional rejection. So I had to get out. I left that note about our sex life, which—I didn't mean to hurt you, but I needed something concrete to convey that we had deep problems. And to me that was a symptom."

"You were right. I can't believe I was so—"

"But it wasn't just your fault. There were so many levels, and it's not— What little sex I've had since then, I haven't. . . ." She fished a cigarette from her shirt pocket.

"So I tried to enjoy working at the soap, but I'd get depressed and drink. You must've realized I had a problem with booze. Anyway, I decided I wanted to try again with you, and that's when I found you already had someone. Which I wasn't surprised, but it still hurt."

She took a drag. "Right after that I went home for Thanksgiving, and all my hostility toward my parents exploded. There was this actually physically violent scene between me and my mother, where she slapped me and I yanked her hair and threw her down." She smiled weakly. "Of course, she was the usual model of rationality, saying that living in Sodom—New York, that is—had perverted my mind, and she'd pray for me.

"That trip shook me badly, and I started doing coke with the Monroe scum and taking pills. I guess I still had some instinct for self-preservation, because after a while I knew I was getting in real trouble and decided to leave New York. I'd been to St. Croix as a kid, and it stuck in my mind as a paradise. That part I told you about."

"Then you went to Paris. Why there?"

"I'd always dreamt of it. I thought it'd be *Breathless*—everyone cool and smoking like Belmondo? I didn't know a soul, but I found a whole scene down in the Metro—musicians, runaways. Some of these kids live there and hardly ever come aboveground. Not much like *Breathless*, except for the smoking.

"I speak high school French, and I guess it sounded cute in my accent, so they let me hang out with them. I had a room in this dump that made the Monroe look like the Pierre. Then I met a runaway named Sylvie and let her stay with me."

"What was she like?"

"Seventeen. Funny, a real clown. But *mon Dieu*, she had problems. When I met her, she'd just kicked heroin, and I thought I could help. We slept in one bed like orphans. When my money ran out, I sold most of my clothes. We started panhandling and scrounging for food. The best was people's scraps at Free Time; that's their McDonald's. You get a sense for who's gonna leave the biggest piece of burger, and you sit nearby and wait.

"Lemme tell you, go hungry for even a week and it changes you forever. That's what your father said at dinner, and he was right. I'll never walk by a homeless person again without thinking. This could be me. Shit, this *was* me."

The river was now dark, though the horizon was bright orange and streaked with nimbus clouds. A breeze kicked up off the water. Bonnie wrapped her arms around herself, and Green shivered. "Gettin' chilly."

Back in the Slatkin apartment, she switched on a wicker lamp beside the couch. He watched her smoke, picturing her digging crusts from the Paris garbage, maybe at the exact moment he was lifting his fork across from a client at Le Cygne. Some year they'd had. "You didn't finish your story. You were the toast of Paris . . ."

"I found a temp job at an American company, as a receptionist—major career advancement, Bonnie. Then I caught Sylvie stealing from me to buy drugs, so I threw her out. By then I'd been in France two months and was already sick of it, hard as that is to believe. The Parisians are annoying. Even the winos think they're hot shit, drinking Bordeaux from a bottle with a *cork*. So I flew back here in March, and I got work waitressing at a restaurant in SoHo called Jack and the Bean Sprout."

She puffed. "'Jack,' as you might guess, is gay, as are most of the waiters. They all love me. They say I have a 'Judy quality,' ha-ha. Anyway, Jack found me a teensy apartment on Prince Street, over a bakery. Like you smell rolls day and night; all your *clothes* smell like rolls. And things seemed great for a few weeks. But I was lonely. Then my mood started to turn. I felt it coming, just couldn't stop it.

"I started drinking again. I'd go to this dive on Spring, at first for a beer, but soon to get plastered. There were some regulars, like the *Cheers* gang, except with nothing even vaguely cheery about them. Just sad fucking drunks. Finally I went on this two-day bender, woke up on my floor, all bruised—I didn't even know what from! For all I knew I might've brought home some freak who hit me." Green flinched; this was becoming agony to hear.

Noticing his expression, she said, "Try and imagine something. I know it'll be hard for you, who's such a godlike figure to his parents, but try and imagine how it feels to believe you have no value as a person. That you don't deserve the shittiest little scrap of happiness. 'Cause that's how I felt while we were living together, and for most of the time since then. And that feeling puts you in incredible danger. Do you understand?"

"I think so."

"Well, I don't know what would've happened to me, but Jack saved my life—checked me into the hospital, where a psychiatrist put me on lithium. Know what that is?"

"I've heard of it."

"It keeps me from going on self-destructive binges. Like, you know I was always accident-prone. I used to burn myself, or I've had maybe five car accidents. Or before I came to stay with you, when I jumped off the roof."

Green gasped. "I thought you fell! Hanging an antenna. That's what you said."

"I *said*. I said anything. Fuck, maybe I even believed that's what happened. Didn't you think it was strange?"

He shook his head. "I didn't know."

"Or when we lived together, how I'd disappear at night. I knew I was hurting you, and a relationship I cared about, but I couldn't help it! Then it was the same shit with the guy in St. Croix . . . until you ask, 'What the fuck is wrong with me?'" Her fingertips were pressing into her chest. "Anyway, with the lithium I feel more in control."

"I'm really sorry. It does sound bad. Wow."

"Well, but things're improving. I'm also in therapy, and trying to work out my feelings toward my parents."

"How is that?"

"Hard." She looked at him for some time. "Lotta real bad memories are coming out."

Had they beaten her? "I'm sorry," he said, unable to think of anything else.

She stubbed her cigarette, then kept stubbing until it was crushed down to the filter. She glanced at him, started to speak, then stopped and shook her head. Then they nodded quietly at each other for a while, until he asked, "Are you still waitressing?"

"Yeah, but Chip suggested I take a few days off and stay here. He thought the quiet would help me decide what to do with myself. I might go back to school. Or maybe give acting a serious try."

Green noticed his watch: eight o'clock! By now he should've been sending the Lee prospectus to word processing.

"A problem?"

"I have to get back to work." He slung his tie around his neck.

"I wish you could stay longer. I've been talking nonstop, and I haven't even heard anything about you."

"But I can't. I'm on a deadline."

"How 'bout dinner? You've gotta eat." He frowned. "Please. I hate to eat by myself." She looked pathetic. And hearing her story had at least gotten his mind off Alfieri. Alfieri: The name alone set his insides rippling.

In the open, wood-floored kitchen were ferns and copper pots hanging on hooks, a long rack of exotic spices, and a shelf of old, stained international cookbooks. Bonnie assembled the ingredients for pasta primavera, then uncorked a bottle of Chianti. "For you," she said.

He leaned against the counter, fooling with a carrot shaver. "I never realized your hair wasn't naturally blond."

She hooted. "Didn't you notice the colors didn't match?" He shrugged, blushing. "I dyed it back to its real shade last month. Y'know, when you're a blonde in New York you stand out, so men hit on you constantly. And I just needed to be anonymous a while. I also started eating like a madwoman. Hey, seems we were having a contest." She poked his belly, her finger sinking in to the first joint. "Anyway here I am, mousy and fat."

"You're not."

"What am I bid for this heifer? Do I hear fifty?"

They ate at a table in a corner of the living room. Outside, the branches whipped around, and raindrops pattered on the leaves. Bonnie asked about his year.

"Well, I learned a lot." He told of the Lee LBO, automatically emphasizing his own role, and then, almost in passing, of the company's recent troubles.

"That's horrible. Holeville depended on the mill."

"Well, the theory is, in the long run the best thing for the workers is to lose these rust-belt jobs. Then high-tech businesses replace them, and they can learn modern skills."

"Who'd put a high-tech business in that shithole? *Lee* was only there 'cause it's near the old plantation. No, without the mill, that town is dead and buried."

"Maybe." He spun some linguine around his fork, sensing her eyes on him, ashamed. "I'm just a lawyer, Bonnie. It's not as if I told Lee to—"

"I know you didn't!" She paused. "Anyway, you still haven't said if you like your job."

"Yes, I do. The money's been great." He had an urge to tell about his bonus, but it would seem boastful. Also, she might touch him for a never-to-be-repaid loan. "And they treat you well. I fly first-class—"

"You know, you always talk about money or the perks, but never your actual work. Is it satisfying?"

"Sure."

"You don't sound very enthusiastic. Tell me what you do, like minute to minute. You go to your desk, and then what? Drink coffee all day and fart? What?"

He envisioned himself marking up documents for hours on end, an expanding lump of flesh in an ergonomic chair. "Well, deals. For example, I just helped sell Angel Face Cosmetics."

"Angel Face? Wow, that takes me back to the mall."

"There were some tough negotiation issues, like an inventory thing. . . ." His voice trailed off. Should he tell about battling over points? Storming out of conference rooms? Badgering and "fucking" other lawyers? Compared to Bonnie's struggles this year, his seemed truly petty.

He sipped his wine. "Frankly, nothing has worked out the way I planned."

"Tell me about it," she said, her face close to his.

Without her glasses, smiling in the lamplight, she'd transformed herself hack into the flirty receptionist who had shaken his world. There was activity in his loins. "Sometimes I think about the start of law school. The thrill when I opened my first book." It had been the torts text, navy blue with gold lettering, paper-cut pages, and heavy as a bowling ball.

"With books like these, I thought, how could I do anything but good? But the minute I began practicing, it all got twisted up. That's why—I'll bet that's why so many lawyers end up committing crimes. And not just lawyers: bankers, accountants . . . anyone who makes a career out of bending the rules."

"If you feel so strongly, why don't you quit? Get into public interest, like you used to say?"

"I might. I've had this idea about joining the U.S. Attorney's office." He flashed on Sterling, of Central Park West, Tom Seaver, and Ping-Pong, and all at once had a powerful desire to trust in him, a boy from his own world who'd made a life separating right from wrong. What was he doing, throwing his lot in with Alfieri? Entrusting his future to an amoral criminal?

Bonnie touched the back of his hand, then laced her fingers with his, saying, "I'm happy to hear you talk like this. I knew you'd make a difference one day. But what'll your fiancée think of the salary cut?"

He thought, with guilt, of Shelly, who had stuck by him without question or complaint; this wasn't how you repaid that kind of loyalty. He withdrew his hand, which flitted around the table, then came to rest in his lap.

"You said 'nice' and 'Jewish' weren't strong enough words for her. What did you mean?"

"Oh, she's—" He stopped, gesturing. It felt wrong, discussing her with Bonnie.

"I'm sorry I made fun before. I really am interested."

He exhaled. "She's a warm, caring person. Also, you know, religious." Bonnie smiled as if in charmed disbelief, an idea formed, and she clucked her tongue. "*You* wouldn't have become religious, would you, Rick?"

"I have been going to temple, yes." His cheeks warmed. "But religious? That depends on how you define it."

"I can define it easy. Belief in God, to begin with. Do you?" He nodded. "Uh-huh, as I suspected. Then there's rituals. You eat kosher food? Wear a beanie?"

"You can laugh at it."

"I'm not! I apologize. It just overwhelmed me. You of all people. Fievel's boy."

"I know. But it's less religious than . . . cultural. And the community aspect. Honestly, it's been mostly for Shelly." He saw himself beside her in shul, chanting and swaying; and now she turned to him, her face a story of betrayal.

"Is God to you a man in a white robe with a beard?"

"Please, can we not—? I have nothing else to say."

"Touchy . . . but of course that's the way."

Setting a candle on the coffee table, Bonnie curled up beside Green on the couch. "Weird year," he said, then closed his eyes, listening to the drizzle. When he awoke, the candle had gone out. "Bonnie," he whispered, shaking her. She jumped, emitting a cry, then fumbled for the lamp.

It was almost eleven, so there was no point in returning to the office. Anyway, he felt pretty drunk. "I have to go home." He tried to push himself up, but sank back.

"Why don't you stay here?"

He shook his head. "It's not . . . good."

She was hurt. "We're friends, aren't we? All that other stuff is history. You're bombed, and look what's happening outside." The drizzle had become torrential rain. "You can stay in the guest room."

She was probably right, he thought. Instead of a long ride uptown, he'd go to sleep, then wake early and head straight to work. Also, he was safe from Alfieri here. Not to get unduly paranoid, but it seemed somehow that the arb could read his thoughts, and knew when he was weakening. The first time, he'd sent Petey in his Porsche. This time, who? A leg breaker?

After finger brushing his teeth, Green went in his room—which had a creaky bed with an orange spread and on the walls more Casals memorabilia and two paintings of Montmartre—and slid under the covers. Soon Bonnie appeared, wearing an oversize Vanderbilt T-shirt. "'Night, John-Boy," she said, and shut the lights.

He woke again when a thunderclap shook the house. The tree outside waved. There was a flash of lightning so near he could hear its buzz, then another crack, like a giant egg breaking overhead. A spray of rain hit the window, as if a mischief-making kid were on the sidewalk with a hose. Green let his head drop back on the pillow.

The door opened, and Bonnie's naked shape moved across the room. Green pretended to be asleep as she crawled in bed. At the next flash and crack, she hid her face in his neck. "I'm scared." He didn't breathe. "Can you hold me?" She burrowed so that his arm was around her, then lay her head on his shoulder.

She whispered, "I always hoped we could be like this again, even for one night."

He still hadn't acknowledged he was awake. It struck him that he could let out a snore and stop this; but he felt the same powerful attraction as before, mixed with sympathy now. She'd been through so much, and all she was asking for was a bit of affection. Would it be *so* awful?

He pecked her cheek. She gripped the back of his head, sliding her lips against his, then pressed her body to his side, murmuring, "Hug me tighter." He got his arms around her plump body and saw her brown hair on the pillow; an erection sprang up. She raised her leg and moved to position him between her thighs, then shifted again and moaned. But he pulled back.

She opened her eyes. "What's the matter?"

"I can't."

"Why? This time I thought we—I really felt we were gonna get it together."

"It's Shelly, though."

"I promise, I'm not trying to steal you back. She'll never know."

"That isn't the problem. I just—I'd be hurting *myself*. How can I explain it?"

She sighed, and they leaned their foreheads together. "I admit," she said, "I do have feelings for you still."

"Me too. That'd make it even worse."

She sat up. "I want you to understand that I didn't mean to make you act sleazy. In my mind, this was between us. It was private, unfinished business."

He got up on an elbow. "We didn't have any unfinished business."

"We did, though. See, I really did love you when we were together, and it hurt to think of you remembering me as this horrible woman. I needed you to know why I acted how I did. Then I thought if we made love, maybe it'd be like closing the book on us, in a happier way."

"I don't think it could be that simple."

"You're probably right." She pulled up the covers. "But at least I got to explain myself, and now it's like a burden has been lifted off my conscience. And lemme tell you from experience: Until you clear your conscience, life is hell."

"I know what you're saying, because I— Because I'm going through it."

"What do you mean?" She sounded intrigued, not malicious at all, but ready, even eager, for a dark tale concerning the good boy. And he wanted her to hear it.

# Chapter 14

Facing Bonnie cross-legged on the bed, Green had just told a story, as close to the truth as he could extract from his confused memory. "I want to make the right decision, but—" He shook his head, then looked out at Grove Street, glowing blue. "What would you do if you were me?"

"I don't know, jump out a window? My traditional reaction to stress." She flicked her ash in a Dixie Cup. "Y'know, you're really putting me on the spot. I don't wanna be responsible."

"Please, just say what you think."

"Well, like I was telling you, you can't *buy* a clear conscience."

"Clear, yeah, but Bonnie, what did I even do that was so wrong? Nothing that hasn't been going on in the market for years! I'm some little schmuck who made a drunken mistake, who didn't even take the money, and I'm the one who gets ruined?"

She nodded slowly. "I hear your words, but your vibe says something different. To me you seem tortured with guilt."

"Well, I swing back and forth. Because I see what other people do."

"Can you forget about other people for a minute, and just look at yourself?"

"Okay, myself then. Sometimes I think—it all fades away. You feel guilty, a month passes and it's less, and after a year? Nothing."

"Maybe in your conscious mind. But as my therapist says, everything you do becomes a part of you." She took a drag, then waved her hand. "Let's say hypothetically you manage to lie your way out of this. Would it really end here? Or the next time you get in trouble, won't lying just come easier? And then what kind of person will you end up, in ten years? A burned-out, corrupted lawyer."

Yeah, fine, he thought, "corrupted," but earning a million dollars, with a Park Avenue co-op and a country place. Going to Crank partner morning meetings, where they'd eat croissants while discussing the fees; maybe taking a young superstar under his wing, as Lou had taken him. Enjoying his status, as the guy who'd brought in the Alfieri business.

And what *about* Alfieri? Now, as Green pictured those merciless eyes, sweat beads popped out on his forehead. "What about Alfieri? I don't wanna overreact, but I could be putting myself in, in danger!"

"He's a businessman! You think—?"

"So was Al Capone! So is everyone a businessman! Do you have any idea what people these arbs are? If you could've seen him when we met. . . ." He shook his head. "Told me he'd just been to Italy. What for? Maybe to meet his Mafia contacts, how the hell do I know? Said he has 'vendettas' against his enemies." Bonnie couldn't hide a smile. "It's not funny!"

"Sorry. But you're all worked up over probably nothing. I refuse to believe we're discussing physical violence." Green began to object, and she suggested he take some deep breaths. He did, thinking that she was right. The shit was definitely flying now, and he had to keep his head.

"Okay, Bonnie, let's assume, um, um—arguendo—that I won't get whacked. What are the consequences of confessing?"

"You'd be sweeping out all the shit, for one. Then you could start over."

"True." If only he could start over! If only Stu Sterling would help. The spirit he'd seen flowing between the prosecutors! He'd have less money, but how much did he need, really, to be happy? His parents had never had any, and—well, bad example. But there *were* happy poor families, certainly.

His ID card would read: Assistant U.S. Attorney Green. "Good morning, ladies and gentlemen of the jury, Rick Green for the United States of America." AUSAs became judges, politicians. Sure, it might sound preposterous that Sterling would hire him, but stranger things had happened. He'd definitely be an asset, having seen securities crime from the inside.

"The hardest part of this," Bonnie said, "is Rosen. You're gonna destroy him. But I can't figure how to avoid it."

"I know. He might save himself, though, if he gives up his boss. The problem is he's easily influenced, and right now Alfieri has him hypnotized. I honestly think he'd be better off out from under that guy." He'd be better off, Green repeated to himself, leaning back in bed. Petey might even thank him someday.

"I see all the pros, Bonnie. The problem is, I'm not sure how the prosecutors would treat me or my father or Rosen. All I can do is speculate."

Bonnie had a brainstorm then. "How 'bout you call this prosecutor? Feel him out? Without admitting anything, you know."

"Oh, forget that." Survivor genes or no, such a call required savvy far beyond any he had ever displayed. Because, in fact, he wasn't too smart. It felt extraordinary—a strangely odd relief—to grasp that his brain lacked whatever connectors were necessary to predict the sequence of events in the world. He was a baby floating downstream in a basket.


After a dazed shower he got back into his suit, feeling like a knight preparing to return to battle. Outside, the city was another sunbath, and a breeze blew along Grove. Bonnie faced him at the top of the stoop. "I wanna say, I'm proud of you. I think you've become a real . . . person since last year. And you're going in the right direction."

"Trying."

"Just stay strong. I know you can. I'll be—" She smiled. "I won't say I'll pray for you. How 'bout I go and make a pagan offering to the river gods?"

"Thanks. Also for your advice. And good luck to you too. I know you'll. . . ." They hugged goodbye, and at Seventh Avenue he turned to find her, waving to him in the bright breeze.

He wandered uptown, unsure where he was going. Back to the office? Home? Maybe he should head down to see Swensen, but what for? The information he needed to make this decision was not in her possession, but Sterling's. If only he could call Stu! Overcome with the urge to trust in the prosecutor's compassion, he stepped to a phone booth at the corner of Sheridan Square, beneath a huge billboard for gay cruises.

He'd punched six of the digits on Sterling's business card before hanging up. He was supposed to clear this first with Helen. To explain his need to contact Stu, however, he'd have to confess to her, and that he could not do. Anyway, how would he convince her that this was a sensible move? Would she comprehend the natural bond that formed between two West Side boys?

Glad to hear Green's voice, Sterling asked how he was doing. "I'm fine. How are you?"

"Fine. Working hard. Are you calling from outside?"

"Yes."

"Oh." Sterling seemed to find this fact important. "Anyway, working hard, though I did manage to catch the last inning of the Mets game last night. See it?"

"No. Who was, was Gooden—?"

"Got knocked out early."

"Didn't see." Green coughed. "So I'm calling with a very strange question. You may even laugh."

"Does this have anything to do with your case? Because if so, you should communicate only through Helen Swensen."

"It doesn't relate—well, sort of indirectly. Maybe I'll start and if you think—I'll stop, if it's too much about the thing. The case."

Sterling paused. "Go ahead."

"Watching you work, seeing what—I'm very interested in the U.S. Attorney. Especially your division. So I've been thinking of changing career paths, from corporate law to something I'd find more satisfying."

"Well, with your resume, you'd have an excellent shot."

"Really? Yeah, I suppose. But contacts are—"

"Aha. I don't know how much juice I have, but I'd be happy to put in a good word."

"What worried me, though, with this investigation, there's an *appearance* of impropriety between me and Rosen. And if things should somehow. . . ." As his voice trailed off, Green heard a knowing intake of breath on Sterling's end, then gripped his forehead. What was he doing on this call? It had been insanity! But it was too late. He had to get through it now.

They were quiet then, listening to each other think, until Sterling said in a careful tone, "I hear you. Obviously people who've run afoul of the law, whatever the circumstances, would have trouble getting a prosecutor job."

"Of course."

"But then there's gradations of guilt. When we talk about blatant violators or when we talk about people who were duped, or inadvertently—"

"Not that I'm in any way saying—"

"I understand. All I can tell you is, if we were to work together on Alfieri, I'd consider you my colleague."

Green mopped his brow. "Stu, that's—I'm very appreciative." He felt his mind going blank. "Speaking of Alfieri, let me ask, because I admit I'm a little nervous. What do you know about him, and any— what's the word—connections to organized crime?"

Sterling paused a full five seconds before saying, "This is completely confidential." Then he hesitated. "Y'know, maybe your lawyer should be involved. I can't be going into all this."

But Green had to hear, and immediately. "I waive! I waive the right to counsel. Tell me!"

"Okay. Alfieri's a bad guy. What he's into, you don't want to know. Your lawyer doesn't know; even your friend Rosen probably doesn't. But I do. And let me put it this way, without rattling you: You'll be better off when he's in prison. Because if you had information about him, you'd never feel safe. But if you were to talk to us, you'd come under our protection." Under their protection, Green thought. He wanted to be under somebody's protection.

"But see, Alfieri's not crazy, either. After you told what you knew, he'd wash his hands of you. Because what reason could he have to hurt you then? Revenge? That'd be irrational. And if there's one thing he is, it's rational." Green's head drooped against the booth's perforated metal canopy. So it hadn't been paranoia; he was in danger. Or was Stu bullshitting?

"Still there, Rick?"

"Yes. But I should probably get going, because I'm on the way to work."

"Okay."

"Thanks again." Leaving a damp handprint on the receiver. Green staggered back into the sun. How much more could his heart stand? That was the deeper issue. A block farther on, he leaned against the window of a surgical supply store, too weary to continue. He passed his eyes over the trusses, elastic stockings, the portable commodes and other invalid needs, and thought: Here were the real problems. Here was the sickness, discomfort, impending death. But Green was absurdly healthy, he had to keep living, and living required you to organize and consider your options. Alfieri, Rosen, Sterling. . . . Which one was lying, or were they all? And how did Fievel fit in? It was a five-way chess game, impossibly complex. Still, he'd drifted as far as possible, and right now, leaning against this window, he had to choose a course of action. More than that, he had to decide who he wanted to *be*. Because it struck him that Bonnie's therapist was right. The questions were, after all, inseparable.

Seen in this light, everything seemed clearer. Who was honest; who was his friend and who his enemy; all the possible moves and countermoves—none of that mattered. All the crimes in the history of the stock market didn't matter. Everything reduced to the simple question: Did he or did he not want to be a mensch?


Swensen stood at her desk, the harbor sweeping wide and glittery behind. "I tried to reach you all yesterday!"

"Sorry, I didn't get your message."

"I was worried. Though nothing new is happening. But what brings you down here?"

"Oh." Heart bouncing around his chest, he lowered himself gingerly into a chair. "Helen. Remember that, um, that hypothetical you gave last week? About me, me—me making a deal with the government? To testify against Alfieri? Would that still be possible?"

A shadow passed over her face. "I'd have to call Sterling and see."

"Because I—"

"Wait, first. I've advised you to come forward. But I want to be sure you know the consequences." She centered a sheet of paper on her blotter, then went on, "It's hard to say without hearing exactly what you have to tell them, but assuming it's more or less what they implied, you may be talking about pleading to a felony. Even if, best-case, the U.S. Attorney needs you so bad that I can get you probation, there'd still be an SEC settlement: fines and penalties."

"Well, as to how bad they need me. . . ." He confessed: "I spoke to Sterling."

"Did he call you?!"

"No, I did. I didn't admit anything! I was just feeling him out."

Swensen rapped a pack of Marlboros against her knuckles. "I can't believe you went around me! That was so dumb. And you of all people."

"I know. I'm sorry."

"If I'm going to keep representing you, you'll have to deal exclusively through me."

"You wouldn't drop me?" He hadn't considered losing her, and that seemed an utter disaster now. "I need you."

"Okay, but no more . . . behind my back. And like I told you, you can't trust Sterling! Tell me the precise substance of your conversation with him."

"Uh-huh. Maybe you should finish what you were saying, about the consequences, before . . ."

She nodded. "I'd do everything to keep you out of prison, but otherwise, you'd get hammered."

Green thought. "I understand, but let's see what deal we can get. Here's the information I've got to offer."

Then he told the truth, beginning with the night of his first tip. "But Rosen wasn't satisfied. I was vulnerable. My girlfriend had left me, and I was depressed, maybe *clinically*. I was also drinking a lot. So he worked on me, saying he was the only person who cared, that kind of stuff. Till finally I gave him the Bolus merger."

Swensen jotted on a yellow pad, balanced on her crossed knee. "Then in early September I tipped him on Orem Petroleum, a hostile takeover. Why I did, I can't say. I still wasn't in my right mind, I guess. Anyway, a few weeks later I told him to leave me alone, and that was the end."

Swensen leaned back, eyes closed, figuring. Green said, "I hope you're not too mad that I misled you."

"What I'm mad about is that you thought you were smarter than me. But you know and I know that I'm stuck with you." She jerked forward in her chair. "Just don't lie to me anymore."

"I swear!" He paused. "You should be aware that when I lied I was out of my mind with terror for Alfieri. How did I know what criminal ties he had? I thought I'd end up in a car trunk!" Green waited for Swensen's agreement, but she just tilted her head skeptically. "He's a dangerous character! And Sterling confirmed it. He said they'd protect me if I testify."

"They'd *protect* you? That little unethical shit. I should get him reprimanded." Swensen lit up. "Anyway, as to Alfieri, what is the basis of your fear? Other than his being Italian."

"It's not that! The basis is, I've met him! I shiver every time I think of the eyes. They're like—"

"You met him? When?"

Green described their Japanese breakfast. "You see the veiled threat?"

She shrugged. "I'm sorry, it's as if you were telling me Bruce Wasserstein took out a contract on you. But let's put the danger aside for a minute, so we don't get confused. I haven't even asked about the money. How much did you get?"

Green nodded vigorously. "Yes, that's important. Alfieri set up an offshore account with my so-called trading profits? But I disavowed it without ever taking a penny. I told them to give it to charity. I don't even know what was in it."

"That helps." She marked it on her pad. "Remind me: Have you spoken to Rosen lately?"

"A couple of times."

"Well, don't talk to him again. They may want you to record a conversation." Green's mind flashed with movie images involving spaghetti, red-checked tablecloths, and Alfieri with a gun, splattering brains against a wall.

"Are you serious?"

"This is all serious," Swensen explained.

Green licked his lips. "Now. About my father."

"Yes." Swensen sighed, flipping to a new page. His crimes were filling an entire pad.

"Let's say I'd tipped him on Lee, too. Could I get a deal that covered him?"

"Oh, I can't. . . . He needs his own lawyer."

"Okay. But I'm telling you, I can't see myself testifying unless he's protected." He leaned over. "Listen. He's a Holocaust survivor. He's sixty-three, or sixty-four years old. Mentally he's not the most stable. What do they want, to put him in jail?"

"I can't make deals for your father. And I'm not sure it's wise to tie your deal—"

"I understand, but. . . ." He rubbed his chin. "All right, first just see what deal I can get. But would you at least get a sense—?"

"Yes. I should be able to tell how tough the government's going to be. Meanwhile, I'll find your father an attorney." She paused. "Before you get your hopes up, I should say that prosecutors don't have the warmest feelings for families who lie to their faces. It's called obstruction of justice."

"I know. But you'll explain how Alfieri threatened me. Won't that help? And as for my father, can they blame him for protecting his only son?"

Swensen appeared to grin, frown, nod, and shake her head all at once. As if to say, Rick, you are too much. "I'll need to hear this in more detail, but speed is key, and I have enough to approach Sterling. Go to your office and I'll call you later. Until then, keep your fingers crossed."

Thomas, Peel's silent, white marble reception area had a direct view of the Statue of Liberty. Green imagined Fievel and Rachel—and Swensen's ancestors, and Alfieri's, and Mandel's—getting their first heart-lifting glimpse, and how it must have felt. The land of opportunity.

.   .   .

Rosa gave an annoyed gum snap. "Mandel's been after you since yesterday. I thought he might fire me. He wants to know, 'Where is the bed-and-bath book?' Also, yesterday Rosen called and said it was urgent. I always meant to ask you, why does he use the name 'Richie Hebner'?" Petey the spymaster, Green thought, unmasked by a secretary in two seconds.

The Lee prospectus lay on his desk where he'd left it, his red markings cutting off halfway down the page. His career as a corporate lawyer had ended in mid-sentence. He stuck it in an interoffice envelope addressed to Lou.

There was nothing to do now but wait, and nowhere quiet to do it but his usual toilet stall. He read the *Journal*, then spent an hour remembering baseball stats, counting tiles, anything to occupy his mind. At one point he held his face in his hands, suddenly feeling watched—haunted—by Fievel. Father and son, he thought.

He returned to his office, closed the door, and stared out the window at taxis, Dial-Cars, limos—up and back, around and around—an ant farm. A young man with a briefcase tore across Park, yellow tie flapping, late for a meeting. Probably thought it was the end of the world.

When the call finally came, the first thing Helen said was, "You're a lucky guy. They must be more desperate than we thought. Sterling has to see his boss, but my sense is I can get you a great deal. We were talking in terms of criminal immunity."

"Thank God!" He closed his eyes as he absorbed the news. Thank God, thank God. "That's so great!"

"By the way, they want you to resign from the firm, and that's non-negotiable. They were adamant."

"Adamant? I mean, not that I thought I could stay, but why do they care so much? Like I'd be spreading some disease around here?"

"It's just the way it is."

Green wanted to debate the issue more, but there was no point in pressing Helen. Whatever happened, he was finished at Crank. "So," she said, "would you accept that deal?"

"Of course." He reflected, then realized: "Wait! Sorry to complicate matters, but see, my father and I. . . ." They were a package. That was the only way it could be.

"Yes," she said. "My gut is that Sterling will have no interest in prosecuting him. And the SEC should settle charges as long as the investment club disgorges its profits. They'll have to pay a penalty." There went the pensions, Green thought, the measly savings, down the toilet. Some Robin Hood he'd turned out. "Okay. But you must know one thing, Helen. I won't make a final deal until I know for sure that my father is safe. I'll go to prison first, I swear it!"

"I understand."

"When will Sterling want my testimony?"

"First we have to reach agreement with the SEC. I've already spoken to Byrne on a preliminary basis. Obviously they'll seize whatever's in your Alfieri account. Also, he'll want a list of your assets and liabilities."

"That's easy enough. I have no liabilities. My assets are a savings account with approximately $19,750, a bed, two TVs, and a few suits. Cheap ones, from Moe Ginsburg. Oh, and my baseball cards. I've got a Tom Seaver rookie, mint condition."

Swensen didn't laugh. "These SEC agreements can take time, but if that's all you have, I think I should wrap something up by the end of the week. And write down this name: Peter Tasch at Elfman, Winkelman. Your father needs counsel, and he's good.

"I guess that's it for now. By the way, Lou Mandel has been trying to reach me, and I've been ducking him. You ought to go in and inform him and Bernie Shapiro, personally, what's going on. Of course, tell them it's still confidential."

"Okay. And Helen, I don't know how to thank you."

"You're welcome . . . though you don't have to thank me. You don't even have to thank God. You saved yourself."


The walk to Shapiro's office seemed eternal. Green's feet dragged along the carpet's nap as through quicksand, and his shoulders were rounded and aching. He stopped at the fountain for a drink, but his parched mouth soaked up all moisture and left him still thirsty.

Mandel and Shapiro were sitting at the big square table. Green lowered himself into a chair, slowly, like a geriatric. Shapiro waited for him to speak, clearly aware what was coming. Mandel, however, hadn't given up hope, his blunt face expectant, fairly anxious. Green unpeeled his lips and began. "Helen Swensen," his voice breaking like a bar-mitzvah boy's. "May I?" He lifted a heavy crystal water pitcher and tried to pour, but his hand shook so violently that he put it back, afraid to do damage.

Dark spots appeared before his eyes as he continued. "Helen is negotiating an agreement with the U.S. Attorney, which is likely to provide that I'll, I'll testify, under immunity, about passing inside information to Vince Alfieri. It's the best way to. . . . It's best."

"But what," Mandel said, tugging at his collar. "It was unwitting. Your friend duped you, tricked you, right?"

"At first."

"There was more than Lee?"

"Bolus and also Orem."

Mandel was stricken. "I can't believe it." Shaking his head, he repeated, "I can't believe it." Green glanced at Shapiro, whose expression was blank. He could believe it.

"I'm sorry. I can't tell you! I was in a horrible state. I was clinically depressed, and drinking." He implored Mandel: "Remember how hard I worked on Lee? It was my first deal, and the pressure . . . I guess I cracked." Tears welled in his eyes. He fought them, but they spilled onto his cheeks.

"I want you to know that I never took any money. It wasn't for money that I did it. It was—I don't know. I don't know what was happening in my brain. I think I may've been—"

Shapiro cut short Green's soul-searching. "Have you reached an agreement with the SEC?"

He wiped his face and sniffled. "Not yet. There'll be a settlement, but I don't have many assets, so. . . ." He brushed his pant legs, trying to smile. "I have a baseball card." But they didn't know what he was talking about, so he just shrugged.

"And they say I have to resign, so I guess I should go now. I mean, today." Mandel's cheeks were red with fury, his eyes glazed. Shapiro, however, seemed calm and, though he barely knew Green, stung; for him, Green later understood, the worst part was the sight of a young attorney, one who'd already functioned competently alongside a Mandel, losing the chance to develop his craft.

When Shapiro began to speak, Green prepared for a lecture, dispassionately delivered, about the lawyer's role in society, and good and evil and betrayal. "You'll need money to live on. And for your legal fees. We'll pay you through the end of the month and give you three months' severance. Will that help?"

"Oh, that's so. . . ." He couldn't finish, covering his face. Shapiro's humane gesture had rendered him conscious, suddenly, of the reality of this moment. How could he have ended up here? It was too crazy to believe.

"Are you all right?" Shapiro asked. "Maybe someone, a family member, should come get you."

"No," Green said, dabbing his eyes again. "I really am okay. I was just grateful."

Unwilling to engage in an emotional exchange, Shapiro glanced away. "I assume your deal is confidential, so nothing will leave this room. Until it's public, we'll tell people you're taking a medical leave of absence."

"What about my matters?"

"Leave the files in your office, and we'll reassign them." Green felt a jealous twinge at the thought of his clients being distributed among the other associates.

"Lou, I got two-thirds through bed-and-bath. I sent you what I've done so far." Mandel nodded once, examining his fingernails. Shapiro's attention drifted to the stock prices glowing on his Quotron, and interest flickered across his face. What did he see? Was a client in play? Green might've worked on the defense if. . . . But that future had been canceled.

He felt himself slipping into a dream; snapping awake, he sensed it was time to leave. He'd hoped that Mandel would first offer some expression of sympathy, some suggestion that he understood, *something*. But all Lou had for him was silent contempt.

He saw that, yet couldn't let it alone. "Before I go, Lou, I want to thank you." Mandel still refused to look at him. "And to say how sorry I am. I can't justify it, except—" He was about to repeat that he'd been clinically depressed, and drinking, but he had grown weary of his own excuses. Instead he said, "My behavior was unforgivable." Mandel studied Shapiro's bookshelf, his lips pursed in an angry little "O." And that was all there was going to be, Green knew, and all he deserved: that angry little O.

Reeling out to the hall, he held the wall for support. *That* was more fun than a day at Monticello Raceway, he was thinking as a hand clapped his back. Hal Wishner, the dumb, detested M & A partner, said, "Y'okay? I've been meaning to catch you about a new deal. I'd like to work with you."

Green licked his lips. "Sure. Catch me later." Wishner continued on his way, whistling through his teeth.

Downstairs, Rosa handed him a message from Shelly. "She's really upset. That's how you treat your fianceé?"

He filled with apprehension. Since last night he'd managed to put Shelly out of his mind. He knew it was wrong not to tell her of his decision, but he just wasn't prepared for the pain and disappointment when she discovered that he was, after all, a felon. And why worry her needlessly, before the deal was even final? In a few days he'd see her and say, "This is it, and where do we go from here?" Now he had to stall.

He began to shout the moment she answered. "Sorry I vanished yesterday! I got stuck negotiating!"

She sounded somewhat annoyed, but mainly concerned. Uncontrolled rage was not in her emotional paintbox. "I'm seriously getting worried about you. Tonight we should have a long talk about . . . I don't know. Stuff."

"I wish I could, but I have to go out of town on business till Friday." That was inspiration.

"But that's sick, with your situation! And what about me? Can't my feelings be considered for once?"

Guilt, the crazed Jewish ax murderer, hacked at his chest. "Please, Shel, just hang on till Friday. Then everything will be resolved. Don't worry! I'll be fine!"

After a minute she was pacified. "I told my mother to postpone the wedding."

"What reason did you come up with?"

"The truth," she replied, her tone startling to Green; she had so casually chosen honesty, an element that now seemed as rare and unstable as plutonium.

He pictured the Feldmans absorbing the news that their daughter's intended was under suspicion. What a letdown! Especially after their initial delight at a Harvard son-in-law. (To celebrate, Marv and Ruth had flown in and taken them to dinner at Lutece, Fievel and Rachel already having treated the engaged couple to pastrami on rye at the Carnegie Deli. Marv was barrel-chested and, unlike Fievel, did not appear to be shrinking with age down to nothing. A Bears season-ticket holder, he'd invited Green to come out sometime to a game.) Now it was all over. "Shelly's fiancé is a crook!" was the piteous howl that would soon ring through the placid streets of Winnetka.

"She took it okay," Shelly added.

"Good, because tell them—" But he could not formulate a statement of reassurance broad enough to cover Marv and Ruth. Really, there was none; simply put, a piece of shit was joining the family. "I'll be okay," he repeated weakly, then promised to call from out of town.

He emptied his briefcase of Crank-related documents, then divided the chaos of paper on his desk, shelves, and floor into foot-high stacks, one for each deal. "Rosa, I'm going." His phone line lit on her board.

"I'll check if he's here," she said, then looked up at him. "'Mr. Hebner' again."

"Tell him I'm out at a meeting."

She hung up. "Where's the meeting?"

"There is none. I'm just not feeling well. In fact I may be out of the office the next week or two."

"What's wrong with you?"

He grinned bitterly. "If I ever figure it out, I'll let you know."


Slippers scuffled along a hall, accompanied by panicked shouts of "Coming!" as if no visitor would wait more than five seconds. Fievel's mixed-up eyes appeared in the crack of the door. "So that *was* you ringing!" he shouted, throwing it open. "What's goin' on? Are you sick?"

"No. I had to talk to you about the investigation."

"*Ja,* come in the kitchen."

Rachel was dragging a wooden spoon around a bubbling pot of pea soup. "Soon we're having dinner," she said. Green took his old seat at the pink Formica table, beneath a laundry-drying contraption that lowered from the ceiling on a Fievel-designed pulley. The empty clothespins looked like birds on a wire. Without asking, Fievel poured two glasses of ginger ale.

Nodding toward Rachel, back over the soup, Green mouthed, "Does she know?"

Fievel said, "She tortured me until I confessed. Right, Ruchel, you tortured?"

"What?" She turned.

"Never mind. Go back to your pot. Continue," he said. "She listens anyway."

Green said, "There's a whole other aspect to this Lee Textiles thing." Fievel rotated his wrist, and Green went on, telling of the Rosen tip and the Alfieri trades. Fievel listened, sipping his soda, punctuating his son's story with barely audible "Vey"s and moans.

"I'm sorry I kept that part from you," Green said. "I wasn't sure how you'd handle it."

"I would've confessed. For sure I would've."

"Well, I guess I realized you were right. It's no way to live, afraid of your own shadow, trapped in lies. So I talked to my lawyer, and she went to the government."

"Who? The Irisher?"

"Yeah, and also the U.S. Attorney And it seems my testimony is very valuable to them at this point. So in exchange we think they're going to give me immunity from prosecution."

"Thank God!" Fievel said, rolling his eyes up toward the tenth floor. Rachel sat and added, "Thank God."

Suddenly she remembered. "What about Daddy?"

"Yeah!" Fievel cried, and then, with a deranged gleam, said, "You'll leave me out, okay? Just stick with that I was a good stock picker. I'm a good analyst of takeovers and—"

"Don't be an idiot!" Rachel shouted, causing the men to flinch. "He has to get a deal for you too. Otherwise it hangs over you!"

"What're you talkin'? He should tell *I* broke the law? Then the club has to give back the money!"

Green waved. "Calm down! Mommy's right; they've got you. I need to use my leverage while I still have some." Fievel stared, his cheeks like Red Delicious apples. "Anyway, why are you fighting me? You were the first to suggest giving up."

"But now that we're oc-tually doing it. . . . One time I made a killing for the pisher. Shit." He puffed out his lips, letting his knuckles drop onto the table. Then he exhaled, nodding slowly in agreement.

"Okay, then. My lawyer can't make deals for you, but I said I wouldn't testify unless you were safe. She thinks they won't prosecute as long as the club returns the profits. And there'll be a fine. Here's a lawyer she recommends."

Fievel inspected the slip. "Tasch? What kind of name is that?" He thought. "Sounds like Tashkent. Could be a Jew from Tashkent."

"Anyway, call him first thing tomorrow."

Fievel winced. "That's gonna be embarrassing when the club finds out. I'll say it was a mistake; I didn't know I was doing wrong. And I'll resign as manager." He rubbed his scalp, anguished. "Boy, I really cocked everything up this time."

"You *should* resign," Rachel said. "Ever since he took over, he does nothing but sit in front of FNN. If a stock he bought goes down, he cries. That I can understand. But he also cries if a stock he didn't buy goes up! 'Look how much I lost!' Is that kind of a mind cut out for speculation?" She stared, waiting for Green to back her. But he'd lost the thread.

Then they all looked at each other, breathing heavily. Green remembered caucusing in these same seats, with these same fatigued expressions, maybe hundreds of times. Usually his parents had been overreacting to modest tsuris, but now, served a huge helping of the real thing, they'd become oddly cool.

Placing his palms flat on the table, Green said, "About my job . . . I'll have to leave."

Fievel reached over and gripped his arm. "I guarantee you'll be okay. You'll get a job you like more. Maybe be a union lawyer; then you'll feel you make a contribution."

"And you know we'll be here to help you," Rachel said. "With money, or whatever you need."

Green was choking up again. "It may sound funny, but I'm thinking I may go work for the U.S. Attorney. To prosecute securities fraud." After exchanging a glance with Rachel, Fievel said, "Possible. You know the inside."

"Right, and Sterling seems to like me. He grew up on Central Park West, you know."

"There's a Sterling in the Bund. A tailor. Couldn't be his father . . . ?"

Rachel said, "What tailor lives by Central Park West? Come on!" She snorted, then cried, "Wait! The wedding!"

"Postponed, to start with. But I'm not sure. . . ." He averted his eyes. "See, I haven't told Shelly yet about the government deal. She still thinks I'm innocent."

"What?" Rachel shook her head. "I'm sorry, but that's not right. She's your fianceé; she's entitled."

"Leave him alone! Maybe he decided she isn't ready to hear, because she's too emotional."

"Like you hid it from me? Saying you're going to Orchard Street to buy pants when really you're going to the SEC?! I could've murdered you!" She checked her pot and sat back down, glaring at Fievel. "Maybe if you came to me right away I would've made you do the smart thing! Because, let's face it, sometimes you're not so bright." She moved a teacup forward as if advancing a chess piece.

"Ach, bullshit! That's a lot of bullssssheet."

Rachel's eyes shone, defiant. "See, Ricky, your father is a *luftmensch*. That means a person who walks with his head in the clouds. From him you inherited some of that. But when we have a practical problem, who has to take care?" She indicated herself. "Who calls the plumber? Who fights with the super?"

"So what?"

"But on the big decisions, suddenly the luftmensch wants control. And I'm tired of it. Because he leads me around by the hand, and all the time we nearly get hit by a bus."

"What bus?"

"Not a real bus. An imaginary bus." Fievel winked at Green: Imaginary bus—you have a disturbed mother.

"That's why, Rickele, the next time you need advice, ask me. Meshuggeh lying to the SEC. You're lucky you aren't both going to prison!"

"Maybe I'd be happier there," Fievel muttered.

"Excuse me?"

"Nothing." He sipped ginger ale and said, "Some speech. The realist takes over. The *knower*."

Green turned to Rachel. "I will tell Shelly. But if I wait till the end of the week, I can go with a *fait accompli.* "

"I think you're wrong, though I admit you know her better than me. If you think she's so fragile. . . ." She eyed him. "But you're still getting married?"

He wheezed. "I'm so confused right now, I can't even say what I'll be doing tomorrow. You know I love Shelly—"

"She's a sweet girl; we always liked her."

"—But in the last couple of weeks everything's changed. It feels like I've stepped into another person's life."

They paused again, gathering *coyekh:* energy-strength. "Out of curiosity," Fievel asked, "this other person, whose life you stepped into? Does he go to synagogue?"

"Who knows? All that doesn't seem important right now."

"That was quick," Rachel said.

Fievel smiled triumphantly. "I knew you'd wake up from that. The opiate of the masses."

"Masses," Green repeated. "Masses of radiologists and litigators, maybe. Anyway, I'm not sure how I feel anymore. One thing I will say: After all my agonizing, I wound up doing what the Torah would've instructed in the first place."

"But this way you made your own choice. Not what some rabbi told you, sittin' in a *office*, with a big beard." Fievel described a waist-long beard with his hand, then reflected. "You know, your story could make a interesting article for *Yiddishe Kultur.* I could call it 'Morality Outside the Torah,' or 'You Don't Need Torah.' Something like that."

Green nodded. "One other thing that's been bothering me. Yesterday, when I compared my situation to yours, in Europe? I was wrong. There's no comparison. None at all."

Fievel blinked twice. "Some. There is." He smoothed his eyebrow with a finger, then was struck by a notion. "I want to ask, but only if you'll agree not to get mad. Maybe for the next couple weeks you should move back in by us." Green began to respond automatically, but then thought, Here he'd be safe from Alfieri. Also, he did have to duck Shelly until Friday.

Fievel detected weakening. "Wouldn't it be better, at this moment?" When Green nodded, his father smacked his hands together. "Now you're talkin'!"

Ladling out a giant's portion of pea soup, Rachel set it before her son. The steam rose, warming his face.

After dinner, heading crosstown for his clothes, Green felt surrounded by menace. His confession had put him in jeopardy—though ostensibly confidential, who knew what moles Alfieri had inside the government?—but he'd so far been able to control his fears. Now, though, he kept checking behind as he walked, running past alleys, and standing back from the curbs, away from moving traffic.

His apprehension increased as he turned the corner toward his building. Here's where the hit man would be, waiting in the shadows; in fact there was something different and weird tonight, as if he really were being watched. But he'd be okay, once he reached the lobby; they didn't kill you in your lobby! He half-ran and then, approaching the doorman, slowed. "Hi, Jimmy," he said, expecting the usual joyless comparison of heat and humidity, but instead the doorman flashed a warning look, calling, "Careful!" A hand seized Green's shoulder from behind.

Wrenching loose, he found Rosen. The doorman shoved between them. "Sorry, Mr. Green. I told him to go away, but he keeps hanging around."

"Shut up, you. I'm his best friend. Ricky, can I come up a minute?" Rosen snatched his sleeve, but he wriggled free, stepping toward the door. "Please!" Rosen cried, pitiful.

"Okay!" But not alone in an apartment. "Why don't we go for a drink nearby?"

"No, we have to talk in private. What are you, afraid of me? How long we been friends?" He waited. "How long?"

Green agreed, though the doorman's suspicion continued, it being his job to assess human nature. "If you need me, buzz," he told Green, with a meaningful glance toward Rosen.

They rode up silently in the elevator, both watching the floor numbers, and only spoke when they had entered Green's foyer. "What the hell are you doin'?!" Rosen abruptly shouted, fists balled.

Green backed against the front door, raising his arms to defend himself. "What do you mean?"

Rosen advanced. "I *mean*, why are you cutting a deal and fucking us both?!"

Green pushed past him into the living room, picked up the TV remote, and took it to the window, as if a flick would change the noisy traffic to a mountain or forest scene. He was a good strategist, according to Mandel, but now hadn't the slightest idea what to say. Rosen followed, yelling, "You figured you'd make your deal, and the first I'd find out is when they came to arrest me!"

Green affected nonchalance. "I really don't know what you're talking about."

"Y'know, you do a lot of things well, but one of them is not lying. If you wanna discuss this like men, that's cool, but if you're gonna lie, then fuck you. I know about your meeting, and your deal, and everything. And don't worry how. Alfieri has connections you never dreamed of."

Green couldn't stand Rosen breathing down his neck. He walked into the bedroom, slid open the closet door, and took out his overnight bag. Rosen reappeared. "Goin' somewhere?"

"I'm leaving town on business."

"Interesting time for it. Your firm must not know about your deal yet or you wouldn't *have* any business, except to clear out your shit." He sat on the bed.

While taking a pile of striped boxers from his dresser, Green furiously pondered what to say. So Alfieri did know; it was as he'd suspected, a rotten egg in the government. "What exactly have you heard?" he asked, folding his underwear with uncharacteristic care, as if acting a packing scene.

"I've heard you offered to— Oh, wait a minute! I am so stupid," Rosen moaned. "You could be wearing a wire."

Green laughed. "Yeah, I'm the big undercover guy. Know what? I haven't changed in two days. You can watch." He took off his shirt. "No wires here," he said, rotating. Rosen signaled that he could stop, but he was annoyed now, and dropped his pants. "Well, my legs seem to be clean. How about under my balls or up my ass?" He stuck his thumbs in the waistband of his shorts.

"All right! I'd consider it a personal favor if you didn't show me your cock or your crack. I believe you."

Green fell into a chair. "So you can tell me what you've heard."

"That you offered to testify and in exchange they'll let you off. And I came to ask if you're outta your mind. I told you, there's *no way* the government can touch us. Everything was holding steady till you opened your mouth. What'd they say to scare you? That they had a 'source,' right?"

Green hung his head. "They're boxing us all in, can't you see that?"

Rosen blinked, then said, "So I was right. I figured you were fuckin' me over, but I wasn't sure. Now I know." Green bit his lip. Tricked again.

"I figured it out because Sterling was after me too, sayin' they had a 'source.' Know what else? That I better talk and fuck you or you'd fuck me first! As if I would rat you out for something I got you into. And also I was thinking, Go to hell, Ricky Green would never give up a friend. But the last couple days, when you started avoiding me, I *felt* something was wrong. I guess we've been friends too long. Like how one twin knows if the other's dead."

Green colored, and Rosen shook his head. "Sterling—what a dick. Played the 'good cop,' sayin' he's from New York, I'm from New York, and did I used to go to Met games. Who gives a fuck? If he's such a nice guy, why does he sic two buddies against each other?"

"Petey, I mean, what's he supposed to do? Say, 'Oh, their friendship is so precious, I can't ruin it by enforcing the criminal laws'?"

"Okay, forget Sterling! Lemme put it differently. Even if you cut a deal, first, you'll be wiped out, and second, your career will be fucked. Where you gonna work? Papaya King, selling coconut champagne? You sure as shit won't get a job as a lawyer or anything like that."

Then he brightened. "I got it! You can change your story! What you do, tomorrow you call and say you were scared and lied because you wanted to see what kinda deal you *could* get, if you snitched." He grinned, as though his scheme were smart.

"It's too late."

"Don't say that! What's—why is it too late?"

Green folded his arms across his bare chest. "Things have gone too far. I can't reverse them now even if I wanted to. And I don't! I told you before, I can't live this way. Without a clear conscience, life is hell."

Rosen sneered. "Who taught you that, some philosopher? Or your rabbi? You know what's hell? Hell is working your ass off your whole life and never gettin' anything for it. Still stuck at a desk when guys like Alfieri are retired and on the Riviera. The guys you admire, you see them riding in a limo, what conscience you think they have?"

"But I don't admire them."

Rosen jerked his head around, frustrated to the point of collapse. "You . . . okay. Let's say a miracle happened and you realized you shouldn't go through with this. Why is it too late?"

"The deal's being made right now. If I back out, they'll skin me alive, and my father. Also they already know at my firm, because I told them today."

"You told 'em. You couldn't even wait three minutes."

"I owed it to them." Green stood. "Listen. It's too *late!* You can talk all night, and you won't change that! And if you're smart, you'll hire a lawyer and call Sterling yourself. I mean, I was a speck in all this, but they're building a major case against you. You could go to prison for years. And why? To protect that sleaze you work for?"

"You know shit about Alfieri! He's great. And loyal. If I stick with him, he—"

"He'd sacrifice you in a second! You've got 'fall guy' written all over your face!"

"You asshole, you asshole," Rosen intoned, his head drooping.

Green paced alongside the bed. "I know you don't see it now, but I'm doing you a favor. What if the SEC *is* working on a source? In that case, they won't need you to bag Alfieri. And then you really will go down with the ship."

"Don't make it that it was about me, okay? It was you first. That's the way you always were, even at Silver Glen."

Green stopped, posing fists on hips like an underwear model. "Please don't start with Silver Glen stories!"

"I have to! 'Cause I only really know you from Silver Glen. And who you were back then is who you still are." Summoning his strength, he rose and approached Green. "Didn't I always protect you? Remember when you broke the casino window?" Green shook his head. "And I took a smack for you?"

"It was fair, because the game was your—"

"Oh, now you remember. So we went outside, and you said thanks. Y'know what I was thinking? That if it was the other way around, you'd never take a smack for me!"

"The situation would never come up! Because I wouldn't get you in trouble in the first place!"

They faced each other, sagging and winded like two old boxers. Rosen said, "What's the use?," walked to the window and looked out. "You do what you want, then find reasons later. Guess that makes you a good lawyer. Oh, sorry, not anymore."

"Believe me, hurting you wasn't my plan." Green lay on the bed, suddenly unable to hold up his head. "I was just tired of living in fear. I wanted some peace of mind."

"Uh-huh."

Green sighed and said, "You could be right. But it doesn't matter, because I am going to testify. Maybe I'm making a mistake. I probably won't find out till I'm on my deathbed and say, 'You know, my life would've been better if I'd kept my mouth shut back in 1988.' But I am going to do it."

He sat up. "With that being the fact, you have to decide what you should do. You can go to Sterling and save yourself. Or wait till they indict you, and Alfieri, and all of you. Either way you'll have to start over. The only question is whether you go to jail first."

Rosen's face was drained of blood. His knees buckled, and he caught hold of the bed. "I'm wiped. I work my butt off, then Ana keeps me up all night with sex." He snapped his fingers. "*She'd* book in five seconds, that's for sure. Right, she'd love me back in a condo in Fort Lee. Well, she's an airhead, anyway." He lay back, staring into space.

"The other thing," Green said, "is there's no reason to be afraid. Sterling told me he can protect us from Alfieri."

"What're you talking about?"

"You know. From his mob connections."

Rosen laughed. "He doesn't have any mob connections!"

"What about him threatening me with vendettas and whatever? And telling me about going to Italy?"

"Vendetta, he meant, y'know, he'd get even. Like someday if your client got in a proxy fight or something, he'd vote his stock against you. And Italy, he has a place he likes on Lake Como called Villa d'Este. Some paradise."

Green had to smile at himself. Idiot! God, he was an idiot. And Sterling—oh, he'd played him like a virtuoso. But it didn't matter. However he'd reached this point, it was over. He dressed and finished packing while Rosen watched, immobilized on the bed.

"Clever, how you tricked me before. But you always were a great bullshitter."

Rosen looked offended. "Tonight was the first time I ever lied to you, except . . ."

"What?"

"Y'know, ha, about gettin' Teri pregnant. I wanted to prove I was a friend and you could trust me. Go ahead and tell me what a scum I am. I deserve it." He paused, awaiting abuse. "So?"

Green just shrugged. "It's my own fault, for being an egomaniac. I mean, who did I think I was, some superhero? Sperm Man?" He zipped his bag.

Rosen repeated, "Sperm Man," then sat up. "I should go before I get mad again. I almost punched you before, and I don't need another criminal charge." He stood.

"Petey, listen. I am sorry. But I promise you'll see it's for the best."

"Sure." He straightened his tie in the closet mirror. "By the way, *are* you gonna get off prison?"

Though Green knew he shouldn't tell, he lacked the energy for further lying. Forever!, forever, because he was, he saw now, no more suited to the liar's life than he'd be to the lumberjack's or the rodeo rider's. "Looks like I'll have immunity."

"Good. Then you can get married on schedule. And don't worry, you won't have to invite me. Because I'll probably be locked up by then."

"I did want to invite you to the wedding."

"Not really. You never liked me, really. I knew, but—oh, forget it." He took a step. "One more thing. I want you to know . . . when all this started, I honestly thought I was helping you. It hurt me to see you dying in that job."

"Okay."

"I guess neither of us wound up doing the other much good."

He left. Green jumped when he heard the front door slam.

# Chapter 15

Green was thorough, explaining about the night at the Shamrock, the staggering home, the vomit, the couch, and the Lee Textiles tip to Rosen. "Wait a minute," Sterling said, chewing the cap of his pen. "That can't be how it happened."

"What do you mean?"

The prosecutor, facing Green across the examination table, checked a sheaf of notes. "My corroborating witnesses have made clear that Rosen got the tip by phone on the morning of the twentieth. That means you would've called him at the office." He glanced up at Green. "Right?"

"No, it was just how I said. I was lying on the couch, drunk—because if I'd been sober, I'd never have done it—and I pulled Rosen down by the sleeve, and I said there'd be a deal the next day."

"It doesn't make sense!" Sterling cried, agitated. "You said you'd passed out on the couch, right? You probably couldn't even remember your name, much less the details of an LBO. Anyway, you were asleep."

"Yes, but I woke up, and I remembered enough to tell Rosen what he needed to know."

Sterling leaned back, folding his arms, then frowned at Byrne beside him. "Let's start again. I have evidence that Rosen received a call on the morning of the twentieth, seemed very excited by it, and immediately ran in to Alfieri. Fifteen minutes later they were taking huge positions in Lee through various entities.

"Now, you say you tipped Rosen. So what makes the most sense, the sequence that's most comprehensible, is if *you* were that caller. In the morning. On the twentieth."

Green stubbornly shook his head. "But that's not—"

Swensen touched his arm; they leaned their heads together, and she whispered, "Think some more. Maybe it did happen the way he says and you've just forgotten."

He kneaded his chin and then, realizing what was desired of him, almost smiled, it was so absurd. He turned back to Sterling. "That's right, I got it mixed up. I passed out, and when I woke, Rosen was gone. It was morning. So I called him at work—"

"Around nine-fifteen?" Sterling asked.

"It would've been about that time. I remember because—" He stopped, afraid to screw things up. "I just remember. I saw the clock. So I said the Lee deal was about to be announced."

"Right. And the price at which it would be?"

"Sixty dollars per share. I told him."

Sterling jotted a note, underlined it twice, then checked the recorder. "Tape's running out," he said and, taking an unbent paper clip, jabbed it into the broken EJECT slot. He flipped the cassette and said, "You can continue."

Green recounted the rest of his story: the meetings with Rosen at Japonica, the calls from phone booths, the sixties baseball aliases. He made no effort to downplay his role or rationalize his actions, and he became emotional only when describing the last confrontation with Rosen. It pierced him to recall Petey sagging onto the bed, sad and weary, ruined.

When he finished, Sterling and Byrne whispered. Green glanced at Swensen, who gave a tight-lipped grin, then at the mirror on the side wall, behind which he assumed lurked more prosecutors, viewing the show. (Did they bring a popcorn popper? Or take up a pool on how many crimes he'd confess, and whether he'd cry?)

"Okay," Sterling said, snapping off the tape machine, and turned to Swensen. "We'll let you know when he's needed for the grand jury."

Green sat back, relieved. That hadn't been too bad. The whole session had taken less than four hours, including the negotiation of the cooperation agreement. "Fine," Swensen said. "And the investigative part?"

"I want him to try and tape a conversation with Rosen "

Green was startled. "But I told you, he figured out that I'm doing this!"

"Well, maybe, or maybe you can convince him you decided against it. Anyway, either he'll talk or he won't, but it's worth a shot."

Swensen said, "Hasn't Rick done enough already?"

"Yes, but still I think he should try."

Green imagined actually taping Rosen. Probably he'd do it from a rigged U.S. Attorney phone, around which the prosecutors would hover, snickering as Petey prattled about his favorite topics: the model he was "doing," a new disco song, memories of Silver Glen. And when the tape was revealed. . . . It killed to think of those hurt eyes and that wounded freckle face. "I can't do it," Green said finally.

Sterling frowned, and Green pressed his palms together, imploring. "I mean, this was hard enough! He's one of my best friends!" Sterling stared, surprised that Green could think that would matter here. Green shifted his strategy. "Anyway, it would never, never work. The last time, he only talked after I stripped to my underpants to show I didn't have a wire. He's not dumb, y'know? He's really not.

"Also, the other problem: You may have noticed that I'm a terrible liar."

"Oh," Sterling said, "you're not so bad." Byrne mumbled to him, and the prosecutor turned to Swensen. "All right, fine. It'd never fly, and we can do without it, anyway.

"So," he went on, "we're going to keep his cooperation secret a while longer, of course." He cocked an eye at Green. "Don't tell *anyone.*"

"I'm—staying with my parents a few days," he said, checking to see if the government was mocking him. "So they're aware—" Sterling nodded. "Sorry, one more person. My fianceé. She's very trustworthy, and I really have to . . ."

Sterling glowered, but Byrne spoke in his ear and he relented, with a warning that she keep her mouth shut. Then he said they were done. Feeling he might float out of the chair, Green gave Sterling a comradely smile. But the prosecutor just stared back, stonefaced, and said, "Helen, thanks."

"Thank *you*," she said, packing up her case. "You too, Gerry." Byrne nodded. She rose, touching Green's shoulder. "We can go." As they left, he tried one last time to catch Sterling's eye, but he was busy fiddling with his busted recorder.

In the hall, Swensen frantically lit a cigarette. Green said, "I'm kind of disappointed."

"Disappointed?!"

"Oh, not with the deal! That was great." It really was. She'd gotten him not only criminal immunity, but also a settlement that let him keep his money (though, as the government knew, it would all go to pay her bill) and, of course, his baseball cards. "It's just, I was hoping for a minute alone with Sterling. I thought there was an outside chance he might—help me."

Swensen led Green away by the arm. "I wouldn't expect anything from Stu. I'm sure he was a peach while he was romancing you. But now he has what he wanted. I always said he was a young man in a hurry. He'll be U.S. Attorney himself one day." She rang for the elevator.

"I'll tell you something else about Stuart Sterling: He was not your big supporter. At first he tried to insist on you pleading to a felony. He thought he'd seem like a hero, sending a Harvard lawyer to prison. It was Byrne who insisted your guilt was minor, and you'd make a good witness. Also, Gerry got the SEC to go easy. No, if you're looking for your angel, he's the one."

Green chewed his cheek. From the moment they'd walked in today, Sterling had treated him like a mangy dog—discussed in the third person and only acknowledged to harass or scold. Green had been praying it was just propriety, but now had the sick sensation that he'd seen the real man.

Downstairs, they signed out in the cheap U.S. Attorney register, a sheet attached with clips to a piece of cardboard. On St. Andrews Plaza it was gray and drizzly. "Walk me to the cabs," Swensen said. Between the bases of the U.S. Courthouse and the municipal building was a brick alley set up with fast-food stalls. All around, people were eating hot dogs, laughing, blowing their noses—oblivious to Green and his disgrace. That was the best thing about New York, he decided.

He buttoned his coat. "So am I definitely going to get disbarred?"

"Well, the government will eventually get around to reporting your settlement, and then it's up to the disciplinary committee. I'd say most likely disbarment, with the right to reapply in a few years. It might be helpful if you could find a heavyweight to write a letter of support. Like Shapiro. Or didn't you clerk for Leo Fineman? He knows everybody." Green frowned; the thought of crawling to the judge was too terrible.

"You want to continue practicing law?"

"You'll laugh if I tell you." Green looked at the pavement. "I'd talked to Sterling about recommending me for a U.S. Attorney job. Prosecuting insider trading," he added, torturing himself with sarcasm.

Swensen was sad. "I think that's a wonderful ambition, Rick. I really do. But Stu is not going to be your entree. You must understand, the AUSAs believe intensely in their mission, and see it as them—the poor, harried prosecutors—against the monsters like Alfieri. And once you've chosen sides, you can't just switch."

"But I—"

"Look. Personally I like you, and I can see how you went wrong. But to them you're just another criminal. They don't want to hear about your psychology. To them it's 'I scrape by on my government salary. Here's this runt, making more than I do, and even that's not enough. He has to steal, too.' You see? I don't want to burst your bubble, but it'd be hard to overcome that attitude."

Green nodded, aware how ridiculous he must seem. Too humiliated to make eye contact, he shuffled his feet, watching a river of rain slide along the gutter.

"Tell you what," Swensen said. "I'll represent you in the disciplinary committee. Free, okay? Just pay my expenses."

"Thanks, he said, and his voice thickened. "Helen, I won't forget what you did for me."

"Oh, sure you will. *All* my criminals forget. They don't write, they don't call. . . ." She was smiling, showing her stained teeth. It was the first joke he'd heard her make.

After she rode off he stood awhile, absorbing the reality of his position. There would never, in his current lifetime, be a place for him at the U.S. Attorney's office. He really was screwed; unemployable.

Watching lawyers hurry up and down the courthouse steps, he got the awful feeling that each move he'd made this week had been stupid. Maybe Petey was right, after all: Everybody was corrupt—look what lies Sterling the Good had been willing to tell, to bag him. Sleaze was an integral component of ambition, and people accepted it just fine. No big deal.

Hands stuck in his coat pockets, he crossed Centre Street, wondering how he'd let a few noble ideas blow all out of proportion and drive him to this foolish confession. Well—Bonnie. He'd made the mistake of believing one of her dramatic scenes, "The Hell of a Guilty Conscience," written by Clifford Odets in 1937. He sighed. Too late, too late.

He approached the subway—no more cabs; he had to save money now—but hesitated. Why not pay the judge a visit? Who could say? Maybe, as a man who'd endured his own trials, he'd come through for an ex-employee in trouble.

A minute later, Green was knocking on the enormous wooden door, which was kept locked owing to Fineman's fear of vengeful ex-cons. His secretary, a pixillated spinster with a hair bun, opened up. "I was passing and thought I'd say hello. Is he in?"

"I'll see."

He waited in the clerks' room. At his former desk sat a gaunt young man whose beaten posture evidenced a full term with Fineman, though beneath the shell shock Green sensed an essential naiveté that reminded him of . . . himself, could it be just a year ago? "Rick Green," he said, and the clerk gave a cold-fish shake.

"T-T-Ted Untermayer." Green almost laughed. Had he come here with his stutter, or had Fineman caused it?

"I used to have your job." In another life, he wanted to add. "So I know the immense power you wield."

"The judge m-mentions you a lot. Makes us read your opinions." Green wasn't flattered; he knew it was bullshit. Every year, to destroy the confidence of the incoming clerks, Fineman used one from the preceding term—even one he'd loved to pillory—as an example of competent work.

"S-so how's law-firm life?"

"It's been an education."

The secretary said he could go in. Green mimed choking himself, and Untermayer laughed. Behind the vast desk sat Fineman, tiny and pecan-headed as ever. Green gripped the liver-spotted hand, feeling the bones inside crackling. "To what do I owe this GREAT pleasure?"

"I was in the neighborhood."

"Why? Are you a criminal defendant downstairs?" Green's face fell. Did he know?! No, of course not, it was one of his witticisms. "So how are you, Judge?"

"Alive still. Sorry to disappoint."

"I'm not disappointed. Actually, I've missed working for you. The good times we used to have."

"Fibber. Like Fibber McGee. How's Molly, Fibber McGee?" Green just nodded, grinning. "So where are you? Crank, Wilson? George Wilson owes me one," he said, accessing his internal favor file. "I got his delinquent son a job in the docket clerk's office. Anyway you must be minting money."

"Can't complain," Green said, rapping on the desk. "I must admit, what you taught me has come in handy, in practice."

Fineman looked skeptical, then pleased. "Good, good," he said, but had nothing to add.

Green uncrossed his legs and leaned forward. "Um, Judge, let me ask a question. *Hypothetically* . . . if I were to have a problem with the disciplinary committee—" Fineman perked up, sniffing blood. "Like, say I overzealously represented a client and was up for suspension from the bar, to what extent if any could you—would you be able to help me?"

The judge broke into a crack-toothed smile. "I always predicted you'd get in trouble. Know why? Because you're a weak man." He adjusted his glasses for a better view of the weak-man.

"See, the practicing attorney has a myriad of opportunities to cheat and get rich. God knows as a judge they tried to tempt me. But a strong man says, 'No, I take the straight and narrow.'" He illustrated the straight and narrow with his gnarled fingers. "I always guessed you'd cave at the first chance, though. Don't ask me how; I have a sixth sense."

Green wasn't especially enjoying ethical lessons from a Funicular-fryer, but there seemed no alternative. "Judge, I—"

"I know, you have an excuse. Ed Koch has been keeping me off the list for the Al Smith Dinner since he's been Mayor and always has a new excuse. I get no invitation to the Bicentennial of the Constitution dinner, and Ronnie Reagan's chief of protocol has an excuse!" Green nodded, thinking that some new trauma must have befallen Fineman, because he was coming unhinged. "Everybody makes excuses!"

"Judge, I'm not saying I did anything wrong! But if I did—never mind what—would you help me? I worked hard for you, and I was hoping if the chips were down—"

"Who helped me when the media raked me over the coals?! I could've been on the Supreme Court, but Eisenhower didn't want to waste capital with the liberals. Oh, he was a politician, don't kid yourself. Talked simple. *Golfed.* All bullshit!" Foam flecked at the judge's lips, but his arms hung limp as two salamis; he was too old to flail them anymore.

"So they had to be executed! They gave secrets to the enemy! The evidence was uncontroversial! The circuit affirmed me, but do you ever hear that? No, all you hear is 'Fineman killed the Funiculars!' Like some fucking child's song! Then since then everything goes against me!" As he continued his rant, Green thought, So, in other words, you're not going to help me.

In a moment he was up and backing toward the door. "I have to run, Judge."

"Wait! I've been meaning to call you. I have to give a speech next month on the federal caseload." He tried to look ingratiating. "Can you do a draft? You were my best speechwriter."

"I'd love to, but I'm sort of—"

"People still tell me how nice my fiftieth anniversary toast was. Not schmaltzy, but sweet. Little Ricky, wait!" Green slipped out, then shook his head at Untermayer. "Has there been some recent thing with the Funiculars?"

"Yes," he confessed. "He saw the v-vigil."

"What?!" On each anniversary of the electrocution, a few diehard lefties still gathered outside the courthouse with candles. The tradition, passed on from one generation of Fineman clerks to the next, was that he must in no event see the vigil or know of its existence. They usually invented some pretext to hustle him out the back exit.

"We screwed up. And it's been h-h-hell since then."

"Well, stick it out. I guarantee one day you'll look back and laugh."

Then he left, empty-handed, but nonetheless glad he'd come. Fineman's tormented face had reminded him that everything you do does, in fact, become a part of you. The judge would find his only peace in the grave.


Green skulked along the Crank hallway. Though he felt he shouldn't be here, he'd ducked in just to grab his boom box and CDs. People he passed regarded him blandly, which meant that word still hadn't leaked—amazing, since the dull-lived lawyers were maniacal for gossip, and his plight was a juicy bit. Shapiro, Mandel, and the litigator, Bluestein, must have wills of iron.

Thoughts of Shapiro and Mandel produced a tiny spark of hope. True, they hadn't seemed overly sympathetic at first, but maybe, upon reflection, they'd see how he'd gone astray and forgive him; and then use their massive clout to help resurrect his career. Well, unlikely. Possible, but unlikely.

All his case files were gone, giving Green's office the cold, naked look of a dog shaved for an operation. He unplugged the radio, threw his CDs into a string-tie folder, began to close it but thought, Fuck it, and stuffed in pens, pads, and his stapler. Then he looked around for the last time. It was hard to believe, after the thirty-five hundred hours and the dozens of all-nighters, that he'd walk out just as he'd come: Elvis poster under his arm, and penniless. End of a young superstar.

Murphy called out from his desk as Green passed. "Get in here! What's this about a 'medical leave'? I'm the one who's sick!" He went on, concerned, "I hope it's nothing serious."

"Between you and me, I'm having a personal problem I can't discuss right now. In a few weeks I'll call to explain."

Murphy's eyes dulled. "I hope you come back soon. I'll miss you. I mean with you out and Josephson gone, I'm surrounded by nerds. Who'm I gonna crack jokes with?"

"You can always go up to Shapiro's office. He's a laugh riot, with his pranks and his garlic gum."

"Speaking of God, it's too bad you won't be able to do that new LBO with him. That was a sure ticket to stardom." He paused.

"Y'know, I was thinking the other day: You've made all the right moves so far, once you got past the receptionist fiasco.

"Even your 'speech' probably had some truth in it!"

"What speech?"

He waved dismissively. "You know, the talk they have with every associate at the end of his first year. 'We know so-and-so didn't make partner, but he wasn't up to snuff. But you!—you've got the brains to succeed here. You're special, you're adorable,' et cetera. They do it to keep the young lawyers from bolting when they see the senior ones being reamed. I'm surprised you haven't gotten your speech yet."

"I did get it, from Lou. Only I didn't know it was standardized." He had to smile: so much for the young superstar. The young asshole was more like it . . . just riding his horse of stupidity from town to town.

"Don't be ashamed," Murphy said. "I bought it too."

Green gathered up his stuff. "I better get going."

"Keep in touch, okay? If I'm not here, I may've taken that offer from Crumb and Crumb."

"What about the guitar-making business?"

Murphy shrugged at his brief folly. "Let's face it. I can't be poor now." It struck Green that affluence was a narcotic as addictive as heroin, and Jeff was hooked. Whereas he would be kicking cold turkey . . . one bright side to disbarment.

"Whatever's wrong," Murphy said, "I hope it works out."

Despite his lack of money, a job, or prospects, Green felt a grand exhilaration as he neared the elevators for his last ride down—like an astronaut about to splash to Earth after a year in orbit. But again he heard his name being called. Why wouldn't they just let him leave?

Ben Lee waved as he emerged from a conference room. Some big meeting must be in progress, without Green, and actually, in the flash of open door he'd spotted Mermelstein, delighted to have reassumed his rightful place at the table. "Tell you," Lee said, "the good Lord must of been in a *hateful* mood when he made bankers. I brought 'em here to make one last pitch for a loan extension and to convince 'em that bed-and-bath is the future, but they won't budge." He sighed.

"But where do you think you're skippin' off to?"

"Didn't Lou tell you? I'm taking a medical leave."

Lee was crestfallen. "Really?"

"It's not serious. But it's hard to talk about."

Lee eyed him funny, perhaps suspecting him of having the clap. "Well, I'm sorry. I was expectin' you to get us through this fire sale. Don't tell me I'm stuck with Mr. Personality," he added, jerking his thumb toward Mermelstein.

McCoy's shouts penetrated the conference-room door. "You won't believe what Joe's fightin' about. They—can we talk somewhere private?" Green led Lee to a vacant office behind the reception area, then set his effects on the bare metal desk.

"We finished the layoffs, and even after the relocations to Louisiana there's a lotta unemployed. Joe, Gilbert, and me have been eating ourselves up—I guess we learned *some* lessons from the LBO—so we decided to take some money from the till and fund a worker-retraining program. But Baxter and the banks say it's an insane expense now, and they got a veto.

"Well, so I insist, and Baxter bluffs, sayin', if it means so much to you guys, will you give up a portion of your stock to pay for it?' So we say sure! If you do, too. And now he's trying to backpedal.

"Tell me, Rick, am I crazy? Am I so completely out of touch with the way things are done now?"

"No," Green said, moved by the almost shocking spectacle of a businessman acting against self-interest, simply because something was right. That the act was on a small scale made it no less admirable. "I don't think you're crazy. But let's back up a second and discuss this 'veto' the bankers have over you. And Baxter's motives." Green took a breath, aware that he was about to extinguish any chance, however slight, of future assistance from Crank, Wilson.

"Remember at Twin Pines you said you were suspicious of Baxter's advice that you sell bed-and-bath? Well, you got it right. He is just trying to get one more fee out in case the company goes into Chapter Eleven.

"The other thing is, the banks are terrified of their loan going bad. The only reason they're talking so tough is Baxter promised them you'll cave."

Lee felt behind him for a chair. "I can't believe Will would screw me like that." After a silence, Lee asked, "So what do you think I should do, for real?"

"Pound the table. You wanna retrain the workers, you insist it's the company's obligation. You wanna keep bed-and-bath, pound the table. Threaten to file for bankruptcy."

"So the banks'll say no. Then what?"

"Right in front of them, you order Lou—no, *Neil*—to prepare a Chapter Eleven. The bankers will pee in their pants."

Now Green felt he really should vacate the premises. "Oh, do yourself a favor and get an independent financial adviser. Morgan Stanley is good." Green smiled when he said "Morgan Stanley," a dagger aimed at Baxter's heart.

Lee worked his jaw and flexed his hands as though gearing up to box someone. At that moment Baxter leaned in the door, grinning dumbly. "The receptionist said you'd come in here. Hi, Rick, I thought you were sick."

"Just going." He shook Lee's hand, then stepped past Baxter and out to the hall. Walking away, he heard muffled shouts from within the office. At the elevator, it occurred to him to remove the stolen supplies from his folder and leave them with the receptionist.

He nearly skipped across the lobby, thinking that he was finally done, finished, kaput. An ex-lawyer. Out on Park Avenue the air smelled like freedom.


All he wanted to do now was go home, get in bed, and read a novel under the old plaid quilt from his childhood. Staying with his parents was turning out much better than expected. First, he realized how much he'd missed the West Side. Fievel was right: living on Second Avenue, in that bumless skyscraper void, you might as well be in Milwaukee or Des Moines. But it was more than the neighborhood.

The night before, after a huge dinner, he'd watched TV in his parents' room, eating tangerines and walnuts. Fievel felt a cold developing, so he rubbed Vicks into his forehead, wrapped a schmatte turban around it, then pulled a woolen hat down to his eyes. The movie *Funny Lady* was on, and the first time Omar Sharif appeared (smiling like an imbecile in the audience at a Fanny Brice show), Fievel said, "Here sits a log. *This* has more emotion," he added, brandishing his backscratcher. From then on, every Sharif entrance was given a backscratcher salute by father or son.

During the late news the family had toasted bagels with cream cheese and, the day's eating done at last, they retired. Before bed, dragging a shoebox of baseball cards from his closet, Green found that the team logos, statistics, even the names of the long-retired players—Kranepool, Monboquette, Amaro—produced serene feelings. Fearing damage to the Seaver rookie that would soon be his sole salable asset, he isolated it from the common cards, pressing it in a book. (Let the SEC turn up their noses, but this three-inch piece of cardboard listed at $1,000.) Then, surrounded by his games and school plaques, he lay on the springy mattress and drifted into his deepest sleep in years.

That's what he needed again tonight, but first he had a stop to make.


A pupil and retina examined him through a peephole, and then Carol Birnbaum opened up, saying, "She should be home soon. Why don't you come in?" He waited on the couch, adjacent to the purple curtain that cordoned off Shelly's sleeping area. Carol—a curly-haired, prematurely motherly but high-strung resortwear buyer for Macy's—fluttered about, bringing seltzer and Kraft caramels. When at last she touched down, it was on the far cushion, as if she feared Green might lunge for her, proclaiming his love. "So you getting excited?" she asked. When he just stared, she explained, "The wedding?"

"Oh, I don't know," he said, then sipped soda.

Her eyes darted. "I guess it's still three months away. July, August, Labor Day. Two and some."

After a difficult silence, Carol ventured, "How's your job?" But Green, incapable of small talk, just shook his head. She started around the room clockwise, adjusting the positions of objects, while Green chewed caramels and tuned out her chatter.

He'd be facing Shelly soon, and had no idea what to say. Should they postpone the wedding further? Or accelerate it? Not only did he lack answers, until now he'd actually given the matter very little thought. He just couldn't get his mind around Shelly in the abstract; he had to see her. Then maybe his heart would tell him what to do.

When she entered, carrying a Zabar's shopping bag, he knew he still loved her. "This is a surprise. I didn't know if you'd be back in time for Shabbes. Wait—what's wrong?"

He stood, walked to her, and hugged her tight. Carol edged to the door, mumbling something about errands, then escaped as from a hostage situation. "Let's sit," he said. Shelly paled. Whatever he had to say, she knew things would never be the same.

"I wasn't out of town. I was staying at my parents'. And this morning I had a meeting with the government."

He spoke dryly, as if repeating an intriguing story, involving other people of course, that he'd heard about at the office. She studied the backs of her hands as he spoke, and when he finished she said, "I can't believe you kept me in the dark."

"I didn't want to upset you before it was—"

"I begged you to! I knew you were hiding something, and it killed me even more." Tears trickled down her cheeks. "And you made all these decisions without the . . . decency to ask what I thought. How could you treat me this way?!" she cried, and his heart ached. How *could* he? Had he been so without sense, and maturity . . . simple humanity?

He caressed her shoulders as she wept, imagining the ways he'd make it up to her, his mind filling with the usual snapshots of their future: a house; their laughing kids; fresh challah; a good car. He felt himself clutching at these visions like a life raft.

"I'm so sorry. I love you, and I want—" He was about to say he wanted forgiveness, wanted things to be as they were, wanted to get married Labor Day, but stopped, struck that he was again failing to do right. And this time he knew why: because he'd asked only what he wanted, what was good for him. Shelly would be his salvation; of that he now felt certain. But what about her? What did he have left to offer her?

She was still crying. Though he yearned to comfort her, he stalled, feeling that the next words out of his mouth would lock in one of their two alternate futures. But it was Shelly, wiping her eyes on her wrists, who spoke. "What hurts most is after all the time we've known each other, how little respect for me you must have. Forget about being engaged. Was my opinion so worthless?"

Green bowed his head, welcoming blame. "I have tons of respect for you. I just didn't want to—"

"Anyway, it's done, and there's no point going over and over it. We need to focus on the future." She sniffled. "I'm so sad for you, you can't imagine. I know better than anyone what a good person you are inside. So it's important to me that you understand what I'm going to tell you has nothing to do with the insider trading. Also, you must believe I'd stick by you, whatever job you had! Money—I don't care for money at all. I didn't want to say so before, but I always hoped you'd quit Crank. I wanted a more normal life, even if we had to struggle."

She sighed. "I've had this feeling for a while, but only in the last couple of weeks it's come clear. And what I feel is, we're really not . . . meant to be. I do love you, but I think you can love someone and just not fit together." She brushed her hair back, looking very beautiful to Green.

"We do fit together."

"In some ways. But I want—I know it's old-fashioned, but I want the things my parents had: a house and kids and friends. Also, temple has become an important part of my life."

"I go to temple with you!" he exclaimed, bouncing the couch.

"But inside you reject it."

"I *question*. Am I not allowed to question?"

"Of course! More—! As far as I'm concerned, you've tried shul like I asked, and if it isn't for you . . . you're against organized prayer, or you're an atheist after all—I'd accept it. What worries me is it's *not* about shul. It's—" She shook her head.

"What? What do you think it's about?"

She looked away. "You're—how can I say this without hurting your feelings?"

"I'm so worn out, Shelly, I don't think I have any feelings left to hurt."

"Okay. You're a very restless person. I feel you're searching for something and you can't find it. So what you do instead is reject every-thing else." Their eyes met. "In your heart you reject me and my friends. You said as much after Wendy's dinner."

"I did not! I just said she and Michael annoy me because they're so materialistic. Anyway, what about Larry and Dvorah? I like them."

She grinned. "You can't stand them. But forget that. The point isn't how you feel about Larry and Dvorah. The point is you reject me."

"I reject you? We're practically living together! We're engaged! In what sense is that evidence of rejection?" When she didn't answer, he repeated, "In what sense?"

Her voice was gentle. "Rick, this isn't a debate, or some court argument. I haven't been to law school, so I can't match you. But if you listen, I'm trying to express how I feel."

"You're right. I'm sorry. It's just, this idea that I reject you, I don't know where you get it from."

"Here's an example. You know I've considered moving to Israel, and you've never once taken it seriously. You belittle it, or laugh at me with your eyes. I knew I'd be giving that up if we got married, but I said, Well, marriage means compromise. Now I've understood that that's only the first of a thousand compromises, because our differences run to our deepest selves."

She paused, reading him. "Say we went ahead with the wedding. In a few years you'd end up unhappy. I just know it. You might go through the motions of being a husband, but inside you'd be struggling. You'd be a prisoner. So I'm giving you your freedom now, *before* the wedding."

Green had an urge to lay passionate kisses all over her face. He put his arm on her shoulders, murmuring, "I don't want my freedom. I want to be with you."

She began crying again, softly. "Why are you making this so hard? Can't you see how much it hurts me?"

"I don't want to hurt you. I want to get married."

"Do you really?" She looked in his eyes, then shook her head. "No. I see that you don't. You can't fool me anymore." She choked out a sob and hid her face in his neck.

He stared into space. She'd torn him up . . . he felt murdered. If only he were able to show her his vision, the kids and the house, maybe she'd see how good they could still be together. But he'd vowed to let her go, if that was best for her; and she seemed so sure. And the sad truth was, she might well be right, and there was no way of knowing today. What if, despite his sincerest wishes, he couldn't be the husband she deserved? The loving, stable, religious man of his imaginings?

Taking his arm from around her, he let his head sink back on the cushion. "Please don't be upset," she said.

"I am upset; obviously I am. And confused. Because I don't know . . . I have no idea what to do next."

"Maybe you ought to get out of New York for a while. Go someplace quiet, where you can rest and think."

He nodded, too tired to discuss it anymore. "I should leave. Can I call you tomorrow? "

"Of course you can call . . . but not tomorrow. Tomorrow is Shabbes." She glanced at her watch. "That reminds me. I have to get ready for services."

They moved toward the door. "Wait! I have a present for you." She went behind the curtain and brought out a rolled-up sheet of art paper. "I finished this last week." It was a drawing of him in profile, praying, wearing tallis and yarmulke; this was how she'd seen him, in shul. His forehead was wrinkled in concentration, and his eyes were lifted, filled with devotion. Really he looked quite happy.

"It's great. My mother will cherish it always."

They hugged. He'd hoped he wouldn't cry, but now found it impossible to hold back, thinking that she'd never be in his arms again, and that months or even years might pass before he grasped the extent of his loss. They stood at the door, sobbing, and finally said goodbye. Then, schlepping his folder, his radio, his Elvis poster, and his portrait, he went downstairs and walked up Second Avenue in the rain, toward the crosstown bus.

# Epilogue

Green nudged the rented Oldsmobile out of traffic, then along the curb until he spotted the building, four stories of metalwork over a modern art gallery. The car stopped with a jerk and muffled screech. Either learn to go easier on the pedals, he thought, or end up a whiplash defendant. The noontime sun beat down brutally on Broome Street, and within five minutes the interior was steamy. Meticulously yanking the parking brake, he got out and leaned on the fender, listening to the engine hiss and clink as it cooled.

He looked up at the third-floor windows. He had seen Rosen only once since the night of their confrontation at his apartment. He'd been leaving the grand jury room, done with his testimony, and Rosen was in the hall, waiting to go on. Though they weren't supposed to talk, Rosen winked; Green wasn't sure if he meant it in a friendly way, or sarcastically, as if to say, Look how you fucked us up.

The grand jury had been fun, sort of. He'd gone in alone, Helen wishing him luck, and sat in a witness box. Sterling led him through the events surrounding the stock tips. The jurors, arranged in semicircular rows like law students, occasionally interrupted to ask Sterling a question, which he would rephrase to Green.

At home a few days later, Green watched a televised press conference at which the U.S. Attorney announced Alfieri's indictment. Sterling stood behind, jockeying to get his face on camera. A young lawyer, whose significance in the world otherwise sounded wormlike, had provided the tip that had broken the case. Well, Green thought with a bitter grin, at Crank he'd always loved making news.

Rosen exited the building, a garment bag slung over his shoulder. "Hey, dude." He laid his bag across the backseat, then stood appraising Green. "Lookin' good."

"You too."

"Guess unemployment agrees with us." Green smiled, but Rosen glanced away and said they should go. He gave the building a final salute. "Goodbye, house. It was fun."

When Green turned on the ignition, Rosen said, "All right, let's see how you do. But no *stunts*, okay? No, like, doughnut turns or wheelies. Easy on the gas!" They lurched into traffic.

Rosen finger-combed his hair in the side mirror. "Um, maybe you should stay in lane, instead of drifting into the middle of the street." Green swerved, but too far, ending up in a parking space. Heart pounding, he nosed back out. "You're doin' fine," Rosen said, seat belt clicking in place.

They were quiet a minute. Then Rosen said, "When we talked the other night, I forgot to mention . . . you see Sterling shoving his face at the TV camera? Told you he was a dick."

"But y'know what? I was a spec*tac*ular witness. The grand jurors loved me, especially that one in the second row, in the miniskirt? From where I was sitting I could see . . . anyway, I wanted to slip her my number, but I figured it broke some law."

Green looked over at him. "So how do you feel? Stupid question, I guess."

"No. I feel okay. Actually it's funny, last month I met a guy who just got out, and he said it wasn't too bad. Also there's like a whole *club* of securities-fraud guys up there. Said he made more contacts at Danbury than at Harvard B School."

Green turned down Broadway, staying right, with the delivery trucks and the creeping buses. "Have you thought what you might do after you're released?"

Rosen rubbed his palms together. "Funny you should ask, because here it is: You and me, partners in business."

"Since our first collaboration was such a success."

"The difference is, this time it's legit, pretty much."

*"Pretty* much." Green gestured at a honking, tailgating taxi. "Pass me, you idiot! Did you see that?" He composed himself, then turned to Rosen.

"Anyway, I'm afraid to ask. What 'pretty legit' business do you have in mind?"

"Check it out: cashew importing. See, Iran grows most of the world's supply, but they only wanna deal with Muslims. So we have an opportunity—"

"I hate to break it, but we're not Muslim."

"Like they know? We go by Ahmed and Hussein. 'Salaam aleikem,' I say when we come in. It means, 'How's it goin'?'"

Green shook his head. "Not a good plan."

Rosen eyed him. "You thought I was serious."

"I never know with you."

"Forget it." Rosen's head lolled against the rest. "I have a few real ideas, but I'm too exhausted to discuss 'em now. Talk to me again in four months."

When they pulled up to the courthouse, Rosen said, "That's my genius over there." His lawyer, waiting at the foot of the steps, was a lanky Hebrew with a battered briefcase and scuffed brown shoes. "All right."

A key dangled from a Mets chain. "This lets you in the bungalow. My grandmother left you a note how to turn on the hot water and shit. You're lucky, I hear the softball team's in a pennant race against Katz's Kottages. And Labor Day weekend they've got a stripper booked to come in, so you're all set."

Green took the key. "Thanks. I appreciate it, especially after . . ."

"Ahh," Rosen said, and waved.

"I really am sorry for everything."

"Me too. But we shouldn't be. Because even if we'd never met, we were both heading for trouble, anyway. Right?" Green nodded.

"So if you have any questions about the bungalow—" He stopped. "I was gonna say call me. Till I remembered, ha-ha."

He stuck a leg out the door, but turned back to Green. Suddenly they caught each other in an awkward hug across the front seat. Rosen broke away, blushing for the first time ever, then hooked his bag on a finger and hopped out. He climbed the steps with his lawyer and disappeared into the lobby.

The West Side Highway was empty, and Green had some fun, changing to the left lane and accelerating to fifty. He cruised up along the river, past the battleship *Intrepid*, the abandoned rail yards, and his parents' building. He picked out their kitchen window as if he might spot them, shuffling in their slippers, cooking dinner while they nibbled on nuts, grapes, and broken cookies.

www.ingramcontent.com/pod-product-compliance
Lightning Source LLC
Chambersburg PA
CBHW051407170626
46809CB00006B/2055